THE

The FOUR

© 2010 by John Jacobsen

Published by John A. Jacobsen

All rights reserved. No part of this publication may be reproduced, stored in a retrieval system, or transmitted in any form or by any means without the prior written permission of the publisher. The only exception is brief quotations in printed reviews.

Unless otherwise indicated, Bible quotations are taken from the New King James version of the Bible. Copyright © 1979, 1980, 1982 by Thomas Nelson, Inc.

Acknowledgements

Many thanks to my readers for their encouragement, feedback and editing, especially to my brother Bill (Jake), Sue and Tracy Villone, Barb Trost, Alan Beeson and my wonderful wife Kristin.

Books by John A. Jacobsen

The End Series

1. The Beginning of the End
2. The End of the Beginning
3. The Beginning of Revival
4. The End of Peace
5. The Beginning of Judgment
6. The End of Judgment
7. The Beginning of Forever

A Tale of Two Sons Series

1. Book One: The Early Years
2. Book Two: Collision Course
3. Book Three: The Visitations
4. Book Four: Hope Deferred
5. Book Five: Ecstasy & Agony
6. Book Six: Evil Rises
7. Book Seven: The Beast Emerges
8. Book Eight: Convergence

Exposure Series

1. Maximum Exposure
2. Over Exposure

For details about these books and for information about new releases, please go to www.johnajacobsen.com

Foreword

This story is fictional, but based on many truths. The characters are strictly fictional and do not represent any actual persons, myself included.

Many direct and indirect Scriptures are employed. Where not specifically noted, the Scriptural references are included in Appendix A.

Statements about Freemasonry, the Illuminati and the New World Order are based on extensive research which can be accessed on my Lion of Judah website at www.lofj.com under the End-Times tab. Some readers will question the truth of demonology as portrayed in this book. However, I have directly experienced quite similar situations in my pastoral counseling career.

Warning: Some readers have experienced physical and emotional reactions when reading details about demons, Freemasonry and the Illuminati. If this should happen to you, seek out pastors or ministries who know how to handle these situations. You can search for them on the Internet.

As for my personal background, which many readers like to know, I was a Director of Management Science at two Fortune 100 corporations, an executive in the software industry and then President of Meals-on-Wheels in Prescott, Arizona. I have a BS in Engineering and an MS in Management Science. I became a pastor in 2001, and was the founder of the Gospel of Grace Food & Clothing Bank and the Lion of Judah ministries in Prescott Valley, Arizona. I also served as the Prayer Coordinator for Yavapai County in Arizona for several years. I was reared a Lutheran, became a pastor in a Pentecostal church, and now consider myself to be non-denominational.

Prologue

The first book, *The Beginning of the End,* concluded the end-time period Jesus called "the beginning of sorrows" (Matthew 24:8) leading up to the seven-year Tribulation. The "covenant with many" (Daniel 9:27) was signed, presumably bringing peace to the entire world. The anti-Christ (Alexis D'Antoni) and the False Prophet (Pope Vladimir Radinsky) were also revealed.

The second book, *The End of the Beginning,* covered the start of the seven-year Tribulation period through the identification of the two witnesses of Revelation 11, namely Pastor Gabriel and Rabbi Abraham.

The third book, *The Beginning of Revival,* took our characters up to the first Great Awakening of the Tribulation period. See next section for a more detailed summary of the third book, *The Beginning of Revival.*

This fourth book, *The End of Peace* will take us further through the first half of the seven-year Tribulation period. Subsequent books of *The End* series will go through the remainder of the Tribulation to the end of the world as we know it, and then on to the New Heaven, the New Earth and the New Jerusalem at the start of the Millennium following the Second Coming of Jesus Christ.

Some readers have questioned the times shown on the front cover clocks. Midnight represents the beginning of the seven-year tribulation period. Thus, the first book takes place a few minutes beforehand, while the second and third books advance through the Tribulation. The clock will cycle around to noon at the end of the seven years to usher in the new Millennium.

Several readers asked for a summary of the pre-Wrath rapture timeline. Appendix B provides both a brief timeline followed by the Biblical rationale. All of this material is scattered throughout the first three books.

****

At the end of the third book, the two witnesses, Pastor Gabriel and Rabbi Abraham, led a revival on Bali and thwarted the Global Czar's attempt to destroy the island, barely escaping as the Agung volcano erupted. Meanwhile, the two new Counter-Insurgency Agencies East and West were reformulating their plans for a new militia following the annihilation of the first group through self-serving and ungodly leadership.

Brandon and Juanita were preparing to visit all the hideaways and remote camps to establish spiritual warfare groups, while Pastor Wally and Michelle were preparing to head out to CIA-West in order to tutor Rev. and Mrs. Braintree, as well as to provide pastoral counseling and training to all the other hideaways as well. Meanwhile, Jerome and Sue were still waiting to get married, and Francine was hoping the Braintrees' restoration would help heal her relationship with Jesse.

Jim and Abby had just completed overseeing the construction of CIA-East and were working with Alan Morrison to rethink CIA operational plans. Jermaine continued to oversee the hideaways and remote camps while his new wife Tara had taken over Havenwood1's prayer team after Juanita left for her national tour.

Global Czar Alexis D'Antoni and Pope Vladimir Radinsky continued to tighten their grip over the one-world government. This followed the successful implementation of the Universal ID/Banking System through the mandatory implantation of RFID chips in every person, without which no one could buy or sell anything. However, Fran was able to infiltrate the global databases and develop a way for those who refused this "mark of the beast" to circumvent the system.

Blaine Whitney, former star TV newscaster and current spokesperson for the Global Governance Committee, was being buffeted back and forth by the forces of good and evil. She would be forced her to make a choice between the guidance of Rev. Boris Wainwright and Pope Radinsky.

Chapter One

Pastor Gabriel, Rabbi Abraham, Aadi and his cousin Komang were eating breakfast at a small inn while the nearby Mount Agung volcano continued to erupt. The ash cloud had turned morning into night, making the proprietors very nervous. Aadi glanced at his watch for the umpteenth time. "The deadline has passed!" he finally exclaimed, and then exhaled in great relief.

"I wonder what Asimoto is going to do now?" worried Komang, not quite ready to accept that the general's threat to annihilate the population of Bali was over.

"Oh, I assume that he doesn't do anything without express orders from the Global Czar," Gabriel noted while scarfing down another helping of "bebek betutu," a very tangy pork dish.

"Well then, I expect our work is not yet done," Abraham said as he wiped off the remainders of the "bubar ayam" off his beard. The chicken porridge was absolutely delectable, just mildly spiced.

They paid the anxious husband and wife proprietors generously and prayed protection over them from any effects of the volcano's eruption, since they were only about twenty miles away.

Abraham and Gabriel were still quite astonished at the amazingly fast spread of the revival to all corners of Bali. Granted, the island wasn't all that large, about the size of Massachusetts. But everywhere they went, it seemed as though most of the population of around three million had been converted in the great awakening.

As Komang drove the taxi westward, back toward the main highway, flaming debris began to fall from the sky. The fiery red embers ignited only a few areas because of the high humidity and robust plant life on the tropical island. The few fiery hotspots that did burn for awhile didn't last very long nor spread very far.

Just before they reached the highway, they saw one particularly bright spot of flames ahead. It turned out to be a lone tree near the junction of the main highway. Just like the tree near Komang's house, it was burning brightly, but the leaves and branches were not consumed.

Komang pulled the taxi onto the shoulder of the road and they all stared at the wondrous tree. "Why is this one burning like the other?" Aadi finally asked, breaking the spell. "This is not a place we have been or staked out."

"I don't know," Abraham finally answered, somewhat awestruck. After all Moses only saw one burning bush.

"I thought the one on my street was due to your presence, you being the two witnesses and all," Komang observed, looking directly at his two passengers in the back seat.

Gabriel chuckled. "Yeah, I guess we were kind of taking credit for it. But it's clear we had nothing to do directly with this one. Forgive us our pride, Lord. It's You and only You."

"But indirectly you did," Aadi offered, "because you obeyed the Lord, resulting in the volcanic explosion that lit this fire."

"Yes, the Lord honors obedience [1], but it is His doing, His miracle," Abraham responded, still staring in wonder at the spectacle.

"Wait a minute," Komang suddenly exclaimed, "that's the same type of tree that's burning in front of my house, a *Waringin* tree. Could that have something to do with it?"

"Tell me more about this type of tree," Gabriel asked quickly, sitting up and taking greater notice of the tree itself. "Does it have any cultural significance?"

"It sure does," Komang replied, and shook his head. "I don't know why I didn't see it beforehand!"

Gabriel waited a moment, watching Komang's gaze turn inward. But he was too impatient to wait longer. "See what?" he prompted.

"Oh, yeah, sorry, I think your God, uhm, mine too I guess, was showing me something. What did you call it before, a revelation?"

7

"Yes, that's the correct term, so what did He show you?" Gabriel asked again, his impatience causing his voice to rise. Abraham laughed, but he too was on the edge of his seat.

Komang took a breath and gathered his thoughts. "Like most things on Bali, trees have a spiritual significance, and the *Waringin tree,* or Banyan in English, is the holiest of all trees. Besides being such a large, beautiful shade tree, it has creepers that drop from its branches that take root and propagate a new tree. So it is said to be eternal, never dying. No important temple is complete without one or more of them prominently displayed."

"Wow," Gabriel exclaimed, "that *is* significant! Is this the tree that I've seen decorated all over Bali?"

Komang nodded. "Yes, these trees are often adorned with scarves or black and white checkered cloths, because people believe they protect the environment from invisible, evil spirits. Some people go so far as to build a whole shrine beneath it where people can make offerings to the spirits."

"This miracle is a direct attack against the demonic gods of this land, showing them to be defenseless against His mighty power," Abraham observed thoughtfully. "Just like Jehovah did to the Egyptians through Moses."

"Yes," Gabriel quickly agreed, "and it also makes the statement that only He is eternal."

They all turned as one to stare yet again at the awesome sight, this time with greater understanding and appreciation. Red embers continued to fall around them and they noticed flames shooting up over the treetops another quarter-mile or so down the highway.

Without a word, Komang slipped the taxi into gear and drove over to yet another Banyan tree shooting flames into the air without a single leaf being consumed. Out of the corner of his eye, Aadi spotted another one down the highway. Then Gabriel saw one down a side street. Komang drove silently down the highway as more and more Banyan trees became perpetually enflamed.

It was then Abraham saw that yet another phenomenon was being wrought by God and the Banyan trees. The nightmarish pallor that had darkened the land was gradually lifting as more and more heavenly torches lit up all around them. "The Lord God, He is our light," Abraham breathed in wonder. [2]

By the time they had reached the outskirts of Denpasar, the capital of Bali and Komang's hometown, all of Bali was lit with a glowing aura of golden light underneath the dome of black soot. It was a surreal, ethereal scene that left them speechless.

Chapter Two

Counter-Insurgency Agency-East, had quickly grown eerily quiet after all its "housewarming" guests shipped out. Alan Morrison returned to CIA-West with a new sense of urgency and tactics; Pastor Wally and Michelle decided to drive west to train Rev. Michael Braintree and his wife Bonnie, turning it into a needed vacation time together.

Brandon and Juanita were off on their tour of all the hideaways and remote camps to build up and train spiritual warfare groups. Jermaine headed back to the Havenwood1 hideaway and his new bride, Tara, from where he would oversee all the hideaway locations to prepare for the coming storm.

Jim and Abby sat in the conference room where so much exciting discussion and revelation had so recently taken place. Instead of feeling energized, they felt lethargic, worn out. Jim glanced fondly over at his wife, always amazed that he of all people had found the love of his life. However, her downcast eyes weighed heavily on his heart.

"What's bothering you, sweetheart?" he asked gently, reaching across the table to take her hand in his.

Abby looked up, a small grim smile acknowledging love for her husband as well as trepidation about the future. "I don't know for sure," she finally answered, "but I imagine it's the same thing that's bothering you."

Jim laughed. "That obvious, huh?"

Abby nodded. "Yes, we both seem down in the dumps. I don't know if it's because we miss our friends already, or because of the danger we face in the days ahead."

Jim nodded agreement. "Probably a little of both."

Then a thought suddenly crystallized in his consciousness. "You know what? I wonder if it's also a letdown following completion of CIA-East? We worked so hard to get it done, and now that it is, the residual fatigue is setting in."

Abby thought about it for a few moments. Jim smiled as he watched her face scrunch up. He loved the way her emotions played so visibly across her countenance. She was a remarkable woman in so many ways, but openness and transparency was perhaps her greatest attribute.

"I think you're right," Abby eventually said, "we're probably just completely drained by overseeing the construction of this place and then overwhelmed by the destruction of the western militia."

Jim jumped up out of his chair and shook off his despondency. "Hey, let's cheer ourselves up by taking a grand tour of our new facility. We can meet and greet all our volunteers and offer them our congratulations on a job well done."

That seemed to strike a responsive chord in Abby. "Yes, but let's also offer the volunteers more than a handshake."

"We don't have any resources to give them bonuses or anything. We'd have to ask Morrison to front us some more money, and we already ran twenty-percent over budget. I don't want to hit him up for more, even though everyone says he's got millions to spare," Jim pointed out cautiously, not want to rain on the parade before it got going.

"So let's throw a grand-opening celebration by using the money in our food budget. We've got a lot of creative people who can cook up some special dishes. Others can decorate using whatever we can find around, and I understand we have a few musicians in our fold, so let's form a praise and worship band," Abby explained enthusiastically.

Jim readily agreed. They set off on the grand tour and recruited the volunteers for the "grand opening" celebration. Soon the entire facility was abuzz with feverish, but welcome, activity. It turned out to be a good way to blow off pent-up steam from the heavy workload, long hours, and lack of sleep.

Later in the day, Abby wandered the halls and was delighted to see all the preparations already underway. The dining hall was being festooned with colorful paper cutouts, streamers of computer-generated graphics, and balloons. Who had those, she wondered? The large, gleaming kitchen was alive with activity and awash with tempting smells.

The sparkling new computer center was devoid of everyone except for two operators manning the computers that hacked into and tracked the global government's key databases. The prayer room had been turned into a rehearsal studio for the rapidly thrown together team of musicians and singers. Judging from the initial attempt to merge their talents, they still had a ways to go. But everyone would appreciate their efforts if not the quality of the music, Abby reasoned and then felt better about it.

She was surprised to find a group in the main conference room preparing what appeared to be a humorous skit, with her and Jim the primary targets. One of the women saw Abby peeking through the slightly cracked door and looked alarmed, but Abby smiled and put her finger to her lips to assure her it was all right. Then she shook her head to indicate that the woman shouldn't tell anyone that Abby had gotten a sneak preview.

Yes, this was just what they needed. Celebrate and get to know one another better, before they had to hunker down to the serious business at hand.

Chapter Three

No one wanted to go near the Global Czar as he continued to rant and rave about the situation in Bali. No one except René, of course. She delighted in seeing Alexis so wound up. For some strange reason, it turned her on. She liked to egg him on and tease him flirtatiously, with a promised reward held out as a carrot of appeasement.

Alexis was on the phone once again with General Falstaff. "I hope you have some good news for a change," Alexis groused into the receiver.

"Depends how you look at it," Falstaff responded evenly. Alexis fumed but said nothing. René grinned in the background, listening in on an extension. She'd sought out the general days ago and used her charms to teach him how to irritate the Global Czar without going over the line, something she excelled in.

"Cut the crap and tell me what I want to know," Alexis demanded stridently.

"Yes sir," Falstaff said, his voice snapping to attention. René was right, this was fun. "Do you want the good news or bad news first?"

"For heaven's sake, man, spit it out," Alexis demanded.

"Yes, sir, the good news is that we now have a sub stationed just offshore. They are now able to communicate with our ground troops under the volcanic cloud on Bali," Falstaff reported.

"Now give me the bad news," Alexis grumped. The only truly good news would have been the complete annihilation of that infernal island.

"Well, sir, it appears that most of, if not all of our forces have defected," Falstaff noted in a matter-of-fact voice that irritated Alexis more than the news itself. How in the world could his chief military man be so blasé about all of this? René almost laughed out loud. The general was turning out to be a quick study. Subtlety was the key.

"Defected to whom?" Alexis demanded to know.

"That's unclear, sir," Falstaff responded, withholding the underlying facts to further stoke the fires raging in the Global Czar. René thought that it was perhaps the imperturbable persona that Alexis presented to the world at large that made it so hilarious to see him sputtering like a common fool. Whatever it was, she was enjoying it immensely.

"And why, pray tell, is it so unclear? If I don't get some real information soon, I'm going to strip you down to a private, do you hear me?" Alexis growled into the phone.

General Falstaff knew that his boss couldn't be pushed any further without severe repercussions. "It seems as though General Asimoto and his troops have converted to Christianity, sir, and are now part of the revival on Bali."

Alexis was stunned. How could this be happening? Was there some kind of hypnotic drug being released in the volcanic cloud? If so, would it similarly infect the rest of Indonesia as it spread out over the area? No, that was ridiculous.

"Perhaps what you're hearing is only what they want us to hear," Alexis observed, a tinge of hope riding atop the mounting despair.

"Of course, that's always a possibility. But we've gotten confirmations from a number of sources, so I really don't think so," Falstaff answered.

"Get General Asimoto on the phone immediately," Alexis ordered. "I want to speak with him myself."

"I'm afraid that won't be possible," the general responded, knowing this would further infuriate Alexis. "He's gone AWOL after telling us that he wouldn't talk to anybody anymore."

"Then let's just use the sub's missiles and blow the island to smithereens and be done with it," Alexis roared in absolute rage.

Now René jumped in. "We can't do that now, because some of the islanders have opened up shortwave communications with people in Jakarta and other nearby locations, which are being retransmitted around the world. Soon everyone will know of the revival there. If we were to wipe them out, a worthy goal to be sure, we'd have to have plausible reasons for public relations purposes."

Alexis threw down the receiver and stormed over to the window, staring out at the Dome of the Rock and the new Jewish Temple off in the distance atop Mount Moriah where Solomon had built the original temple. The view usually gave the Global Czar solace, knowing that soon all of these would be replaced by a temple devoted to worshiping Lucifer through him, the true god of this age. [3]

However, he drew no comfort from the view this time. Turning, he burned his eyes into René, the only one he'd found who could withstand his demonic, withering gaze. "Since you seem to be enjoying this so much, why don't you and Blaine get together and come up with some plausible rationale we can present to the world. I'll be glad when we get to the point that I don't have to justify everything I do."

"There, there, sweetums," René purred. "It will all come about soon enough. After all, it's in the Bible isn't it?" [4]

With that she swept grandly out of the room just before the statue of Napoleon crashed against the nearby wall and shattered into pieces. It was so easy to goad the leader of the entire world that sometimes it got a little boring.

Well, she'd just have to see if she could have a little more fun with Blaine. Right now, she was a whole lot more interesting as she bounced back and forth like a ping-pong ball between Satan and God.

Chapter Four

Blaine Whitney had been kept prisoner in the Global Palace since Alexis had forced her to drink the blood out of the skull and prayed some evil spirit back into her. "What's your name again?" she asked out loud.

"Mephistopheles," a hoarse, whispery voice responded. Was it her imagination? Was it all in her mind? Or was she really hearing audible responses from some ghastly ghost? She didn't know, nor did she really care.

She knew from Rev. Wainwright that such demons could be dispatched in the name of Jesus Christ. At least by someone as full of faith as him. Though she'd tried herself, it had only brought about severe repercussions of headaches, stomach disorders, and weakness. When she cooperated with this Mephistopheles demon, things went a lot smoother.

So she bided her time, waiting for the day she would be released so that she could go see Rev. Wainwright and truly be set free. Yet again. How many times would he take her back, she wondered and shivered in fear. In the meantime, she'd pretend to cooperate with the unholy trinity of Alexis, René and Pope Radinsky, and get back in their good graces.

The "prison" was actually a guest suite that was sumptuously furnished. Though she was locked in, wonderful food was brought in for each meal like clockwork. There were nice clothes to wear, books to read, and a TV to watch. She tried to believe she was on vacation.

Having a plan made her feel better, but those good feelings evaporated quickly when the door was unlocked and René sashayed into the room, a wicked grin on her face. "How's our little girl doing today?" she inquired as her eyes consumed Blaine's body.

Fear spread across Blaine's countenance, a delicious topping on the cake for René. "Listen up, dearie, before we get to this evening's entertainment, we have a little work to do."

René sat down beside Blaine on the couch and tingled as her prey slithered away. She enjoyed the chase more than the conquest.

After explaining the situation in Bali, she asked, "So, Blaine, our public relations wizard, what should we tell the world?"

Blaine's mind was churning in several different directions at the same time. How was she going to hold René off? If she went along with her, as horrible as that seemed, would that facilitate her release? If she were to come up with a brilliant plan for the media, would that get her off the hook?

It was quite disconcerting trying to sort it all out under René's wicked gaze, so Blaine arose from the couch and began to pace back and forth.

"Okay, how about this?" Blaine stopped and faced her adversary. "What if we said that it wasn't so much a revival as an insurrection? That the frenzied mobs have overthrown the government, killing many people along the way."

René nodded. "Yes, but we'd have to provide some evidence. Otherwise it would just be our word against theirs."

"What if we sent in some black ops troops undercover and they blew up government buildings and assassinated key officials? We could have one of them digitally record the events and then we could give copies to the media."

René was impressed. Clearly this was more than the old Blaine Whitney talking. Mephistopheles must have attained a strong foothold inside her. Alexis would be pleased.

They ironed out a few more details before René declared an end to the business portion of her agenda. She gave Blaine her best "come hither" look and laughed as Blaine retreated out of the living room and into the bedroom. She chuckled as she heard Blaine fruitlessly attempt to lock a door that had no lock, and then push furniture up against the door.

Chapter Five

When Morrison got back to CIA-West, he found it in sheer bedlam. Rumors and panic were spreading like wildfire. Morrison spoke to three different people and got four different stories. One person had an either/or scenario.

Since the common thread had to do with their computers, he rushed off to find Francine. She was at the main console barking out orders and babbling at the computer, her fingers flying over the keyboard while incomprehensible code whisked across the screen. Others were running around in comical confusion, reminding Morrison of the Three Stooges. Surrounding them was a mob of residents who nervously tried to interpret what they were hearing and seeing.

Morrison pushed through the mob, dodged scurrying technicians, and tapped Fran on the shoulder. She dismissively waved him away without turning around to see who was there. So he grabbed her arm and turned her around on the revolving chair.

"What's going on?" he demanded to know.

Francine twisted free and turned back to the keyboard. "Can't talk now. It's the height of the battle. Ask Fred, he'll fill you in."

Morrison turned around and scanned the technicians' name tags as they scooted by in a pattern choreographed by Fran's rapid-fire commands. He finally spotted Fred and called out to him, but the heavily bearded young man either didn't hear him or was too terrified of Francine to deviate from his appointed rounds.

So Morrison grabbed him, but Fred's momentum carried him forward and they toppled over together to the tiled floor. Neither one was hurt, but Morrison had to grab hold of Fred to prevent him from escaping.

"Fran said I should talk to you to find out what's going on," Morrison yelled over the hubbub.

Fred's face screwed up in puzzlement. "She did? Who are you?"

"I'm the guy who owns and finances this place, that's who!" Morrison snapped back, annoyed not to be recognized. He realized this was probably his own fault for not spending time with the troops.

"Fran really said I should talk to you?" the flustered young man said as he gave Francine a worried glance, but she was too engrossed in her own tasks to notice him.

Morrison struggled to his feet, lifted Fred up and pulled him out of the computer center into an adjacent conference room. "Sit," he commanded and Fred did so, his fear transferring to the visibly agitated Big Boss.

"Now, take a deep breath, and tell me what's going on," Morrison ordered as he sat down across the table from Fred and fixed him with his best no-nonsense stare.

Fred did exactly that. He breathed in very deeply, held the breath a few moments, and then exhaled across the table. The stale aroma of coffee, pizza and garlic bread caused Morrison to fan away the noxious odors with both hands.

"Oh, sorry about that," Fred grinned lamely.

"Just get on with it," a very frustrated Morrison said between gritted teeth.

"Well, let's see, how can I explain this so you'll understand. Hmmm. Okay, I think I've got a way. It's like we've been secretly sending commandos into the enemy's camp and they've been secretly communicating back the enemy's plans. That's been working out fine, but this morning we thought we detected that the enemy was monitoring our communications and trying to track down the commandos as well as their headquarters, which is here, of course."

Fred had been talking to the far wall, but now he looked over at his audience to see if he'd been understood. Morrison nodded at him and said, "So I assume you've been taking evasive measures, disguising IP addresses, using our botnet of remote PCs," he replied.

Fred was taken aback. Then he remembered Fran telling him and the rest of the technicians not to underestimate Mr. Morrison, because he'd built one of the world's biggest Internet companies.

"Uhm, yes, sir, that's correct. But we're also going on a counterattack, destroying some of their data and embedding Trojan Horses in their software." Fred was now warily watching Morrison out of the corner of his eye.

"To what end?" Morrison asked.

"Ahh, to distract them from locating us and to disarm them entirely if we have to," Fred replied cautiously.

"But won't this make us *more* visible? I thought the objective was to remain below the radar," Morrison snapped at Fred as if he were the enemy.

Fred leaned away from the angry man across the table. "It's too late for that. They were very close to tracking us down. They already know we're somewhere in the western United States."

As Fred braced himself for another attack, Morrison leaned back in thought. "So that's why the rumors grew to the point where people think we're under imminent danger."

"I guess so," Fred replied carefully. "I really don't know what people are thinking, I've been too busy."

Morrison studied the young man. A typical computer nerd. Guileless, transparent. "Okay, you better get back to work before Fran has a cow."

Fred ran off, visibly relieved. Morrison sat alone for awhile. Were things falling apart? First the militia, now potential discovery? Was he at fault? No one knew of his underlying insecurities, which he covered over with a confident demeanor that he put on and took off like a well-worn hat.

It took a lot of energy to maintain the façade which was why he was so reclusive. That air of mystery had served him well over the years, but sometimes it was his Achille's heel. As his recently departed mentor always told him, "Your greatest strength is also your greatest weakness, because it will make you blind."

Had he been blind? Blind to General Wycliffe's foolish pride that led to the militia's demise? Blind to Fran's seeming invincibility? What if he'd taken the time to get to know them better? Could he have foreseen the problems and warded them off? But that would mean they would get to know him better too, and that would mean….

Well, he didn't exactly know what that would mean. It was too scary to contemplate. He had too many skeletons in the closet, too many personality deficiencies. If everyone knew him well, no one would respect him. They wouldn't accept his as their leader.

Morrison sighed. The same old dilemma. No matter what he did, he always wound up back at this same place with the same issues, the same questions, and no answers.

Chapter Six

Brandon and Juanita had, for the most part, enjoyed their little "vacation trip" down south through old memories and past childhood haunts. So much had happened since they'd left their dysfunctional families behind and become successful in Yankee territory. It was both refreshing and depressing, so it was with some sense of relief that they arrived in the Florida Panhandle where there were no memories and no one to avoid.

Havenwood3 lay outside Tallahassee, just inside the Apalachicola National Forest. The remote camp was situated in the southern portion of the vast preserve near Boggy Jordan Lake. Even with detailed directions, the hideaway was difficult to find. Darkness was setting in when they finally spotted a large stand of Cypress trees with the red dot on the trunk of the largest specimen.

Although they were welcomed effusively, Juanita felt in her spirit that there was an air of resentment they would need to overcome. Brandon told her later in the private underground "guest suite" that it was similar to the time he was promoted to be

Director of a Human Services department in which he'd never worked before. Mr. "Big Shot," who also happened to be black, had to patiently win the trust of the people who'd been passed over. "Maybe that's what the prayer team down here is feeling now." he suggested.

Juanita nodded. "Yes, that's probably it. I'm so used to being in charge and having people know who I am. I'll have to be real careful not to step on their toes," she agreed.

However, as she lay awake long into the wee hours of the morning, she knew how hard it would be for her to hold back. It just wasn't her nature to do so, and time was of the essence. The matters at hand were too important for coddling prima donnas. But she promised the Lord to try. She asked over and over again for patience[5] and wisdom.[6]

After a communal breakfast, Howard Jenkins, the hideaway's leader, brought Juanita down a dimly lit hall whose earthen walls dripped muddy water in many places. The floor was made out of metal grating above the slime below. She appreciated Howard's warning to not wear heels.

"Is it always this damp?" she asked carefully, not wanting to seem like she was disparaging their hideaway, but it really did pale in comparison to Havenwood1. She'd never fully appreciated how well it had been constructed. This clammy air and dank smell would take some getting used to.

"Hmm? Oh, yes, we're right next to a swamp. But it stays nice and cool down here in the summers, so that's a real advantage," Howard answered distractedly.

When he opened the prayer room door and led Juanita inside, she was immediately struck by three things. First, she saw the prayer stations scattered around the large room. She was quite impressed. They were as good as the ones she had set up back in Virginia. Each one had a theme, but before she could study them further, Howard began the introductions.

As Juanita nodded and mouthed hellos, the second thing that struck her was the resentful, obstinate face of a heavyset white woman with puffed grey hair over a reddened countenance. With her arms folded tightly across her massive chest, she was quite an imposing woman, one to be reckoned with.

The third thing she saw was that the other five women and two men were completely subservient to the red-faced woman. They were nervous, but their eyes pleaded for help. *Oh my, what have I gotten myself into?* Juanita thought as she sat in the proffered chair at the opposite end of the table from the obvious leader of the prayer team.

Howard quickly scrambled out of the room, mumbling something about things to do. Even he seemed fearful of the commanding presence who slowly rose to her feet. Juanita had been too distracted by the circumstances to pay much attention to all the names during Howard's introduction. However, she would never forget the name of the leader, Lenore, who now began to speak.

"I'm not sure what you hope to accomplish here," Lenore began as she unfolded her thick arms and leaned forward toward Juanita, placing her hands on the table to support her massive body.

"But I can assure you that we have things well in hand." Lenore threw out the words like darts. "Howard tells me that you're visiting all of the hideaways and remote camps to check up on things and provide assistance and direction where needed. While we welcome your presence here, you'll soon see that we have no need of such outside interference."

With that, Lenore proceeded to boast about all the things that they had accomplished. She rattled on and on and on. Finally, she said they would begin to pray and that she'd start off. Fifteen minutes later she was still going strong with no end in sight. Juanita watched the faces of the prayer team as they sat motionless, heads bowed, hands folded, muttering amens from time to time.

Meanwhile, Howard had taken Brandon aside into a smaller conference room down another damp hallway, where he proceeded to spill out his anguish and frustrations over Lenore who had apparently cowed everyone in the hideaway. While Howard was the titular head, it was really Lenore who made the major decisions. Morale was at an all-time low, and Howard didn't know what to do about it. Brandon leaned over and put his arm around him when Howard looked like he was going to cry. Then he prayed over him for the Holy Spirit to provide comfort[7] and to show them how to deal with this situation.[8]

Chapter Seven

Gabriel, Abraham, Aadi and Komang were exhausted when they finally returned to Komang's house. The Banyan tree outside was still burning brightly, as were many others in the immediate vicinity. The military presence had faded away to be replaced by the sight of children playing joyously in the street while happy, grinning parents and elders visited in small groups up and down the block.

After collapsing into an eighteen-hour sleep, Aadi was the first to stir. He made coffee and began to prepare a traditional breakfast out of the odds and ends in Komang's refrigerator and cabinets. The golden glow from all the trees continued to provide sufficient light, although Aadi couldn't tell if it was day or night.

While the coffee brewed and the meal warmed in the oven, he stepped out onto Komang's small front porch and took a deep breath of surprisingly fragrant air. It wasn't quite the smell of a Banyan tree, but similar with a hint of a flower he couldn't remember the name of, a delicious aroma that had him briefly wondering whether this was heaven on earth.

He heard some noises back within the house, and saw Abraham and Gabriel stumbling out of their room, lured by the scent of coffee and food. Their stomachs rumbled with hunger, but Aadi insisted they first go outside and breathe in the aroma of heaven.

"Who would have thought that underneath a dark cloud covering the sky with soot, that we'd have such beautiful, warm light and such wonderfully fragrant air?" Gabriel said as he shook his head in wonder.

When the community saw that the two witnesses had arisen, they flocked over to greet them with great enthusiasm. They also communicated the latest news and rumors. It was hard to distinguish between the two.

As best the 'gang of four' (as some called them) could make out, General Asimoto and most of his troops had been swept up in the revival, but someone was blowing up key government buildings. Reports of black figures slinking through the shadows revived traditional fears of evil spirits.

Gabriel and Abraham assured everyone that no evil spirits could withstand the mighty presence of God on this island, so it must be the work of ordinary human beings. If so, then perhaps they too would succumb to the Holy Spirit and come in out of the dark. They led the community in an impromptu prayer meeting to that effect, and then retreated back inside to finally partake of the breakfast Aadi was keeping warm but not overcooked.

After breakfast, they set off in Komang's taxi once again to see for themselves what was fact and what was rumor. Sure enough, several buildings in the capital had been decimated. Fortunately, or thanks be to God, no one was hurt. The government sector had closed due to the national holiday that had been proclaimed to celebrate the revival and their deliverance from General Asimoto's threatened doom.

They were seated on a bench outside the main municipal building, or what was left of it, when two of those rumored black bodies emerged from a shadowed alleyway between two buildings across the street. Komang and Aadi stood up in front of the two witnesses to protect them, but all Abraham and Gabriel did was laugh and push them aside so they could see for themselves. They had finally grown accustomed to the fact that they still had around three years to go before they would be killed and resurrected.

As the two black bodies stepped out into the light of several burning Banyan trees, the four observers could see that they were wearing dark, skin-tight wetsuits. The two held up their arms in surrender and slowly crossed the street. Aadi and Komang stepped around the bench and stood behind the two witnesses, not wanting to get in the way of what felt like a fateful confrontation.

"We mean you no harm," the man on the right said in a thick accent, as the two came within ten feet of the bench.

Abraham waved his arm back at the ruins behind him. "Harm enough, it would appear."

A woman's voice came out of the wetsuit on the left. "We made certain no one was around."

"Nevertheless, an evil deed to be sure," Abraham stated emphatically.

"Yes, and for that we are truly sorry," the man asserted. "We have been watching since the explosions and do not understand what is happening here. But we feel so ashamed of what we've done, that we want to be part of it. It's like some external force is compelling us to surrender and accept our punishment."

"We'd rather you surrendered to Jesus and accepted His forgiveness," Gabriel quickly interjected.

"We're from Russia," the woman said, "where Christians are despised as being weak-willed fools."

Gabriel laughed. "Yes, the devil's favorite characterization, but one devoid of substance. In fact, it is human reasoning that is too narrow-minded and locked into the religion of secular humanism to be open enough to receive the truth."[9]

"It takes an enormous amount of courage to be a Christian, so it is not the avenue of choice for the faint of heart," added Abraham.

"Can you tell us about your Jesus, then?" the man asked sincerely. "We wish to be open-minded."

"We'll do better than that," Gabriel said as he stood up and walked toward them. "We'll introduce you to Him."

"You mean He is here?" the woman gasped and looked around.

"Most certainly," Abraham said as he and Gabriel embraced the two terrorists and guided them toward the taxi. "Squeeze in the car with us and we'll take you to Him."

Chapter Eight

General Falstaff put down the phone and glanced across the bed at René. The raw scratches on her face made her seem just a tad more vulnerable. She saw the flame of desire flicker to life in the general, so quickly rolled out of bed and pulled on a heavy terrycloth robe.

"What was that call all about?" she asked, sauntering over to the window of his quarters in Brussels. As the former head of NATO's forces, and now of the entire globe's military might, he truly held the world's fate in his hands. That kind of power caused her knees to grow weak with longing, but she had to hold back in order to maintain her control over him.

"Not good news, I'm afraid," Falstaff said with a sigh as he too arose and pulled on the pair of slacks that had lain crumpled beside the bed.

"I thought they had successfully infiltrated the island and blown up numerous government buildings throughout all of Bali," René noted as she turned to face him.

"Yes, but now it appears that two of our operatives have also defected," Falstaff regretfully reported.

"Damn it to hell!" René cursed bitterly. "Those two clowns are way too much trouble. We should have dealt with them when we had them under our thumbs."

"But I thought you said they couldn't be killed, or at least not yet?" Falstaff asked, genuinely puzzled about all this supernatural claptrap. Truth be told, he thought she and Alexis were every bit as irrational as the two so-called witnesses. However, he wasn't about to say anything that would drive René away or cost him his lofty position.

"Yes, but we could have kept them from running loose," she snarled.

"So, what now?" Falstaff asked, striding toward her with renewed purpose.

René stretched out her arm and held him off. "So, now you call Alexis. I thought you were the big cheese here, not me."

Falstaff felt stung by her mocking tone. Nevertheless, a small price to be paid. "And how do you think I should handle him this time?"

René scooted away from Falstaff. "Oh, he's going to be beside himself this time, so now you become his buddy, his confidant, someone he can talk to about all his frustrations."

"Me?" The mighty general was incredulous. He'd never been known for his soft side.

"You can fake it, can't you? He needs a friend right now. He's had it with me and Vlad, and is starting to withhold information from us. You can be that buddy he opens up to and then you can fill me in."

A wicked smile holding the promise of things to come convinced Falstaff to go along. "My, my, you are the cunning one, aren't you?" he said as he reached for her.

She backed away yet again. "It's time to make that phone call," she coaxed.

Falstaff stopped and sighed. "Okay, but not until you tell me where you got all those scratches."

René's face darkened and she glared at the general. Without further word, she turned into the bathroom and slammed the door shut.

27

Chapter Nine

Blaine stood behind the bedroom door of her exquisite prison and waited anxiously. She simply had to get out of this place. It took all her strength to hold off René last time and now Alexis was making his move on her. And all her Papal counselor would say was to "give in to the inevitable and start enjoying life."

Even worse, the demons were driving her batty, tormenting her mind and pushing her emotional buttons.[10] She couldn't hold out much longer. She'd tasted more of the dark side than she cared to imagine, and it left her queasy and unsettled. If this was what Satan had to offer, she no longer wanted any part of it.

Or at least the sane part of her felt that way. However, other parts of her thirsted for more. Somehow, though, she knew if she went back down that dark alley once more she'd never return. So now she would play the last card available to her, a plan to escape hatched more out of desperation than hope.

The muscular guard who brought her food had become somewhat of a friend. He knew nothing of the circumstances that led to her incarceration, but he remembered her quite well from TV when he used to fantasize about her. Now she had him wrapped around her finger, bringing her food on a tray as she lolled in bed.

She knew that he expected one of these days to join her there. That had weakened his watchfulness. And so she now waited behind the bedroom door, with the sturdy, gold-encrusted leg of the living room chair in her sweaty, shaking hands. The chair was propped up in the corner of the living room, but she knew his eyes would focus only on the bedroom door.

At last came the sound of the main door unlocking. She took a deep breath and held it as she raised the chair leg above her head, gripped tightly in two hands. She glanced over at the bed where spare pillows and a large comforter were bundled under the blanket, looking a whole lot less believable now that the moment of truth had arrived.

Nevertheless, Bruce sashayed into the room without a clue. As he passed through the doorway holding the tray of breakfast food in front of him, he called out, "Hey, cutie-pie, sleeping in today?"

Blaine shoved the door aside with her foot and swung the heavy leg squarely down on Bruce's head. He instantly collapsed to the floor, his head gushing blood and her breakfast splattering all over.

She stood over him with trembling legs, the chair leg held high, waiting for him to move again, but he lay still, except for the blood which continued to flow copiously. She hadn't expected so much blood. Now she was torn. She hadn't wanted to kill him, but she hadn't known how much force was required to knock out someone so big and strong. Apparently she'd used too much.

Was he dead? Or was he going to bleed to death? She stood immobile in her disguise. Her long blond hair was gone, replaced by a crew cut of mottled hair she'd attempted to color with grape juice. She'd woven the bedroom drapes into a sarong something like she'd seen the Moonies wear at various airports.

Before she backed out of her plan, she felt Bruce's neck for a pulse as she'd seen on the TV crime shows. To her surprise and thankfulness, his heart was still pumping. She gathered up a sheet and wrapped his head in it, not really knowing if it would do any good, but it made her feel better to try.

Then she ran to the main door, opened it cautiously and peeked into the hallway outside. No one was in sight, nor did she hear any sound at all. She hadn't paid much attention when they'd dragged her down to this guest suite, but she'd heard Bruce's footsteps always coming from the left, so she headed to the right.

She tried to walk slowly as if she belonged there, but her legs were shaking and her lips quivered. Many foreigners in all their traditional regalia were common sights around the Global Palace. If she could only get to the public areas, she thought she might have a chance of getting away.

There was an elevator at the end of the corridor and a door that said "Stairs." She vacillated a moment, and then pushed through the door and started down the steps. At the next landing, there was the number "8" on the door, so she guessed that was the floor number.

And then door number eight opened. Blaine gasped and pulled back. Two Muslim men dressed in tunics and turbans briefly looked over at her and then averted their eyes. They mumbled some words of apology and then went down the stairs.

She grabbed the handrail to keep from falling over, her heart pounding furiously, her head spinning. She listened to the quiet voices of the two men until a door opened and closed several flights below and then there was silence. Slowly she made her way down, renewed by the apparent acceptance of her disguise.

When she got to door number one, she couldn't get her hand to reach out for the doorknob. Then she noticed that this door had a small, thick glass window. Although it distorted the images, she could see the main lobby to the palace spread out before her.

Blaine tried to remember how the lobby was laid out and figure out where she was. It made her head hurt and she got lightheaded again. Spatial relationships and directionality had always been a weakness. So she took a quick breath, opened the door and strode out into the busy lobby with feigned confidence.

She attracted the usual number of casual glances from the men she passed by, but that was normal. The look on the guard's face behind the main counter was not. He poked the guard to his right and pointed her way. She tried to appear nonchalant.

Just then the phone rang at the counter. The first guard picked up the red receiver and listened for a moment, his face wrinkling in shock. In doing so, his eyes lost focus as they do when someone is concentrating or mentally paying close attention to something else.

In those few seconds she dashed for the front doors, pushing into a group of Muslim women in their burkas and veils as they made their way through the two revolving doors. Just as she stepped out onto the front portico, alarms began to clang loudly.

There were two long limousines stretched out at the bottom of the stairs, awaiting the Muslim women who panicked when guards started running frantically to and fro with drawn guns. Blaine ducked down and stayed within the group of women as they shuffled quickly into the limos. Surprisingly, no one objected when she got inside with them.

When two guards came over to the limos and tried to peer inside the windows, Blaine ducked down again and one of the women leaned forward to block the view of the guards who apparently couldn't see much anyway through the darkly tinted windows.

The limo driver began arguing and cursing loudly at the two guards. "Infidels are not allowed to look upon Muslim women," the lady who'd helped to hide Blaine said with a cultured English accent as she sat back in the seat.

When the limo pulled away, the woman lowered her veil. Blaine glanced up front toward the driver, but a dark sheet of glass prevented even him from looking upon his passengers.

"Why did you help me?" Blaine asked, still shaking and breathless.

"It is atrocious what men in all cultures do to women. We have to stick together."

Chapter Ten

It was not a good day to be the Global Czar. Defections and escapes thwarted his plans. René and Radinsky were nowhere to be found. At least General Falstaff had been more supportive and conciliatory. So he'd invited him to come up to Jerusalem where they could put their heads together and determine how to handle the situation in Bali.

Without Blaine's availability, he'd made a rare appearance at the daily news conference to spin the clever story she and René had come up with. Exuding confidence and charm, he had the media eating out of his hands by the time he was done. Now the news was all about the Bali Insurrection. Video of government buildings being blown up conveyed the message better than any of his words. At least something was going right.

Although opposing points of view were being broadcast surreptitiously out of Bali, the mainstream media decried it all as typical Christian hysteria and lies. So far, world opinion remained in his camp, but the fact that he still needed to even consider world opinion infuriated D'Antoni.

At last his assistant showed the general in, bedecked in his dress uniform with scads of medallions. "Have a seat General Falstaff. I hope you bring good news, or at least a plan of action."

Falstaff saluted Alexis smartly and took a seat, sitting rigidly on the edge.

"At ease, soldier," Alexis said and smiled with satisfaction. He was pleased that the general had learned the value of respect.

"Thank you, sir. And yes, I do have good news as well as a plan," Falstaff said as he leaned back in the leather covered wing chair.

"Let's hear it," Alexis requested as he sat down behind his desk. It was still too soon to show familiarity with this as yet unknown X-factor that he'd inherited when NATO was merged into the Global Governance Committee. Though highly recommended, Falstaff was known to be headstrong, which Alexis had experienced at the other end of the phone line. But in person, so far, so good.

"Well, first of all, the volcanic cloud is dissipating somewhat as it spreads out over the entire region. Although Mount Agung and the lesser volcanoes are still erupting sporadically, there is far less debris and ash. I believe we can now launch an attack on Bali. The only question is how strong of an attack. Surgical air strikes can take out key facilities and render the island uninhabitable. Or, we can blast the capital as a warning."

Alexis smiled. Not that he agreed with the general's approach, but at least he was moving in the right direction. "I don't want to just provide a lesson. I want to obliterate the entire island."

Falstaff's eyes widened. "What about civilian casualties?"

"You mean collateral damage?" Alexis egged the general on, enjoying the turnabout.

"Well, yes, but not just civilians on Bali, but also Java to the west and Lombok to the east. There would be a lot of fallout from an attack that destroyed the entire island." Falstaff was sure that Alexis was simply posturing.

"I don't care one whit about fallout or collateral damage. Give Java and Lombok a 24-hour warning to take cover, and then blast Bali into kingdom come," Alexis growled, leaving no doubt about his intentions.

Falstaff was quite taken aback and struggled to maintain his composure. He'd heard Alexis say similar things before, but thought it was all overwrought hyperbole. Now he could see for himself that the Global Czar was quite serious and possibly insane. He briefly wondered whether this is what it was like reporting to Hitler.

Alexis saw Falstaff's struggle and laughed. "What's the matter general? Too weak for real combat?"

Combat? Bombing innocent victims isn't combat, it's genocide. Falstaff forced himself to reply, "No sir, I've proven myself in Vietnam and the Gulf Wars. This is quite different."

"Yes it is," Alexis surprisingly agreed. "But it's what we should have done in those wars like Truman did to end World War II. Bomb them into oblivion. We have the power and the might but are always too timid to use it," the Global Czar declared with surprising vehemence.

Falstaff was at a loss. René's little plan had flown out the window. This wasn't a time for silly games. "I agree to some extent, but those were actual wars. We're not at war with Bali."

"No, but we *are* the world's peacekeeper, and Bali is suffering from an insurrection that has shut the entire government down," Alexis declared.

Does he really believe his own smokescreen? Is he that far gone? Or is he simply adhering to the plan? Falstaff repositioned himself in his chair to gain some time. "Well, yes, that's the cover story. However, if we have collateral damage on innocent, adjacent islands, I'm not sure the rationale will stand."

"Okay," Alexis agreed, but a sly curl of his mouth worried Falstaff. "I'll leave it up to you to figure out how to completely destroy Bali without damaging Java or Lombok. But I want it taken care of in the next twenty-four hours, is that clear?"

Oh boy. Now the ball's in my court. Alexis is a lot more formidable than René led me to believe. Was she just setting me up? Using me?

"That's an order, soldier, from your Commander-in-Chief. Alexis stood up at attention and looked for Falstaff to do the same. The general arose and snapped a salute. "Yes, sir!"

"That's all. Dismissed."

Falstaff saluted once more, pivoted sharply and marched out the door. *Now what? Mutiny or genocide? But I have to speak to René first.*

Chapter Eleven

Morrison took the time to dispel all the rumors and shoo all the people out of and away from the computer center. Then he retreated to his ranch house and hid away in his office with dark, hooded eyes. His housekeeper and ranch hand knew that look and steered clear of the boss. Although each had been with Morrison for over ten years, neither really knew him.

Behind the closed doors, Morrison sat in his desk chair and stared out the window at the mountains in the distance. He sighed deeply and rubbed his eyes. Born to wealth into a family that had a long history of CEOs, Senators, Generals and Admirals, the expectations for him had been so high that he'd found it impossible to achieve. Not just in his own mind, for his family told him so constantly. Well, not so much now that he'd become a Christian and they'd shunned him entirely.

Graduating from Princeton in the top 10% of his class wasn't high enough. Failure to follow through on his PhD was a mortal sin with no margin of forgiveness, despite the psychiatrist's diagnosis that he'd suffered a nervous breakdown. Off to war as an enlisted private only brought further familial condemnation. An honorable discharge due to Post-Traumatic Stress Disorder put the final nail in the coffin. He was a loser, a reject.

The success of his first software company was much too small to impress any of them. His marriage to a lower-tier socialite was only mildly accepted. When the marriage failed and, even worse, didn't produce any offspring, he became the black sheep that everyone joked about and held up to the younger family members as a model of how to waste your life.

There was surprise, at first, when his software company grew into a mammoth conglomerate, including one of the largest Internet companies in the world. There were a few muted congratulations, but mostly whispers in the background that he was sure to louse that up too. And then came his conversion to Christianity.

The family were all nominal Episcopalians, attending church often enough to impress world opinion. Behind closed doors, their true religion was capitalism. Morrison saw it as a lust for greed and power, a key ingredient he seemed to lack. Creating a highly profitable company had only been an exercise to gain his family's respect. He cared little about the money, except for the privacy it bought.

One night as he was being driven home to his Denver penthouse, he was dozing when he heard a deep, loud voice. "Alan, do you want true peace in your life? Love? Acceptance? Forgiveness?"

Morrison looked around but there was no one there. He pressed the button that opened the window separating him from his long-time driver. "Otis, did you hear that?"

"Hear what sir?"

"That loud voice."

"No sir, I didn't hear anything but the usual traffic noises," Otis reported.

Morrison pressed the button again restoring his privacy. Had he been dreaming? Must have. Now he was too awake to doze so he watched the traffic and people out his window, speculating on who was happy and who wasn't.

Just before they entered the underground garage in his apartment building (literally his, because he owned it as well as many other real estate properties), he heard the voice again. "Alan, God loves you. Seek Him and you will find Him."[11]

There was no doubting it this time. He could see that Otis didn't react to the voice, so only he was hearing it. Once safely ensconced in his penthouse, he asked the voice to come back and explain itself, to no avail. Nevertheless, it had a profound effect on him. Not just the words, but the voice itself had pierced his heart.

That set him off on a two-year spiritual quest that took him to Tibet and an ashram in India where he studied and practiced many forms of Eastern religion. That led him to Virginia Beach to study and experience the writings of Edgar Cayce, the "sleeping prophet." Then it was on to Sedona, Arizona, the so-called New Age Capital of the world where he discovered *The Course in Miracles,* presumably dictated by Jesus Christ.

That, in turn, led to an interest in Jesus. The many claims in the *Miracle* book about Jesus forced Morrison to actually read several translations of the Bible that convinced him *The Course in Miracles* was a fraud. He was never the same after that. Finally, he accepted the Bible's veracity and knelt one night to surrender his heart, mind and soul to Jesus. No sooner had he done so than he felt instantly changed and fulfilled. Born again, according to John, chapter three. Filled with the Holy Spirit.

That's when the angel came and told him to contact Pastor Gabriel and start building the remote hideaways. The rest was history, as they say. Morrison plunged himself into living out the Christianity he'd found in the Bible, Unfortunately, his visits to many churches and denominations led him to believe that most had imposed their own rituals and regulations that were not supported by Scripture. He decided to simply be a Christian on his own.

Looking back now, he could see how that decision was heavily influenced by his fear of people and what they thought about him. In isolation, his faith withered on the vine and became simply one of works, devoid of love and compassion. He was trying to earn God's acceptance just as he'd failed to win his family's approval.

Speaking with the Braintrees, awakening them to love and compassion, had stirred his own heart and soul. Then came the militia's demise and now potential discovery. *What are you doing, Jesus? What do you want from me? What do you want me to do?*

Chapter Twelve

Fran burst into Morrison's office without warning and came to an abrupt stop when she saw him on his knees praying and weeping. She tried to tip-toe back out, but he turned and looked at her forlornly. "It's okay, please stay. I want to hear where things stand with the government's infiltration of our computers."

He arose slowly, almost painfully, and shuffled back into his desk chair. Fran's feet were glued to the floor by the office door. Morrison chuckled at the sight of the hyperactive motor-mouth frozen in place. For her part, Fran couldn't get over seeing the always composed and controlled leader with his defenses down.

"Please, sit down, and fill me in." Morrison waved Fran toward the chair on the other side of his desk.

As she shyly settled in place, he was surprised at the lack of guilt or shame he felt at being seen in his most vulnerable state. He thought that perhaps the Lord was already at work in him in response to his prayers.

When Fran didn't begin her report, he opened his mouth to coax her to start, but was surprised at what actually came out. "What do the people here think of me?"

Fran was quite taken aback and didn't know how to respond, so she remained uncharacteristically still.

"What do you think?" Morrison continued to probe. "Do you really know anything about me? Do you trust me as your leader, given the recent fiascoes?"

Fran's eyes were bulging out of their sockets, even as her lips seemed to be stapled shut. "I'm not sure I really want to get into that," she finally said.

"That's okay, if you don't. I understand that it's an uncomfortable topic. But I guess I thought you, of all people, would give me the straight scoop," Morrison said as he sighed and leaned back in his chair. "I thought maybe God had sent you in answer to my prayer."

Suddenly the dam broke and the words spilled out of Fran like a freight train with no brakes rushing down a mountain. "I can't speak for anyone else, but as for me, well, you're right, I really don't know anything about you. From what I've seen and experienced, I think you're a strong leader, maybe a little too strong. But most of my respect comes from what you've done, not what you've revealed about yourself, which is precious little. I admire that you financed the hideaways and remote camps and respect your leadership based on your successful business ventures. I truly appreciate your intercession with the Braintrees. That seemed to be really anointed. But when push comes to shove, you're so aloof that you might as well be like the Wizard of Oz, shouting out directions from behind the curtain. Without any kind of personal relationship, I do feel uncomfortable and even a bit afraid, not knowing who or what you really are, especially with our fate now in your hands. Well, of course, it's really all in God's hands, but I think you know what I mean."

Morrison couldn't help but laugh, even though the truth stung. "So, what do you think I should do about it?"

"Well, you could allow us to call you Alan, for starters," Fran said, and smiled back in relief when she saw he was not angry about her appraisal.

He nodded somewhat apologetically. "I guess I've kind of used that as a barrier," he admitted. "I never really thought about it before, it just came to seem natural that everyone would address me by my last name."

Fran opened her mouth again and then clamped it shut.

"What? What were you going to say? I promise I won't get offended or angry about anything you say," he prompted her.

Fran judged that he appeared sincere, so she took a deep breath and removed the filter. "It's way more than just hiding behind your last name. You don't ever hang out with us nor have a single friend, from what I can see. Even your housekeeper and ranch hand tell us they don't know you very well either. You stay locked away here in your office and don't appear to have social interaction with anyone outside the ranch either. That's just not normal."

Morrison sighed. She was right, far more so than she realized. Was this the time to finally come out of hiding? Then a thought suddenly popped into his mind. He assumed it was from the Holy Spirit because it was not the kind of thing he would have ever thought on his own.

"Fran, I really appreciate your honesty. How about you and Jesse, plus Jerome and Sue, join me for dinner tonight?" Morrison couldn't believe that this minor step caused his heart to pound furiously as fear of exposure rose within him.

Her eyes lit up and positively sparkled, not exactly the reaction he'd anticipated. "That would be wonderful… Alan."

He found himself grinning like a fool, but couldn't stop. *Good Lord, what are you doing to me?*

"Okay, then," Fran said as she got up to go. "Oh, what time?"

"How about six o'clock?"

"Super, see you then." Fran was nearly to the open office door when she remembered the original purpose for her earlier violation of his boundaries.

She turned, her head tilted slightly to the side and her hands on her hips. "Don't you want to hear my update on the crisis?"

"Oh, that," Alan sputtered, embarrassed that he'd placed his personal issues above the more significant matters at hand. But the unbidden thought came into his now open mind. *Nothing is more important than your relationship with others and with Me, for you are just as aloof with Me as you are with them.*

Fran watched as Morrison's normally unexpressive face twisted through a variety of emotions, culminating with a single tear that traced down his right cheek. "Yes, of course, please tell me."

Fran's adrenalin kicked into gear again. She scampered over and sat down on the edge of the chair, her face flushed with excitement. Alan couldn't help but smile again. *I don't ever recall smiling so much. What in the world is happening to me?*

"Well, we finally figured out how the infiltrators had tracked us down. Rather than employ direct countermeasures, we hid away some false information about who we are and where we are. I knew if they were that good, they'd eventually find it on their own and think it was for real. When I hacked into their system and saw that they'd taken the bait and run with it, I then modified the way we trick their databases into allowing us to continue to buy and sell without the RFID chips. So now they're looking for a group of terrorists who are holed up somewhere in Wyoming, and we've got some of our people on their way to Denver to test out whether we can still circumvent the Universal ID System."

Alan sat back and processed the information that had come at him as if out of a shotgun. "Good job," he finally said. "Assuming our people get back from Denver all right, let's have a celebration tomorrow night over in the dining hall."

The corner of Fran's mouth curved up in a sly smile. "And you'll actually come?"

Alan sighed. "Yes, I will, and I'll even talk to people and be sociable."

Now a tiny tear trickled out of Fran's eye. She could see how difficult this was for him. She, like the others, had thought Morrison acted like he was too good to mingle with the troops. Instead, she realized he had his own personal deficiencies, just like everyone else.

Chapter Thirteen

Back at Komang's house, Gabriel and Abraham had been up all night with the two Russian operatives who'd surprisingly surrendered to them in downtown Denpasar. Alyosha, an intense, wiry woman with piercing eyes, questioned them relentlessly about Jesus, Christianity and God to the point that both witnesses were completely spent as the light of dawn began to seep into the kitchen.

Vyacheslav, a large, brooding hulk with heavy eyelids and an insolent sneer, had mostly watched and listened, only occasionally asking for more clarification. At times, they thought he might even be dozing behind those wary eyes, but it was he who finally broke down in wrenching sobs, gave his heart to Jesus and repented from a long and horrifying list of sins.

When they turned back to Aly, the early sun broke across her face giving it an angelic appearance in sharp contrast to the stern mask that had been her trademark in a dark, secretive world populated by violent, Alpha males. Her eyes were wide with shock as she'd watched Vy break down. She fought hard to cling to the unbending, unyielding veneer that was her last line of defense.

Abraham stood up and stretched his arms to the heavens. "Almighty God, we thank You and praise You for Vy and his acceptance of Your Son as His Savior. I ask now for Your Holy Spirit to immerse Aly in the great love You have for her. Speak to her in a way that only her omniscient Father can. Reach past her mind, and penetrate her heart."

Gabriel placed his right hand on her head and began to pray in his unique prayer language. Slowly, gradually, the hard, stone face melted like wax in the sunlight, unveiling a delicate, wounded little girl. Her eyes moistened even as she fought to maintain some semblance of control.

With a loud wail, she cried out, "Daddy, daddy, why did you leave me? It was so hard to survive without you. Didn't you love us?"

Then her eyes flew open in shock and she fainted into Gabriel's arms. He and Vy carried her over to the living room couch and laid her gently on the cushions. Vy knelt down beside her and took her hand. "Aly, Aly, it's okay, we are all here with you. Whatever it is, we and Jesus can see you through it."

She was out for several long minutes before she began to stir. When she opened her eyes, she looked around as though she had no idea where she was. Then they could see recognition and memory begin to take hold. The sweet, angelic face started to quiver. "Oh, God, I didn't know, I didn't know. I thought you'd abandoned us, daddy. I didn't know that they'd taken you away because you stole some food to feed us. Forgive me, daddy, for doubting you."

With that, she flung herself into Abraham's arms and wept on his shoulder until he felt he couldn't hold her one more moment. Then she pushed back from him and looked deep into his eyes. "Your God showed me other things too. Things that nobody knows. Things that I'm terribly ashamed of.[12] Do I need to confess them out loud or can I just ask Your Jesus to forgive me for those things, just between me and Him?"[13]

"As long as you're honest with Him, and truly repent from those sins, that's His business, not ours," Abraham answered gently. He took her aside sensing that she needed privacy to make that final commitment to Jesus. Gabriel grabbed Vy and dragged him into the kitchen.

"Are you two lovers?" Gabriel asked pointedly.

"What? No, not at all," Vy answered. "I don't think she's ever been able to let her guard down enough to be with a man."

"But you have feelings for her?" Gabriel continued to probe.

Vy's brow furrowed. "Up until a few moments ago, I would have said no. But now, my heart yearns for her. I don't know if that's your brotherly love or something more."

Gabriel put his hand on Vy's shoulder. "You're both very open and vulnerable to things of the heart right now, so go very slow. The devil would love to come and use you to hurt one another right now."

Vy nodded his assent just as Abraham and Aly came into the kitchen. Gabriel couldn't believe the transformation in Aly. Even her hard, stiff body had become soft and compliant, graceful movements replacing the previous, exaggerated swagger.

"So what now?" she asked with a twinkle in her eye.

Before Gabriel could answer, Vy jumped in. "I want to become part of your team," he said earnestly. "We could be bodyguards, or go out on dangerous missions for you and God."

Aly's soft laughter filled their hearts to overflowing. "Yes, it would be a shame to waste all our training. Maybe your Jesus has some way to make good use of us?"

"He's not *our* Jesus, He's *your* Jesus now," Abraham gently corrected her. "And in my spirit, I sense that the Lord does indeed have a plan for you to help us out. I just don't know how quite yet. Let's have some breakfast and then pray about that afterward."

Chapter Fourteen

When General Falstaff finished explaining his dilemma to René, he gave her a steely look as if to say, *see what you've gotten me into!*

Of course, that only made René laugh, a wicked grin letting him know that was her plan all along. There was nothing she enjoyed more than pitting people against one another with her controlling the puppet strings.

Falstaff's face was growing redder by the second. She let him get close to the exploding point and then said coquettishly, "I don't see what the problem is, my dearest. Blow the whole island up and who the hell cares about Java and Lombok. We need to thin out the Muslim herd, anyway. Then we can get back to doing what you do best."

She ran her finger along the general's cheek and over his lips. Despite all his efforts to the contrary, he was overcome again with lust. Except with René the roles were reversed. He'd always had several mistresses at a time who catered to his every whim, attempting to satisfy his voracious appetite. Now, all he wanted was René. With her, he finally felt fulfilled. At last he had someone to whom he could surrender *his* will.

Without another word, he rushed out of her office at the Global Palace and flew back to the Command Center for the Global Forces in the old NATO building in Brussels. Along the way, he gave the orders to prepare for an attack on Bali using tactical nuclear weapons.

He'd ruled out strategic nuclear weapons because he was still worried about too much collateral damage. He still had a few loyal eyes on the ground in Bali who could plant the homing signals for short-range air-to-ground missiles before the sub retreated back out to sea. Then the missiles would be fired from bombers just above the dissipating ash cloud in sufficient numbers to wipe out almost all of Bali's population.

Since there were no defensive forces to contend with, it should be easy picking, if he could manage to keep thoughts of morality out of his mind. Nuclear fallout would cause thousands, if not millions, more deaths throughout Indonesia. *Morality, that's a joke. Who am I to worry about morality. Just my childhood ghosts coming back to haunt me.*

As a former Catholic altar boy, he'd rejected the guilt-ridden, idol-worshiping ways of his family long ago with nary a look backward. He couldn't understand why it would surface now, of all times. Then he was jolted by a strange memory of a long-forgotten Bible story. Was he to be like King Saul and fail to completely annihilate the population and fall into disfavor with Alexis just as Saul was rejected by the prophet Samuel and his God? [14]

He felt somewhat queasy, but pushed those disturbing thoughts aside even as he pushed his way into the command center. Taking charge, he was back in his element and deftly orchestrated the movement of soldiers on the ground and birds of prey in the air.

As the countdown to launch transitioned from minutes into seconds, Falstaff broke out into a cold sweat that he strove mightily to conceal. A flurry of doubts and extraneous Bible verses flooded his mind and heart. His hands shook. He thought his staff was looking at him oddly, but he kept trying to focus on the plasma screens showing radar, satellite and on-plane camera views of Bali.

When the countdown reached zero, he hesitated and then gave the order to launch with a quavering voice that shocked those around him who'd always seen him as unflappable. He had to grab the edge of the long table to keep from falling over.

"Are you sick, sir?" his aide said, rushing over to him and helping him into the nearest chair.

Before he could answer, their eyes were drawn to the screen showing the trace of thirteen missiles plunging into and through the black volcanic cloud all across Bali. Everyone waited breathlessly while the missiles continued on their deadly track through the cloud, intact and operational. The most troublesome part was past. The relief was palpable.

It would be a couple of minutes before the missiles struck their appointed targets on the ground. The aide turned back to General Falstaff, expecting him to look pleased. Instead, his face was pasty white and a slight bit of drool was threatening to drip from the corner of his mouth. The aide wiped it off quickly with his the general's own tie and hoped no one had noticed.

"Hey!" a voice cried out. "What's that?"

The screen indicated a premature explosion. Then another. And another. Soon, the black cloud was lit up with thirteen bright spots of spreading luminescence that hurled the darkness away in all directions, revealing some kind of transparent golden-hewed dome in the reflected light.

"What the hell?"

"Do you see what I'm seeing?"

"This can't be happening!"

"Delta Angel, what in blazes is going on?"

The lead pilot didn't answer for a few moments. Then, in a careful monotone, he reported, "There appears to be a transparent dome of incredible strength over all of Bali. The ordinance didn't even make a dent or any apparent mark on the surface. We have two bombers that went down from the ash and debris that was thrown back at us. Two other aircraft suffered damage as well. What are your orders now?"

Everyone looked over at General Falstaff who just stared off into space. Each one speculated about the source of his breakdown, but most felt it was because he would have to report failure to the Global Czar. As near as anyone could remember, Falstaff had never failed at anything. Apparently, it was more than he could bear. Had he had a premonition, the aide wondered?

Meanwhile, back down on the surface of Bali, it seemed as though the entire populace had run out to get a view of the spectacle in the skies, drawn by enormously loud concussions of sound that rattled their windows and shook their souls.

The gang in Komang's house shielded their eyes from the bright points of light that appeared to banish the dark cloud they'd almost gotten used to. Now the soft glow of all the burning Banyan trees merged with the crisper white light from above. Shimmering reflections bounced off the surface of what appeared to be a giant golden bubble encompassing all of Bali.

Many people fell to the ground on their knees in awe and fear over the spectacle. "What in the world is going on?" Komang asked in a hushed whisper.

No one expected an answer, but it was Vy who spoke up. "Those were nuclear missiles that exploded against a protective shield of some kind, beyond the scope of our technology. Surely this must be the work of your… that is, our God."

Chapter Fifteen

Juanita and Brandon had spent two days at Havenwood3 outside Tallahassee, deep in the woods on the edge of a swamp. As the hideaway's leader, Howard, had noted, they'd finally gotten used to the damp, sour aroma. However, the bitter stench of excessive control ran amok and permeated every aspect of the hideaway's existence.

Lenore, the erstwhile prayer leader, had apparently browbeaten everyone into total submission. Even when she was not around, the residents crept about sneakily and spoke in guarded whispers. It was eerie and painful to watch. There was no joy, no freedom, just dread and oppression. Most people were afraid to be seen talking with Brandon or Juanita, who felt led by the Lord to hold their peace until He opened a door.

By the third day, though, the tension abated somewhat as everyone surmised that the two outsiders were not going to interfere. Lenore became a little friendlier and her prayer warriors a bit more relaxed. Over breakfast in the dining room, one of the intercessors, Samantha, suddenly lurched out of her chair and fell to the floor where her frail body jerked around spasmodically.

"Stand back," Lenore ordered and slipped a tongue-depressor into the pale girl's mouth. The hideaway's doctor arrived and gave Samantha a shot of something which caused her to settle down into unconsciousness. They then carried her off to sick bay. From the reaction of the residents, this apparently was a somewhat common occurrence.

Juanita looked over at Brandon, her eyebrows raised slightly in question. He nodded. This seemed to be the opening they were looking for. Juanita followed the small group down to the small infirmary where Samantha was placed on a cot and then left there alone. Lenore disappeared as did all the others except Doctor Wilson.

"Does this happen often?" Juanita asked the doctor.

"Yes, fairly frequently. She's had epilepsy since early childhood. She hasn't adjusted well to the stress of the times and being underground, so it's been getting progressively worse," Dr. Wilson noted impassively.

Juanita hesitated a moment, but then felt impelled to proceed. "You know, doctor, Jesus healed an epileptic by casting out a demon."[15]

Wilson looked up from the lab work he was studying. "You don't really believe in such things, do you?"

"You mean you *don't* believe what the Bible says?" Juanita asked pointedly.

The doctor smiled condescendingly. "Look, we all know that the Bible is filled with metaphors, parables and symbolism. It's the principles that matter. We can't take it all literally."

Steam was practically visible rising off Juanita's furrowed brow. "Oh really, well watch this!"

She turned toward the cot, praying in tongues for guidance from the Holy Spirit. "Awaken, sleeping beauty!" she cried out as Wilson backed away in sheer terror, thinking Juanita insane.

When Samantha's eyes flew open, Wilson grabbed the edge of his desk for support.

The young girl's anorexic face was white as a ghost in stark contrast to her long, black hair. As she began to seize again, she looked like something out of a horror movie.

"In the mighty name of Jesus Christ, I command you unclean spirit to release your grip on Samantha's body and come out of her now!" Juanita ordered.

Samantha began to shake even more violently. Several residents stopped in the hallway to peer inside at the commotion.

"Come out now, you filthy demon of epilepsy, and go where Jesus tells you or incur His wrath!" Juanita commanded as she poked her finger into Samantha's flailing chest.

"Stop this right now," Lenore demanded from the doorway. "Get her out of here," she ordered the doctor and the other residents.

Just as the doctor and residents started forward, hesitant and alarmed, an unearthly scream pierced the air, sending chills up everyone's spine. Samantha gave one more violent shake and then collapsed back onto the cot, her eyes glassy but open.

Those who had stepped toward Juanita froze in place. "Grab her you fools, before she kills the girl," Lenore demanded from the doorway.

"Wait," came a small voice into the shocked silence. Everyone turned to look at Samantha as she sat up. "I think I've been healed. All my anxiety and fear seem to be gone. Juanita has cured me."

"No, child, it wasn't me, it was Jesus," Juanita gently corrected her.

The color was flooding back into Samantha's face as she stood up to face the small group. The delicate girl began to swirl around, laughing gleefully.

"She's not cured," Lenore growled as she pushed her way into the infirmary. "She's been deceived. You'll see, she'll have another seizure before the day is out."

"Who are you to deny the power of God?" Juanita demanded to know.

Now it was Lenore's face that was turning red. "Don't you dare talk to *me* that way! You are nothing but a fake, a charlatan, come here to undermine my authority," she shrieked.

Lenore began to shake in fury. She reached out to grab Juanita, who stood her ground as she peered into Lenore's blackened, glazed eyes.

"In Jesus' mighty name, I bind up you demons and command you to cease and desist!" Juanita declared. [16]

Lenore's hands had just grabbed onto the front of Juanita's blouse when it appeared that the angry woman had turned into a statue. She and Juanita stood still, eyes locked in combat.

With a grunt and a shudder, Lenore slunk to the floor slowly, like a large balloon with a small leak. Juanita reached down and grabbed her head before it hit the floor, gently laying it down.

Juanita looked up at the flabbergasted residents. "Please lay her on the cot."

Turning to a visibly shaken Dr. Wilson, she said, "Doctor, please call me as soon as she awakens."

Chapter Sixteen

Blaine stayed with the Muslim women for several days. They'd given her a burka and kept her in the background at the compound in the new Islamic Center in Jerusalem, now the capital of Palestine. The woman who'd protected her in the limo kept Blaine under her wing, befitting her name, Asimah, which means 'protector.'

"Good morning, Blaine," said Asimah as she entered the side tent for the harem, which was attached to the large tent of

Abdullah, 'servant of god.' Abdullah was the sheikh who was in charge of security in the new Muslim sector of Jerusalem.

"Good morning, my protector," Blaine smiled back. She still found it ironic to be sheltered by the Muslim women, particularly within the harem of the chief of security. But Asimah had promised to help her escape before it was her turn to spend the night with Abudullah.

"Today is the day," Asimah whispered, nodding to the other women who nodded back in understanding.

"I still can't believe all you've done for me, an infidel," Blaine said in wonderment at it all.

Asimah's face turned serious. "You only lack enlightenment," she replied. "We have been praying to Allah that you would see the truth."

Blaine frowned. Yet another camp trying to get her to see things their way. First Rev. Wainwright, then Alexis and his crew, and now the Muslims.

Before Blaine could respond, Asimah hurried on because time was short. "Soon the Mahdi will be revealed, the twelfth Imam, Muhammad al-Mahdi, who was hidden by God at the age of five. He is still alive but has been in occultation, awaiting the time that God has decreed for his return."

"Occultation?" was all Blaine could stammer after this unexpected indoctrination.

"It means hidden away until the prophetic signs have been fulfilled. Now that the Great Deceiver has been exposed, we await only the lunar and solar eclipse during Ramadan, when a star with a luminous tail will rise from the East and the Mahdi will emerge to convert the world to Islam and the worship of Allah," Asimah explained in urgent whispers as she adjusted Blaine's veil.

"The great deceiver?" Blaine stuttered, quite taken aback by this verbal assault.

"Alexis D'Antoni, the Global Czar! And that blasphemous false prophet, Pope Radinsky," Asimah said with a hoarse snarl.

Well, at least we agree on one thing, Blaine thought.

"The only reason we put up with this Global Governance Committee and its Universal Religion is that we know the Mahdi will soon appear and overcome this evil world government."

Before she could formulate an appropriate response to her protector, a male voice called out in Arabic from outside the tent.

Asimah held her finger up to her lips. "It is time to go. Do not say anything more or they might discern that you are not one of us."

The women climbed into the same two limousines that had transported Blaine away from the Global Palace. They were taken to the Arab sector in East Jerusalem and dropped off at an open-air market that encompassed a large cobblestoned plaza as well as some of the side streets.

Blaine silently followed Asimah around as she bought various food items, placing some in a woven grocery sack that she then handed to Blaine. "Take this and walk slowly down this side street. Pretend you are examining the merchandise in each stall. When you get to the end of the street, turn right. That is a residential area where a woman in a Burka carrying groceries will not seem out of place. Then continue north, which will take you out of the Arab sector."

Blaine nodded her assent and wanted to give her protector a hug, or express her thanks in some way, but knew that would call attention to them, so she simply whispered a thank you, bowed her head slightly, and proceeded down the street.

As she slowly made her escape, she could think of only one place to go where she would be safe. But she couldn't remember Rev. Wainwright's address. Nor did she know how to get there from wherever she was now. She tried to clear her head, but Mephistopheles was filling her mind with reasons to go back to the Global Palace, so she silently prayed to Jesus to come and help her.

She could tell she'd reached the end of the Arab sector because the pot-holed streets and rundown buildings of the Shuafat neighborhood in north-eastern Jerusalem were separated by an ugly concrete barrier from a nicer area where she could see women dressed in normal western clothing.

Blaine stood staring uncertainly out toward freedom, but with no idea of how to find Rev. Wainwright. With the Burka cutting off all peripheral vision, she didn't notice the handsome, well-groomed Arab man approach from the right. She flinched and drew back when he suddenly appeared before her.

"Don't be afraid, Blaine," the smiling Arab said with a tenderness that touched her heart. "I will guide you to Rev. Wainwright. Just stay three paces behind me for appearances sake."

She was too shocked to answer right away. Then he set off at a brisk pace. She scurried forward in the flopping burka and settled in the requisite three paces to the rear wondering whether this was a trick or a trap of some kind.

But he knew my name and where I was going! An angel? How exciting!

As they walked, Blaine was in a daze of some kind. She couldn't get her eyes to focus. All she could see clearly was her guardian angel in front of her.

In what seemed like a very short time, he stopped suddenly and pointed up the front stairs of an apartment building, twenty-three Achad Haam the letters on the front door said. *That's it! Rev. Wainwright's address!*

She turned her head back to thank her angel, but he was gone. Twisting her veiled head this way and that, she couldn't catch sight of him. He'd simply disappeared.

Blaine gathered up the front of the burka, climbed the steps and pushed through the glass doors into the lobby where she saw Wainwright's name next to one of the buzzers. She pressed it once and then waited, her heart pounding anxiously. Mephistopheles was not pleased. In fact, she thought he felt terrified.

Her body began to shudder and twitch, her vision growing hazy. She heard an answering buzzer from the door, but couldn't move. Instead, she fainted into a black heap on the tiled floor.

After the buzzer sounded twice more, heavy footsteps pounded down the inside stairs. Rev. Boris Wainwright's eyes bulged in shock and puzzlement at the sight of a Muslim woman collapsed in the lobby. What was she doing ringing his doorbell?

He opened the door and knelt beside her, not sure what to do. Would he be violating her honor to remove the veil and take her pulse? He looked quickly around, saw no one and reached for the veil. As he lifted it up, his eyes almost burst from their sockets.

"Blaine!" he cried out as the veil slipped from his fingers. He looked around once more. Still no one in sight. He quickly gathered her up in his arms and lumbered back up the stairs to his second floor apartment.

After setting her down on his couch, he lifted the veil again and felt her pulse. It was weak, but she was alive. He rushed into the kitchen area of his small one-bedroom apartment and ran cold water onto a clean dishcloth, then returned to her side and placed it on her forehead.

Blaine's eyes fluttered open. "Oh, thank God, it's you!" Then she fainted again.

Chapter Seventeen

Carmelita was sitting behind the teacher's desk in the classroom of the Havenwood1 hideaway, daydreaming about her husband Gabriel while the students worked quietly on their tests. She missed him terribly and wondered if she would ever get to be with him again now that he was one of the two witnesses. It was really all quite unbelievable. Imagine, her Gabriel.

The thought of not being with him, not even knowing where he was, made her sad and restless. She got up to walk around the classroom and see how the students were progressing. She smiled contentedly to see the children eagerly working on their Bible exams, using material Carmelita had developed over the years for her Sunday School classes. Now they studied the Bible every day, in addition to the normal curriculum of academics she'd purchased through the homeschooling co-op. The studies and exams were geared to the various age levels in their one-room 'schoolhouse.'

Suddenly the door flew open and a wide-eyed Tara burst into the room. Carmelita was about to scold her for disturbing the students without even knocking when she saw the strangest expression on Tara's face.

"What is it, Tara, what's wrong?" Carmelita called out urgently.

Tara was so excited she couldn't even speak. Instead, she held out a piece of paper, waving it at Carmelita who came over and grabbed it anxiously.

It was the standard message form used by the control-center technicians for incoming calls. Carmelita couldn't believe her eyes. It said it was a short-wave radio transmission relayed from Pastor Gabriel in Bali. The hand-written message read:

> *Carmelita, I love you and I am sending two Russian commandos to bring you to me here in Bali where we are having the most wonderful revival, despite what you hear in the media. Their names are Vy and Aly. They will come in the dark of night. Alert the guards to let them in when they hear the words, "Jesus is Lord." Then go with them. They will take care of everything. See you soon my love. Gabriel.*

Carmelita couldn't contain herself. She shrieked with joy and ran a circle around the baffled but laughing students. Soon the entire hideaway was alive with excitement. Although no one had felt it wrong that Gabriel hadn't sent for her sooner, everyone sensed that a dark hole had now been filled, a missing piece of the puzzle found at last.

Carmelita's joy soon gave way to worry over who would take her place since she wore so many hats within the hideaway. But so many of the women stepped forward to volunteer their services that she realized she'd kept so busy to avoid dwelling on her husband's absence that she'd wound up thwarting the desire, the need for others to take on more responsibility. Her departure would actually be a good thing for all concerned.

A sleepless night passed without an appearance by the mysterious Russian commandos. Carmelita realized that it would take time for them to get from Bali to Virginia, especially having to do so undercover. Still, the waiting was hard, even harder than the separation had been.

Another day and night came and went. Carmelita was exhausted from lack of sleep and found herself dozing off during class time. That night she couldn't stay awake even if she'd tried. Haphazard dreams alternated between nightmares and glorious reunions. When Tara shook her awake, she had trouble remembering what was real and what was only a dream.

"They're here!" Tara kept repeating to the dazed pastor's wife. "The Russians, they're here!"

Finally Carmelita's brain kicked into gear and she leaped out of bed, grabbed her flannel robe and ran out of the bedroom, down the hall into the central area of the hideaway. A sleepy crowd of residents was gathering around a man and woman dressed entirely in black.

"Ah, so you are the wonderful wife who Pastor Gabriel loves almost as much as Jesus!" the thick-chested Russian man said in his heavy accent.

Carmelita didn't know what to say, so she just stood there with her mouth hanging open. Everyone laughed. The Russian woman came over and hugged Carmelita tightly, tears streaming down her cheeks. "Your husband, he save my life."

All at once, Carmelita, Tara and the others began to bombard the two commandos with all kinds of questions about Pastor

Gabriel, Bali, the revival, and how they were going to transport Carmelita back.

"Whoa, hold on," Carmelita finally shouted. "Let's cut our guests some slack. They must be hungry. Let's rustle up some food and all enjoy a midnight snack together and then let them tell their story. Unless, you'd rather sleep first and join us for breakfast?"

Vy and Aly looked at one another and then Vy answered. "Eat first, tell story, sleep long time."

The cooks began quickly preparing sandwiches and a crudités platter. After Jermaine prayed a blessing over the food and for Carmelita's safe journey with the commandos, the guests led the way in digging into the welcome sustenance. They hadn't eaten or slept in two days, except for a couple of energy bars.

When Vy and Aly had replenished themselves, they sat back contentedly. "Now is time for story," Vy sighed and then proceeded to mesmerize the hideaway residents with their personal conversion story and then information about the Bali revival and the global government's attempts to blow up the island.

It really was an incredible tale that almost defied belief. Carmelita finally broke the awed silence. "Wow, wouldn't it be wonderful to live under a golden dome of God's divine protection!" [17]

Then she looked sheepishly out at her friends and compatriots, realizing that she would be the only one of them to do so. She quickly added, "And I hope and pray that the Lord provides a golden dome over this hideaway."

"But we don't have any Banyan trees," Jermaine lamented in an exaggerated moan, providing some comic relief to break the tension.

"Seriously, though, we need to be grateful for the divine protection that He *has* provided for us during these difficult times, for it's only by his grace that we have survived this long without being discovered," Jermaine added. The sleepy heads nodded agreement as everyone traipsed off to bed.

Carmelita showed the two commandos to two rooms they had recently set aside for guests, not knowing that the need would be so soon fulfilled with such exotic visitors.

Chapter Eighteen

Alexis, of course, threw a fit when he heard the news about the failed attempt to destroy Bali. He was frustrated at not being able to vent his fury on General Falstaff who had lapsed into some kind of coma. At first, Alexis didn't believe it until they'd hooked up a video feed into the hospital room. He railed at the inert body anyway, just to get it out of his system.

The doctors felt it was stress-induced and suggested, ever so politely, that Falstaff be allowed to rest and recuperate in peace. That was fine with the Global Czar who fired him over the remote connection and washed his hands of the matter, replacing him with one of the four-star NATO generals who had risen through the ranks even as he'd advanced within the Illuminati.

Perhaps it was for the best, Alexis reasoned to René, because now they would have one of their own in charge, someone who wouldn't suffer doubts at ridding the world of Christians or anyone else who stood in the way of Lucifer's plans. "That was Falstaff's problem," Alexis declared knowingly, "he still had a conscience."

Fortunately for those who worked at the Global Palace, the next few days were busy with all kinds of meetings that kept the Global Czar busy and out of everyone's hair. When he was in one of his moods, anyone could be a target of his rage for any reason, real or imagined.

However, the Group of Twelve insisted upon a meeting of their own with Alexis, Pope Radinsky and René because of the situation in Bali as well as restlessness in the Muslim community and growing resistance in the North American Union, primarily in the western part of what used to be the United States. Although Alexis was the one chosen by Lucifer himself to be the leader, each of the Twelve were far enough advanced in Satanism to not live in abject fear of the Beast, as they liked to call him.

Sure, Alexis still had more power than they did, politically and spiritually, but only by a small margin, or at least that's what they thought. In any event, if they stood united, they felt that they were the ones who would hold sway when push came to shove, and that time might just have arrived.

They met late one evening in one of the many Masonic lodges that had existed in Jerusalem long before the New World Order was established. In fact, they considered Jerusalem to be the "Cradle of Freemasonry" because it was the ancient Masons who built the Temple of Solomon. They were traditionally called the first Freemasons and that era marked the birth of Freemasonry.

The Ein Hashiloah Ari Lodge #26 at 13 Ezrat Israel Street had been specially prepared for such meetings after D'Antoni took up residence at the Global Palace. It was used exclusively by the Global Czar and was soundproofed and bug-proofed. Alexis didn't trust Masons any more than he did the general public.

Besides the unholy trinity of the anti-Christ (Alexis), the False Prophet (Pope Radinsky) and Mother of Harlots (René), the other nine members comprised the heads of the Club of Rome, the Tri-Lateral Commission, the World Bank, the International Monetary Fund, the Secretary-General of the United Nations, the exalted leaders of the Illuminati and Masons, as well as CEO's of the largest media empire in the world, and the world's largest financial conglomerate.

After delivering a white-washed summary of the events in Bali, Alexis addressed the increasing agitation of the Muslim nations. "We are reaching the point at which we either need to give them their Mahdi or simply wipe out all the Islamic power centers around the world," he pronounced as though he didn't care which option prevailed.

There was much debate, of course, and then Alexis was asked to explain how they might raise up the Islamic 'savior' and still retain overall control. "Glad you asked," he replied smugly, having decided it was better to wait for the question than force it on them.

"I believe we have a suitable Mahdi already in place. Many of you know Pope Radinsky's private secretary, Mustafa. He has been raising up a suitable savior, a young man who has been programmed just for this purpose. Mustafa has already been the primary liaison between us and all the major Islamic players who respect him very much. However, of course, that is not enough. We would have to stage a supernatural emergence that fits most of the prophecies concerning the Mahdi in order for them to accept the young man as the Twelfth Imam."

"Most of the prophecies? Why not all of them?" asked the IMF Chairman.

"Because there are many different prophecies across the various Islamic sects, just like there are major divisions in the Christian community," Alexis explained. "We'll focus on the major, most accepted prophecies and then produce such a supernatural spectacle that the Muslims will believe it could not have happened without divine intervention."

"So, is that the option you're proposing?" pushed the U.N. Secretary-General.

Alexis sensed the trap. The Twelve would love to catch him superseding his authority and be "forced" to replace him. "No, I'm just laying out the alternatives. We'll all commune with our master Lucifer in a short while to see what it is he would have us do. But beforehand, I'd like to quickly address a few other topics for which we will also seek our master's guidance."

"As you know, the various environmental catastrophes that we've been inducing over the past decade or so have been coming to a head. So-called global warming, fed by our low-frequency HAARP, ELF and GWEN towers around the globe, have now melted more than half the earth's glaciers and caused the oceans to flood many low-lying areas. This has wiped away much of the coastlines that were havens to millions of poor people in the third-world nations. We are housing them in refugee camps where we are infecting them with malaria and tuberculosis, diseases for which those we care about have long been inoculated with appropriate vaccines.

"In order to reduce the population of undesirables living inland, the localized famines we have been able to produce through refined weather manipulation techniques are finally beginning to take hold. Even as we rush in shipments of food and medicine as the 'good guys,' we are ensuring that supply falls well short of demand. These same weather control techniques are funneling the increasing precipitation caused by global warming to the areas where we need it to be for our own people and purposes. All of this is on plan and on schedule. We should net a population reduction of ten percent this year, climbing to one-third in another two years.

"Finally, we are stepping up our response to the pockets of resistance that have been building up around the world. We didn't want to get too heavy-handed right away, lest we seem like the bad guys. But now that the media have been stoking the fires, and a big thank you goes to Geraldine and her media empire for leading the way, we will pound them under the guise of anti-crime and anti-terrorism measures. By out next quarterly meeting, I don't expect this to be an issue at all."

Alexis glanced around the room, his proud chin protruding just a tad more, his eyes boring into each attendee, daring them to challenge him openly. A tiny smirk creased his mouth when he saw them all whither under the stare down.

"All right, then, prepare your hearts and minds to welcome and receive lord Lucifer into our midst. Master Lucifer, we come before you tonight as your humble servants, seeking only to do your will. I know you have already been here with us, listening to our discussions. Now it is time we listened to you. So before we vote on a number of items, speak to us, to our minds, our hearts, our souls. Give us visions and direction. Give us strength to stay the course. Bring us into unity."

Alexis pressed some buttons on his console. The lights dimmed and a fragrant aroma was released into the room carrying with it just the right amount of hallucinogens and dopamine enhancers.

Candles on the walls were automatically lit and strident metallic music beckoned their leader. When a sudden rush of wind blew the candles out and mussed their hair, several looked over at Alexis in question. He closed his eyes and spread his arms. Abbadon and his horde of demons had arrived.

Chapter Nineteen

Back at Havenwood3 in the Florida Panhandle, Lenore had refused to speak with anyone for several days. In her absence, the prayer team asked to meet with Juanita and have her teach them about spiritual warfare, the very thing she had come to do. The sessions were going very well because the team was comprised of experienced intercessors.

Toward the end of the third day, Brandon knocked lightly on the prayer room door and peeked inside. When Juanita turned around he beckoned her to come out. "What is it?" Juanita asked with a scowl. "We were right in the middle of an important lesson."

"Lenore is asking for you and is creating quite a fuss," Brandon quickly replied as he placed his hand on his beloved wife's broad shoulder. "Lord, I pray that You would give Juanita wisdom, revelation and strength to deal with this situation successfully."

"Amen," the chastened prayer warrior agreed, gave her husband a quick peck on the cheek and set off down the hall.

Brandon smiled as he watched his powerful yet loving wife set off for her next battle. He had grown accustomed to her unwavering intensity and unlimited passion, although adjusting to it had been somewhat difficult over the years.

Even before she got to Lenore's room, she could hear a deep voice yelling and screaming behind the closed door. In front stood the wide-eyed, visibly shaken doctor surrounded by some of the hideaway residents who looked like they were ready to run and hide at any moment.

Juanita pushed the doctor aside and threw the door open. Lenore was jumping up and down on a now collapsed bed, waving her arms and cursing up a storm in what clearly was not her own voice. Spittle drooled down her chin and blood was trickling out of eyes that had morphed into black holes with a deep red center.

"Demons, I command you in Jesus' name, power and authority to shut up and come out of Lenore this instant!" Juanita declared as she pointed her finger at Lenore.

A deep raspy voice responded, "We don't have to listen to you because Lenore wants us to stay."

"Liar!" Juanita bellowed. "You have deceived her with your lies, but I now speak the truth of the Word of God into Lenore. Lenore, you are a child of God, heir to the riches of His Kingdom. He loves you and does not condemn you, for there is no condemnation for those who are in Christ Jesus. Do not listen to the lies, Lenore. Do not hate or reject your God, for He is not the source of your problems. It is time for you to renounce all pride, fear and anger, which give the devil a foothold in you. Seek the Lord's forgiveness and He will cleanse you from all this unrighteousness."

A mighty roar thundered out of Lenore as her body trembled and her head shook violently back and forth. But then her eyes closed, and a little girl's voice cried out. "Help me, help me."

"Lenore, there is no fear in love.[18] Receive God's love. It is a lie that He doesn't love you. He wants to hold you and cherish you. It doesn't matter what you've done or think you've done. Let Him wash you in the water of His Word.[19] Receive His living water.[20] Receive the shed blood of Jesus Christ to cleanse you of your sins [21] and cleanse your spirit, soul and body."

Despite the violent shaking of her body, Lenore opened her eyes and looked up toward the heavens. "Jesus, Jesus," she cried out mournfully. "Come and save me. I'm sorry, so sorry."

Juanita rushed forward. "Tell the demons to go, Lenore. Renounce the false comforts they have brought you. Rebuke and reject them!"

Lenore's lips moved and Juanita could see her mouth forming some of those words. With Lenore's agreement, Juanita proclaimed, "Demons, you lying unclean spirits, I now command you to come out of Lenore right now. She has rejected you. You no longer have any rights to her body. Leave now!!!"

With that, Lenore's body was flung backward against the wall and the headboard. A loud wailing sound comprised of many voices sent chills up the spine of every onlooker as Lenore slowly slid down the wall and finally collapsed into a heap on the sweat-soaked mattress.

Juanita watched carefully. "All of you," she declared. "Every last one of you demons, get out right now!"

Lenore's body gave one last twitch, moaned softly and then was still.

The sudden silence was deafening. It was as if the world had stopped spinning and everyone was frozen in place. The temperature had literally dropped ten to twenty degrees. The light was dry and brittle.

Slowly the temperature rose back to normal and a warm glow enveloped Lenore and spread out into the room and the hallway. The manifest presence of God filled the room and their hearts to overflowing. Fear turned to love, doubt to belief.

Lenore began to move. Her eyes fluttered open. They were bright green. The doctor gasped. He hadn't known she had normal eyes, so dark and angry they had been ever since he knew her.

"What happened to me?" a soft, tiny voice asked.

"You have been delivered from the hands of the enemy," Juanita said tenderly. "And now you're experiencing God's love. Don't push it away because you think you don't deserve it. None of us do. But He wants you to have it anyway. Embrace the love."

Juanita waved to the large crowd outside the door, beckoning them inside. "And these people all love you too. They are your friends and they want to help you."

Two of the prayer team came and knelt beside the bed. One of them stroked Lenore's hair and face while the other squeezed Lenore's hands and held them to her lips.

"We love you, Lenore," many began to say. One of the praise team began to sing a spontaneous song about God's great grace and love. Soon everyone joined in as he repeated the chorus over and over again.

As the voices filled the hideaway, Juanita slipped outside the room, unnoticed. "I think the Lord's work is done here," she said to Howard Jenkins. Then she took Brandon's hand, kissed him gently, and they quietly left the hideaway to set off on their next adventure.

Chapter Twenty

Sir William was not happy, not that he ever was really happy. Just momentary times of bliss within the spectrum of general, undefined discontent. Unhappier than usual, he groused to himself. Just when things seemed to be proceeding properly, the Global Computer Center in Brussels had to trace the world's worst computer hackers to his territory. Jehovah's Witnesses in Montana. Who woulda thunk.

In fact, he himself didn't quite believe the report. He wasn't sure why. Sure, the JWs had been vehement resistors, but never had gained much traction because they were so despised and rejected by all the other Christian denominations. What a blessing it was to have such division in Christ's Kingdom, rendering them no match for Lucifer's finely-tuned army that was kept in line through fear and severe reprisals.

He had studied up on the JWs a bit. He could only tolerate reading such garbage a little at a time. But as near as he could figure it, the primary source of disagreement about the JWs was their refusal to declare Jesus as the Son of God. Even Sir William knew they were off base on that point. Being a Satanist didn't mean not believing in Jesus as God, but rather desiring to live in freedom separated from God without having to obey all that 'shall not' garbage.

Lucifer, Satan, was right to seduce Adam and Eve by pointing out that we could all be gods ourselves. Why let Him have all the glory! Since sin separated us from God, Sir William worked very hard to be as sinful as possible and enjoy *all* the fleshly pleasures. Of course, his ample flesh was visible testament to that proclivity.

Still, he had expected those who were more devoted to Jesus as the Son of God and Son of Man to be the ones to cause the most trouble. The JWs were loners, isolationists. It just didn't make sense. But, of course, he'd have to look into it and prove his case before anyone would listen to him.

Thankfully, he had an army of troops at his disposal. He no longer went anywhere himself. Why bother? With high-tech communications, he could literally go anywhere right from his earthly throne, just like God. A few phone calls set numerous people in motion, from spies to computer nerds to black ops killers. Soon he'd know for sure whether the JWs were the source of the cyber crisis.

He smiled to himself as a delicious thought surfaced. Even if the JWs weren't the ones, he'd wipe them out anyway. After all, you need to be sure. Eliminating troublemakers, or potential troublemakers, was never a bad thing. Population reduction was a key objective.

With that settled for the moment, he turned his attention to a report that had really perked his antenna. Two Russian commandos and a Hispanic woman had been caught offshore from Virginia Beach in a motorized, black rubber raft that was favored by the special ops types. Presumably, they were seeking to rendezvous with a larger vessel out at sea.

The Coast Guard was off to find the mother ship while the captives were being rushed back to Sir William's own interrogation center in the basement of his mansion. Could this be the opportunity he'd been looking for? Ever since Pastor Gabriel had slipped out of his grasp and gone on to bigger and better things, he'd been obsessed with finding the location of the merry band of agitators he'd left behind. He'd assumed that most of them were Hispanic, so maybe this woman might know something.

Just then the phone on his desk rang. The caller ID indicated it was his detested boss, Franklin Montrose. With a deep breath and great trepidation he picked up the receiver. "Yes?"

It always grated on Montrose's nerves how Sir William was able to sound insolent without actually being insolent. One of these days, he'd slip up and Montrose would hang him out to dry, permanently.

"Why didn't you tell me about those Russian commandos and the Hispanic woman?" Montrose snapped into the phone.

Sir William was momentarily taken aback. "I just heard about it myself a little while ago."

"Well, Alexis says it's Pastor Gabriel's wife and he wants us to ship them out to the Global Palace in Jerusalem."

"How did *he* know about it?" Sir William was stunned, giving Montrose the opening he needed to put his large underling back in his place.

"Do you think Lucifer has millions of demons all over the place for no reason? That network can communicate a message around the world in a matter of minutes, as you should well know by now," Montrose scolded.

Sir William sighed, signed off and slumped in his oversize desk chair. There went all his fun right out the window.

Chapter Twenty-One

Pastor Wally and Michelle took their time driving to CIA-West, enjoying their first vacation without the children since their honeymoon. Wally had started his first job in the ministry shortly afterwards and threw himself into his life's work with great passion and intensity. Too much so, he realized now. God had never called upon him to shortchange his family. With hindsight, he saw it was a case of misplaced priorities and blind ambition.

He wanted to be the best pastor possible for his Lord and Savior. Little did he realize that this also meant being a shepherd to his wife and children too. All he could do now was try to make up for lost time. In fact, didn't the Scriptures say that we could redeem those times?[22] Well, he would surely try.

It was such a blessed time together that Michelle was actually disappointed when they finally arrived at Morrison's ranch in Colorado. She had been dreading the time away from the hideaway and her kids, and now she didn't want it to end. Clearly they were on the right path, the Lord's yellow brick road.

Their first surprise was the marked change in Morrison's demeanor, who now insisted they call him Alan. Having just seen him less than a week ago, they knew something major had happened. An encounter with the Lord of the best kind. However, he didn't talk about it, nor did they ask.

Instead, they enjoyed a long, multi-course dinner with him, Jesse, Fran, Sue and Jerome. By the time the evening ended, Wally and Michelle felt comfortable and at home. The tour of the underground facilities was a real eye-opener. Having just come from CIA-East which had just been constructed, it was amazing to see a counter-insurgency operation in action. The depth and scope of activities was mind-boggling. The guest quarters were more than adequate and they fell quickly and deeply asleep after a long, satisfying day.

The following morning, Alan had them over to the ranch house for a southwestern-style breakfast with Rev. Michael and Bonnie Braintree who were the reason they had made the long journey in the first place. After a green-chili omelet, breakfast burrito, spicy fried potatoes and some special kind of sausage with a real kick to it, Wally suggested that the two couples take a stroll together around the beautiful ranchland.

Wally and Michelle couldn't stop staring at the Rocky Mountains in the distance. 'Big Sky' country was both awesome and intimidating for lifelong easterners who seldom saw the horizon for all the trees. Wally suggested to the Braintrees that they spend the entire day together getting to know one another, but without any talk of theology or counseling. "Let's become comfortable with each other before we get into the deep stuff."

Michael and Bonnie were relieved, but somewhat taken aback. Socialization was not their forte. In fact, they were actually terrified to let people see inside their crusty shell. Sure, the Lord had used Alan Morrison to crack the shell open, but there was still a long way to go to overcome a lifetime of hiding behind a manufactured persona.

Wally led the way in talking openly about his background, the mistakes he'd made and what he was doing to rectify those errors. Michelle shared her story about how fear had turned her into an angry shrew, but more importantly how the Lord reached her through a vision and an angelic visitation. The Braintrees were flabbergasted to hear such openness, but they also felt a growing desire to see similar changes in their own lives.

They enjoyed a picnic lunch together under a huge old cottonwood tree and took a drive around the expansive ranch in one of Alan's ATVs. They ate dinner with the rest of the residents in the underground dining room and relaxed together in one of the lounges. By the end of the day they all felt like old friends. It was certainly a different experience than the Braintrees had expected.

However, they were still nervous about where Pastor Wally's counseling would take them the following morning. Even though they'd let their guard down more than ever before, there was still a long way to go. For her part, Michelle was excited that Wally had asked her to be part of his counseling sessions.

"I can't hope to properly advise a married couple by myself," Wally explained. "Besides, without you I'd never have become the man and minister I am."

Michelle was actually shocked to hear those words. She'd come to believe that she had been a hindrance, not a help. Wally saw the look of disbelief on her face and added, "If I had performed my husbandly role correctly from the very start, you would never have had all the problems you did.[23] We're one flesh.[24] What we do affects each other much more than we think. When you had your breakthrough, you helped lead me to higher ground."

Chapter Twenty-Two

Back in Jerusalem, Alexis couldn't believe that his vast network of spies hadn't been able to locate Blaine. He had been certain that, if she was still alive, she would have made her way by now to Wainwright's apartment, which had been under surveillance since the very day she escaped.

Not trusting people one bit, he insisted that a team review all the video over the past few days. The subsequent report was quite interesting. Yesterday, there had been a sudden white light that blinded the lenses of the camera focused on the front door of Wainwright's apartment building. Simultaneously, the captain of the surveillance team was embarrassed to report that his two operatives had dozed off, their heavy breathing appallingly apparent on the accompanying audio.

That flash of light, presumed to be the reflection of the sun off some car window, had damaged a portion of the digital disk and about ten minutes of video was just static. Alexis dismissed the captain with a disgusted wave of his hand. When the door closed behind him, Alexis stood and stretched his arms out wide. "Oh mighty Lucifer, can you confirm that Blaine is indeed at Wainwright's?"

The Global Czar's body suddenly flinched spasmodically, throwing him to the floor. "Why did you not inquire of me sooner!" a voice bellowed in D'Antoni's head. "You have become too busy and have been using your own resources rather than relying on me! I am the one in charge! I am the one who made you!! I am the one you must turn to more and more each and every moment of every day!!!"

Alexis thought his head was going to explode. He moaned, rolled onto his side and threw up on the $1,000 per square yard carpet. Yes, he had to admit, it was true. It was hard to maintain his perspective when he was running the world like its god. Except he wasn't a god, it was Lucifer who was and who desired to live more and more through the Global Czar.

Briefly, Alexis bemoaned having become party to such a deal. It wasn't turning out quite like he thought it would. He had to do the hard and dirty work, and then Lucifer grabbed all the glory. Well, not all, he had to admit, and then was glad his master couldn't read his mind.

But suddenly there was another wrenching spasm that lifted him off the ground and threw him face forward into his own vomit. "I may not know what you're thinking," the harsh voice scolded, "but I can snese your emotions and you had better not go down that path again or I will have to replace you."

And then it was over. Alexis felt empty, abandoned. Lucifer had gone for the time being. Thankfully, as an angelic being, Satan could only be in one place at a time, unlike that blasted Holy Spirit. Fortunately, though, the Holy Spirit was a so-called 'Gentleman' who would not impose his will on human beings, and that was the flaw in God's plan.

It was also embarrassing that it was Pope Radinsky who'd gotten the word during his meditation time that Pastor Gabriel's wife had been apprehended on the coast of Virginia. Altogether, not a good day, although he was glad to have possibly gained some leverage with those annoying witnesses.

Alexis got slowly to his feet and buzzed for his private secretary. When she came inside, she took one look and understood exactly what had happened. She'd been with Alexis for too long, and been chastised by her own spirit guide too often, to not recognize the aftermath. She rushed out to call the cleaning crew and sent for another suit of clothes for her boss who stumbled into the private bathroom to shower off the filth.

Well, at least his hunch had proved correct. Somehow, an angel must have caused the blinding flash of light and induced sleep on the surveillance team. That could mean only one thing. Blaine had indeed made her way into Wainwright's apartment.

****

When Blaine awoke out of her stupor, she was disoriented at first. Then as Rev. Wainwright gently prodded, she was able to recall all the horrific events of her imprisonment, the miraculous escape, the assistance of the Muslim women and the guidance of the handsome angel.

Wainwright had been sitting on the edge of the nondescript beige couch cattycorner to an identical couch on which Blaine lay stretched out with the cold compress still on her forehead. He sat back with an appreciative smile. "That's quite a story. Jesus really is watching over you."

Blaine's eyes shot open. "It was an angel, not Jesus."

Wainwright laughed gently. "The angels are under Jesus' authority. They don't listen to me, to you, to the Global Czar, or anybody but Jesus. He has saved your body, now it's time you gave him your soul. Unless, that is, you wish to continue to be tossed around like a wave on the sea, subject to any wind that comes along. According to God's Word, to be double-minded means you'll be unstable in all your ways." [25]

Something rose up inside of Blaine that gave her a splitting headache. She clutched her hands to her face and groaned. "I'm not up to dealing with such things quite yet."

Wainwright nodded. His enthusiasm often caused him to lurch ahead of the Lord. He silently asked His forgiveness, and then changed the subject. "You must be hungry and thirsty after such an ordeal. That was quite a long walk you took with your guardian angel."

Blaine shook her head. "The thought of food makes me nauseous. Besides, we only walked a short distance."

"You must drink some water, though," Wainwright gently insisted. She nodded her consent. He knew she had come more than a short distance, but he decided to let it pass for now. Perhaps the angel had carried her unconscious for most of the way.

When he returned from the small kitchen area with a large glass of water, he helped Blaine to sit up on the couch. That made her head spin awhile. When things settled down, she took a sip of water. That awoke her thirst, so she gulped the rest down.

Finally, her headache and dizziness subsided. She focused her eyes and saw the reverend on the edge of the other couch again. She glanced around the living room area. Very sparse, like a cheap hotel room. At the far end, a wood-veneer table and two matching chairs formed the dining area.

She rose unsteadily to her feet. Wainwright came to hold her up. "Easy now, don't push it."

Blaine nodded and waited till the dizziness settled down again. She was determined to get herself back together as quickly as possible, although she wasn't quite sure what her sense of urgency was all about.

With Wainwright's help, she walked to the opposite end of the living area and glanced into the kitchen which had a small refrigerator, a minimal electric stovetop, a microwave and a toaster oven. It was antiseptically clean. She walked down the short hall and peeked into the bedroom with its single bed, a small nightstand and nothing else. Nowhere did she see any personal items.

Blaine looked questioningly at Wainwright. "Have you lived here long?"

He chuckled knowingly, having been expecting a comment of some kind. "Yes and no," he answered.

Blaine shot him a scowl. "Rev. Wainwright, you're not being open and honest with me, so how do you expect me to trust you?"

"Boris, call me Boris," he reminded her and then sighed. "Come, sit back down and rest. And then I'll tell you what you need to know."

When she was settled back down on the couch again, with another cold compress on her forehead and another glass of water in her hand, Boris sat down on the opposite couch and took a deep breath.

"While it is true that I am a minister and a counselor, that's only a front. Prior to the global government, I was a spy for the CIA based here in Jerusalem." He paused to let that sink in.

"When the Global Czar took over all the world's governments, I was given a choice to be part of the new order, or to go my own way. Of course, I took the latter option fully knowing that I'd signed my own death warrant. However, the good Lord has seen fit to protect me all this time for some purpose, I suppose. I only wish He would let me know what that might be."

Even as Blaine's eyes were wide with wonder, Wainwright's focus had turned inward. She held her tongue and waited for him to return from his reverie.

Gradually, his attention refocused on Blaine and he picked up the story. "I became a spy after the death of my two children. I had become bitter and despondent, and was no support to my wife who justifiably left me. It turned out, some of my ministry contacts in the local government were on the CIA's payroll and they recruited me, knowing I needed an outlet for my anger. As I healed, my counseling ministry took off. Then the world fell apart. Since then, I've been working with some local Christian groups that have formed an underground resistance movement."

When Blaine didn't make any comments, he continued in a spare monotone. "I leased this place to have a legitimate residence, but I spend virtually no time here. I also rent space and pay for a secretary at a local church to take calls for my counseling ministry, but for the most part I stay elsewhere with various friends and compatriots. I've become somewhat paranoid about discovery."

Boris stopped and sat back. Blaine was clearly stunned, so he waited quietly for her to digest the unexpected information. "Have I blown your cover by coming here?" she wondered aloud.

Boris shrugged. "Oh, they know where I live and they keep a watch on me from time to time. But I'm strictly small potatoes to them. Up till now, that is. I suspect you're considered to be a very high priority fugitive, so I'm sure they've got eyes on this place even as we speak."

Blaine sat up quickly and then held her head in her hands for a few moments before it cleared. The effects were wearing off. "So, what should we do? Will they be knocking down the door any minute?"

"The fact that they didn't do so immediately, tells me that they don't know you're here. Maybe they weren't keeping watch when you arrived, although I'd think they would, knowing we've had a counseling relationship. Perhaps your guardian angel got you in here undetected somehow. In any event, I'm sure they're watching now."

"So, we're trapped?" Blaine moaned mournfully, not relishing going back into captivity or worse. And yet something inside was compelling her to run out of the apartment and give herself up. *Oh, hush, Mephistopheles. I'm tired of you.*

Boris smiled, a cunning, conspiratorial grin creasing his face. "No, Blaine, we're not trapped. The owner of this apartment building is one of the key players in the resistance movement. He had long ago constructed an underground tunnel back into the basement of the building behind us. I use it all the time to escape detection."

Chapter Twenty-Three

Back on Bali, Pastor Gabriel and Rabbi Abraham had slipped comfortably into the role of itinerant ministers and teachers, traveling from one end of the small island to the other. Since virtually everyone in Bali was now a Christian convert, the government opened its facilities for the use of the two witnesses. Sometimes, they would preach to large crowds in school auditoriums. At other times, they would conduct smaller classes in Hindu temples that were being reconstituted as churches.

Komang would drive them from place to place, and then go on ahead to make arrangements at their next stop. Aadi stayed with them to attend to their needs, and they would sleep in whatever home or shelter that was made available to them. There was no lack of people who wanted to share their homes or food with them. They felt truly blessed. Gabriel was growing impatient to see his wife Carmelita once again, eagerly awaiting Vy and Aly bringing her back to him.

The Banyan trees continued to burn, miraculously giving golden light to the transparent dome that continued to shield the revived island from all outside forces. It appeared that, for the moment, the Global Government had given up their attempts to destroy Bali, though the two witnesses knew that the Global Czar would never totally give up striving to do so.

Both knew that their time on Bali was not going to last much longer. However, they had no idea what was to come, having prayed fruitlessly for such advance information. "Just like the Lord to keep us in the dark till the last minute," Gabriel griped one night in the spacious bedroom of a wealthy benefactor.

Abraham laughed. "Not without cause, for if we knew what was to come, we would head out in our own wisdom and strength, not understanding the larger picture, sure to mess things up. We must depend on the Lord for day-to-day, moment-to-moment guidance. We need to remain as a small child who takes his father's hand without knowing or questioning what is to come."[26]

Gabriel frowned, but nodded agreement. "I heard a good analogy that's worked well for me. We are like a waiter in a restaurant with God as the customer. We stand at the ready off to the side while He studies the menu to decide what He wants to order. Then, when He's ready, He beckons us over and sets us in motion to fulfill His desires."

"Yes, that is a good analogy," Abraham acknowledged. "I guess that's why the Scriptures say over and over again to wait upon the Lord." [27]

Just then, a sharp knock on the door startled them. "Yes?" Gabriel called out, his pulse quickening. He had a sense something was wrong.

Aadi rushed inside, his countenance wrinkled in worry. He stood before them unable to find the words to begin.

"Spit it out, man," Abraham growled, knowing bad news was coming.

"Uhm, well, we, uh, got a communication, uhm, well, from... from the Global Czar," Aadi was able to get out before his mouth snapped shut once again. Tears began cascading down his cheeks.

Gabriel arose and went over to Aadi, holding him tight. "No matter what it is," he said soothingly, "the Lord will see us through it."

Aadi's sad eyes stared deeply into Gabriel's soul. "They've got your wife," he whispered despairingly. Then he held out a handwritten note from their main shortwave radioman.

Gabriel read it twice and looked up at Abraham, ashen-faced and clearly troubled. Now Abraham and Aadi embraced Gabriel who haltingly explained, "Alexis says if I don't go to Jerusalem and meet with him, I will never see Carmelita again."

Abraham remembered back to how the Global Czar had tried to use his wife Tezla as a bargaining chip, only to have her die of a heart attack. A blessing, actually, for now she was safe and sound in heaven with the Lord of Lords. But he wisely kept quiet.

"We have to go at once," Gabriel exclaimed, pushing Abraham and Aadi aside. "Call Komang, have him arrange transportation."

Aadi left immediately, glad to have something to do, some way to help. No one had attempted to fly an airplane out through the dome, and he didn't think now was the time to experiment. So he had Komang contact the same shipping company who had arranged to take Vy and Aly out of Bali.

Within less than twelve hours, the two witnesses were aboard a small freighter looking back off the stern, pleased to see that the golden dome remained steadfastly in place over Bali despite their departure. It truly was of the Lord, not of them.

They then made their way forward, staring anxiously off the bow into an uncertain future. "I think it's time to pray about this," Abraham gently prodded. "The Lord always has a way of escape from any situation." [28]

Chapter Twenty-Four

Subsequent stops on Brandon and Juanita's journey to the hideaways and remote camps did not have the same heavy-duty drama as their visit to Florida. While each had its minor problems, they were each able to work comfortably with leadership for a couple of days and then move on. Brandon would help them with organizational and management issues, while Juanita would teach and mentor the prayer team, focusing most on spiritual warfare, but also covering various forms of intercession as needs arose.

As they were driving from the outskirts of Cincinnati, Juanita was lost in prayer while Brandon drove through the early morning light on the way to Wisconsin. The CD player was blasting some loud gospel music and Brandon was singing along. That's why he didn't hear Juanita when she first called out to him.

She shook his arm, startling him, causing him to veer almost out of the highway lane. When he'd gotten back under control, he snapped, "What?"

Juanita said, "I'm sorry, but I just heard from the Lord that we need to go to Las Vegas immediately."

"What?" Brandon said again, frowning and pulling over onto the shoulder.

"We need to go to Las Vegas," Juanita reiterated.

"I heard you the first time. But why now? And why Las Vegas? We don't have a facility there."

Brandon didn't like sudden changes in plans. He had gone to great lengths to scope out the most logical route between the various locations, having to modify that somewhat to fit the schedules of each place. Making such a drastic change was not a pleasant prospect.

Juanita took a deep breath to slow herself down. When she heard from the Lord, she got excited and wanted to proceed immediately. It was hard to try and explain it to people not so well-attuned to receiving such clear direction. Not that she was better than others, simply that she'd put in more time and training.

"While I was praying," she began softly, "I felt the Lord say that we need to go to Las Vegas right away to intercede about some urgent matters there. This is as strong a word as I've ever received."

Brandon sighed. He knew there was no use opposing Juanita and the Lord when they got together like this. Still, it was irritating. "Any idea what the urgent matters might be?"

"Not specifically," she admitted, "but we need to pray both salvation and judgment over that city. I think something bad is brewing there, but I don't know what."

Brandon sighed again. "Okay, get out the maps."

The GPS unit was not an option, because they didn't want anyone tracking their movements. It was hard enough having to take country highways and byways to avoid the random roadblocks the government used to keep citizens under surveillance and control.

After they laid out a route, Juanita took the wheel while Brandon used his next-to-last prepaid, untraceable cell phone to apologize to the Wisconsin hideaway for having to change their plans.

****

Things were more upbeat at CIA-West. The delayed wedding of Sue and Jerome was drawing near, while Jesse and Fran worked out their issues. So a double wedding was now in the offing. Even as Pastor Wally and Michelle had been making their way westward, the transformation of the Braintrees had lifted the black cloud from Jesse's shoulders.

To Fran's surprise, it turned out that Jesse's reluctance was not due to his love growing cold, but rather to fear overwhelming his love for her. Jesse was afraid that he wouldn't measure up as husband to the whirlwind genius he adored. While she continued to be revered by all the residents for her fantastic computer skills, Jesse was floundering to find his niche.

He felt he was just the pseudo-manager of the underground campus, but it was really Alan Morrison who made the major decisions. Like most men, Jesse's self worth was defined by his career. Back when he was a lead FBI agent, and then a middle manager in the main office, he felt both fulfilled and worthy of respect. However, he didn't feel worthy of Fran.

Then, Alan called him over to the ranch house for a meeting. Jesse thought it was going to be the usual weekly update about the mundane functioning of the facility which mostly seemed to run itself, so well-designed and built it had proven to be. After the usual detailed run-through, Alan threw him a big curve. Right out of the blue, Alan asked, "So, how would you like to start up and head up our militia?"

Jesse's jaw hung open for a few moments before he was finally able to gasp, "Who me? I don't have that kind of experience."

Alan leaned forward across his desk. "No, but the Lord told me that you're the man for the job. You're a strong Christian, devoted to our cause. You fought in the first Gulf War and have had all kinds of training with the FBI that's applicable to the task. Weaponry, tactics, etc."

Jesse sat back in the chair and stared back at Morrison. He certainly seemed serious, and it was true that he had a better background for the job than anyone else at CIA-West. But surely there was someone outside with far more experience and better leadership qualities. Still, if it was of the Lord....

"I've been in touch with some of the militia leaders around the area," Morrison continued. "None of them, however, are true believers, and after the fiasco with our first militia, they don't want anything to do with us. However, there are a number of good Christian men and women who've served in the military or various militias who would like to join up if only we had a leader."

Jesse nodded to show he understood what Alan was saying, but not yet ready to accept such a surprising and humbling offer.

"I believe that we need the militia to operate on a smaller scale," Alan added. "Wycliffe was too interested in size and importance because of his own ego. Instead, let's build a small, highly-skilled strike force that can do guerilla warfare for the Lord much as Satan has used terrorists and insurgents so successfully."

"What exactly would you see us doing, then?" Jesse asked, beginning to warm up to the idea. Already his mind was starting to envision the possibilities.

"Well, I think Wycliffe's destruction of our former San Gabriel hideaway to keep it out of enemy hands is a good example of what we could do, while his misguided attempt to attack a large detention center by brute force was an example of what not to do," Morrison answered ruefully, still feeling overall responsibility for such a tragic loss.

"So you think we shouldn't try to release Christians from the detention centers?" Jesse asked with a surprised and disappointed tone.

"I do, but not that way, and not unless the Lord tells us to do so," Morrison answered quickly. "It needs His direction and a lot of prayer covering. We learned that the hard way."

"What about intercepting all those buses they use to transport detainees?" Jesse suggested.

"Yes, that would be just the type of thing a small force could accomplish," Alan agreed, holding back a smile. It appeared Jesse was hooked.

"And what about taking down some of the regional computer centers that the Global Government uses to enforce the 'mark of the beast?'" Jesse offered intently, leaning forward onto the edge of the desk.

"Yes, you've got the idea, so now you need to go back and pray about all this. I don't want you taking just my word that this is from the Lord. You need to know in your heart that this is His commission."

Jesse nodded solemnly and strolled back toward the underground center, taking his time and praying along the way. By the time he got there he knew for sure that the Lord had answered his prayers for something truly useful to do for Him, albeit in a most unexpected way.

That evening over dinner, Fran couldn't help but notice the change in Jesse. His whole manner and appearance had started to change. He was smiling instead of moping, animated instead of repressed. When he suddenly asked her once again to marry him immediately, she burst out in tears screaming, "Yes, yes, yes!"

All the diners burst out in applause having been well aware of the couple's relational difficulties. There were virtually no secrets in such tight quarters.

Chapter Twenty-Five

When Pastor Wally and Michelle finally convened with Rev. Michael and Bonnie Braintree in the small conference room, everyone was a bit on edge. However, each was thankful for the time they'd spent getting to know each other without the pressure of having to get into pastoral counseling right away.

Wally began the session as he always did, with prayer. "Heavenly Father, we come together today in the name of your precious Son Jesus, seeking only Your wisdom and guidance. Your

Word says that You are our Counselor.[29] We ask, according to Your Word, for words of wisdom, knowledge and revelation directly from You.[30] We surrender ourselves into Your hands today. Lead and guide us in every way, we pray in Jesus' name, amen."

He smiled gently at the Braintrees and said, "As you now know, I made just about every mistake in the book. I learned my lessons the hard way. Seminary didn't prepare me for the realities I faced on a day-to-day basis. All the theology I learned enabled me to preach and teach, but not to counsel. I quickly found that just telling people what the Bible said didn't seem to be of much help. In fact, many people resented being told what they already knew. What they really wanted and needed was the ability to make the Scriptures come to life in the midst of their trials and tribulations."

The Braintrees both nodded in understanding. "As the youth in my church used to say, been there, done that," Michael sighed.

"It was hard to do within our own lives as well," Bonnie added regretfully. "The only way we seemed able to cope was to become rigid and inflexible, with ourselves and with others. We see that now, but still don't know how to get past it."

Michelle glanced at Wally to see if it was okay to add her two cents. He smiled and nodded, quite pleased to now have a true partner in his life's work.

"Looking back, I now understand how and why Wally and I both got off track. He plunged ahead to do what he'd been trained to do, and actually did it quite well. But the church, the people, ate him alive, leaving nothing for me and the children. I blamed him, but he was only doing what he knew to do. Meanwhile, because of my own personal history and problems, I bought into the materialistic mentality to try and fill the void. But the emptiness remained. I was so consumed with fear and guilt that I literally became a basket case."

Tears pooled in her eyes as she recalled those bitter days. "Then, when Wally began to seriously study and practice counseling techniques that actually worked, I fought and resisted it with all my might. It took a mighty move of God to break down my walls of resistance. But I can tell you now that this stuff works. Not just for me, but for everyone who's willing to put in the time and effort. And much as I appreciate my husband, it's not that he's such a good counselor, but that the Word of God and the power of the Holy Spirit are true and they work!"

"But we know the Word inside out, so why didn't it work for us?" Bonnie lamented.

Wally grinned. "That's exactly where I wanted to start this morning. The problem isn't the Word, it's our minds. Biblical knowledge isn't mental, it's a matter of the heart."

Michael's eyebrows raised. "How can knowledge not be of the mind?"

"There are two kinds of knowledge, according to the Bible, head knowledge and heart knowledge," Wally began to explain. "The trouble with the English language is that some spiritual concepts don't translate well from Hebrew and Greek. In the original Greek, the New Testament has two different words for 'knowledge' – *gnosis* and *epignosis.* All our English versions translate both of these as knowledge, but there's a major difference. *Gnosis* is head knowledge, while *epignosis* is heart knowledge, information that is taken in through the mind and then metabolized until it becomes part of us, deep in our heart, our spiritual center."

Michael and Bonnie looked skeptical, so Wally plunged ahead. "Many Scriptures that refer to knowledge or wisdom reference the heart, not the mind. For example:

- *Apply your **heart** to **understanding*** (Proverbs 2:2b)

- *When **wisdom** enters your **heart**, and **knowledge** is pleasant to your soul.* (Proverbs 2:10)

- ***Wisdom** rests in the **heart** of him who has understanding.* (Proverbs 14:33)

- *The **heart** of the prudent acquires **knowledge**.* (Proverbs 18:15)
- *Incline your ear and hear the words of the wise, and apply your **heart** to my **knowledge*** (Proverbs 22:17)
- *My **heart** has understood great **wisdom** and **knowledge**.* (Ecclesiastes 1:16b)
- *So teach us to number our days that we may gain a **heart** of **wisdom**.* (Psalm 90:12)

"Wow, I never made that connection before," Michael admitted.

"Neither did I until Pastor Gabriel showed it to me," Wally likewise admitted.

"It must've been wonderful to have one of God's two end-time witnesses as your mentor," Michael said with a touch of jealousy.

Wally laughed. "Yes, it was. He opened up the eyes of my heart to see and understand things that were right there in Scripture. God has sprinkled golden nuggets of wisdom throughout the Bible for those who desire to seek them out."

"I guess that's why the Word says, *And you will seek Me and find Me, when you search for Me with all your **heart**.*" Michael added.

"Exactly!" Wally exclaimed, thankful for Michael's openness to see things in a new light. "Mark 4:22-23 in the Amplified Version says: *Things are hidden temporarily only as a means to revelation. For there is nothing hidden except to be revealed, nor is anything temporarily kept secret except in order that it may be made known. If any man has ears to hear, let him be listening and let him perceive and comprehend.*"

"Isn't that the same reason Jesus spoke in parables?" Bonnie asked. "He was always saying, *He who has ears, let him hear.* If we're not making the effort to understand and if we're not open to new revelation, then the parables make no impression."

Wally couldn't have been more pleased. He thought he might have encountered resistance at this point. "Right. The other thing we need to keep in mind about the Bible is that it has many levels of understanding. There's the surface idea or information. But then, when we reread the same verse, the Holy Spirit brings new revelation about how it applies to our own lives, or to specific situations. Then later, we begin to connect Scriptures from different areas of the Bible to paint a tapestry that tells yet a deeper story."

He waited while Michelle and the Braintrees seemed lost in thought. That was another thing he'd learned. If the Holy Spirit is going to bring wisdom, knowledge and revelation individualized for each person, there needs to be time when the teacher remains silent, giving the real Teacher[31] the time and space to do His job. He especially enjoyed watching people's faces when the 'aha' moment came. Now he got to see it in triplicate.

When everyone's focus and attention had returned to him, he introduced his second topic. "Another thing about all these golden nuggets of wisdom and knowledge in the Scriptures is that they also have a great deal to say about counseling. When this revelation was first unveiled to me, I began searching through the Bible on my computer for all kinds of topics that addressed how to deal with all kinds of issues. I don't know how anyone could do that effectively without the computer. I give a lot of credit to our ancestors who had to do it by hand and by memory."

"Yes, that would be me," Michael laughed. "I just could never get the hang of using a computer. But tell me more about these counseling Scriptures."

"There are far too many to go though today in our first session. That's why I've been writing a book entitled, *The End of Bondage*. I'm well along with the draft and I will give you some of the key chapters for your reference. Just remember, that these are draft copies. I still have to go back and edit the whole thing."

Wally handed copies to each of the Braintrees. "Later today, we'll look at some of my specific cases that illustrate the use of these Scriptures in counseling. But for the moment, we need one more foundation of understanding before we really dig into it. And that's what I call demonology."

Bonnie literally shivered and recoiled at the very word. Michael abruptly sat back in the chair. "Now that might be taking things too far," he cautioned.

Wally had anticipated this response, having encountered it many times before. "You do believe in the truth of the Bible?" he asked.

"Yes, of course, we believe it is literally true, all of it," Michael said defensively.

"I'm sorry to say that's a mistake," Wally said and then quickly added. "The Bible is *inerrant*, that is without error. However, Jesus' parables are not literally true, because they're stories. The symbolism in Ezekiel and Revelation are not literally true, they are metaphors. However, the principles are true."

Wally could see the Braintrees struggling with that concept. He gave them time to sort it out. "Well, yes, I can see what you mean, but that could be a slippery slope," Michael finally intoned with a touch of fear in his voice.

"It's a slipperier slope not to understand each verse within the context of its intent. If we literally interpret the verse that says we should not cast our pearls before swine, then we wouldn't give it much thought, because who would think to throw actual pearls to pigs. However, if we realize that the context is addressing wisdom, and that swine represent those who do not wish to hear such wisdom, then we realize that this verse is telling us not to waste our time trying to convince people who refuse to be convinced."

"Yes, well……" Michael's voice trailed off. Wally knew there were mental roadblocks that needed to come down before the enlightenment of the Holy Spirit could be fully received.

"Context is everything," Wally declared. "We must interpret every single verse within the context of the entire Bible. Otherwise, we can come to wrong conclusions. For example, Jesus says that we will receive anything we ask for in His name. But this is not literally true. John 5:14-15 amends this statement: *Now this is the confidence that we have in Him, that if we ask anything **according to His will**, He hears us. And if we know that He hears us, whatever we ask, we know that we have the petitions that we have asked of Him.* When Jesus invokes the use of His name, He is doing so in the Hebrew/Greek context in which His name refers to his entire character, nature and will."

Michael and Bonnie were now paying rapt attention, but not responding, so Wally hurried to complete the concept. "In addition, each verse or section of verses must be interpreted within the context of what precedes it and what follows. An example of this is when Jesus rebuked the disciples and told them, *Assuredly, I say to you, if you have faith as a mustard seed, you will say to this mountain, 'Move from here to there,' and it will move; and nothing will be impossible for you.* Was Jesus literally talking about causing a physical mountain to move? No, he was addressing the disciples unbelief, or lack of faith. He was using hyperbole to make a point. The context shows us what that point is."

"And to further refine that point, and as a segue to our next topic, the context shows us that Jesus was specifically referring to the disciples' inability to cast out a demon," Wally concluded and sat back to see how Michael and Bonnie were doing. Not too well.

Wally knew the look, having seen it many times before. Their minds were now spinning in turmoil because he'd hammered at a major stronghold in their minds in preparation for attacking even bigger strongholds.[32] When these begin to come down, the mind flounders, having no firm foundation. That's why these truths needed to become written on the tablets of our hearts, just like the Bible says. But first, the mental barriers had to come down, a most uncomfortable process.

"Let's take a break," Wally suggested. "Why don't we go get a snack and something to drink in the dining room?" And so they did, much to the Braintrees relief.

Chapter Twenty-Six

Alexis got tired of waiting, so he sent his personal SWAT team to break into Rev. Wainwright's apartment. He was furious when he heard that neither Wainwright nor Blaine was there, and dumbfounded that there was no visible evidence that either had *ever* been there. The team retrieved a water glass and a damp towel to take back to the lab to check for fingerprints and DNA.

He then ordered the team to dismantle the entire apartment building and find out how they got out. Lucifer assured him that they had indeed been there, but his demon scouts had been taken out of commission when Wainwright prayed to bind them up, striking them deaf, dumb and blind in Jesus' name.[33]

Thankfully most Christians didn't know how to avail themselves of this power. That's why Lucifer's overall strategy of encouraging disbelief of Satan and all things demonic was so effective. Dealing with someone who understood how the spiritual realm worked, who knew that Jesus had so much more power than the archangel Lucifer, was a perpetual thorn in the Global Czar's psyche.

In the end, however, most powerful Christians were worn down by the unrelenting onslaught of a demonic horde who kept the pressure on every aspect of their lives. Eventually, most of them cracked and became discouraged. The few who remained steadfast they left alone, seeking instead to isolate them by driving their supporting cast away.

The telephone startled Alexis out of his reverie. Sure enough, the team had found an underground tunnel beneath the basement that led into the building behind it, giving them access to the parallel street. "Arrest the owners of those two buildings and search every apartment," Alexis ordered and felt somewhat better. One nest eliminated. He wondered how many more there were right here in his backyard.

****

Rev. Wainwright and Blaine were now ensconced in an even deeper nest with many others, much closer to the Global Palace. Instead of just a tunnel below an ancient, historic building, an entire underground shelter had been constructed over the past two years, anticipating the arrival of the Beast in God's capital city. These were mostly Messianic Jews who were already outcasts from their own friends and families.

Wainwright was worried about Blaine. She was shivering and lethargic. While the subterranean hideaway was somewhat damp and chilly, they had bundled her up in several blankets and had a portable electric heater blowing on her. Moreover, she was almost unresponsive when he tried to question her. It was either shock, or a demonic attack.

In case it was the former, he wanted to be extra careful. When David, the head rabbi of this Messianic sect, arrived, Wainwright took him aside and gave him a brief summary of who Blaine was and what had happened to her. The tall, distinguished middle-aged rabbi had a sharp angular face with deep, piercing eyes.

"So, Boris, the Beast's official spokesperson is our captive," David said with a satisfied smirk. "That might make her very useful to us."

"No, David, not our captive," Boris quickly corrected him. "She came to me of her own volition after being held prisoner by the Global Czar. She risked her life to escape. I believe she's ready to become one of us and then be useful to us as an ally, not as a pawn."

David chuckled. "I like you, Boris. You're one of the few who will stand up to me. How do you suggest we proceed?"

"We need to see if she's still under demonic influence or just suffering from shock," Boris noted.

"Well, then, let's surround her with love, worship, prayer and the Word of God. That will either cure her of any physical ailments or drive out any lingering demons," Rabbi David decided.

Soon, two musicians led a group of ten worshipers surrounding Blaine with songs of praise and healing prayers. In between the songs, Rabbi David read from Psalm 91 and Revelation 21 & 22.

Right from the start, Blaine's reactions were revealing. At first, her eyes opened to glare at the small crowd. As the worship continued, her body shook more and more. Her eyes turned dark and flitted wildly back and forth. Suddenly, she leaped to her feet, a deep growl rising from the depths of her soul.

Rabbi David signaled for the group to raise the intensity of the worship and prayers while he grabbed Boris by the arm and led him to stand right before the demonically possessed woman. "I bind up the strongman according to the Word who is Jesus Christ," the rabbi intoned forcefully.[34]

"You do not have the authority to bind me," a deep, raspy voice shouted back out of Blaine's spasmodic body.

"And who might you be?" Rabbi David asked, a glint in his eye.

"I am Mephistopheles, reporting directly to Lucifer. I am married to Blaine, sanctified by blood, an inviolate contract," the maniacal voice resounded within the underground chamber. "

Rabbi David's voice suddenly bellowed, "The blood of Jesus triumphs over you and the devil, and trumps any other blood sacrifice. I declare, in Jesus' name and by His blood, that your marriage contract is null and void and I command you and all your cohorts to come out of her now and go where Jesus sends you!!"

With a scream of anguish and defeat, Mephistopheles and his horde of henchman flew out of Blaine and out of the building, accompanied by the rush of a cold breeze. Blaine sank to the floor in a heap. Rabbi David motioned to the musicians to continue playing and singing.

Now as they worshipped their Deliverer[35] and prayed over Blaine, she gradually regained her faculties. With teary eyes, she looked up at the loving faces surrounding her. Then she gazed into

Boris' eyes. "I'm ready," she said in a small, soft voice. "I want, no I need, your Jesus."

Chapter Twenty-Seven

Brandon and Juanita were halfway to Las Vegas from Cincinnati when their trusty old Toyota van hiccupped and died in Kansas. It was early evening, the winter sun having just sunk below the western horizon. In the dim light, they could see nothing but depleted corn fields.

"I thought you prayed for a safe trip?" Brandon grumped to his prayer-warrior wife as he fiddled under the hood.

"You're still safe and well, aren't you?" she snapped back.

"Not for long, if we don't get this vehicle running again, or get some assistance." Brandon stood up and stretched his aching back. Not much of a mechanic, he had quickly determined that it wasn't a loose sparkplug or battery wires, so it wasn't likely he'd get the hunk of metal rolling again.

"You know, this trip to Vegas is probably more important than we thought. The enemy has redoubled his efforts," Juanita commented as she gazed off toward a small light in the distance.

"So what do you think we should do?" Brandon asked in a disgusted tone of voice as pitch darkness settled over them. He didn't want to call for roadside assistance because that would attract government attention.

"We'll pray for guidance, of course," she said and came over to squeeze Brandon's hand. "And we'll call Tara and have her get the prayer teams all around the country covering us. Then we'll be okay."

As Juanita prayed, Brandon stared into the darkness feeling scared and vulnerable. And guilty. He felt responsible for providing reliable transportation, and now he felt like a failure. He tried to remember when he'd last had the van serviced. Not all that long ago, so it wasn't really his fault, was it? He probably should have had Barry, the hideaway's resident mechanic, give it a quick checkup before they set off on this trip.

"Brandon Woodbridge, did you hear anything I prayed, or anything from the Lord?" she gently scolded.

"Huh? Oh, no, I guess not. I was thinking," he answered lamely.

"Yeah, kicking yourself because you think all of this is your fault, right?" she stated rather than asked. "But it's not your fault. The devil has attacked us, that's all. Now the Lord has shown me what we should do."

As Juanita gave her beloved husband a big hug, he saw the same light in the distance that had first attracted her attention. "There's a light over there. Maybe it's a house where we can get some help," he suggested.

"Yeah, that's what I thought too, but the Lord showed me that we need to turn right up ahead at the next intersection."

"What intersection? I don't see a stop light or any intersection," Brandon complained, desperately desiring to go to the light, anticipating a nice warm, cozy farm house with a helpful loving family.

"Oh, I saw it in my vision," she answered. "Tell you what, I'll make you a deal. Let's start walking. If we don't come to an intersection, then we'll keep on going to whatever that light up ahead is."

"Okay, deal," Brandon responded quickly, hoping there wasn't an intersection. But as they walked, hand in hand through the black, moonless night, he apologized to the Lord for possibly opposing His plan.

They had gone about half way toward the light that now gleamed twice as bright and seemed all the more alluring, when they almost walked past the intersection of a small, dirt road. In the darkness, they could barely see it even though they were right next to it, unless they shone their flashlight right at it.

"That's your road to safety?" Brandon exclaimed skeptically. "It seems more likely a road to hell."

"I agree that it doesn't look promising, but the Lord's promises are sure and certain,[36] so even though my brain says no, my heart says yes, this is the way." Juanita tried to sound confident.

Fortunately, they had both been through similar episodes where the Lord's way didn't make sense on the surface. So, with not a small amount of trepidation, they set off deeper into the darkness. They could hear animals of some kind rustling along in the bushes that now lined the road as it climbed gently upward.

The unpaved road was full of ruts and rocks, causing them to stumble several times even with the flashlight pointing the way. An hour later, they stopped to catch their breath. The temperature was dropping rapidly. Juanita was shivering and beginning to doubt that she'd heard the Lord rightly.

"What's that?" Brandon suddenly whispered and pointed further down the road. A single headlight was bobbing and weaving down the small incline toward them.

"Maybe that's our help coming," Juanita said, hope rising in her voice.

"Or, maybe it's another attack of the enemy," Brandon worried. "Let's hide in the bushes to see what's what before we expose ourselves."

Before Juanita could respond, he grabbed her arm and pulled her off the side of the road behind some prickly bushes that tore at their skin and clothing.

Soon they could hear the clacking of a diesel engine as the headlight slowly traversed the torturous path. Finally, a gap in the clouds allowed the half-moon to shine through. They saw what appeared to be someone, or something, wrapped in a dark hooded robe riding a tractor. The apparition was quite devilish in appearance.

Brandon whispered to Juanita to stay put and keep quiet. As the tractor bumped slowly past, they could see it was towing a small hay wagon. Then it suddenly stopped.

The wraithlike figure climbed down off the tractor and trotted ahead into the beam of the headlight. Then he squatted down examining the ground. *Oh no,* thought Brandon, as he held his breath. *It sees our footprints in the dusty road.*

They ducked down further as the dark ghost followed the tracks to the side of the road. "Don't be afraid," a kindly man's voice said. "I'm from the monastery. We heard from the Lord that you were coming during our devotions. The abbot sent me to pick you up."

Truth or lie? Before Brandon could decide, Juanita leaped out from behind the bush and rushed over to the monk. "Praise God! I thought the cavalry would never arrive."

"You can ride in the hay wagon," the monk said apologetically. "We don't have any regular vehicles because we never go anywhere. I put a bale of hay in for you to sit on."

As the monk climbed back on the tractor, Juanita jumped up on the wagon excited as all get out. Brandon was still suspicious, and climbed in reluctantly.

"I'll have to drive down the road a bit further until I can turn around," the monk advised before putting the tractor in gear.

Juanita and Brandon bumped and jostled along for about a quarter of a mile until the tractor pulled into a semi-circular turnaround that obviously had been dug out for just this purpose. Brandon surmised that the adjacent fields must belong to the monastery, if there actually was one and not some nefarious trap.

The laborious return trip took longer than they would have liked. Juanita was so pumped up about the joint visions that she could barely contain herself. Brandon moped in silence awaiting the verdict.

Finally, at the top of the small rise, they turned off the dirt road onto a gravel driveway. Up ahead they could see some faint lights. As they came closer, candles in the windows of a larger-than-expected building became visible.

As if hearing their silent questions, the monk explained, "We don't have any electricity or running water. No modern conveniences of any kind. We're divorced from the world, waiting for Jesus' return."

When the tractor and wagon stopped in front of the pair of large oaken doors, they swung open and a monk in the same kind of dark robe stepped out. In the faint light of the candle he carried they could see white stripes around each arm cuff, and a red stripe on the hood.

"Greetings my fellow spiritual travelers. We have been expecting you for some time. I am Brother Charles, the Abbot of the Holy Trinity Monastery. We have a late supper prepared for you. Please come inside."

In the faint glow of the Abbot's candle and others in a few windows, it appeared to Brandon that the monastery building was much like a stone castle, although it was too dark to see any turrets.

"Come on," Juanita prodded as she grabbed his arm. "I'm starving, and we don't want to keep the monks up all night."

Chapter Twenty-Eight

Neither of the two witnesses had turned out to be good sailors, fighting nausea the entire way. After the freighter dropped them off in Hong Kong, they were met by two 'guides' who looked more like bodyguards or even assassins. They were whisked away in a limo to Hong Kong International Airport where they boarded a private jet, bound for Jerusalem.

As Rabbi Abraham and Pastor Gabriel buckled themselves into two comfortable, roomy leather seats, a reedy, almost inhuman voice called out to them from behind. "Pastor Gabriel, so nice to see you again."

Gabriel turned around and saw an anorexic, pale, platinum-haired man striding toward them with a tray of finger food. "Karl, you do get around don't you? "Gabriel answered.

"That's what makes this job so much fun. Every day is different, and I get to see the world," Karl said as he held the tray out to his two guests.

Abraham nodded at the strange-looking man and took a small plate off the tray and filled it up with chicken wings, meatballs, and veggies.

"But don't you get tired of being around so much evil?" Gabriel asked pointedly.

Karl's eyes narrowed, turning completely black. "What you call evil, I call enlightened. While you pine away for the empty promise of the future, I fully enjoy the pleasures of the here and now. It is you whose sanity is in question, not mine."

As Karl turned quickly and disappeared behind a cabin door, Abraham chuckled. "Charming fellow."

The flight was long and uneventful, enabling the two witnesses to catch up on their sleep.

When they finally landed at Ben Gurion International Airport in Israel at two a.m., their two guides hustled them through customs into a waiting limo which took them once again to the King David Hotel. The irony was not lost on them. The last time they were here, Abraham's wife died. Here they were again to find out what would happen to Carmelita, Gabriel's wife.

The guides told them to be ready to be picked up at seven a.m. for breakfast with the Global Czar, same as last time. After they settled in, Abraham peeked out the door. The guides were now guards standing at attention on either side of the door.

"Well, I guess all we can do for now is see what the situation is tomorrow," Abraham sighed. "With no information, there's really nothing we can do, so we might as well get a few hours sleep."

Gabriel agreed, but lay awake in bed till six in the morning and then got up to take a shower. He was pacing around the suite's living room when Abraham awoke to the smell of coffee.

"We need to pray so that the Lord will visit us like last time," Gabriel said in a rush when Abraham emerged from his bedroom. They did so, but there was no visitation. This time, everything seemed dark and dangerous. Disappointed, they forlornly followed the guards down to the limousine.

When they arrived at the Global Palace, they were quickly escorted into the same dining room. They couldn't resist looking over into the corner where the holographic image of Abraham's wife Tezla had been, but there was no sign of Carmelita anywhere in the ornate room.

"Sorry to disappoint you," Alexis called out as he entered from the opposite end. "No more fun and games, just serious business. So please sit down so that we can begin."

The two witnesses hesitated, not wanting to feel as though they were subservient to the Global Czar They then sat down and immediately prayed a blessing over the food. Alexis shrugged. "Don't expect me to get caught up in any drama this time."

As Alexis piled food on his plate, he explained, "If you wish for Carmelita to remain unharmed, you will do as I say. We will not kill her, but rather afflict her with torture every day that you do not cooperate. I know that you think it would be best for her to die and go to heaven like Tezla, so we will do everything possible to keep Carmelita alive."

The Global Czar dug into his food as though he didn't have a care in the world. The two witnesses were not hungry at all. "How do we know that you actually have her?" Gabriel asked. "Or that she's still alive?"

Alexis nonchalantly picked up a small remote control device, pointed it at the wall and clicked. Two panels retreated to either side, exposing a large flat panel TV which was showing a live feed of a naked woman strapped down to a metal table. A guard nodded at the camera, turned and held a small medicinal stopper over Carmelita and squeezed a drop of liquid onto her stomach. She shrieked and writhed in pain.

"Sulfuric acid," Alexis commented, and then filled his mouth with soufflé.

Gabriel continued to stare at his precious, suffering wife. Alexis was right. He would rather her be killed, knowing she would then be home in heaven with the Lord, fully healed and full of joy. But this… this outrage. How could he allow her to suffer like this?

He wanted to call fire down from heaven to consume the Global Czar, but knew from Scripture that the "Beast" would live until the Day of Wrath.[37] *Please, please, Lord God Almighty, do something!*

Suddenly the image on the screen changed. Flashes of lightning blinded their eyes, a roar of thunder closed their ears. Alexis cried out in pain and writhed in his chair, slowly slumping to the floor.

Gradually, sight and hearing returned to the two witnesses even as Alexis continued moaning on the floor. Gabriel hurriedly looked back at the TV screen. He was astonished to see Vy and Aly untying Carmelita from the table.

Gabriel heard his exhausted, disoriented wife ask the two Russian operatives, "How did you get free?"

"It was amazing!" Vy exclaimed as Aly held Carmelita upright. "There was a burst of light and a loud explosion. Then the shackles fell off our hands and feet, and the prison door flew open. Outside the guards were unconscious. Your door was also open and those guards knocked out as well."[38]

Aly grabbed a robe hanging behind the door and helped the dazed woman slip into it while Vy averted his eyes. Then they both held onto Carmelita as they cautiously made their way out into the hallway, out of the camera's viewpoint.

Abraham and Gabriel rushed out of the room atop the obelisk of the Global Palace and raced to the elevator. "Do you think they were being held here in the Palace?" Abraham asked as the elevator proceeded downward.

Gabriel was punching the floor buttons to no avail. "I think we just got our answer. This elevator is under someone else's control. I think the Lord is taking us to them."

Sure enough, they bypassed the lobby floor and watched the numbers light up for the two basement levels, but they continued downward even further. When the elevator stopped, the doors opened and there were Aly and Vy, each holding onto Carmelita.

"Mi amor!" cried Gabriel. Carmelita's heavy eyelids flew open, wide with surprise and longing. With a sudden burst of strength, she leaped into his waiting arms.

As Gabriel held her tightly, Abraham asked the two Russians, "Is there any way out of this level?"

Vy shrugged his shoulders. "We were unconscious when they brought us here."

Abraham closed his eyes and prayed for guidance. What he saw made him chuckle. So much like the Lord. "We're not going to leave here as fugitives but as kings and queens."

He beckoned them back into the elevator. Before he could touch the buttons, the number one lit up. The doors closed, they ascended and then stared warily out into the lobby when the doors reopened.

"It's okay," Abraham assured them. "I saw it in my vision. Just follow me."

With that, Abraham sashayed out of the elevator into the bustling lobby as though he owned the place. Gabriel followed, holding Carmelita tightly around the waist as she shuffled along, a huge grin plastered across her face.

Vy and Aly trailed behind, their trained eyes searching for trouble. Instead, absolutely no one seemed to notice them. The guards behind the front counter were busily engaged with the phones and two visitors. A vast assembly of foreign visitors in their national garb moved to and fro intent on their own business. Even as they pushed their way through the front doors, the guards on either side appeared to be watching other things.

Out front, they made their way down the portico steps onto the main sidewalk and turned northward, slowly leaving the Global Palace behind. Abraham laughed as Vy and Aly still kept a wary watch, their countenances fixed with both worry and astonishment.

"Relax," Abraham advised them with a merry smile. "We've done this before, just like Jesus walked unseen through the crowd." (39)

Chapter Twenty-Nine

It turned out somewhat easier for Jesse to recruit militia members than he'd anticipated. He used the same conference room in the bank building in Denver where Alan Morrison had first connected with General Wycliffe. Jesse first called each one from Morrison's old list of those who'd previously expressed interest in joining their first militia team. He wisely informed them up front that they were only accepting true born-again believers this time, offering to lead those unbelievers to Christ.

As expected, many were offended at the criteria and the offer. Some even tried to force their way into the bank building to confront Jesse, but the security guards kept them at bay. Those who were invited in for interviews were more accepting of Jesse's status as leader when he explained upfront his vast experience and training with the FBI, just as Alan had advised him to do.

Jesse didn't like to blow his own horn, but it did prove useful to get quickly beyond any resentment about his being designated as the new militia general. General? He detested the title but Morrison insisted he use it to maintain military discipline.

He was pleased that those with prior militia leadership experience didn't appear to resent his position, but he cautioned himself to keep an eye out for that in the early stages of training the troops. However, when he told these experienced members that he would be relying heavily on their expertise, they seemed to appreciate his openness and honesty. Jesse was determined to develop a militia built not so much on fear and discipline but rather on collaboration and cooperation.

As he awaited another interview, Jesse had one of those "Aha!" moments. He quickly called Alan Morrison for confirmation and then placed a call on his untraceable cell phone to CIA-East. As he waited for someone to answer, he silently blessed his talented wife-to-be for her technological savvy that enabled them to convert standard cell phones approved by the Global Government into untraceable units.

After the secretary passed the call on to Jim, they exchanged pleasantries until Jesse couldn't wait any longer. "Look, Jim, as I sit here pretending I'm a general, it suddenly occurred to me that if I can do it, so can you. Stop looking for a sold-out Christian militia leader and do it yourself!"

Jesse allowed the ensuing silence to continue for a few moments before further interjecting, "Your training at the CIA makes you every bit as capable as me. Besides, I'm finding lots of good men and women with all kinds of skills. As a leader, you know from experience that you don't have to be able to do every job, but rather coordinate and manage everyone into a cohesive unit."

Jim grunted on the other end of the phone, mostly to let Jesse know that he'd heard the proposition, but also because he thought he'd left that kind of life behind. He was happier than he'd ever been before. Free from the devil, free from a life of lies and distortion, free from dealing daily with life and death. But mostly, he was happy because of his life together with Abby. How much would such an undertaking take him away from her? How much danger would he be in?

As though Jesse could read his mind, Jim got some immediate answers to his unspoken questions. "Jim, I know what's going through your mind right now because I just went through that whole mental process myself. I was worried that it would interfere with my upcoming wedding and marriage. I was happy to be away from the battlefield. But when push came to shove, I felt that the Lord was telling me that I should do this and that it would all turn out right."

Jim found his voice at last. "I hear you, buddy, and I'm happy for you. But I'm not sure that the Lord is calling me like he called you. I need to pray and talk to Abby about it all."

"Of course," Jesse quickly agreed. "I wouldn't expect any less. I'm just putting the proposition out there. Alan Morrison agrees that you're a perfect choice given our new criteria and mission, but you have to be sure that it's what Jesus wants you to do as well."

As soon as Jim got off the phone, he pulled Abby out of a meeting with the technical team and explained the new job offer. Abby smiled tenderly. "I was wondering how long it would take before you or Alan or Jesse would see that you're the right man for the job."

Jim was flabbergasted. Abby never failed to amaze him. She took his hand and began to pray for the Lord to reveal His will in the matter. It didn't take very long before they both simultaneously opened their eyes and looked at one another. The answer was clear. The CIA-East had a new general.

Chapter Thirty

Back at CIA-West, Wally, Michelle and the Braintrees reassembled to continue Wally's introduction to counseling. He knew that Michael and Bonnie needed some personal assistance as well, but first they needed to understand the Biblical foundations for such counseling before they would accept it for themselves.

After they'd gotten settled around the conference table, Wally started off in prayer, asking the Holy Spirit to be a mighty presence and speak to each one as they had need, to be their guide and fount of wisdom. He waited to see if anyone else felt led to add to his prayers, but Michelle, Michael and Bonnie were silent. Wally sensed trepidation and fear, so he prayed inwardly for God's perfect love to cast out all fear.[40]

"As I indicated before the break, in addition to ingesting Scripture via the heart, not the mind, a second foundational pillar is understanding the role demons play in our lives. I know this is not a pleasant nor accepted topic in traditional Christian circles. Certainly not in seminary. The prevailing view is that demons are a thing of the past, not applicable today."

"But that's true," Michael objected. "We have the Holy Spirit within us, so we cannot be possessed by demons."

Wally smiled and nodded. "Yes, what you've stated is true. However, the key word is 'possessed.' That means totally under the control of a demon or demons, such as the Gadarene who was possessed by a 'legion' of demons."[41]

"Right, and when he was saved, the demons had to leave," Bonnie asserted.

"Not quite," Wally answered gently. "Jesus cast out the demons and *then* the man was saved. But the important point is, when we're saved, the Holy Spirit takes up residence within us. But where within us?"

Wally waited while Bonnie and Michael processed the question within the cloud of doubt that veiled their understanding. Then Michael's eyes widened, his mouth falling open, one of those great 'aha' moments Wally loved so much. *Thank You Holy Spirit!*

"In our hearts?" Michael asked cautiously.

"Right on," Wally grinned encouragingly. "Again, the heart is the key. Most people confuse the English word 'heart' with emotions, However, in the Bible, one of the Hebrew words for heart actually means 'bowels,' This is meant to imply the center of our body. Context across many Scriptures shows that the heart is our spiritual center."

Now Bonnie was looking confused. "How then do our emotions come into play?"

"Our emotions are actually part of our soul," Wally answered. "The Bible always defines us as being comprised of 'spirit, soul and body.' When we are saved, the Holy Spirit takes up residence in our spiritual center. However, our soul is made up of our mind, emotion and will. Each of these can and are influenced by demons. In fact, some people such as those addicted to alcohol or pornography, have a portion of their souls that become fully controlled at times by demons, regardless of whether they are saved or not."

Again, Wally waited while Bonnie and Michael processed this information. He continued to pray that the Holy Spirit would bring insight and revelation to them, that the strongholds in their minds would be exposed. He watched as Michael's face mirrored the internal struggle against a major stronghold of deception.

Finally Michael looked up, his brows furrowed in deep concentration. "So," he began deliberately, "that's why some Christians, pastors even, can't overcome their addictions, in spite of being saved and regardless of their attempts to adhere to Biblical truths."

"Exactly," Wally responded solemnly. "There are strongholds in their minds that open doors and windows into their souls that demons use to gain entrance and influence over us. And let's not forget that even the Apostle Paul had a *thorn in the flesh, a messenger of Satan,* which the Lord would not remove despite Paul's prayers, so that he would not become consumed with pride, his particular area of weakness." [42]

"But that was a physical affliction, not a mental or emotional condition," Bonnie pointed out.

"Correct. Demons can afflict our bodies as well as our souls," Wally quickly agreed. "That's why Jesus was able to cure muteness and deafness by casting out demons." [43]

"So, then, is all infirmity the result of demons?" Bonnie wondered, her mind churning in disruption and confusion as her own strongholds were cracking and crumbling.

"No, there are obviously physical causes such as viruses, bacteria, even accidents," Wally answered. "However, all imperfections, physical or otherwise, open doorways for demonic influence and infestation."

Michael and Bonnie stared off into the confines of their own souls as the Holy Spirit began to show them individually where they too had come under the influence of demons.

Wally knew that this was a key juncture in the process of breaking down their unbelief in demonic influence, a stronghold very much reinforced by the devil who wanted all people to be unaware of both their presence and their mode of operation. Now it was time to start taking those confused thoughts into captivity by Jesus Christ, replacing Satan's lies with God's Truth. [44]

"Before we further discuss how demons function," Wally began, "we need to keep foremost in mind that Jesus gives us power and authority over them. It's only when we remain ignorant of their devices that we become victims."[45]

Wally saw that he now had their full attention again. "Jesus says in Luke 10:19 that He gives us authority to *trample on serpents and scorpions and over all the power of the enemy, and nothing shall by any means hurt you.*"

"But that was just for His disciples," Bonne protested.

"Well, not just the twelve Disciples," Wally gently corrected, "but rather the seventy who were sent out two by two. But more than that, Mark 16:17 says that *those who believe* can cast out demons — that is *all* believers."

"But that verse isn't in all of the ancient manuscripts," Michael further objected. "At least that's what we were told in seminary, so therefore we shouldn't put too much stock in it."

Wally laughed remembering his own seminary instruction that, looking back, seemed to go to great pains to explain away Biblical injunctions about casting out demons and all forms of supernatural healing. "Yes, that's what we've been told, but it's only partially true. After Pastor Gabriel challenged me on this, I went and did a little research. If I recall, only about six manuscripts out of around eight hundred did not include Mark 16:17-18. So, in fact, the preponderance of Scripture is in favor of this interpretation."

Michael and Bonnie drifted further back into soulful reflection. Wally waited a few moments before picking up the thread. "So let's focus a bit on how demons, or unclean spirits as they're sometimes called, actually affect us. I look at them as spiritual germs. Like their physical counterparts, they are everywhere in vast numbers. So the first thing we need to do is make sure our spiritual immune system is fully functional. This means a steady diet of the Word, our spiritual food. We need to ingest Jesus."

That last comment provoked a look of shock on Michael and Bonnie. "Ingest?" Michael finally asked.

"Yes. Jesus Himself told us that we should eat of His flesh and drink of His blood.[46] That caused many of his early disciples to become offended and disgusted. However, He meant spiritually. He is the Bread of Life.[47] Therefore, we need to partake of Him daily. How? By opening the door of our hearts, because Scripture says He's knocking at that door and wants to come in and dine with us."[48]

"Okay," Bonnie said playfully, "I'll bite. How do we dine with Jesus?"

Wally laughed, relieved to see the barriers coming down. "We must *commune* with Him, *partake* of Him, as several Scriptures enjoin us to do.[49] This means we must open our hearts to Him, surrendering our wills to His Holy Spirit to work within us in any way He sees fit, allowing Him to take down mental strongholds, to perfect His strength in our weakness.[50] To be *filled with the Spirit*, as many verses instruct us to do." [51]

Michael and Bonnie simply nodded as they attempted to open their own hearts to Jesus. Wally saw, or rather sensed, that some deep work was being performed by the Holy Spirit. He silently prayed for guidance in how to wrap up this session.

"When our spiritual immune system is weak through lack of nourishment, the devil sends his demons in to tempt our flesh and deceive us with lies. Because the demons watch us carefully, they know just the right temptation and lie at just the right moment. Often, this is when we're down or depressed, or when we've been hurt emotionally. The demons attack any crack, any open wound," Wally explained.

"However, they sugar-coat these lies to make them seem true or feel right. That's why the Bible says the devil comes *disguised as an angel of light.*[52] They provide us false comfort. For example, a favorite tactic is to feed on our anger by encouraging us that it's all right to be angry, after all God feels anger too. But the Bible says, *Be angry, and do not sin. Don't let the sun go down on your wrath.*"[53]

"Then, day after day, the demons poke and prod and encourage that anger to grow into resentment and bitterness. Scripture says that the *root of bitterness* causes trouble and defiles many.[54] It's a destructive force that can become an all-consuming fire. That's why the Bible says anger gives an opening or foothold to the devil," Wally explained.[55]

He could see that Bonnie and Michael were now under the conviction of the Holy Spirit as tears of remorse formed and ran down their cheeks. The anointing, the presence of God, was strong. Wally sat back down and closed his eyes, praying for the Holy Spirit to speak to and work within these two precious ministers. Soon, he heard his wife Michelle sniffling herself. He thanked and praised the Lord for being the true Counselor.

Michael and Bonnie weren't quite sure what was happening. Certainly Pastor Wally's words had opened their eyes. Now, each was hearing things, sensing things, feeling things that stripped away layer upon layer of their own garbage and baggage.

Wally remained in prayer until he sensed that the Lord was finished doing whatever it was He was doing. He opened his eyes and saw Michael and Bonnie embracing each other, their lips quivering with heartfelt emotion. He waited until the two sighed deeply and sat back in their chairs. Their once pale, stern faces were now aglow with life, much like Moses appeared after convening directly with the Lord.[56]

"If it were up to me," Wally began gently, "I'd plow ahead. But I strongly sense that the Lord wants to continue whatever He is doing in you and for you. So, if that seems right with you, I suggest that you two go back to your room and commune with the Lord for the rest of the day. Then we can pick up again tomorrow."

Unable to even speak, Michael and Bonnie nodded, grasped their hands together, and left the conference room. Wally glanced over at Michelle who was glowing as well.

"I never expected counseling to go like this," she said, wiping away the last remaining tears. "This was so beautiful, so…. Well, I don't know quite how to describe it, but it was wonderful."

"Yes it was," Wally agreed. "But it doesn't always happen like this. All the parties need to be open to the move of the Holy Spirit and be in one accord.[57] However, this is what we must always seek in every counseling session, because a move of the Spirit is worth more than ten thousand words."

Chapter Thirty-One

After a plain but filling breakfast, Brandon and Juanita met with the Abbot, Brother Charles, in his sparse yet functional office.

"I know that you have many questions," Brother Charles began as he settled his elongated, almost emaciated frame down into the wobbly, creaky desk chair. "But as with most spiritual things, beginnings and endings are not always as clear as we would like."

He leaned forward onto the desk, his bony elbows protruding through the robe and making dents in the blotter. With Brother Charles' hood back on his shoulders, Brandon thought the Abbot looked like Abraham Lincoln might have had he lived long enough to go completely gray.

"Your presence here," Brother Charles continued as his eyes glazed over, "is neither a beginning nor an end, but rather the continuation of a process that began a couple of years ago."

Brandon was somewhat confused. He liked things to be clear, and this didn't sound like it was going to very lucid at all. Juanita, on the other hand, smiled knowingly. She strongly sensed that something important was going on, something of spiritual significance that could not be understood in worldly ways.

"So please excuse me if I jump around a bit chronologically and grope for words to convey my very limited understanding of what is happening," Brother Charles apologized off into some distant view beyond the walls of his office.

"We are, or at least were, Jesuits. We feel that we still are, but the powers that be excommunicated us when we strongly protested the existence of a militaristic group of Jesuits who were conspiring with Pope Radinsky to enforce changes in our core beliefs," the Abbot explained.

"There have always been rumors of such a group within our ranks over many centuries dating back to the Crusades and the Knights of the Templar. Back then they were instrumental in the Inquisition, uncovering and capturing supposed heretics. In modern times, they were rumored to be cooperating with the so-called New World Order in establishing Catholicism as the one-world religion."

Brother Charles' eyes came back into focus and he glanced over at his two enrapt listeners. He'd almost forgotten they were there. "You may not be aware of how many Jesuit organizations and principals have risen into the very power centers of the world. I'm not going to bore you with a detailed history, but rather try to paint an overall picture, to weave a tapestry of understanding, if you will."

"And what exactly does this have to do with us?" a somewhat frustrated Brandon asked.

"Oh, a great deal, to be sure. A very great deal. For we are to become spiritual partners in a very important undertaking for the Lord God Almighty!" Brother Charles intoned seriously.

"Glad you cleared that up for me," Brandon sniped sarcastically, but the Abbot had refocused on some distant spiritual horizon again.

As they waited for the Abbot to continue, Brandon and Juanita both began to sense the presence of the Lord to such an extent that they each got goose bumps on their arms. Brandon decided that maybe, just maybe, there was something going on here that was indeed significant.

Finally Brother Charles began to speak again to some far away vision that only he could see. "What the world refers to as Jesuits is actually the Society of Jesus. We are the largest male religious order in the Catholic Church, founded in 1534 by St. Ignatius of Loyola. But just like the Freemasons evolved out of the Illuminati, so too did our ranks become infiltrated and corrupted by a dark, shadowy group with Templar roots.

"We are best known in the world for our schools, colleges and universities, as well as for our intellectual research and our work for social justice, human rights, interreligious dialogue and cooperation. It is this latter activity combined with secretive works of renegade Jesuits that have perpetrated a false Pope and a Universal Religion that is more like the ancient mystery religions the Bible warns us against."

Brandon and Juanita had many questions come to mind but felt led by the Holy Spirit not to interrupt the Abbot's stream of consciousness.

"When the Global Czar and Pope Radinsky established the Global Governance Committee under the guise of world peace, a new Superior General of our Society was named, one of the rogue, black priests who worship the devil, not Christ Jesus."

Brother Charles was breathing heavily now, impassioned by a righteous indignation that almost consumed him. "New directives of policy and belief were issued to which we could no longer abide. When we refused to obey, we were totally cut off. A virtual army of these renegades descended upon us one day and took away all our vehicles, our appliances, everything they claimed we had received from the Society. It didn't matter that we had labored hard ourselves to purchase these items. We were left destitute with no more support or funding from our very own Order."

Brother Charles attempted to blink away the tears of outrage that had formed, but continued on with his tale of injustice. "In the end, though, it was the best thing that could have happened to us. No longer able to travel out into the world, we became self-sufficient and totally reliant upon the Lord. Our relationship with Him grew deeper and deeper, both individually and as a group.

"When we realized we would survive, we began to pray and ask the Lord what He had in mind for us. After several weeks of intense prayer, each of us had a vision one night, slightly different but with a common theme. The Lord was sending two emissaries of African descent who would appear one night on foot in the dark of night, who would connect us to a new mission, a new purpose."

Brother Charles' eyes now refocused on the flabbergasted couple on the couch. "You are those emissaries and we now await your direction."

Chapter Thirty-Two

Alexis had been furious and almost out of his mind over Carmelita's miraculous escape. Pope Radinsky and René were quite concerned about the Global Czar literally going bonkers, so they arranged for a series of events to mollify D'Antoni's overly inflated ego.

The first event was a ceremony marking the fulfillment of the program to generate holographic images of the Global Czar in the centers of every major city in the world. With the local systems in place, linked by a new network of satellites to a projection center in the Global Palace, previously recorded messages from Alexis had been running on a continuous loop. Now it was time for a live broadcast.

All the nations and cities of the world had been notified that an important announcement would be made at five p.m. Friday, Greenwich Mean Time, noon EST. Alexis was at first annoyed that Blaine was no longer available until René pointed out that they no longer needed her. The Global Czar himself could now speak to the entire world, virtually in person, anytime he wanted. Better yet, this would bypass the media and go directly to the people with no one around to harass him with potentially embarrassing questions.

Furthermore, René also found a blonde bimbo with a modicum of intelligence and network TV experience to replace Blaine for more minor announcements, or when they need to throw someone to the wolves. "Christine is much more suited to our purposes than Blaine ever was," René pointed out. "She's already given herself over to Lucifer and his ways. A real opportunist, out to get what she wants at any cost."

René knew Alexis would be quite pleased, without getting attached to her as he had with Blaine. This one was a real throwaway, easily replaced if she got out of line. After an evening and night working and playing with Christine, Alexis heartily agreed.

Alexis was eager and excited Friday morning, more so than in a long time. Although largely symbolic, he knew this first live broadcast was a major step in the eventual subjugation of all humanity who would one day bow before him, not just as the Global Czar, but also as god.[58]

He had to suppress such anticipation from his address, however, because the sheep must not be allowed to see the future before they were fully prepared for it in advance. Instead, he'd decided to summarize all their achievements to date, and announce the finalization of and conversion to the new global currency, the DEY, a combination of the Dollar, Euro and Yen. Most people, though, would use the Terra, equivalent to one hundred DEYs.

"At midnight, tonight, all currencies in every account in the world will be switched over to the DEY," D'Antoni proudly proclaimed. "Now that everyone has an electronic account through the Universal Banking System, one hundred Terras will be deposited in the account of every single person in the world as a reward for participating in the global system and putting up with some of the earlier wrinkles," Alexis beamed into the special cameras that encircled him and transmitted his holographic image around the globe.

"The blessings of worldwide peace and prosperity will now reach down into every squalid corner of the planet to lift each and every person out of the bondage of poverty. In the future, a basic subsistence level will be distributed electronically to everyone every month. No more poverty. No more war. What a wonderful world," Alexis intoned as the broadcast signal was terminated.

Of course, he had purposely neglected to tell about the Terra Tax that those not in poverty would have automatically deducted out of their accounts as a percentage of their wealth. With all finances now under complete control, the sheep could be manipulated with the click of a mouse. He'd let Christine tell the press about that next week.

Chapter Thirty-Three

Blaine Whitney was not herself, and that was just fine with her. What a fool she'd been not to surrender herself to Jesus back when Rev. Wainwright first suggested it. However, from her new divine perspective, she had eternity ahead of her, so the relatively brief slings and arrows of the past were quickly and easily forgotten.

She realized that her stumbling block had been thinking she'd have to give up her personality when she put off the old self and put on the new self in Christ.[59] She had not wanted to become a brain-dead robot, nor did she want to give up the essence of who she was.

Fortunately, Rabbi David and Rev. Wainwright were able to show her that the so-called 'new self' was the one God the Father had originally designed and intended for her to be.[60] It wasn't new in the sense that it was a totally different self, but rather her core being — that had been corrupted and covered over by the garbage of a fallen world — was being released from its bondage.

The newness was more a matter of being awakened spiritually. We were born spiritually dead, separated from God because of our sinful natures.[61] By accepting Jesus as her Savior and repenting of her sins, Blaine had been reconciled to God.[62] In addition, she had received the Holy Spirit to fill that void that everyone spends most of their lives trying to cram with worldly substitutes. Her substitutes had been prestige and respect, to replace the sense of unworthiness she'd acquired through her father's abuse.

Now her true Father in Heaven had given her a sense of worth beyond what she'd ever hoped for or imagined. She felt whole and at peace for the first time in her life. And it was still her, not some other strange being. It was her without all the heavy baggage that had sublimated her real self, her God-given self.

Neither Rabbi David nor Rev. Boris had enough time to fulfill Blaine's ravenous appetite for understanding Scripture and the ways of God. Several other members of their underground group spent hours a day with Blaine until she finally felt she'd reached a foundational level of knowledge.

Even as the world was mesmerized by the image of Alexis all over the globe, she sat on a pillow in a corner of the large basement trying to figure out where she went from here. All the publicity about Alexis brought back memories of her recent association with the unholy Trinity. How had she been so blind not to see through the evilness of Pope Radinsky's satanic services? Why had she allowed her drive for success and recognition to overshadow her early feelings of wariness regarding the Global Czar and the Global Governance Committee? At least she'd been able to see René for who she was right away.

However, she refrained from beating herself up about the past despite a strange desire to do so. Boris said the devil would never give up trying to reopen those doors, so she had to strengthen herself in the Lord, resist Satan's lies and he would flee.[63] Having done so yet again, she prayed for the Lord to give her a glimpse of what she should do in the future.

Surely He didn't want her to remain hidden below ground accomplishing nothing of any value. *There you go again,* she sensed a voice deep inside saying to her. *Your worth is not defined by what you do.*

"Yes, Lord," she mumbled quietly, "but I want to do something for You! Your Word says we should become a servant, which implies that we have duties of some kind. I only want to begin fulfilling my role as a humble servant."

A Scripture came to mind. *But those who wait on the LORD shall renew their strength; they shall mount up with wings like eagles, they shall run and not be weary, they shall walk and not faint.* [64]

"Yes, Lord, I will wait."

****

Rabbi Abraham, Pastor Gabriel and Carmelita were growing restless in the safe house Vy and Aly had led them to in the heart of Old City Jerusalem. The Old City is a 0.9 square kilometer (0.35 square mile) walled area within the modern city of Jerusalem, Israel. Until the 1860s this area constituted the entire city of Jerusalem. The Old City was now roughly divided into quarters, one each for the Muslims, Christians, Jews and Armenians.

The Russian safe house was in the Armenian Quarter and had not been used much since the advent of global peace. Largely forgotten, the safe house was within the small sector behind high walls and a gate that traditionally closed nightly at 9:30 p.m. There were only a few thousand Armenians still living in the Old City. The Armenians originated in Turkey, Iran and the Caucasus

Mountains, first coming to Jerusalem in 95 BC as a result of a trading relationship. Subsequently Christianity spread to the higher echelons of Armenian royalty. In AD 301, Armenia was proclaimed a "Christian state" under King Terdat III.

One of the central reasons for the continued existence of an Armenian quarter was their strong and stubborn desire to retain their cultural and religious heritage. They had remained a homogeneous group, intermarrying over the years and keeping their culture intact. The Cathedral of St. James and its monastery remained the center of all life within the walled sector.

Surprisingly, there were over one million Armenians officially living in Russia. Including guest workers, some estimate the Armenian population to be almost three million. Regardless, Russia possessed the largest Armenian population outside of Armenia proper. There had been an Armenian presence in Russia since the Late Middle Ages, when various artisans, merchants and traders ventured north to the Crimea and the northern Caucasus in order to set up trade ties and conduct commerce.

Consequently, the Armenians in Old City, Jerusalem, reluctantly allowed the KGB to establish a safe house within their walled sanctuary so as not to cause trouble for their brethren in Russia. It had only proven to be a minor inconvenience, easily overlooked. Although the gatekeepers were surprised at the appearance of the two Russian operatives, they had been there before and knew the passwords and protocols, so they'd been allowed inside the gated sanctuary.

Their three companions, hidden under hooded robes, were not identified and the Armenians knew better than to ask. Still immersed within their traditions and separated from the mainstream, the Jerusalem Armenians cared little about the global government, even though they existed within the shadow of the Global Palace. They gave no thought to alerting anyone about their visitors.

Now that a few days had passed, Gabriel and Abraham were sensing it was time to move on, but to what? They hunkered down that morning and prayed for guidance. They were startled when there was a knock on the door. The Armenians never approached the Russian safe house. Who could it be?

Standing in the archway was a tall, blond, handsome man dressed in a white robe. There was a certain glow about him that made everyone gasp. "You're an angel, aren't you?" Gabriel finally inferred.

"Come," the man said without answering the question. "Follow me."

The man strode off purposefully, leaving them little time to gather up their few belongings and rush out after him. They caught up to him just as he passed through the open gate. Their hurried movements attracted quite a bit of attention. Carmelita noticed, however, that no one seemed to be looking at the man ahead, the angel. She supposed that he was not visible to anyone but them.

Abraham, Gabriel and Carmelita were still dressed in their monk's habits that Vy and Aly had "borrowed" from the monastery. Nevertheless, they caused little stir outside the Armenian walls as they rushed after the rapidly striding angel. They supposed that now they were all made invisible to prying eyes.

They twisted and turned deep into the Jerusalem Quarter toward the Western Wall. A few blocks short, the angel trotted down some steps to the basement door of one of the crowded, stone buildings. He walked right through the door, leaving the five breathless followers wondering what to do.

"I guess we're supposed to go inside too," Abraham observed. "Too bad we don't yet have our glorified bodies so we too could pass through solid objects like the angel."

Gabriel chuckled and knocked on the door. A small panel opened, revealing a young, cherubic face. "Who are you?"

For a moment, Gabriel was caught short. How to explain their presence? Obviously, the angel had not deigned to do so.

But then he realized it was time to identify who they really were. He threw off the hood and pulled Abraham's off as well. "We are God's two end-time witnesses, the world's most wanted fugitives."

The young man's eyes bulged wide with shock and recognition. The panel quickly closed. They could hear voices behind the door arguing for awhile before the panel was reopened. This time a wizened, skeptical face peered out at them.

"So, it *is* you!" The man flung the door open. "Quickly, come inside." He slammed the door closed behind them. "Come, follow me."

They trailed the man through a typical basement complex of storage areas, a furnace room with several water heaters, and a small living area for the apartment building superintendent. The old but agile man pushed through another door in a dark corner behind a pile of old furniture and led them down some steps into a dimly lit corridor that led to yet another door.

They were startled by the light and loud voices raised in worship beyond this final door. Once inside, the old man stopped, a little out of breath. "Welcome, I am Rabbi David. This is the headquarters of our Messianic congregation. We are the center of resistance in Jerusalem to the satanic Global Government. You've come to the right place and we are honored to have you here. But how did you find us? Why are you here?"

"An angel of the Lord led us here," Rabbi Abraham replied. "As to why, you'll have to ask the Lord yourself, because we haven't got a clue."

Chapter Thirty-Four

Brandon and Juanita had spent two of the most enjoyable days of their lives at the Holy Trinity Monastery. The sense of peace, separation from the world, and connection with God were so intense, that a seemingly permanent, palpable joy settled over and within them.

Or course, Juanita's presence at the male-only monastery caused a little consternation before certain adjustments were made. After all, she was one of their "emissaries." Brandon and Juanita were allowed to eat with the monks in their dining room as long as they did not speak with them. While the monks' private devotions were still off-limits, the two emissaries were allowed to attend the morning and evening services.

The Abbot left them alone for the most part, not out of neglect, but rather to give them the time and space for them to hear from the Lord the mission and directions He had for the monastery. Normally, Brandon would have felt anxious about such expectations, but the presence of the Lord was so deep that a supernatural calm unlike anything he'd ever known filled him to overflowing.

So the two emissaries simply walked around the beautiful grounds, labored in the vast vegetable gardens, helped tend to the cows, goats and sheep, and forgot all about the world outside the idyllic refuge. From the top of the hill where the abbey stood strong like an ancient castle, they could see for miles around — not that there was anything to see other than vast acres of corn and winter wheat fields. There were some farmhouses on the far horizon, but only one visible structure was within several miles. That one was the source of the light Brandon and Juanita had seen when their vehicle first broke down.

When they asked Brother Charles about their nearest neighbor, he grew solemn, perhaps even fearful. "We don't have anything to do with them. We tried to visit them once but were driven off by two angry young men who pointed shotguns at us. Fortunately, they've never come up here to cause us any trouble. I think that they're perhaps fugitives or maybe they have a meth lab or something like that."

Brandon marveled over the self-sufficiency of the monastery. They grew all the food they needed and their well had plenty of water. All that was required was manual labor which took up all the monks' time save for eating, devotions and services. In the winter, they sold excess food to buy enough gasoline to run their sole tractor through a farmers market that came out to pick up the produce and bring the gasoline for a cut of the profits. They also bartered produce for firewood to feed the several fireplaces that were the only sources of heat in the winter.

Brandon and Juanita hadn't minded the cool evenings because they would snuggle up together under several blankets in the guest quarters. The daytime sunshine kept the stone structure warm enough that the fires hadn't yet been necessary. But on their third day there, the early winter's first cold front blew through with frigid winds and dark brooding skies. Despite the fires, they shivered through the night. Juanita despaired of hearing from the Lord because her many prayers for revelation and enlightenment for them and the monastery had gone unheeded.

The following night was even colder and further dampened her spirits. Images of warm Las Vegas dominated her dreams. She awoke with a start, and when she groped for Brandon she came up empty. She put on her robe and slippers and slipped down the hall into the main room just off the entrance. It was what the monks referred to as their 'great room,' with its sturdy couches, chairs and tables that were used primarily for visiting with guests.

She found Brandon sitting before the roaring fireplace that cast its heat down the narrow hallways toward the living quarters. He seemed lost in thought and jumped slightly when Juanita sat beside him on the frayed couch that faced the fire. "Can't sleep?" she inquired.

Brandon turned and looked at Juanita, a strange expression on his face. "No," he finally answered in a soft, faraway voice.

"Bad dreams?"

Brandon stared back into the flames. "Not exactly."

This wasn't like the straightforward Brandon at all. "Well, then, exactly like what?" she asked, growing a bit exasperated.

Brandon sighed. "I think I had a dream-vision."

"Really? What about?"

Dreams and visions were Juanita's specialty, her domain. Brandon felt like an interloper. Surely it meant nothing. And yet he knew it did. But he was hesitant to give his interpretation because it was somewhat ludicrous, probably way off the mark. He slumped back in the sofa and gazed down at the floor.

Juanita began to surmise the problem. Brandon had always felt inadequate in his prayer life, even his relationship with the Lord, when compared to his precocious wife. This was really a first for him, so she understood that he was besieged with a sense of inadequacy.

She put her arm around him. "Honey, I haven't heard a blessed thing from the Lord. I think this time He's chosen to speak through you. I sense that whatever you saw and heard is important, so please tell me about it."

Brandon felt somewhat encouraged, so he haltingly began to describe his dream-vision. "It was quite vivid, unlike any dream I've ever had before. The colors were so bright and crisp. When I awoke from it, I had a sense of joy that was so strong, so profound, that it was quite overwhelming."

Juanita nodded. That's exactly what separated a dream-vision from an ordinary dream. If the predominant emotion had been fear, then it would have either been a nightmare or perhaps a warning from the Lord.

"In the dream, I was exploring the rest of the monastery that's off limits to us," Brandon continued, his eyes turned inward, reliving the experience. "It was as if none of the monks could see me. I just walked right past them in the hallways. I don't know if the various rooms I saw are real or not, but I followed one particular hallway that was longer than the others. At the end was a large red door. I could hear a noise coming from behind the door, so I looked around to see if anyone was watching me, but no one was there."

Brandon's eyes widened and his breath quickened. "I placed my hand on the large gold doorknob but quickly withdrew it because it was quite hot. When I looked around for something to use as a hot pad, there was nothing at all in the hallway. But then I noticed I was wearing one of the monk robes with long rolled-up sleeves. I unrolled one and grabbed the doorknob again through the thick material."

Juanita watched Brandon's face, transfixed by his transformation as his jaw flopped open and his brow furrowed in wonder. "I couldn't see anything at first because the light coming from the center of the room was so bright, but I could hear the monks chanting above the deep throbbing of a powerful engine. Gradually, my eyes came into focus and I could see the monks busily at work around a very large, gleaming motor that took up half the huge room."

Brandon started pointing this way and that as he described the monks' activities. "Over to the left side, some monks were shoveling fuel into the side of the motor. However, the fuel wasn't black like coal, but shiny like silver or platinum. On top of the motor, two monks were operating a feeding tube that came down out of the high ceiling. The tube was transparent and I could see liquid gold pouring into the top of the motor. Off to the right, several monks were chanting and turning a large crank protruding from the side of the motor."

Brandon's breath caught and his body twitched as he continued reliving the dream. "A voice suddenly startled me. It seemed to be coming out of the motor itself, but then an angel in a long white robe descended through the vaulted ceiling, coming to rest on top of the machine. 'This is the engine that will empower you to defeat the enemy,' the angel proclaimed. I was immediately filled with a great joy far beyond anything I've ever experienced. Then I awoke and came out here to ponder what it all meant."

Now it was Juanita's eyes that bulged. "I just heard the Lord say that just as we are now in the geographic center of the country, so too is this monastery at the very center of all that we do."

Brandon blinked several times trying to refocus on the present. "The motor, what do you think it represents?"

Juanita's face slowly lit up with a huge grin as the interpretation flooded into her mind from the Lord. "It's the prayers of the monks. The silver represents the purity of their lives while the chants are their actual prayers. Those prayers are then answered by the Lord above who empowers the motor with gold from heaven."

Brandon's brow furrowed in confusion. "I thought the prayer groups in the hideaways and remote camps were empowering and protecting us?"

"Yes, to a degree," Juanita answered as though in a daze. "But now, as the warfare escalates in scope and intensity, the Lord is saying that we need even more force behind us, and that will come from this central power generating station. We'll need to keep them informed of everything we're doing or intending to do, because without them, we will not achieve all that the Lord has in store for us."

The pair sat in awed silence as the light from the fireplace flickered across their faces. They marveled over the series of steps that had led them through the darkness to this holy site. "So, I guess we really are the two emissaries," Brandon finally acknowledged, aglow with the satisfaction of having been the receptor of the vision.

Chapter Thirty-Five

Pope Radinsky and Mustafa stared through the one-way glass at their protégé, the soon-to-be announced Mahdi, the 'guided one' who is supposed to rid the world of error, injustice and tyranny, who will usher in worldwide Islamic rule. The young man was beautiful, his every movement fluid and graceful, his voice both commanding and soothing. His olive complexion was set off by incredibly blue eyes, a prominent, aristocratic nose and natural platinum hair and beard which outlined a broad forehead that communicated both strength and wisdom.

"The years of training have come to fruition at last," Radinsky said as a sly smirk played across his face. "You chose well, Mustafa."

"No, master Lucifer chose well and merely led me to the baby before it was terminated because of its unusual appearance," Mustafa replied with honest humility. "We'll have to die his hair and beard black soon to comply with Islamic prophecies."

"Well, he certainly looks the part, but are you sure you can sell him as the actual Mahdi?" Radinsky asked pointedly, cutting to the heart of the issue. Theory was one thing, but carrying out a conspiracy of this magnitude was going to be very difficult.

Mustafa nodded solemnly. "We will be able to fulfill most of the signs, but by taking advantage of the differences in expectations of the Sunnis and Shiites, we will also create elements of confusion that will take the focus off the Mahdi and fuel internecine strife. In fact, the advent of the Mahdi is not a universally accepted concept in Islam, since it is not mentioned specifically in the Qur'an. It is only referenced in one of the six books of hadiths which are based on the sayings and deeds of Muhammad."

"Yes, quite clever," the Pope agreed, "but we want to foster belief not war."

Mustafa withheld several irritated comebacks. They'd been over this ground numerous times, but Radinsky always had to play skeptic in order to maintain his perceived authority. Mustafa wished that a real Mahdi would come and do away with the Pope and all of Christendom, but he knew that was not to be. Lucifer was the true Mahdi who would empower their protégé just as he was empowering the anti-Christ, Alexis D'Antoni.

Instead of replying, Mustafa signaled Radinsky to follow him into another viewing room. There on the other side of the one-way mirror was the Masih ad-Dajjal, the Great Deceiver. Even as Radinsky had marveled upon finally seeing their fake Mahdi for the first time, so too did he now recoil from his first sighting of the one-eyed Islamic Dajjal, the evil, false messiah who will war against Jesus in the final days.

The young man on the other side of the mirror paced erratically around his bedroom, his long, skanky dark hair falling over broad, hunched shoulders. When the Dajjal turned around, Radinsky gasped. Although knowing he would be "one-eyed," he was not prepared for the sight of a viscous film covering the right eye socket while the left eye bulged outward like a grape about to explode. The man's dark brown complexion was clouded by facial expressions that flitted randomly from cunning to rage to insanity.

Across his forehead were raised red letters, k.f.r. A tattoo? Birthmark? Or had Mustafa branded him? "The letters stand for the Muslim word, *kaafir,* meaning infidel," Mustafa explained. "Just as the hadith foretells."

"Uhm, yes, quite believable," Radinsky finally mumbled. Then he regained control and went back on the offensive. "But can the Mahdi and ad-Dajjal keep up the act?"

Mustafa smiled benignly, willing away the smugness that sought to surface. "That's the best part of all, it's not an act. We have programmed them to truly believe they are these two divine characters from Islamic mythology."

Radinsky flinched. This he hadn't heard before. "Doesn't that make them uncontrollable in the long run?"

Mustafa beamed, his ultimate surprise to finally be revealed. "No, for two reasons. First of all, they have been hypnotized to respond to certain words and phrases in pre-programmed ways. If they're going off-script, we can verbally redirect them."

"And if that fails?" Radinsky asked sharply, not liking to be upstaged by his underling.

"Then, we destroy them with an implanted device that will release a deadly poison into their bodies with a simple cell phone call," Mustafa concluded and awaited the earned adulation.

Instead, Radinsky's eyes darkened and narrowed ominously. "Don't be so sure we don't have similar fail-safe measures with you, should *you* get too cocky or arrogant."

Mustafa stumbled backward as waves of demonic hostility pounded on both his body and his psyche. He'd wondered how far he could push Radinsky. Now he knew.

Chapter Thirty-Six

The excitement over the impending double wedding spread all the way from CIA-West to East. Jim and Abby would fly out for the festivities in the new Cessna that Morrison had purchased for the eastern campus. He'd even sent one of his pilots to become permanently stationed there in the Tennessee Valley.

Francine, however, was somewhat conflicted over the latest insider news she'd gleaned from hacking into the Global Government computer systems. Her ruse of deflecting their cyber identification northward away from Morrison's Colorado ranch had worked only too well. While pleased to have thwarted the enemy, she was distraught that it had resulted in the deaths of a whole community of Jehovah's Witnesses in Wyoming.

In addition, she'd read that the Global Government was going to make an example of all the Jehovah's Witnesses, rounding them up and carting them off to various detention centers, while putting several leaders on trial for treason to be hung publicly as a deterrent to further Christian resistance.

Of course, the anti-Christ global government empowered by Satan detested all things Christian and didn't care much to distinguish between its various sects and denominations. That the Jehovah's Witnesses were not true Christians didn't matter at all to Jesse, but Alan Morrison rejected his pleas to unleash their newly formed militia on some of the caravans carrying the captives to western detention centers.

"Don't pull a Wycliffe on me," Alan Morrison warned. "These folks aren't even Christian. They believe Jesus is Michael, the archangel, and not the Son of God. They also believe that salvation is earned through good works, in direct opposition to the Bible which states we are sinners saved only by the grace of God through the atoning blood of His Son Jesus Christ."[65]

"Yeah, I know but the Global Government and the general public don't understand those distinctions," Jesse argued. "So this is seen as a direct attack on all of Christianity. Isn't it time we took a stand and showed we aren't going to take this outrage sitting down?"

"Perhaps," Alan admitted. "But we're not going to do anything without confirmation from our prayer teams. We're not going to make that mistake again."

"Right, but no one knows where Brandon and Juanita are," Jesse pointed out, a worried frown creasing his face. "Maybe we should send some of our scouts out to track them down."

"Yes, that's a good idea," Alan agreed, "but it needs to be addressed by the prayer teams as well. Without Juanita available, let's get Tara coordinating it this time. Then talk with Jim and see whether it makes more sense to send out scouts from there or from here."

With the last known communication from Brandon and Juanita placing them near the Nebraska-Kansas border, CIA-West was closest and a three-man team was sent out. However, one of Brandon's friends, Mike Bishop, now an officer in the CIA-East militia, requested permission to join the hunt, which was granted. Mike arranged to meet the three scouts in Lebanon, Kansas, the geographic center of the contiguous United States.

****

Midst all the excitement, Wally, Michelle, Michael and Bonnie reconvened for what Pastor Wally said would be his last formal class on counseling. After that, he would begin real counseling sessions with the many residents who'd so requested, and the Braintrees could attend to get a first-hand feel for how it all worked.

After Michelle led them in an opening prayer, Wally began. "Up to this point, we haven't actually talked about specific counseling techniques. I feel it's appropriate to leave them for last because we don't want to get technique oriented. The Holy Spirit needs to drive the sessions, not methodology. However, it's good to have an established plan to follow until and unless the Holy Spirit sends us in another direction."

The three 'students' nodded, so Wally pulled the cover sheet off the flip charts he'd prepared in advance. "The first thing we need to do is make a quick determination whether we're going to take a long-term approach or treat the immediate symptoms up front. If the problems are severe enough to require urgent attention, then we need to take what I call a 'top-down' approach. This gets us right into dealing directly with the symptoms immediately, employing techniques that I'll outline later. Then, after getting the person to the point where they can focus on the deeper issues below the surface, we can switch to the normal 'bottom-up' approach."

Over the course of a long day, Pastor Wally presented in detail the counseling techniques he'd learned and developed over the past few years. He was pleased to have spent the time preparing the series of detailed flip-charts which he now could use in his counseling book, *The End of Bondage*.

Pastor Wally waited as Bonnie finished her note taking before beginning the final segment of the course. Just as he opened his mouth to introduce the final topic, a gentle tapping on the conference room door left his jaw hanging open for a few seconds. The door cracked and Francine's face pushed through.

"Excusez-moi si vous plais," Fran called out in her best imitation French. Wally saw a twinkle in her eye that made him laugh at the ill-timed intrusion.

"Okay," Wally chuckled, "you're too cute to resist. What do you want?"

Fran burst through the door followed by an embarrassed Sue. "We wanted to catch you four all together because we have an important question to ask you," Fran explained in a rush.

"Well, here we all are," Wally replied, somewhat bemused and more than a little curious.

Fran turned and gestured for Sue to do the formal request. Sue blushed. "Uhm, well, what we wanted to ask you, but please don't feel obliged, and I hope you won't be insulted, but, well, as you probably know, we've decided on a joint wedding, and we were wondering whether, uhm, if both you Pastor Wally and you Pastor Braintree would consider officiating the ceremony together?"

Before either could reply, the impatient Fran jumped back in. "And, we'd like for Michelle and Bonnie to be our matrons of honor!"

That caused a moment of silence that seemed to drag on interminably for Fran and Sue. "It's okay if that wouldn't work out for you," Sue felt necessary to repeat.

Wally looked over at Michael and they nodded to each other. "I think we can work that into our busy schedule," Wally intoned in an ultra-serious manner that broke the tension.

Meanwhile, Michelle and Bonnie looked at one another with big grins on their faces. "And we'd be delighted, actually honored, to be your matrons of honor," Michelle answered as her eyes moistened up.

"So, when's the big day?" Wally asked, which launched Fran into a tizzy of details. When Michelle and Bonnie began to join in with their own ideas, Wally and Michael excused themselves and retreated almost unnoticed out of the room into the calm of the dining room, where dinner was just being prepared.

"You know, it's just as well," Pastor Wally conceded. "I tend to go on and on for much too long. We really covered all the important stuff, so let's call it a day and begin actual counseling tomorrow."

Michael smiled gratefully. So much material had been presented that his mind had turned to jelly hours ago.

Chapter Thirty-Seven

Rabbi David led the two witnesses, Carmelita, Vy and Aly into the center of the large basement shelter. Off to one side, a small group of people were praying intensely and loudly. In the front corner, a worship team was practicing. Several individuals here and there were reading or studying. Another group toward the back was having a meeting of some kind with a few of the participants arguing vociferously. In the back corner, a blonde woman was eyeing them suspiciously.

The rabbi took out a large whistle and blew it three times, producing a shrill, piercing sound that brought all activity to an immediate standstill. Rabbi David waved for everyone to gather round him in the center of the vast room.

"Come, come, I have very exciting news. I would like to introduce to you Pastor Gabriel Ramirez and Rabbi Abraham Cohen, God's two holy end-time witnesses!"

Gasps of wonder were the only sounds as reverential awe took everyone's breath away. Voices were stilled by the majesty of the moment. Rabbi David wisely allowed the holy hush to fulfill its purpose before continuing his introductions.

"Also with us is Pastor Gabriel's wife, Carmelita, who just miraculously escaped from the clutches of the anti-Christ thanks to the Lord God Almighty and his two soldiers, Vy and Aly. They were led here by an angel of the Lord, so we know that there is a reason, a purpose why they're here, even though neither they nor I understand what that might be."

Rabbi David allowed that to sink in for a few moments. "Therefore, I am asking each of you to come together as one and join in non-stop prayer right now until we discern the mind of God."

At first, no one moved or even seemed to comprehend what Rabbi David had requested. Then, in a sudden burst of activity, people scattered this way and that. It appeared to the five guests as though there was rhyme and reason within the apparent chaos, that this was a fire drill and everyone knew their roles.

Then order began to materialize as the worship team played soulful, spirit-filled music. Some people gathered together and formed a circle, holding hands, singing hymns and praying. Others paced about or knelt on their own, quietly or wailing in loud, pleading cries. No one, though, felt comfortable or confident enough to step forward to join the guests except one.

The strikingly beautiful blond woman looked familiar to Pastor Gabriel. Familiar, but different. Carmelita's eyes widened in recognition. "Blaine Whitney? What are you doing here?"

Blaine smiled repentantly, recognizing the accusing tone in Carmelita's questions. Before she could answer for herself, Rabbi David rushed to her side and put his arm around her. "Yes, Blaine Whitney, the Global Czar's spokesperson has come to the light of truth and accepted Jesus Christ as her Lord and Savior. Yet another wonderful miracle."

"Well, the Lord certainly does appear to be up to something," Abraham observed and held his hand out to Blaine. "Come, join us in prayer to see what it is the Lord has for each of us, or perhaps for all of us."

Blaine was both humbly grateful and greatly intimidated as she was pulled into the embrace of such august company. At first, she couldn't do anything more than listen to the powerful, beautiful prayers and absorb the incredible sense of holiness that enveloped her entire being.

Then her ear was attracted to the melodic, heavenly but unknown prayer language of Pastor Gabriel. Though she couldn't comprehend a single word, somehow she was drawn into the midst of it. The language itself began to fade into the background as a bright, vivid vision overwhelmed all her senses.

She saw herself standing before a large group of people, her back against a high stone wall. When she looked closer, she could see that many in the crowd were from the various media that she used to address for the Global Government. Most of these were jeering her with obnoxious words and tones. However, there were also curious people of all stripes mingled within the crowd, while armed soldiers watched over the proceedings in the distance.

She began to introduce two men standing on either side of her, both dressed in hairy tunics, but she stopped because she didn't know who they were or why they were there. Flooded with anxiety and a sense of failure, she saw the faces of Alexis, Radinsky and René glaring down at her from high above to her left. Then the Global Czar signaled to the troops who raised their rifles and grenade launchers in unison.

Blaine gasped aloud and her body jerked convulsively. Her eyes flew open in alarm as the vision faded away. When she refocused on the present, she saw the two witnesses staring at her with bemused smiles even as Rabbi David looked at her quizzically.

"Tell us what you saw, my dear," Abraham gently coaxed.

After she'd recounted her vision, Abraham and Gabriel exchanged knowing glances. "And so it begins," Abraham sighed.

Gabriel feigned a mock look of horror. "Oh no, you mean we really do have to dress in sackcloth and ashes?"

Abraham nodded gravely. "I'm afraid so. Your worst nightmare is coming to pass."

Blaine glanced anxiously back and forth between the two witnesses. "What begins? What nightmare?"

Gabriel laughed. "Sorry, it's an inside joke. But it appears that you're now on the inside, so I'll tell you what it all means. Abraham and I each saw this moment some time ago. We thought it was to come sooner, but we were unexpectedly shuttled off to Bali where the Lord did some amazing things which we'll tell you about later."

Abraham picked up the narrative. "We both saw ourselves dressed in those hairy outfits in your vision, like John the Baptist wore. Gabriel apparently has sensitive skin, so he was not looking forward to this day. We too saw ourselves standing below that wall, what is popularly known as the Wailing Wall, just below the Temple Mount and the Dome of the Rock."

"However," Gabriel interjected, "I knew I'd have to do it someday, so I've grown accustomed to the idea. We also saw in our visions that there was some unknown woman there. We were waiting for her to begin, but our visions stopped there. Now we know that you're that woman, so it's time to go forward and see what the Lord has in store for us."

"What about those soldiers?" Blaine asked worriedly.

Abraham chuckled. "We've had enough encounters with soldiers to know that we'll be protected and empowered somehow to overcome any situation."

Blaine pondered that for a few moments. "But what about me? What's my role? What am I supposed to say? Will I survive?"

Rabbi David cleared his throat. "I believe what I saw answers your questions. You, Blaine, once the spokesperson for the anti-Christ, will now become the spokesperson for the true Christ. I saw you going to many places to tell about your remarkable conversion and then to introduce the two witnesses. Apparently, you will be protected as well as the two witnesses."

Blaine was overwhelmed. Her roller coaster ride from worldly highs to spiritual depths back to glorified heights left her speechless. She staggered over to the nearest folding chair and sat down heavily. From the moment she'd told the Lord that she would wait upon Him to reveal her assignment, she'd expected something more mundane. After all, she was just a baby Christian. But this? She didn't deserve such a role given her past history.

As though reading her mind, but actually responding to a word of wisdom from the Holy Spirit, Rabbi David squatted down next to her and took her chin in his hand, forcing her to look deeply into his eyes.

"God didn't choose you for this job because you deserved it, but rather because nothing will reveal His power and His glory better than to show the world how He reached down and pulled a sinner out of the enemy's camp through His great love and mercy. People will listen to your story because they knew you when you were an atheist, then the devil's spokesperson, and now the Lord's handmaiden."

Rabbi David took her two hands in his. "Do not worry what you will do or say, because the Holy Spirit will lead and guide you in every way.[66] Put your faith and trust in Him, as well as in His two mighty witnesses."

Blaine's features dissolved from worry and unworthiness into tears of joy and amazement. She recalled several examples from her recent Bible studies of ordinary people being chosen to do miraculous things, not out of merit but rather out of willingness, obedience and availability.

She looked up at the glowing faces of the two witnesses. Her heart overflowed with gratitude and expectancy. What an honor to be included in their midst, let alone in their employ.

Chapter Thirty-Eight

Brother Charles waited expectantly as Brandon and Juanita settled into the spongy, uneven surface of the old, musty couch in his sparsely furnished office. He could sense something momentous was going to happen, but he squelched his eagerness because he saw the nervousness of the two emissaries.

Juanita finally finished smoothing out her dark pants suit even as Brandon adjusted his tie for the third time. They felt they ought to dress up a bit for this important occasion. One of the monks had made the long walk down to repair and retrieve their SUV, enabling them to change their clothes at last.

"So, have you heard from the Lord about our monastery's role during the Tribulation?" Brother Charles asked, unable to contain himself any longer.

Brandon and Juanita haltingly retold the vision and their interpretation. What had seemed so clear during the night, now felt more uncertain. For Brandon, he was not accustomed to such a spiritual role. Juanita, on the other hand, felt a sense of inadequacy in attempting to describe the intensity and power of Brandon's vision. They also were concerned that the Abbot would think them fools or opportunists to claim that the monk's mission was to support the hideaways and Counter-Insurgency campuses..

Brother Charles nodded a few times but otherwise kept his thoughts and reactions to himself until they eventually wound down. Then he bowed his head for a few moments as Brandon and Juanita nervously awaited his response.

"Thank You Father," Brother Charles finally intoned as he raised his head to the heavens and spread his arms in gratefulness. "You have indeed answered our prayers. That which You promised in our vision has been delivered through theirs, just as You said."

The Abbot then turned his moist eyes upon the two relieved and somewhat reluctant emissaries. "What a beautiful picture. A prayer engine! A power source for the remnant! God's earthly battery! Perfect!!"

Juanita and Brandon were too overwhelmed to speak as tears filled their own eyes. Confirmation was always gratifying, but in this case it was also uplifting. They all sensed the power of the Holy Spirit filling them and the office to overflowing.

After they'd all expressed their thanksgiving to the Lord, Brother Charles sat back and asked, "So, tell me about your plans so we can fire up our prayer engine."

The two emissaries went back and forth describing not only the mission they were on, but also the status and plans of all the hideaways, remote camps and the two CIA campuses.

"Of course, we've been out of touch for awhile because you have no cell-phone service out here," Brandon observed. "As soon as we re-establish contact, we'll have someone come out and hook up a satellite dish that will be able to receive transmissions from CIA-West. I don't know how they do it, but Francine set up a way for us to communicate through the global government's satellites without their knowing. It's worked so far."

"Great!" Brother Charles responded with much enthusiasm. He only now realized how bereft of purpose he and the rest of the brothers had felt over the past few months. Just to survive was not enough. They wanted to serve and now their opportunity was at hand.

"Tell me a little more about what you feel you're supposed to do in Las Vegas," the Abbot inquired. "Until we get the communications established this will be our major focus, in addition to covering all the locations with a blanket of prayer, of course."

Juanita's gaze drifted inward. *A blanket of prayer. The very same metaphor I've seen all this time, keeping our people hidden from view and covered with the favor of God.* She began to sob tears of gratitude.

Brandon put his arm around her and held her tight, and tried to answer Brother Charles' question since his wife was temporarily immersed in the Holy Spirit, a condition he knew would last at least a few minutes.

"My wife was impressed by the Lord to not only visit Las Vegas, but other cities as well, each representing a specific form of sinfulness that has brought our country down from its glorious Christian foundations to the very depths of perversion. Las Vegas, the self-proclaimed 'sin capital' of America, is to be the first stop. After that, we don't know if we're to resume visiting the hideaways or go on to the next city. I guess we'll only know that after finishing our business in Las Vegas."

"And what precisely is that business?" the Abbot prodded, needing to know the full extent of the mission to more specifically direct their prayers.

Brandon laughed nervously. "Well, I think Juanita has a better grasp of this than I do. She says it's like the Israelite priests carrying the Ark of the Covenant into the Jordan River.[67] They had faith that the Lord would move and dry up the river if they were obedient. Like them, we have only a glimpse of the specifics, but we have faith that we'll be told more when we step out into the center of Las Vegas."

Juanita stirred out of her spiritual immersion. She felt refreshed and alive, ready to move on into battle. She picked up where Brandon left off. "The only direction we have is that we are to pray both judgment and mercy onto Las Vegas. The two-edged sword of the Lord[68] is poised over that sinful city. When it crashes down, it will destroy the city but also save those who are open to receiving the truth, even at the very last moment. Exactly what we are to pray and when the sword comes down is unknown to us now, but will be revealed when we are in the midst of the enemy's camp."

Brother Charles nodded. "But isn't Las Vegas more of a symbol than the actual center of sinfulness?"

"Yes, you're right," Juanita agreed. "But in my dream-vision, I saw ripples of judgment flowing outward from Las Vegas across the entire country. What we do there will have an effect somehow on sinfulness throughout all of America."

"If so, then you will undoubtedly meet strong spiritual resistance," the Abbot observed with a hint of concern in his voice. "I can see now why you will need our support and covering."

The three sat in silence awhile pondering it all. Then Brother Charles asked, "Brandon, you indicated that other cities were on your list. I'd be curious to know what those might be as well. It's never too early to start praying about it. We might hear something useful before you go there."

"Yes, that would be wonderful, knowing that you and your monks are paving the path ahead of us," Brandon said, lighting up as the heavy burden he'd been feeling about it all began to lift off his shoulders. He nudged Juanita to answer the Abbot's question.

"Each of the cities we're being called upon to visit represents a particular aspect of the enemy's strongholds here on the earthly plane. Hollywood represents the media which cranks out all sorts of ungodly filth and lies that are used to further the devil's agenda. Dallas represents the energy center of the country with its oil wells, refineries and natural gas pipelines. I believe these are metaphors for the spiritual energy sources that empower the one-world government. If these are disrupted, both physically and spiritually, the control of the global government in our country will be significantly reduced."

"New Orleans is another sin center, but different than Las Vegas. It is the center of perversion, which became so great that the law of sowing and reaping brought Hurricane Katrina to destroy a great deal of it. However, instead of heeding the warning, they have been rebuilding it all over again. The next time, there won't be anything or anyone left to rebuild it," Juanita noted ominously, sending chills up all their spines. These were indeed perilous times.

"Washington, D.C., of course, represents the government itself, which has become so corrupt that it is totally devoid of any redeeming qualities," Juanita continued. "Judgment will fall heavily, but the Lord wishes to save as many who will respond to His offer of mercy and salvation as possible. New York City is the financial engine of the United States, and is rife with greed. The Lord wants to turn off the money spigots to dry up the enemy's supply lines, which I saw as veins of blood spreading outward across the entire country. Finally, in Chicago, the so-called 'Windy City,' God wants the Holy Spirit's breath of judgment and salvation to sweep through the city and out across the entire country. That's all I know for now."

Juanita had chosen to leave out descriptions of the catastrophic disasters that would soon fall upon these areas that she'd seen in her dream-vision. She wasn't sure if they were metaphors or true representations of what was going to happen.

"I thought Hollywood was destroyed by the tidal wave?" Brother Charles noted. "Why would the Lord have you go there now?"

Brandon chuckled. "Oh, you've been out of touch here. That was one of the first places the global government rebuilt afterwards. After all, they need to keep their propaganda machine running. Shows what the enemy's priorities are. Lies before truth, sinfulness over righteousness."

"How soon do you think all of this will occur?" Brother Charles asked.

Juanita shook her head. "I don't really have any idea. I only know we're to go to Las Vegas now. What the future holds, well, we'll just have to rely on the Lord to lead and guide us."

The Abbot nodded solemnly. "I suspect that all of this will loosen the devil's hold on people's minds, freeing them to hear and respond to the Holy Spirit's call to salvation and service. Before you leave, and before I bring all of this to the monks, let's pray and be joined together in the Spirit. Perhaps we won't even need that satellite dish."

Chapter Thirty-Nine

After Pope Radinsky left with a few parting shots at his increasingly independent chief-of-staff, Mustafa finally exhaled the pent-up anger that was growing harder and harder to suppress. His body shook with rage for a few moments before he was able to gather himself and go check on the Mahdi.

"Did all go well, Isa?" the Mahdi inquired as Mustafa bowed before him.

"Yes, your Lordship. Pope Radinsky now feels that he knows all our secrets," Mustafa answered with great deference.

"And I assume he did not take that well?"

"No, just as we expected. But it is becoming more and more difficult to submit to his preening arrogance." Mustafa once again shook with rage.

Muhammad bin Abudullah, the Mahdi, the 'guided one,' reached out and placed his hand on Mustafa's shoulder. "It won't be long now, Isa al-Maseeh. Soon you will be able to be who you really are, who destiny has called you to be. But for now, you are in the perfect position to keep an eye on the infidel imposters."

Mustafa bowed his head once more and backed out the door. "As Allah wills."

Before checking in on the Dajjal, a much more difficult and odious task, Mustafa returned to his small corner office in the underground complex near the revered Ka'ba in Mecca, the holiest site in all of Islam. The Ka'ba is a small building within the courtyard of the al-Haram mosque, and is the *qibia*, the point all Muslims face when they pray from anywhere in the world. It is also the focal point around which they circumambulate on their *hajj* pilgrimage.

The Ka'ba is the location where the Mahdi is first prophesied to appear. Soon he would. But there were several other signs that needed to occur first. It was really a menu of signs that different sects and various Imams disputed. However, the most prominent and accepted sign was a solar and lunar eclipse within the same month of Ramadan, the ninth month of the Islamic calendar. According to Islamic scientists, this would occur next month.

In the meantime, there was a lot more preparation required to provide enough signs that there would be little dispute that the Mahdi, the Twelfth Imam, the Redeemer of Islam, had indeed returned. Mustafa was torn between belief and the necessity to create the signs himself.

When he'd first heard of the blue-eyed, platinum-haired infant whose mother had been stoned to death for presumed infidelity, he'd been first curious and then emboldened. Raised among prominent Iranian Shiites who did not believe in the Mahdi, Mustafa had felt for some time that the Muslim world needed its Redeemer, fake or real, to unite the sects and Muslim nations. When he saw the unusual child, it was as if Allah himself had sparked the revelation for Mustafa to raise the child to be the Mahdi. The infant's father was glad to get rid of the embarrassingly strange-looking child.

Mustafa hired a nursing mother to care for the baby and provided her family with enough money to keep them quiet. Meanwhile, way back then, he had been torn between joining a local terrorist group or a delegation to the United Nations, which was available to him as a result of his father's lofty standing in the Iranian government.

With the plan to raise the Mahdi up himself, he felt the U.N. was the better venue to reach across the Islamic world that now literally circled the globe. Eventually that led to Brussels and to the European Union and Alexis D'Antoni who encouraged him to become part of his Luciferian cabal. Advancing rapidly up the ranks of the Illuminati, his spirit guide further encouraged Mustafa to become a priest and conduct black mass for new initiates.

Eventually, his spiritual passion, intelligence and good looks led to partnering with Cardinal Radinsky as both priestly assistant and lover. He assisted Radinsky in poisoning the Pope and then helped orchestrate Radinsky's succession to the Papacy. But it wasn't until afterward that Mustafa told him about the Mahdi.

After Alexis and Radinsky conferred with Lucifer, they realized that this was Satan's plan all along to gain ultimate control over the Muslims, who otherwise would be a major obstacle to world peace. However, unbeknownst to them, Mustafa had become a believer. When the child he'd named Muhammad bin Abdullah, in accordance with Islamic prophecy, became five years old, a most unexpected development occurred. The child pronounced himself the real Mahdi, accompanied by numerous small, but nonetheless impressive miracles.

The boy seemed able to exert control over the local wind and rain, turning the bleak desert where he was hidden into a virtual oasis. Mustafa's extensive studies of Mahdi literature showed him that this too was prophesied. "Believe in me," the five year old child said in his haunting, almost hypnotic way. "It was not you who discovered me, but rather Allah who led you to me."

Now Mustafa remained stuck between the proverbial rock and hard place. He truly believed the young man was indeed the Mahdi, but would the additional signs need to be manufactured or would they really occur as written in the hadiths? The Mahdi seemed unperturbed by it all, devoting himself to prayer, study and meditation, leaving Mustafa to ascertain Allah's will.

He sighed yet again, shrugged his shoulders and went off to see the Dajjal who required a lot more attention. He too had come to Mustafa's attention in a most peculiar way. Mustafa had been on a diplomatic mission for the U.N. to Syria. After evening prayers, he had been strolling through the streets of Damascus when he encountered a group of boys stoning a large man down a side alleyway.

After chasing the ragamuffin gang away, he found that the big man was in fact a huge boy. He was heavily cut and bruised, with his right eye smashed in with the letters kfr branded on his forehead. Mustafa brought him to a hospital where they patched him up, but were unable to save the eye. The boy, Sayed Hashemi, begged Mustafa not to send him back to the orphanage where the administrator had purposely revealed to the other children that the troublesome boy was, in fact, the bastard child of a sinful Muslim woman and a Jewish father.

Sayed didn't know if it was true or not, but he felt his life was in danger if he were to return to the orphanage. Aware of the Islamic prophecies concerning the Dajjal, Mustafa knew that the Dajjal was supposed to appear in or near Damascus, be one-eyed and have the word *kafir,* or infidel, on his forehead. Sans the vowels, he wondered whether Allah had now led him to the Dajjal.

Since he already had the Mahdi hidden away, he arranged for Sayed to join him deep in the Iranian desert.

Troublesome, though, was just what Sayed was. Manic, hyperactive, schizophrenic and more, requiring Mustafa to ultimately imprison him at a sequestered site. It had taken several years of high-tech brainwashing for Sayed to accept that he was the Dajjal, the Great Deceiver, the false messiah to the Jews. Once he did, he became impatient to fulfill his role and chafed under continued bondage.

Only recently had he moved the Mahdi and Dajjal to Mecca in preparation for their upcoming debut during Ramadan. Now Mustafa was consumed with raising up the Sufyani and Yamani. The Sufyani is a supposed tyrant who will spread corruption and mischief on the earth before the Mahdi returns. He is also a reputed descendant of Abu Sufyan, a staunch opponent of the prophet Muhammad before accepting Islam later in life.

The Sufyani is prophesied to emerge from the depths of Damascus along with the equally reprehensible Yamani from Yemen. Two promising candidates awaited him later that evening. Was Allah doing all the raising up and Mustafa simply being led down the prophetic path? So it was beginning to seem. Perhaps he really was Isa al-Maseeh after all.

Chapter Forty

It took a few days for the two witnesses to acquire their sackcloth and ashes as well as other supplies for their public debut in Jerusalem. Shopping was difficult when you were the world's most wanted fugitives. Fortunately, Rabbi David's organization was able to procure all that they needed.

In the interim, they worked with Blaine to plan what they felt sure was just the first of many appearances together. At first, Blaine was too overwhelmed and humble to fully grab hold of the role Abraham and Gabriel wanted her to play.

Abraham became a little exasperated with her. "Goodness gracious, child, if you had the chutzpah to stand before the world as the devil's spokesperson, surely you can do the same for the Lord God Almighty!"

Blaine was crestfallen and confused. How could she explain how she felt? How could someone never at a loss for words or audacity come to this?

Gabriel chuckled. "Abraham, do you not remember how we felt when we were appointed by the Lord as His two end-time witnesses? At first we refused to believe it. Then we were so humbled by the awesome responsibility that we ran and hid. We were terrified, not by the enemy, but by the fear of not being able to live up to God's expectations."

"Yes, that's it, exactly," Blaine exclaimed in relief. "I want so much to please my Savior that I feel incapacitated by fear of failure."

Abraham nodded and smiled contritely. "Yes, yes, I remember. It all seems so long ago. Now we feel that we can go anywhere and do anything without worrying about the consequences."

Gabriel leaned forward and took Blaine's hand. "The Lord doesn't choose us because we're worthy, but rather because we're willing and obedient. He takes care of the rest."

Abraham took her other hand. "And He uses the foolish things and people of the world to confound the wise.[69] He chooses fishermen and tax collectors as His disciples, not the leaders and shakers. He will even give us the words to say if we simply show up."

Blaine laughed and shook her head. "This is so hard to get used to. It's so different."

"God's Kingdom is upside down and inside out," Gabriel said quite seriously. "Worldly values and ways are generally the opposite of God's ways. Since the devil is the god of this age,[70] that's to be expected. God's Kingdom is within us,[71] so we need to think and act from the inside out. We are spirit, soul and body, not body, soul and spirit. Instead of gratifying the flesh, protecting the ego or seeking materialistic goals, we need to make our mind, emotions and will conform to the things of the spirit, the ways of God."[72]

Blaine squeezed Gabriel's and Abraham's hands. "Thank you. That was just what I needed to hear. I'm ready because the Lord is ready, so let's go do it."

The next morning, Blaine emailed a press release to all the major news media outlets inviting them to come and meet God's two end-time witnesses who had an important announcement to deliver tomorrow morning at 9 a.m. at the Wailing Wall. With a stroke of boldness, she even copied all the Global Governance Committee.

No longer afraid, she felt imbued with God's Spirit and favor. She was so excited she barely slept that night, spending the time communing with her Lord and Savior her newest, yet closest and dearest friend.[73] She awoke abruptly early that morning out of a dream in which a giant Jesus towered over all of Jerusalem.

Her eyes had a hard time adjusting to the glare of the early morning sun. The sun? Blaine bolted upright in her cot. The large subterranean basement had no windows! Where was the light coming from?

She could barely keep her eyes open, the light was so intense. It seemed to be coming from Abraham and Gabriel. She leaned forward toward the comatose witnesses and squinted carefully. Sure enough, their bodies were glowing with brilliant light. She smiled and lay back. Peaceful sleep descended upon her like a gift from heaven.

****

Alexis was beside himself. Literally. He had become so apoplectic after reading Blaine's press release, that he'd collapsed in a heap. Briefly he found himself floating up above his own body. Had he died? Was this when he'd come back to life as foretold in the Bible?

"Not now, you idiot," he heard Lucifer scream within his mind. Immediately he rejoined his body and felt his heart pounding erratically.

"Come back to us," he heard René's voice call down sarcastically. "It's not your time yet, dingbat."

Alexis felt like strangling her, but she was right. Why was he allowing Blaine and those irksome witnesses to bother him so much? Lucifer had things under control. Why should he worry?

The Global Czar sat up and stared into René's scowling face. Then he started to laugh uncontrollably, unable to stop. René resisted as long as she could, but then crumpled to the floor in hysterics.

When the merriment finally subsided, they arose, dusted themselves off, and attempted to regain a more serious perspective about the press release.

René took a long slow breath, exhaled slowly and stared out the window overlooking the Dome of the Rock and the third Jewish Temple from the Global Czar's office high above the Global Palace.

"Prophetically, there's no way we can touch the two witnesses, but it would seem that Blaine and their audience would be fair game," she finally observed.

Alexis' eyes lit up with anticipation. "Yes, we can prevent any outflow of information through the media by destroying them all and blaming it on the two fugitives."

Chapter Forty-One

The festivities at CIA-West were ramping up rapidly. Nearly everyone was swept up into the upcoming double wedding of Jesse and Fran along with Jerome and Sue. Alan Morrison was pleased to see euphoria replace the prior prevailing sense of doom and gloom.

In return, the inhabitants of the underground Counter Insurgency Agency were delightfully surprised to see the formerly aloof and reclusive Morrison join in the planning of the major event. He seemed a totally different person, as did Michael and Bonnie Braintree. Everyone took this as a sign that the heavens approved what they were doing, not just with the wedding, but their overall end-time mission.

Everyone, however, except Fred, Fran's assistant who had felt humiliated at Morrison's treatment of him during the crisis when it appeared that their location had been discovered by the government. As a Christian in name only, he had joined Fran's computer team solely for technical reasons, not because he believed in their mission. He was no lover of a government that had taken away his individual freedoms and he enjoyed the challenge of infiltrating and undermining their electronic networks. However, the zealous radicalism was not his cup of tea.

At first, when he'd complained about Morrison's supercilious attitude he'd gotten agreement and confirmation from Fran and others on the team. But now, he detested watching everyone fawn over Morrison as though he was a brand new person. Everyone knows a leopard can't change his spots, so Morrison must be up to something. Fred sensed it was time to move on and maybe extract a little retribution along the way.

When Fran left to get fitted for her wedding gown that several of the women were sewing from scratch, she left Fred in charge. With nothing of consequence occurring out in cyberspace, Fred dismissed the other two restive technicians who seemed more interested in the upcoming festivities than their job responsibilities.

Fred waited a few minutes and then opened the folder of purloined contact information for various government officials and technical leaders. He scanned the list of names, not sure who would be the best one with whom to trade information for asylum and immunity. His eyes lit up when he saw the name of Sir William Tyron, the man who'd led the previous cyber attack against CIA-West and who was responsible for wiping out the surrogate group of Jehovah's Witnesses who'd paid the price for Fran's deception.

Now Fred's blood was really boiling. Innocent people had died because of their subterfuge. What kind of Christian behavior is that? And now Jesse was rebuilding their militia to wreak who knows what kind of mayhem. Yes, the time was ripe to expose this bunch for the hypocritical, self-righteous maniacs they really were.

Fred dashed off a quick email to Sir William outlining what he wanted, but sent it through the algorithm that bounced it around the globe to disguise the originating IP address. Afterward he got the shakes. What had he done? He prayed that he hadn't opened up the door to hell.

****

Back in Washington, D.C., Microsoft Outlook dutifully ding-donged the arrival of an email for Sir William, who of course had his lackeys screen all incoming communication beforehand and weed out the unnecessary and uninteresting. When his office door burst open unexpectedly, Sir William's corpulent body jerked upward and almost destroyed the overburdened desk chair on the way back down.

"God dammit, man, knock before entering, remember?" Sir William scolded as he rearranged himself, silently praying that the reinforced chair wouldn't give way like the previous one had. At least that had occurred in private.

The young man froze in the open doorway, awaiting yet another tirade. Sir William, unable to remember the intruder's name and nervous about the status of the chair, simply waved him over.

Greatly relieved, cheeks aglow with embarrassment, the young man rushed over. "Sorry 'bout that, but this email is from some guy with those underground Christian zealots out west."

Sir William's eyebrows and ears shot upward. He reached out and snatched the paper away from the startled messenger. Quickly digesting it, Sir William sat back pensively. Was it real or a trick? His demonic instincts were buzzing dramatically.

"Traceable?"

"No sir, we tried, but came up empty."

"Okay, then, send a reply back saying that I'm willing to meet with him. Ask him to propose a time and location, then we'll see if that makes any sense," Sir William said.

"Yes sir, right away, sir," the young man said as he backed toward the open door. "I'll be sure to knock next time," he said as he disappeared from view.

Chapter Forty-Two

Brandon and Juanita had been lulled into a bored stupor as mile after mile of barren desert floated past the windows of their SUV. Highway 93 out of Kingman, Arizona was apparently the only highway leading from I-40 to Las Vegas. Just as she was about to drift off to sleep, Juanita's eyes caught a dramatic change in scenery. Brown mounds rose up all around them, spreading out in all directions. It looked as if some giant ants had built large nests.

While still quite barren, the other-worldly landscape was riveting to the tree-starved easterners. As they began the descent toward Hoover Dam, Juanita wanted to stop and see the Depression-era wonder, but Brandon was intent on getting to their destination. Fortunately, the recently-constructed highway overpass afforded an eagle's eye view from high above. Quite spectacular. Juanita was appeased.

The rest of the trip toward Las Vegas was uneventful until they were driving into Henderson and the skyline of Sin City came into view.

"Get off here," Juanita suddenly demanded.

"Huh?"

"This exit, take it now, we're in danger," Juanita exhorted him urgently.

A quick glance into the rearview mirror, and then Brandon swung the SUV across two lanes of traffic and shot onto the exit ramp. He'd learned the hard way to heed his spiritually-attuned wife when she had those sudden inspirations. Still, it galled him to be put on the spot like that when he was driving.

He slowed and merged onto a five lane street running past one shopping center after another. "So, what was that all about? I thought we were fully covered in prayer, what with the Jesuits and the hideaway intercessors."

Juanita hesitated. It wasn't always easy to convert her spiritual senses into words. "I'm not sure. Something about it not being the right time yet. I think hearing that warning was a direct result of the Jesuits' prayers."

"Well, it *is* late in the day," Brandon observed drily, still a bit miffed. "It's probably for the best that we find somewhere to hole up overnight and get an early start tomorrow." He just wanted to get the job done and then beat it out of town.

Juanita didn't answer. Instead, she drifted off into that place somewhere between earth and heaven, where her mind became a blank slate for the Holy Spirit to write upon. Brandon knew that look and realized further conversation would get him nowhere.

He came to a major intersection with North Boulder Highway and turned left to keep going in the general direction of Las Vegas while Juanita sorted out the spiritual stuff. Soon he was passing several small casinos and lots of billboards touting the major gambling centers in Las Vegas itself.

As he pondered why anyone would want to sit and feed their hard-earned money into a slot machine, a large tall sign for Sienna Suites caught his eye. He turned in and parked in front of the office. Juanita was still staring off into space and mumbling to herself, so Brandon got out of the vehicle and went inside to see what was what. He sensed that this was where they were supposed to be. That made him feel better.

He was surprised how cheap a suite with a kitchen was, but was told that food and lodging were artificially low in the area to attract the gamblers. He winced yet again as the scanning wand was passed over his wrist, silently praying that Fran's workaround was still viable.

With a sigh of relief, he took the two key cards, drove around the back past several two-story buildings to their unit in the rear. Apparently a lot of people lived here full-time. He saw lots of families with little children and even smaller dogs walking about in the mild winter weather.

He parked and started to unload their suitcases when Juanita piped up: "Have they got Wi-Fi here? If so, bring in the laptop. I've got to do some research."

She carried in their suitcases while Brandon rummaged through the piles of stuff in the rear of the SUV. It was hard being on the road for so long. He finally grabbed the laptop and went inside. He hooked it up quickly while Juanita got their stuff organized. She even put on a pot of coffee in the well-equipped kitchen. But they had no food, so Brandon headed back out while Juanita began exploring the Internet with their fake ID. Praise God for Francine.

When Brandon got back with a pizza, sodas and a bag of groceries, Juanita sat back and smiled at him. "Now I know why we had to stop before going into Las Vegas. We would have gone in blind and that would have been a disaster. I thought we'd just roll in and get to work with the Holy Spirit guiding us every step of the way, showing us where to go and telling us what to pray. Instead, I have to do some research first."

Brandon served her a couple of slices of pizza and a cola. "Isn't that something like spiritual mapping?"

Juanita laughed. "I didn't know you were aware of that concept. I've never had to do it before and thought it wasn't necessary if you were fully plugged into the Holy Spirit. But I guess I've learned a lesson. We almost blew it. The Lord showed me that we have to know the spiritual roots of the city so that we can close the doors that allowed the devil and his demons to establish such a strong presence here. Simply driving off the surface level demons would only have a temporary effect."

"That sounds logical," Brandon replied, his brow wrinkled in thought. "But you said it would also be dangerous?"

"Oh yes," Juanita quickly replied. "Because the Lord also showed me that if we came directly against the satanic strongholds instead of the roots, we would have experienced extreme backlash."

"Backlash? How so?"

Juanita hesitated, but then decided to tell Brandon everything. "Most likely killed in an accident. The devil is very good at using demonically controlled people to unconsciously do his bidding. In our case, I saw a sixteen-wheeler whose driver was temporarily blinded and failed to see a red light. He ran right into and over our SUV, killing us instantly."

Brandon plunked down on the couch, speechless. His wide eyes refocused on his precious wife, feeling somewhat guilty about his unspoken annoyance over her sudden warning on the highway. "Well, then, by all means do your research and take as much time as you need."

Juanita smiled to herself as Brandon exhaled in relief over what might have been.

Chapter Forty-Three

Mustafa returned to his Mecca hideout stunned. The Sufyani and Yamani he'd met with were clearly those prophesied in the hadiths, the sacred writings of what Muhammad said and did. So all the pieces were literally falling into place without Mustafa's having to do a thing. Belief was growing by leaps and bounds. Relief as well, since it was now obvious that he wouldn't have to force prophetic alignment of his own accord.

He reported back to Mahdi Muhammad bin Abudullah who simply smiled tolerantly. "Just as I was shown when I was but five years old. But you had to come to belief on your own, and I surmise that you have just now attained that exalted place of complete confidence in Allah."

"Yes, your majesty, I have indeed," replied Mustafa with a deferential bow.

"So then, instead of staying here trying to contrive the major and minor signs yourself, I suggest you return to the Vatican where unbelief needs to be addressed," the Mahdi said as he put his arm around Mustafa's shoulders.

"You want me to convert Pope Radinsky and others?" Mustafa said, his face wrinkled in confusion.

"No, my son, not convert but subvert. The seeds of revolution and conquest need to be sown now so that they will blossom at the appropriate time."

Mustafa looked even more confused. "What seeds?"

"Allah will guide you," said the Guided One. "Go now and leave the signs in my hands."

Mustafa bowed and backed out of the door, his mind churning in consternation. The Mahdi seemed to have more faith in him than he did himself. Belief might be growing, but he was quite unsettled about what he should do when he got back to the Vatican.

Pope Radinsky solved the problem for him. "So you've returned at last," the Pope said as he imperiously waved Mustafa into the inner sanctum.

"I think you're becoming too enamored of your creations," Radinsky observed, his beady eyes burrowing holes into Mustafa's psyche. "The Muslim card must be played, but our goal is to create confusion and a failed uprising, not to overly worry about fulfilling false prophecies."

Mustafa was incensed. Even as he sensed his blood boiling to the surface, he felt Allah's hand upon him bringing serenity and wisdom. "Yes, Your Eminence, you are right. It is difficult for me when I am back under the black cloud of Islam. It is as though the roots re-grow when I'm there."

Radinsky nodded sagely. "Yes, that's just what I thought. I'm glad you see it for yourself. You'll have to be more careful. Perhaps it's best for you to remain here. I can look after your creations from this point forward. You've done such a good job with them that you can take your hands off the controls now. Instead, you should focus on creating the other signs. So tell me, how are you progressing in manufacturing them?"

Mustafa was astounded. Allah had confirmed the Mahdi's directions, apparently even in control now of the Pope himself. Greatly emboldened, Mustafa answered, "I have enlisted two men who will fulfill the role of the Sufyani and Yamani, although they are not aware of the prophecies. They are mean, hardened criminals who will stir up intense disputes between the various sects. I have provided the Sufyani with the financial wherewithal to spread increasing violence between Sunnis and Shiites, not only through suicide bombers but with weapons of mass destruction."

"Good, good," the Pope nodded, "the greater the mayhem the better. But what about other sects?"

"Well, the Sufi's aren't really a sect, but more of a mystical way of approaching the Islamic faith, somewhat like the Jewish Kabbalists," Mustafa replied. "They seek divine knowledge through personal interaction with Allah. Most Muslims revere Allah but do not believe that he is approachable. The Yamani, who is himself more spiritually focused, is preparing some experiences for the Sufi's that will stir them up into extreme jihad against the Jews."

Mustafa was amazed at the newfound confidence he had that these things would now come to pass without any further guidance from him. The prophecies were real and Allah was in control.

"What about that other sect, the Ahamadi's, or something like that?" Rakinsky prompted, seeing that Mustafa seemed to have drifted off into a mystical state himself. His concern ratcheted up again.

"Oh, you mean the Ahmadiyya," Mustafa hastily replied. "Because they believe that Mirza Ghulam Ahmad was the messiah, they will be greatly stirred up when the real Mahdi is revealed."

"The real Mahdi?" Radinsky said, his voice rising in reprimand.

Mustafa realized he'd have to be more careful. "What they will *think* is the real Mahdi," he corrected himself and then plunged ahead. "Since they are already denounced by orthodox Islamists as heretics, the Yamani will foment further strife by encouraging Islamic fundamentalists to slay many of the Ahmadiyya' around the world for blasphemy."

"What else?" Radinsky asked, somewhat mollified.

"The Sufyani will ensure a major battle in Mina, another preceding sign. And I have already planted a mountain of gold on the banks of the Euphrates that will soon be 'discovered.' It is in a location between Sunni and Shia towns which will start yet more internecine strife that only the *fake* Mahdi will be able to resolve."

"I'm concerned about the star with the luminous tail that is supposed to rise from the East before the Mahdi emerges," Radinsky further probed. "How do you intend to pull that off?"

Mustafa couldn't help smiling, sensing that his careful plans were no longer necessary. Allah really would take care of it with a real star or meteor. So now he'd need to lie, but that was no problem. The Qur'an allowed, even encouraged, deceit when dealing with infidels. Fortunately Radinsky took Mustafa's attitude as a sign of his acquiescence rather than his rising confidence in Allah.

"I have arranged with a fringe Islamic group in Kazakhstan to acquire and fire a specially constructed missile I've obtained from a former Soviet arms dealer," Mustafa truthfully reported. "It will sizzle brightly across the skies of Iran, Iraq and Jerusalem before turning south and passing over Medina and Mecca in Saudi Arabia and then crashing into the Red Sea." The lie was that he wouldn't need to see this plan through.

Radinsky grinned. He loved subterfuge, pulling the wool over the eyes of the very sheep that had been shorn. Little did he realize that in this case he was the blind lamb. "Excellent, excellent. It would appear that we are ready for the next phase. Good job!"

Normally such praise would have ignited passionate allegiance in Mustafa. Now, he was filled with hatred for the man who had given him false spiritual direction for so long. *Allahu Akbar!*

Chapter Forty-Four

Blaine awoke refreshed and raring to go. Abraham and Gabriel exchanged a knowing smile. They retreated to the bathroom and donned their sackcloth and pasted damp ashes on each other's forehead. When they emerged, the awaiting crowd in the basement applauded their approval and encouragement.

Their transformation was remarkable. Despite the ungainly costume, there was a certain glow that gave the distinct impression that the two had stepped out of time, out of the pages of the Bible.

"All you need are locusts and honey!" Rabbi David exclaimed, referring to John the Baptist's wilderness attire and diet.[74]

Gabriel hadn't shaved in a couple of weeks and his dark beard over light brown skin gave him a distinctly Old Testament look. Coupled with Abraham's whitish-gray beard, the two now appeared much more like Elijah and Moses come back to earth.

Indeed, they knew it was the Elijah spirit that had anointed and empowered them for their role as the two end-time witnesses. Just as Scripture foretold, Elijah had now returned in spirit before Christ's second coming just as he had done in John the Baptist before Jesus was born. [75]

However, both witnesses felt somewhat self-conscious and not a little foolish. Without a word they headed out of the basement followed by all fifty or so inhabitants. No one had said anything about their accompanying the witnesses, given the need to keep their resistance movement and location a secret. However, all seemed to be moved by the Holy Spirit to step out boldly to proclaim their faith. To be martyred this day would be an honor.

The procession attracted a great deal of attention as it wound through the narrow streets toward the western Wailing Wall. At 8:30 a.m., the area was already alive with activity. By the time they had traversed the short distance, hundreds of people followed in their wake.

Several Jews were already praying at the wall and backed away in alarm, not knowing what to make of it all. Most of the media had already assembled and were scrambling to record this unexpected initial procession. Several reporters began talking into their microphones and a general hubbub arose in anticipation. A few recognized Blaine and shouted both words of acknowledgement as well as pejoratives.

When armed Global storm troopers appeared shortly afterward, a hush descended over the crowded plaza. The minutes clicked off slowly, the only sound coming from the late-arriving media frantically setting up their equipment. When nine a.m. chimed in the distance, Blaine stepped forward confidently to stand at the portable podium they had carried with them.

Prior worries over not having a microphone or a prepared script were replaced by a certainty that her voice would be supernaturally amplified just as she imagined happened when Jesus spoke to large crowds. She was further heartened by how close the scene before her was to the vision she'd had just a few days ago. She glanced up to her left and sure enough, there was the Global Czar and René staring down from the Temple Mount.

"Ladies and gentlemen of the media, bystanders, soldiers, René and Czar D'Antoni, I welcome you on behalf of Jesus Christ, Lord of Lords and King of Kings," Blaine began boldly, pleased to hear her voice echoing off the walls of the buildings in the distance.

A few jeering voices briefly interrupted before Blaine continued. "You are here on an historic day, one that will be debated in homes across the entire globe for some time."

As she spoke, Blaine was simultaneously analyzing the mystery of how the Holy Spirit was speaking through her. It was not as she had imagined. Far from being taken over, she was speaking from a sense of knowing, choosing her own words to describe what she felt deep within, all of her own volition. She was even free to not speak or say something different, all up to her own volition.

However, to deny the power, enlightenment and yes, even love that she felt would have been inconceivable, so she continued forcefully. "Today, the two whom you have labeled the "world's greatest fugitives" stand before you here in Jerusalem, the capital of God's Kingdom on earth. Nearby is the restored third Jewish temple, rebuilt without room for the outer courts, just as Scripture foretold."[76]

Griping and mumbling arose from some of the crowd, disliking the overly religious tone, an affront to universal tolerance. "These two men have been chosen by the One True God to be his primary two witnesses on earth during these last days."

Boos and hisses. "Yes, I too was skeptical at first. An atheist to the core, I wholeheartedly supported the goals of the New World Order and the Global Governance Committee, as you all well know. However, God orchestrated a series of events that led me to Jesus and His mercy, grace, forgiveness and salvation. I have tasted His goodness, experienced His love and seen His power. It is real. It is true. Jesus is the only way."

A great disturbance swelled in volume, yet somehow Blaine's every word was clearly heard. She felt no fear as she saw the animosity and even the soldiers' weapons aimed at her. "Although the Global Government has conspired to keep the truth about the events in Bali from you, I can report factually that great revival fires were started there by these two witnesses that all the military might in the world has been unable to extinguish."

A wave of shock rippled across the constantly growing crowd, silencing them as they contemplated the implications. Glancing fearfully at the soldiers surrounding them, they became aware of the thumping of helicopters in the distance, headed their way. Was there going to be a confrontation? While many wished to see Blaine and the two witnesses destroyed, they were thrown off by the report about Bali.

"Now these two witnesses are here before you, openly, unafraid," Blaine continued with increasing passion. "They seek only to speak to you, a freedom that has been lost because of men like Alexis D'Antoni, the 'beast' prophesied in both the Old and New Testaments, along with the false prophet, and counterfeit Pope, Vladimir Radinsky."[77]

The crowd nervously looked up to where the Global Czar stared down hatefully at his former spokesperson who continued on unconcerned. "God's witnesses do not wish to cause anyone any harm, only to enlighten you to the real truth, not the phony substitutes you are being fed. They wish to alert you to the imminent danger in the days ahead. We will all wind up soon in the Valley of Decision[78] with our eternal lives at stake. Heaven and hell literally stand before us. The Lord God Almighty does not wish to see anyone perish but wants everyone to receive His free gift of redemption."[79]

That was the last straw for Alexis who raised his right arm, fist clenched, as the signal for the storm troopers to move in to disperse the crowd. The strategy was to provoke a response within the crowd that would justify the use of force. In truth, Alexis didn't care whether it was supporters or detractors of the two witnesses who initiated resistance, only that someone did. To that end, he had his own plants in the crowd to act up should no one else do so.

As the troopers moved forward, Abraham called out, "We seek only peace. It is the Global Government that seeks conflict. Do not resist."

The cameras were rolling as the troopers moved into the crowd and began herding them out of the plaza with their shields. Two of the dupes on opposite sides of the crowd began hurling bottles and rocks at the troopers. "Down with Global Government, up with

Jesus," they began a chant that other stooges in the crowd took up immediately.

Soon there was mayhem as the troopers began using stun guns on the crowd which panicked and stampeded. Alexis and René grinned in satisfaction. But then Gabriel raised his arm and waved it at the troopers, whose stun guns immediately imploded, sending the current directly into the soldiers who fell to the ground writhing and screaming.

Abraham's voice then boomed supernaturally above the hubbub: "Oh Jerusalem, Jerusalem, you have turned your heart from God and seek only to destroy His prophets.[80] The time for mercy and grace is over for you, for from this day forward you shall see no rain, and your rivers, creeks and lakes shall turn to blood."[81]

With that, Blaine folded up the portable podium, glanced up triumphantly at the seething Global Czar, and followed the two witnesses out of the plaza followed by Rabbi David's congregation. Alexis waved for the helicopters to move in but suddenly the witnesses and their procession disappeared entirely from view. Vanished into thin air, all recorded on video for the world to see.

Alexis couldn't allow that to happen, so he ordered the helicopters to release their missiles into the remaining crowd, and watched as they and the downed troopers disappeared within a cloud of destruction. He then alerted Christine to contact all media outlets and forbid the use of any footage that had already been forwarded from the plaza.

Chapter Forty-Five

Fred's nerves were quivering as he contemplated an excuse to leave the underground shelter at CIA-West. It wasn't all that unusual for someone to have a family matter to attend to, or the need to purchase new clothing or other supplies not provided by the central stock room. The substance of the excuse wasn't the problem, it was being able to say it believably. He was afraid his frazzled nerves would be his undoing.

Fortunately, the shelter was in a heightened state of agitation over the footage Fran had been able to surreptitiously download off the Internet before the video had been completely eradicated. While it was inspiring to see the awesome display of God's power working through the two witnesses, it nonetheless reminded them what a target they all were for the Global army.

Fred told Fran how disturbing it all was and how he felt he ought to stock up on a few personal items before the global clamps tightened and made such forays into the world too dangerous. She gave him the keys to one of the vans and even asked him to pick up a few things for the stock room. As he drove off the ranch toward the meeting with Sir William in a Denver hotel, he was struck by the thought that he probably wouldn't be returning. Although he had intellectually recognized that outcome, it didn't touch his soul until the comforting vistas of the ranch faded away in the rear view mirror. He wondered if he was making a major mistake.

Furtively parking away from the hotel, Fred pulled on his cap and turned up the collar of his winter coat against the frosty air, but more so to disguise himself. He walked quickly with his head down, although there wasn't really anyone out there who would recognize him. Continuing through the hotel lobby and up the elevators, his heart was pounding so hard he thought he might faint. When he got his first look at Sir William he almost did.

"Please be seated, Fred," Sir William smiled from a severely sunken couch. "Can my man James get you a drink or snack?"

Fred shook his head no, too frightened to even speak. He sat in the straight back chair set up for him on the opposite side of the coffee table. James, young and obsequious, stood off to the side.

"So Fred, you've been a bit cryptic in your emails," Sir William said, getting right to the point. "I've made a long uncomfortable journey to see you, so I hope you're going to make it worth my while."

Fred heard the veiled threat and felt a wave of hostility that was distinctly unsettling. He almost ran out the door, but then worried that they would follow him wherever he went. Suddenly, his anger toward Morrison seemed very petty.

"What's the matter, Fred, having second thoughts?" Sir William growled.

"Uhm, no sir, it's just that, well, I'm very nervous about all of this," Fred finally answered.

"Yes, it is an important decision you've made, and let me emphasize, it has already been made. There's no turning back at this point. We're going to get the truth from you one way or another," Sir William said, actually smirking in anticipation.

The sound of a gun being locked and loaded startled Fred. He looked over at James who now held a semi-automatic pistol at his side.

"And while we're at it," Sir William continued, "let's be up front about everything. I have two men parked in a car down the street from your parents' house in Sarasota. If need be, they'll use a little coercion at their end to ensure your cooperation at this end, is that clear?"

Fred was aghast. Here he was trying to be a good citizen, desiring to cooperate with the global government in ensuring peace on earth and right off the bat he and his family were being threatened with violence? This wasn't right. Suddenly his anger turned toward Sir William and intensified dramatically.

He tried to consider his options. He couldn't run. They'd shoot him and torture him or his parents. *Oh Lord God if You're still out there, do something, please!*

Sir William waved James over and signaled him to provide Fred with some encouragement. James grinned sadistically, glad for some real work to do. He slammed the pistol against the side of Fred's head and stepped back, keenly watching the flow of blood trickle down cheek of the terror-stricken snitch.

Fred's eyes suddenly widened and peered upward, a beatific glow on his face. Then with a shudder, his body slowly fell sideways off the chair and thudded onto the thick carpet.

"Get some cold water and wake him up," Sir William ordered. James rushed to do so as Sir William eyed the pitiful tattletale. *These Christians are such hypocrites and wimps,* he grumped to himself.

James splashed water on Fred's face and slapped him, to no avail. Then he shook him hard. No reaction.

"Check his pulse," Sir William demanded, suddenly concerned about Fred's wellbeing.

James felt Fred's wrist, then his neck and shook his head. "He's dead."

"You goddamn fool!" Sir William thundered as he hoisted himself to his feet.

James backed away, terribly frightened. "But I didn't hit him that hard," he whined.

Sir William threw the coffee table aside and kicked Fred's inert body several times until his fury diminished to a manageable state. He backed away, took several deep breaths and glared at James.

"No, you didn't hit him too hard," he admitted, much to James' relief. "Get his keys and find his vehicle. Then check to see if there's a GPS unit. Perhaps we can trace his steps backward to find their hideout."

James gratefully ran off on his new assignment. Sir William followed James out the hotel room door and signaled for the two goons he had stationed at each end of the hallway to come inside.

"Get the local forensic team here and see if we can't find some evidence of where this man or his vehicle came from," he ordered. *And why this creep died so easily.*

He then called the helicopter pilot who had been his eyes in the sky. "Did you get any video of the guy in the red ball cap and gray coat that came into the hotel a little while ago?"

"Yes, sir, I did," the pilot quickly responded. "He came from a few blocks away. He was behaving quite suspiciously and drew my attention. As you requested, the three of us took continuous ongoing video of the surrounding area, so we were able to trace him back to the garage three blocks east of here. Shortly before he came out of the garage, a white van went inside. So we traced the van westward for several miles before it was out of camera range."

"Good, good," Sir William muttered. "Get in touch with the local police and have them check any surveillance or traffic cameras they have along that route. Maybe we can track that van back to or at least close to their hideout."

Sir William grabbed the tray of snacks, popped open a beer and settled back carefully onto the couch. He was getting close, very close. He could feel it in his bones.

Chapter Forty-Six

"Thank God they haven't totally censored the Internet," Juanita said to Brandon as they enjoyed the breakfast she had prepared in their suite.

"It's tough to find anything Christian out there, but anything sinful, like Las Vegas, is a piece of cake," she said sadly as she took a bite of the coffee cake Brandon had purchased the previous day.

"So, tell me what you've found out," Brandon encouraged as he wiped the remaining vestiges of the scrambled eggs, bacon, home fries, and orange juice off his face. He picked up the cup of steaming coffee and settled back contentedly. He'd slept like a baby while Juanita labored into the early morning hours.

She set aside her dishes and pulled out the notes she'd made from her online research. "I was surprised to learn that this area used to be part of Mexico until 1855. They named it Las Vegas, which is Spanish for 'the meadows' because back then there was abundant ground water and extensive green areas, unlike the dry desert we see today."

"Wow, that is a total surprise," Brandon exclaimed and almost spilled his coffee. "Things have sure changed around here in a very short time." *That's what sin will do to a person and a place,* he thought.

"The Paiute Indians occupied the land until thirty Mormon missionaries established a fort near the current downtown area that same year," Juanita continued, simultaneously highlighting in yellow key points on her numerous pages of research. "However, they abandoned the fort two years later after mistreating the natives who then drove them away."

Rifling through her notes, she began organizing them chronologically. "In 1865, Octavio Gass drilled irrigation wells and established a 'wine ranch' which was called the 'best stop on the Mormon Trail.' Octavio lost the ranch in 1881 due to mismanagement. The land was later acquired by the San Pedro, Los Angeles and Salt Lake Railroad. The State Land Act in 1885 offered surrounding land at $1.25 per acre, bringing in a lot of farmers, so farming became the primary industry until 1901."

"Farming? Here? Who woulda thunk," Brandon joked, but was seriously amazed.

"The Mormons returned in 1895 and in the early 1900s water from wells was piped into town and the railroad was completed. Las Vegas became a primary water stop for both wagon trains and the railroad. Mining started up in earnest around then, and so did gambling, which was outlawed in 1910," Juanita continued, pausing here and there as she scanned all her notes for the more relevant events.

"A nationwide railroad strike in 1922 left Las Vegas in desperate shape until 1926 when U.S. 91 was completed, connecting it with California. But it wasn't until President Hoover signed an appropriation bill in 1930 to build Boulder Dam that the area really began to take off. The dam's workforce quickly swelled the population of Las Vegas from 5,000 to 25,000. Gambling was legalized in 1931 and soon casinos and showgirls appeared to entertain all the male workers," Juanita reported with undisguised disgust.

"And so it begins," Brandon murmured, finding himself far more interested in this background information than he'd expected.

"After the dam was completed in 1936 and renamed Hoover Dam, Lake Mead became a major tourist attraction, bringing even more people to Las Vegas. Then, in 1940, U.S. 95 opened and connected Las Vegas to the south. In 1941, an Army base was established which later became the current Nellis Air Force Base. It was the Army that forced an end to the widespread prostitution trade within Las Vegas where it remains illegal today," Juanita read.

"Really? I thought prostitution was legal within certain establishments," Brandon wondered aloud.

"It turns out that the boundaries of Las Vegas are much smaller than people realize, with most of the surrounding metropolitan area part of Clark County where prostitution is also illegal. However, in eight of Nevada's rural counties, brothels are legal but heavily regulated. There are currently twenty-eight legal brothels employing about 300 registered prostitutes. However, there are also apparently several 'escort services' within Las Vegas that manage to circumvent the law," Juanita concluded, anxious to move on to another topic.

"Although the first casinos were built on Fremont Street, El Rancho Vegas, a resort hotel offering the first 'all you can eat buffet' opened in 1942 in the area that became the Las Vegas Strip, which is actually in Clark County. Then in 1946, gangsters Bugsy Siegel and Meyer Lansky built the Flamingo Hotel. Organized crime then moved in with a vengeance building many more hotels and casinos on the 'Strip' between 1952 and 1957. Interestingly, many of these were financed by the Mormon-controlled Bank of Las Vegas. Many stars started performing there and by 1954 Las Vegas had over eight million visitors."

Juanita flipped through more pages. "Atomic testing was carried out in the area with hundreds of atmospheric explosions through 1963 and then further underground tests till 1992. Las Vegas actually advertised these as yet another tourist attraction. It wasn't until later that officials realized the radiation was causing increased incidents of cancer as far away as Arizona."

Brandon shook his head in revulsion. "It seems Las Vegas revels in a culture of death and destruction."

"That's absolutely right," Juanita concurred. "Satan comes only to 'steal, kill and destroy'[82] and I guess we could say gambling that is preprogrammed to generate profits is legalized robbery, often resulting in destruction of lives and even suicide."

"Not counting those who died from radiation poisoning and mob killings," Brandon added.

"No wonder we find it so spiritually depressing and oppressive here," Juanita observed before sifting through her notes again. "The infamous and reclusive Howard Hughes bought the Desert Inn in 1966 after refusing to leave their penthouse suite. He subsequently invested hundreds of millions in local real estate, becoming the most powerful man in Las Vegas, changing its image from Wild West to cosmopolitan city."

"From the 1970s to the recession of 2009, Las Vegas experienced explosive growth, doubling in population every decade and it became America's 28th largest city with over 550,000 residents. Mega resorts began to be built in 1989. However, since the recession, gambling revenues declined drastically and many properties went into foreclosure, from which Las Vegas has not yet fully recovered," Juanita concluded with a big sigh as she turned over the last of her notes.

Armed with that information, they set off later that morning and drove through the two "downtowns" in Las Vegas – the Strip and Fremont Street, where the smaller older hotels and casinos were located. On their first reconnaissance swing through the area, they were surprised to see how many law offices there were, while they only spotted one church, a damning indication of life in Sin

City. They also saw lots of homeless people wandering aimlessly about the surrounding area.

Of course, the Strip itself was impressive on the surface with the Statue of Liberty, the Eiffel Tower, Caesar's Palace, Circus Circus, the Stratosphere, Streets of New York, Paris and Venice, all quite extraordinary. But they each felt what Brandon called an "icky feeling" as they made their second pass through. Juanita thought it was "creepy, with a strong spirit of depression and hopelessness."

They pulled into a McDonald's just past the south end of the Strip, had some lunch and made final plans for a drive-through prayer attack. "As the Lord showed me awhile ago, we've been assigned to bring the Lord's two-edged sword down on Las Vegas. On the one edge, we'll pray for mercy, forgiveness and salvation for all the people here. But the other edge of the sword is judgment. I see tornados with giant hailstones descending soon here and fire falling from heaven, perhaps in the form of lightning. And just as the plentiful water that was here not too long ago dried up, we'll pray that their gambling revenue streams would also dry up."

Brandon nodded in agreement, having himself seen visions of destruction raining down on Las Vegas. "But what about the spiritual roots?" he asked.

Juanita nodded and pulled out a small piece of paper where she'd written down the key issues. "Yes, we'll need to bring the ax of the Holy Spirit down on the bad roots and trees that have grown here[83] from Mormonism, organized crime, gambling, prostitution, addictions, radiation, death, destruction, depression and oppression and then burn them in fire so that they no longer sprout here and send their shoots off all across the country."

Afire with the Lord's righteous anger and consumed with Godly sorrow, they spent the rest of the afternoon walking and driving through Las Vegas praying these things and more as the Spirit led them. Afterwards, they were thoroughly drained, too tired to even eat dinner. They collapsed into bed, eager for the next day to come so they could leave this sad, sad place.

Chapter Forty-Seven

Excitement over the double-wedding was reaching a crescendo even as concern was ramping up over Fred's disappearance. Fran was the most conflicted since she was one of the brides as well as Fred's immediate supervisor. To say that Fran's nerves were quivering was a vast understatement. The result? Ultra-hyperactivity and motor-mouth.

Fortunately, Jesse understood the situation and slipped into the background. Planning social events was not his forte anyway. So he and Jerome found various excuses to stay out of the way. The situation with Fred was a great opportunity to leave the compound entirely. Fran had modified the GPS unit on their vehicles to send out an encrypted signal that only she could decipher. She hacked into a government satellite and located Fred's van in the Denver garage.

Since Jesse was now the 'generalissimo,' as his security team and militia liked to call him, it was natural that he would take the lead in the investigation. He took Jerome, who was one of his sergeants, with him. They enjoyed their drive into Denver, relishing the time 'above ground' as the residents called it.

As they approached the parking structure, they shifted mental gears and went into stealth mode, their antennas up and senses heightened. They drove through the main level and then saw the parked van up ahead on the second story. Without turning their heads, they continued on by and parked on the third level. A good thing, because parked directly across from the van was one of Sir William's goons.

As a former FBI agent, Jesse knew all about surveillance, so they took the elevator down to the first level, back up to the fourth and then slipped carefully down the stairs to the second level. They emerged on the other side of the parking garage, well away from the van. Jesse led them to the center aisle where they took up positions behind two large supports.

Jesse took out his small but powerful binoculars and located the snoop in the black SUV about three rows down. They watched the watcher for some time to be sure that he wasn't just a bored husband waiting for his wife to return laden with packages from her shopping excursion. It was when the goon took out his own binoculars to scan a newly arriving vehicle that Jesse knew all he needed to know. It was a stakeout, all right. Somehow, they had identified Fred's vehicle.

For whatever reason, Fred was a target of the global government. A turncoat or a victim? Hard to say, and they'd have to be extra careful now in case Fred was providing the enemy with details about CIA-West, whether voluntarily or not. Jesse and Jerome backed away to the stairs and returned to their vehicle. Jesse then took a tiny GPS tracker from his purloined FBI kit and snuck back to the second level, crawled between the rows of cars and placed the magnetized unit on the undercarriage of the SUV.

After returning to the nondescript CIA sedan, Jesse called out on one of their modified, untraceable cell phones to a similar unit in Morrison's office and left a cryptic message that only Alan would understand. That would put the counter-insurgency compound on high alert with the militia taking up defensive positions throughout the ranch as well as on the roads leading there.

Then Jesse and Jerome took turns keeping an eye on the stakeout. Around six p.m. another black SUV pulled up, signaled to the first goon to leave, and then took his spot. Jerome hustled back to rejoin Jesse who was adjusting his receiver to follow the departing SUV on a Denver street map. They waited a couple of minutes before exiting, not wanting to cause undue attention.

The tracker showed that the SUV had gone a few blocks and then entered the underground garage at a nearby hotel. Jesse parked on the street a few blocks away and then strolled into the hotel. Jerome wasn't sure what Jesse expected to find, but tagged along obediently, his heart pounding. With no apparent leads in the hotel lobby, Jesse led the way down the elevator to the garage and located the black SUV among several others in a reserved parking area.

It was clearly a government operation on a fairly large scale. Now they'd have to wait until someone came along to provide them with further clues.

Upstairs, Sir William reassured his stakeout detail that it would still be productive to keep an eye on that van for at least a few more days. Then he called his away team who had used video from various street and commercial cameras to retrace the van's trail into Denver from Colorado. The trail ran cold, however, on the west side of Colorado Springs. His techie experts were still trying to decipher the modified GPS unit.

Sir William had gone into an intense meditation session in an effort to receive demonic information and was rewarded with assurances that the pesky Christian hideaway was somewhere in the western foothills. So he'd ordered satellite surveillance and infrared imagery to find any hotspots in the remote areas. Several possibilities had already emerged.

****

Back at CIA-West, one of Fran's best cyber-snoopers caught wind of the satellite surveillance. Now Fran and Alan Morrison were trying to decide what to do about it. Fran had been throwing ideas out a mile-a-minute. Alan tried to suppress his frustration, not that she'd notice. "What about doing something like submarines do where they release some material to confuse the sonar on torpedoes," was her next gambit.

That sparked an idea in Alan's worried mind. Perhaps they could feed counterfeit information to the satellites. He waited until Fran had to take a breath and then jumped in. "Great idea. Let's upload some alternate data!"

Fran's eyes widened as she held onto that breath. Intriguing. She could take some old satellite imagery, retag and modify it, and send it through the satellites to whoever was monitoring the output. That wasn't much different than what she had to do to make changes to the scanning data on the satellites relaying purchasing information to the various databanks.

Alan chuckled as he watched Fran's wheels spinning. Finally she nodded emphatically. "Yes, we can do it." And she headed back from the ranch house to the underground shelter to do so.

However, on the way inside she was waylaid by several people who were working on various details for the impending wedding, now two days hence. The seamstress needed her to try on the gown again after the recent alteration. The cook wanted her to taste a few cake samples. The organist was complaining about having to change keys to accommodate the singer's low register. The six year old ring-bearer was throwing a tantrum about having to wear a dress.

Pastor Wally saw the mayhem and wisely stepped back as Fran let out a long, howling scream. "That's it! I'm going to elope!" she snapped and stormed off.

Soon afterward, Alan came to tell Pastor Wally what was happening externally. "We need a lot of prayer on this one. Can you get the various prayer teams going?"

"You bet," Wally replied and immediately rushed off to do so. When he contacted Juanita he was delighted to find that they were coming down from Las Vegas for the weddings. Meanwhile, she contacted Abbot Charles via the satellite link that had just been installed.

Chapter Forty-Eight

When Blaine, the two witnesses and the rest of the procession made their way back into the sub-basement, Vy and Aly took up positions at opposite ends of the street to ensure that they hadn't been followed. They were beginning to get used to the supernatural and weren't overly surprised this time to see that they had been hidden in plain sight.

However, back in the plaza outside the Western (Wailing) Wall, the massacre was attracting many media types and ordinary onlookers who attempted to take pictures and videos as additional troops arrived to begin the cleanup and cover-up. Despite more shooting and killing, a few people had gotten away and transmitted their images to the Internet where millions had already viewed the carnage.

This was an extreme affront to the Jews, because the Western Wall was one of their holiest sites. It was a remnant of the Herodian retaining wall that once enclosed and supported the Second Temple. It came to be called the "Wailing Wall" by European observers because for centuries Jews gathered here to lament the loss of their temple. Now that the third temple had been built incorporating the Western Wall, lamentations had changed to prayers of thanksgiving.

No one was giving thanks now, though. Especially since blood red water was running out of every faucet in Jerusalem. The false sense of peace was shattered once again in the capital of God's heart, but outside the city boundaries people weren't sure what to think.

The public relations arm of the Global Governance Committee quickly manufactured lies and phony photographs to bolster their claim that Muslim terrorists had attacked the Christians and Jews because of the Temple's encroachment on Dome of the Rock property.

"Such intolerance will not be allowed under the Universal Religion Directives. Not only have they killed hundreds, but now they have poisoned the water supplies as well. The full weight of the Global Peace Army will be brought to bear to hunt down and capture these Islamic extremists. We remain confident that this does not reflect the attitude of most Muslims, but represents the reprehensible actions of a very small contingent of fundamentalists," the press release read.

Pope Radinsky was ecstatic over this serendipitous turn of events that played right into their hands, as he was quick to point out to Mustafa who was a bit more unsure about it all. He hoped and prayed that this was Allah's will, but felt serious misgivings that this would stir up Islamic conflagration before the time was right.

Rabbi David just shook his head in disgust over the way the media kowtowed to the Global Government and bought their pathetic explanations hook, line and sinker. Turning away from the TV monitor, he asked the two witnesses what trouble they were going to stir up next.

Abraham pretended to take offence, but knew Rabbi David was trying to lighten the mood. "I beg your pardon? Pastor Gabriel and I didn't get a chance to even say a word. It was all Blaine's doing!"

Blaine was startled out of her stupor. "What??"

Gabriel continued the deflection. "Why if you hadn't aggravated the Global Czar so much, none of this would have happened!" Then he grinned to let her off the hook.

Blaine growled at them in fun, but then grew serious again. "How can we go do any more outreaches if they're going to result in so much bloodshed?"

"Yes, that is the crux of the problem," Abraham admitted.

Gabriel sighed deeply and held Carmelita even tighter. "Perhaps we should have remained there to fend off the attacks that occurred after we left."

Abraham nodded in agreement. "Yes, I think you're right. We acted hastily without seeking the Lord's immediate guidance. I was too concerned about all the people who had followed us there and wanted to get them out of the plaza, but perhaps that was not God's plan."

"Well we won't know until we pray, so let's gather everyone together again before heading out on any more missions," Gabriel suggested. And so they did.

Once again they were flooded with images that only made sense when they gathered later to put the pieces together. The result was clear. They were to retrace Jesus' path of ministry, eventually circling back to Jerusalem where they would carry a cross up the Via Dolorosa, the route Jesus took on the way to his crucifixion on Calvary, or in Aramaic, Golgotha, literally 'place of the skull.'

More significantly, they saw that if they stayed on the assigned path, the Lord assured them that all the believers who followed them would be fully protected.

Chapter Forty-Nine

The big day finally arrived. Fran was greatly relieved that her diversionary tactics had so far kept the global forces chasing shadows. She also realized that the distraction had held wedding jitters at bay. Now the dam burst, flooding her with nervous apprehension.

She wasn't so much worried about whether Jesse was the right man, but rather that she was the right woman. Would Jesse tire of her hyper personality? Would he put up with all her eccentricities? Should she try to change? Could she?

Fortunately Sue was as calm as Fran had ever seen her. She had a regal glow about her, a princess about to marry her prince. Fran stuck like glue to Sue as they prepared for the ceremony, finding peace and comfort in her presence.

On the other side of the dining room that had been transformed into a dazzling ballroom, Jerome was so excited that he couldn't contain himself, driving Jesse crazy. He paced around the small dressing room like a wild, caged animal.

"What if I can't remember my vows?" Jerome worried aloud.

"Pastor Wally will prompt you, if necessary," Jesse reminded him. Each of them had written out their own personal vows and Jesse had made sure Pastors Wally and Michael Braintree had copies.

"Where's my bow tie?" Jerome wondered, madly sifting through his jumbled pile of clothes.

"Around your neck, where I tied it," Jesse answered, shaking his head. They had found old-fashioned, used tuxedos at a thrift shop in Colorado Springs.

"What time is it?" Jerome asked for the umpteenth time.

"About five minutes later than the last time you asked," Jesse sighed in frustration. "Look, the ceremony is going to begin in ten minutes. You're all dressed and ready to go. Why don't you sit down, close your eyes, and relax until then."

"Okay," Jerome quickly agreed, sat down, closed his eyes, only to pop up again ten seconds later. "Are you sure Alan has the rings?"

Yes, Jerome, I'm sure," Jesse responded in a carefully modulated monotone. He didn't want his exasperation to further stoke Jerome's agitation.

Before Jerome could say another word, Jesse followed his own advice and sat down on one of the spare dining room chairs and closed his eyes. He also closed his ears as best he could, determined to ignore any further Q&A with Jerome.

"Jesse, Jesse, wake up! They're calling for us to go now!" a frantic Jerome cried out as he shook Jesse out of a deep slumber.

"Huh? What's going on?" Jesse mumbled and shook his head back and forth to try and clear the cobwebs.

"It's time to get married!" Jerome exhorted.

"Oh, yeah. I can't believe I fell asleep," Jesse muttered, struggling to his feet. He wondered about the psychological implications. Shouldn't he be nervous? But he felt so calm, so right. He decided it was a good thing and so allowed Jerome to lead him out the door.

They joined up with their mutual best man, Alan Morrison, up front where the buffet line usually formed. However, the serving stations had all been covered over and decorated so cleverly that a visitor would never have guessed this was their dining room.

The two pastors stood side by side, grinning like two Cheshire cats. Wally was beside himself with joy to be able to marry his fellow easterners and good friends. Michael Braintree was ecstatic to feel finally free of the baggage he'd carried around for so many years. Free to experience the joy and share this moment with those he'd previously alienated.

They looked out upon their brightly dressed compatriots who filled the dazzlingly decorated dining room with excited energy. Brandon and Juanita waved cheerily from the back, having arrived just fifteen minutes ago. The dining room chairs formed a semicircle with a red carpet fragment running down a center aisle.

Wally nodded at the organist off to the side who began playing Mendelssohn's Wedding March on an antique organ carried over from Morrison's ranch house. It was the organ his mother used to play. Tears welled in Alan's eyes for more reasons than he could count. Mostly he was thankful to have finally shed the carefully constructed façade that had separated him from all these people he now called dear friends.

Oohs and aahs rippled through the crowd when an adorably dressed and coiffed flower-girl, Clarissa, strode imperiously down the carpet, casting rose petals this way and that. The tantrum-prone ring girl had been replaced by a smug seven-year old boy who stuck out his tongue at his mocking friends, but otherwise stuck to the task at hand.

The guests all gasped when Fran and Sue appeared in their wonderfully crafted white gowns, transformed into angelic apparitions. Sue slowly strode like royalty down the aisle, her head held high and eyes sparkling like champagne. Fran was firmly focused on resisting the urge to scamper up the carpet, instead keeping pace with the agonizingly deliberate tempo set by Sue.

Pastors Wally and Michael each briefly shared some Scripture and insights about marriage. Then the four exchanged their personal vows, Jerome only needing one prompt. The heartfelt words were so right, so beautiful, that tears were overflowing and noses were gently honking in one accord.

Sue and Fran both lamented the absence of their fathers to give them away. Both dads had rejected their daughters' pleas to accept Jesus as their Savior, as did the rest of their families. Just as the Bible foretold, the last days would drive a wedge between family members.[84]

But on this joyous day, the pangs of separation were overshadowed by the love and acceptance of their new family. Just as Jesus had said, *"Here are My mother and My brothers! For whoever does the will of My Father in heaven is My brother and sister and mother."*[85]

After the exchange of rings, the pastors pronounced them husbands and wives, and told the men to kiss their new brides. Everyone laughed heartily when Fran practically leapt into Jesse's waiting arms while Jerome stood nonplussed at how to embrace Sue without wrinkling her exquisite gown. She reached out, grabbed his lapel, and pulled him close.

Fran dispensed with decorum and skipped merrily back down the aisle pulling an embarrassed but happy Jesse behind her. Emboldened by Fran's breach of etiquette, Jerome swept Sue up in his arms and carried her down the red carpet grinning madly. Sue felt it was kind of appropriate, her knight in shining armor rescuing her once again.

Then came the most miraculous transformation anyone had ever seen. The men sprung into action as they had rehearsed several times over the past few days. Tables were quickly carried out, unfolded and set up according to marked spots on the floor. Chairs were swiftly set in place while the women rushed in with all the table decorations and place settings. Up front, the two pastors and Alan Morrison whipped the covers off the steam tables while the cooks and their helpers carried out the sumptuous feast.

The worship team set up quickly in one corner and were soon playing danceable tunes that had many happy people up on their feet. The brides and grooms joined the two pastors and Alan Morrison at the head table and soon glasses were clanking and kisses forthcoming.

Maybe it was the atmosphere, but everyone agreed the food was the best ever. Prime rib, roast duck, spiced ham, Caesar and Waldorf salads, plus twice-baked potatoes, steamed veggies, coleslaw and corn fritters for the main course. Of course there was a multi-level chocolate wedding cake gloriously decorated for dessert.

Months of pent-up anxiety were released in one of the best weddings anyone could ever remember attending. And for once, no menacing crisis interrupted the party that lasted into the wee hours of the morning. The two couples slipped away shortly after midnight and rode away in festooned ATVs, dragging along the proverbial tin cans for their honeymoons at two hunting cabins on opposite ends of the vast ranch.

Chapter Fifty

After much prayer among themselves and together and with Rabbi David's subterranean congregation, Abraham, Gabriel, Blaine and Carmelita received another surprise from the Lord. They were not only to follow the path of Jesus' ministry, but also his entire life beginning in Bethlehem.

"That could prove quite dangerous," Blaine worried. "Bethlehem and other areas Jesus went are controlled by Muslims now."

"If the Lord has ordained it, then He will go before us and be our rear guard as well," Abraham replied.[86]

"What about Jesus' journey to Egypt as a young child?" Carmelita asked.

Gabriel looked lovingly on his devoted wife, so grateful to have her with him once again. He was also pleased that she had taken Blaine under her wing. There was no one better equipped to lead a young woman on the Godly path than she.

"It seems as though that's to be part of the mission as well," Gabriel answered, feeling somewhat unsettled about it though. Had they heard right? If so, was it going to be a difficult journey?

Carmelita had a glint in her eye that alerted Gabriel to pay special attention to her next question. "What about Jesus' journey from Nazareth to Bethlehem?"

Blaine's face scrunched up in confusion as the newbie Christian tried to recall when in Jesus' life He had made that particular journey. Gabriel, however, knew what Carmelita meant.

"Ah yes, the pre-born child still in Mary's womb," he explained. "Now that you mention it, I think it would be quite appropriate to affirm life within the culture of death being promoted by this New World Order. Not only do they encourage abortion, but euthanasia as well, all in the name of population control for the greater good."

Group prayer confirmed Carmelita's suggestion and also answered two other critical questions: how would they travel and where would they stay? Fortunately for them, they did not have to walk the entire journey as Jesus and His disciples had. "After all," Abraham observed, "they had no alternatives back then. What would He do today? Hard to say, but I'd guess He'd use public transportation, since He and His disciples didn't seem to carry much money with them."

"And what money they *did* have," Gabriel laughingly noted, "Judas Iscariot, their treasurer, extorted according to the Apostle John."[87]

Unfortunately, the Lord told them that they could not stay in hotels, but like Jesus they would have to rely on local hospitality or sleep under the stars. "As Jesus said Himself, *'Foxes have holes and birds of the air have nests, but the Son of Man has nowhere to lay His head.'*[88]

Blaine gulped in spite of her efforts to contain her trepidation. "I never liked camping. Too many bugs and snakes and stuff."

Although everyone laughed, each was discomfited to varying degrees by the prospect of traveling in dangerous areas with little money and no places to stay. They better appreciated what the twelve disciples had gone through.

"Well, I for one could use a vacation," Carmelita snickered, recalling her recent kidnapping and miraculous escape.

"I don't think this is going to be much like a vacation," Blaine grumbled quietly. "Say, will Vy and Aly be gong with us too?" she asked hopefully.

"Yes, of course," Abraham answered. "They are our permanent bodyguards."

Somehow that brought relief to Blaine. Gabriel and Abraham exchanged glances. They knew full well that the situations they would encounter on this journey were beyond what even two special forces agents could counter. Divine intervention would be a necessity.

Interlude

Brandon and Juanita enjoyed the company of their friends awhile before leaving for Hollywood, California, the next stop on their prayer journey. Juanita also held workshops on spiritual warfare for the prayer team at CIA-West. She didn't see them as just classroom training because she put the intercessors to work right away practicing what she was teaching.

Pastor Wally counseled many of the residents there along with Pastor Michael Braintree, who himself continued to receive personal guidance from Wally. Michelle and Bonnie became good friends and started up a women's group to help them cope with their unique difficulties living as fugitives in the underground shelter.

Meanwhile, Brandon started up a men's group he called the Mighty Men patterned after David's mighty men as chronicled in first and second Kings. Since he'd be leaving shortly, he also spent extra time with Lawrence Little, who would be taking over as group leader.

Fran's countermeasures kept Sir William at bay, but his persistence was worrisome, so Jesse continued to train the militia for both defensive tactics as well as pre-emptive offensive strikes.

Back at CIA-East, Jim and Abby finally were able to raise up their own militia led by former General Randy Klingsmart, who had served in both Iraq and Afghanistan, and was well acquainted with guerilla warfare tactics. Jim was glad that the Holy Spirit hadn't chosen him as militia leader, but rather someone with the appropriate experience.

The Lord continued to grow Jermaine and Tara as strong leaders of the ten remaining hideaways. Their evangelistic outreaches, although more and more dangerous, were reaping greater and greater fruit. Soon they would have to establish more remote camps to accommodate all the new believers.

In Jerusalem, Abraham and Gabriel worked with Blaine to research and prepare for their mission to retrace Jesus' life journey through the Middle East. Through much prayer and mutual visions, they perceived it would be a monumental time with ripple effects that would reach out to the entire world, despite the Global Czar's efforts to interfere every step of the way.

René was growing increasingly concerned about Alexis, as the Global Czar's behavior became more and more erratic and unstable. He now spent a large portion of his time speaking out to the world through the holographic images now present in the center of almost every city of the globe.

Pope Radinsky was driving Mustafa to distraction during the run-up to the Mahdi's appearance in Mecca toward the end of Ramadan. Although everything was in place and in order, Mustafa worried that Radinsky would interfere at the last moment. He couldn't wait for the momentous occasion to finally free him to become Isa al-Maseeh and forever abandon the shell that had been his worldly disguise.

Chapter Fifty-One

Nazareth lies about sixteen miles to the west of the Sea of Galilee in Northern Israel, nestled in a natural bowl below Mount Tabor along the southern ridges of the Lebanon Mountains. It is known as the "Arab capital of Israel," with a population of about

65,000 that is predominately Arab, of which two-thirds are Muslim with the other third Christian.

Blaine thought it quite odd that the Israeli city of old should now be almost entirely bereft of Jews. Abraham grumbled something in Hebrew as he stared out the bus window, not at all pleased with the modern situation from a Judeo-Christian perspective. Although Nazareth is the largest Arab city in Israel, Christians and Muslims lived together mostly in harmony. Now, under the aegis of the Global Governance Committee, both groups chafed under the homogenous Universal Religion Directives.

As bus number 955 out of Jerusalem completed its two-hour trip to the Central Bus Station in Old City, Nazareth, the traveling party of six was surprised that no one recognized the two witnesses or Blaine, the once famous TV news anchor. While not exactly disguised, they all wore hats of some kind, and Blaine tucked her blond hair out of sight. Gabriel's new, dark whiskers rendered him generic Hispanic while Abraham's bushy white beard and yarmulke were common anywhere in Israel. Of course, the public didn't know what Carmelita, Vy and Aly looked like, especially dressed like ordinary tourists.

As Blaine's research pointed out, Nazareth has attracted hundreds of millions of Christian pilgrims from around the world. The historic Old City had been extensively renovated, preserving and restoring its original beauty and unique character of narrow lanes and alleys. Some considered it to be among the most beautiful historical destinations in the world.

While Nazareth was not specifically mentioned in the Old Testament, an early Hebrew inscription was found in Caesarea that mentions it. In Jesus' time, it had a population of about five-hundred and was really nothing more than an obscure backwater town. That's why prospective disciple Nathaniel is quoted by John as remarking, "Can anything good come out of Nazareth?"[89]

Nevertheless, Nazareth was home to Mary and Joseph and the site of the "annunciation," Gabriel's pronouncement to Mary that she would give birth to the Messiah. Jesus grew up there and was often called the "prophet from Nazareth in Galilee."[90] Others said of Jesus, "Is this not the carpenter, the Son of Mary, and brother of James, Joses, Judas, and Simon? And are not His sisters here with us?"[91] So they refused to believe that He was the Son of God. This attitude caused Jesus to observe, "A prophet is not without honor except in his own country, among his own relatives, and in his own house."[92]

Since the angel's pronouncement preceded Mary's impregnation by the Holy Spirit, the group set off on foot across the southern edge of the Old City to the Church (or Basilica) of the Annunciation. This was where, according to tradition, Mary was spoken to by Gabriel. The current church building was fairly new, having been constructed in 1969 to replace a Crusader-era structure. They walked through the latticed gate and followed a small tour group through the front door and immediately down to the lower level where the Grotto of the Annunciation presumably marked the location of Mary's childhood home.

The first annunciation shrine was probably built in the middle of the fourth century. A larger structure, commissioned by Emperor Constantine, was destroyed in the seventh century following the Muslim conquest of Palestine. The Crusader church was never fully completed but was later used by Franciscan priests to conduct services until it was once again destroyed by the Sultan of Egypt and Syria in 1260. Emir Fakr ad-Din granted the Franciscans permission to return in 1620, at which time they constructed a small structure to enclose the grotto.

In 1730, Dhaher al-Omar permitted construction of a new church, which became a central gathering place for Christians in Nazareth. The church was enlarged in 1877, but then completely demolished in 1954 to allow for the construction of the new basilica, which was completed in 1969. It remains under the control of the Franciscans, and is the largest Christian sanctuary in the Middle East. It was dedicated in 1964 by Pope Paul VI.

Blaine's reporter-trained eyes quickly surveyed the grotto. Immediately before them was an altar, rectangular and covered with a white tablecloth atop a rough-hewn stone talbe resting on a somewhat larger tile base raised about a foot off the floor. Two candles and an open Bible were the only adornments. Beyond the altar, behind a black wrought-iron fence, was what appeared at first to be an enormous stone fireplace fronted by several stone pillars holding ornate oil lamps.

On closer inspection, she could see the stone walls housed not a fireplace, but the entrance to a cave. "A cave?" she whispered to Gabriel.

"Yes, some traditions believe Mary's home was in this cave," Gabriel replied softly, not wishing to disturb the hushed atmosphere or the reverent tourists. "But the Greek Orthodox Church believes the annunciation occurred at a spring a little north of here and have build their own Church of the Annunciation there."

They were both startled, as was everyone else, when Abraham's booming voice suddenly cried out, "Behold, you will conceive in your womb and bring forth a Son, and shall call His name Jesus. He will be great, and will be called the Son of the Highest; and the Lord God will give Him the throne of His father David. And He will reign over the house of Jacob forever, and of His kingdom there will be no end."[93]

The tourists turned to gape at Abraham whose eyes seemed to have glazed over. "George, that's one of the witnesses!" an enraptured woman called out to her husband.

Soon all eyes flitted from Abraham to Gabriel. "Yes, Matilda, you're right. They're both here and I bet that's Blaine Whitney!"

The tourists crowded around and then backed away as Abraham's eyes refocused on them. Video images of fiery destruction played across their minds as they contemplated God's powerful messenger and one of the world's two greatest fugitives.

As several priests came running to see what the commotion was all about, Abraham spread his arms over the small group of people and proclaimed, "His mercy *is* on those who fear Him from generation to generation. He has shown strength with His arm; He has scattered the proud in the imagination of their hearts. He has put down the mighty from their thrones, and exalted the lowly. He has filled the hungry with good things, and the rich He has sent away empty. He has helped His servant Israel, in remembrance of His mercy, as He spoke to our fathers, to Abraham and to his seed forever."[94]

The Holy Spirit was so strong that the tourists and the two priests fell to their knees. Some began to cry. One woman fainted. The atmosphere was electric. Blaine stood frozen in place, awed, overwhelmed. Carmelita began praying softly in a strange tongue. Gabriel moved slowly from person to person, placing his right hand on their heads and praying a blessing over them.

When he had finished, Abraham abruptly turned and marched up the steps and back outside. The rest of the group followed behind trailed by the tourists and the priests. Abraham never broke stride, seemingly intent on another destination. He turned right and marched down Al-Bishara street, past the Terra Santa High School and up to the front entrance of St. Joseph's Church, also known as Joseph's Workshop because it is believed that the cavern in the basement was Joseph's carpentry shop.

The white-bricked exterior looked a little rundown and tired, but inside Blaine was surprised to see a magnificent sanctuary under a high-vaulted ceiling supported by numerous pillars and archways spanning four rows of polished wood pews. There were already some people there, a few praying in the pews and at the altar.

Abraham marched right up to the altar and raised his arms to the fresco of Joseph and Mary above the golden cross. "Joseph, son of David, do not be afraid to take to you Mary your wife, for that which is conceived in her is of the Holy Spirit. And she will bring forth a Son, and you shall call His name Jesus, for He will save His people from their sins. All this was done that it might be fulfilled which was spoken by the Lord through the prophet, saying: 'Behold, the virgin shall be with child, and bear a Son, and they shall call His name Immanuel,' which is translated, 'God with us.'"[95]

As before, the anointing of the Holy Spirit was so strong that people fell to their knees, fainted or cried reverential tears. Without another word, Abraham turned and strode up the center aisle and back outside, followed by a retinue of nearly two dozen people who were dazed but determined to remain close to the presence of God.

Chapter Fifty-Two

Unbeknownst to the two witnesses in Nazareth, a divine journey of a different sort was underway on the western coast of the United States. Brandon drove the SUV off exit 8A of the nearly deserted 101 Hollywood Freeway onto Sunset Boulevard and pulled off to the side.

The devastation from last year's tsunami was still quite apparent, despite a major federal effort to bring Hollywood back to life. Midst new and ongoing construction was a wake of destruction that boggled the mind. More troubling was the spirit of oppression that Juanita felt blanketing her soul.

"Why would anyone want to rebuild this God-forsaken place?" she wondered aloud.

Brandon suspected she already knew the answer, but voiced his own opinion. "They have to keep the myth alive."

That cryptic response caused Juanita's eyebrows to arch questioningly, so Brandon elaborated. "Our entire post-modern culture was built upon a foundation of lies that the film industry foisted on us, guided unwittingly by Satan, the *father* of lies.[96] The primary deception was that reason, science, nature and tolerance could overcome all things, even God."

Juanita's head tilted to the side. "My, you're erudite today."

Brandon chuckled. As he became more emboldened, thoughts he'd once kept to himself now tripped lightly off his tongue. Even he was surprised at what came out sometimes.

Juanita thought about Brandon's comments awhile before carefully replying, "Yes, I see your point, but isn't it also a case of Hollywood promoting immorality?"

Brandon was focused on the famous Hollywood sign that had been reconstructed bigger and better than ever up above on Mt. Lee in Griffith Park. "Yes, that and prideful arrogance," he said with a disdainful, dismissive wave of his hand at the sign.

Down below, Juanita shook her head in exasperation. "I wonder how much of this area has been rebuilt after the tsunami?" Juanita pondered, glancing around the immediate area, but unable to see much from their vantage point on Sunset Boulevard. "What a waste of time and money when there were so many more pressing and productive projects that should have come first."

Brandon grunted in agreement as he pulled the SUV back onto the road. "Well, let's have a look and see what's what."

Juanita played navigator with the maps they'd printed off the Internet back at CIA-West. They didn't want to take a chance on using the GPS unit in case it could be used to track them. Their trip had been duly filed with the authorities through Fran's magical computer routines and they had the appropriate bogus paperwork should anyone question them. But still, it was less nerve-wracking to avoid such situations.

On Hollywood Boulevard they saw that the area containing the Kodak Theater, Grauman's Chinese Theater, Ripley's Believe It Or Not Museum and the Hollywood Wax Museum had been resurrected, but most of the surrounding neighborhood was still desolate.

"Want to see the famous foot and hand prints?" Brandon asked, tongue firmly planted in cheek.

"Infamous is more like it," Juanita snorted. "With our role models being narcissistic, overpaid movie and sports stars, no wonder the world is such a mess."

As they continued on, sure enough there was a bunch of tourists oohing and aahing over the Hollywood Walk of Fame, eyeing the stars of the various celebrities inlaid in the sidewalk.

Sunset Strip, home to L.A.'s hottest and hippest bars and clubs, had also been largely reconstructed. Brandon headed north on Highland out past the Hollywood Bowl where people were already lining up for a concert by a group neither Brandon nor Juanita had ever heard of.

They continued on out to Universal Studios, the land of make believe, which was a beehive of activity. The "World's Largest Movie Studio and Theme Park" looked like nothing had ever touched it, despite most of the surrounding area having been destroyed. Even with the debris cleaned up, it was a surreal – and disheartening – sight.

Brandon sat back in the SUV and closed his eyes. "Okay," he sighed, "let's do what we came to do and get out of here. It's way too depressing – not only because of the devastation, but also to see what it is our government really values – and that most people think these things will satisfy them."

Juanita rubbed her eyes as though she could wipe away the bizarre images. "Well, it's late in the afternoon. Maybe we should first find a place to stay for the night."

Brandon took another look around. "I suppose they must have rebuilt enough lodging for all these tourists, but I think I'd rather pitch a tent out in those hills, rather than participate in this sickening charade."

"Yes, that sounds a lot better," Juanita heartily agreed. "Let's get out of here."

After consulting his Google map of the area, Brandon took Bantham Boulevard.to Lake Hollywood Drive which led them to the north end of the Hollywood Reservoir. The former development of homes to the east was still in shambles, so Brandon drove further south along the reservoir until they couldn't see anything but water and vegetation that had grown lush after the tidal wave.

It was just before dark and the early spring temperatures were dropping rapidly. They quickly set up their tent, fired up the gas grill and soon sat eating their dinner in the blessed bosom of resplendent nature. The only sounds were those of wild creatures whose population was expanding rapidly with no human beings around.

With their stomachs satisfied and their minds clear, Juanita pulled out the research notes she'd printed out from the Internet back at CIA-West. Under the soft glow of the kerosene lamp, she began reading selected portions aloud to Brandon, who sat back in his camp chair and closed his eyes. He loved Juanita's strong but tender voice. It was like music in the wind.

"When Spanish explorers first entered the area now known as Hollywood, Native Americans were living in the canyons of the Santa Monica Mountains, but were later forcibly moved into missions. Legend has it that in 1853, only one adobe hut stood in this area. The Spanish government divided the land into two parts: the western portion was named Rancho La Brea while the eastern acreage was called Rancho Los Feliz."

Juanita glanced over at Brandon who appeared to be asleep, but probably wasn't. It had taken her quite some time to get used to Brandon's habit of listening to her with his eyes shut. He said he could concentrate better that way and, for the most part, it was true, although on occasion he did fall asleep.

"I'm listening," he said to keep her going, knowing she was trying to figure out if he was still awake.

She smiled to herself and continued. "By the 1870s, an agricultural community was flourishing with crops ranging from hay and grain to subtropical bananas and pineapples. In 1886, Harvey Henderson Wilcox bought an area of Rancho La Brea that his wife Daeida christened Hollywood after the ample stands of native Toyon or Holly, that covered the hillsides with clusters of bright red berries each winter."

"So that's what we were seeing on the way here," Brandon remarked.

"Yes, but it was actually Hobart Johnstone Whitley's wife Gigi who originally coined the name. However, Wilcox was the first to record it on a deed. Whitley was a banker and one of the nation's most successful land developers. During the westward construction of frontier railroads from the late 1870s to the early 1890s, he founded scores of towns in the Oklahoma Territory, Dakotas, Texas and California. HJ was a good friend of Theodore Roosevelt. He became known as the 'father of Hollywood.'"

"So he's the one to blame," Brandon muttered, sounding very sleepy.

Juanita pressed on, suspecting her droning voice was serving more as a lullaby than a fountain of information. "Within a few years, Whitley had devised a grid plan for the new community, paved Prospect Avenue (now Hollywood Boulevard) for his main street and started selling large residential lots to wealthy Midwesterners looking to build homes so they could winter in California. As president and major share holder of the Los Angeles Pacific Boulevard and Development Company, Whitley orchestrated the building of the Hollywood Hotel, the opening of the Ocean View Tract and construction of a bank which was located on the corners of Hollywood Boulevard and Highland."

A snort alerted Juanita that Brandon had succumbed to sleepiness. However, she knew from past experience that if she stopped now, he'd wake right up and insist he'd never fallen asleep. She liked the fact that her voice was so soothing to him.

"Prospect Avenue soon became a prestigious residential street populated with large Queen Anne, Victorian and Mission Revival houses. Mrs. Wilcox raised funds to build churches, schools and a library. By 1900, Hollywood also had a post office, newspaper, hotel and two markets for the population of 500 people. The thriving community incorporated in 1903, but its independence was short-lived due to a lack of water. Los Angeles, with its surplus of liquid gold from the Colorado River, annexed Hollywood in 1910."

She paused as she scanned more of her notes and then was startled nearly out of her skin when Brandon piped up. "So when did all the movie moguls come to town?"

She laughed. "You got me. I was sure you were asleep."

"I was, briefly," he confessed, "but I woke myself up when I snorted."

Juanita sighed in contentment. Why couldn't life be like this all the time? Why had the world gone so far astray? She knew the answer, but wished it wasn't so. One day, after Jesus returned to claim His Kingdom, all would be well at last. But for now.... well, she'd just have to keep on keeping on.

"In answer to your question, it was 1911 when the Nestor Company opened Hollywood's first film studio in an old tavern on the corner of Sunset and Gower. Shortly afterward, Cecil B. DeMille and D. W. Griffith began making movies in the area as well because of its open space and moderate climate. This created a clash between the older and newer residents. Acres of agricultural land south of Hollywood Boulevard were subdivided and developed as housing for the enormous numbers of workers the movie-making industry required. Next, high-rise commercial buildings began to spring up."

"So the newbies took over," Brandon observed, staring down at the pockets of light in the rebuilt areas. "And now they own it entirely."

"Yes, it took a few decades, but soon many movie stars moved to Beverly Hills to the west, with elegant shops and restaurants following along. Then, much of the movie industry dispersed into the surrounding areas such as Burbank and Westside. Significant ancillary industries such as editing, effects, props, post-production and lighting remained in Hollywood. Many historic theaters were built as venues to premiere major theatrical releases and host the Academy Awards which began in 1929," Juanita read.

She thought Brandon had drifted off again, but continued on, "The famous Hollywood Sign originally read Hollywoodland when it was first erected in 1923 to advertise a new housing development in the hills above Hollywood. For several years the sign was left to deteriorate, but in 1949 the Chamber of Commerce took it over, repaired it and stripped out the last four letters."

She paused, heard him lightly snoring, but decided to finish her lullaby, if only to enter the information into her mind so that tomorrow she'd know how to pray, as led by the Holy Spirit. "The first commercial TV stations west of the Mississippi began operating in Hollywood in 1947, and in the 1950s music recording studios began moving in as well. In 1952, CBS Television City was built and the famous Capital Records building near Hollywood and Vine opened in 1956."

There was, of course, a lot of other detailed material but none that sparked any spiritual connections. It was always the roots that were significant. The branches were mere symptoms. But then she came across a sad commentary, which she also read aloud. "A serious problem for Hollywood since the 1960s was its attractiveness for desperate runaway adolescents fleeing broken homes across North America. They flocked to 'Tinsel Town' hoping to become movie stars only to discover that their chances were slim to none. Many of them sunk into homelessness on Skid Row in downtown Los Angeles or became prostitutes and panhandlers. Others wound up in the large pornography industry in the San Fernando Valley."

That put an exclamation point on the underlying, unspoken theme running through Hollywood's modern history. Surface glamour covered over a foundation of greed, lust and immorality. Stars sleeping around became a way of doing business, feeding a growing hunger in America for salacious gossip. The pity of it was that it desensitized moral sensibilities and made immorality desirable. What was good became bad, and what was bad became good. Perhaps that was the subconscious genesis for young people starting to use the word 'bad' as an adjective of praise.

Following the tsunami, those in charge had reconstituted the false façade that had led so many astray. It wasn't God's hand of judgment that had wiped it clean, but rather His law of sowing and reaping. "Sow to the flesh and reap corruption," the Bible warned.[97] Just as the voodoo centers of Haiti and New Orleans were rebuilt following 'natural' catastrophes, so too was Hollywood.

Ignoring God's laws might seem attractive for awhile, but in the end calamity strikes. When it did, cause and effect were ignored, with the so-called 'acts of God' attributed to random misfortune. Wouldn't humanity ever learn that God's spiritual laws are every bit as real as His laws of nature which govern gravity and the structure of the entire universe?

Juanita sighed in frustration, woke Brandon gently and led him into the tent. She prayed that they would continue to be protected from a very active enemy who would like nothing more than to destroy them before they could complete their mission.

Chapter Fifty-Three

"Where are they now?" the Global Czar inquired of his spy in Nazareth.

"They're just standing around, sir," Colonel Jankovic replied. As a chief officer in the new Global Security Agency, he resented his current assignment, but knew he couldn't let it show. Dressed in a hooded sweatshirt and jeans, he'd followed the two witnesses and their entourage from Jerusalem to Nazareth, something any number of lower-ranked agents could have done.

"Doing what?" Alexis demanded, his agitation resonating over the secure satellite phone.

"Well, Abraham is just kind of staring off into space and his followers are just milling around," Jankovic answered, puzzled about this whole episode.

"Followers? You mean the other five?"

"No sir, about thirty more that they picked up after going inside those two churches." Jankovic really wanted to know what had transpired inside, but hadn't wanted to blow his cover by getting too close. Those new followers appeared to be completely enraptured by the two witnesses. It just didn't make any sense.

Before Alexis could frame another question to feed his insatiable addiction about the activities of his two nemeses, Gabriel all of a sudden started shouting toward the heavens in some foreign language, arms spread apart and waving rhythmically.

"What's that noise? What's happening?" Alexis asked urgently.

"I don't know sir, Gabriel seems to be in some kind of trance. Wait, what's that? Some kind of whirlwind has formed around them and the air is shimmering. Hard to see what's happening. I'm moving closer. It sounds like a freight train. I can't see anything at all…. Huh? They're gone! The six of them have disappeared into thin air!!"

"No, no, you idiot," Alexis ranted into the phone. "They can't just have disappeared. That dust devil must have blurred your vision. Go find them. That's an order!"

Jankovic ran over to the spot where the six had last been standing. His trained eyes roved over the area, sector by sector. They were nowhere to be found.

He turned to the enraptured followers. "Where did they go?" Matilda pointed upward.

Colonel Jankovic looked toward the sky in spite of himself. This was crazy. He grabbed Matilda and shook her out of her stupor. "Tell me right now where they really went. I know you're covering for them."

George shoved the intruder away. "Get your hands off my wife!"

Jankovic held back his trained response. The flabby, red-faced husband clearly was no threat.

"They really did go up," George confirmed. "Just like Elijah!"[98]

"No, George, they were translated, transported, just like Philip," Matilda interjected.[99]

Other voices piped up in agreement. The Colonel could hear the Global Czar's voice screaming out of the phone in his hand. His head was spinning. How was he going to explain this?

****

"Where are we?" Blaine asked, her eyes wide with amazement and excitement. She felt as though she'd been on a rollercoaster ride.

Vy and Aly, acting on instinct, had drawn their weapons and thrust themselves in front of the two witnesses, ready to take a bullet for them if necessary.

Carmelita simply spread her arms in great joy. "Praise God!"

Gabriel was still entranced and mumbling in his prayer language.

Abraham chuckled. "Okay, okay, you can stop praying now. We've arrived on chariot's wings right in the center of Bethlehem. Now that's the way to travel!"

Vy and Aly relaxed a little, although the stares of several dozen people around Manger Square were somewhat worrisome, even though they all appeared to be just tourists.

Traveling to Bethlehem usually required special permits because it is now a Palestinian city in the central West Bank, approximately six miles south of Jerusalem. It is the capital of the Bethlehem Governorate of the Palestinian National Authority. However, the city of about 30,000 is inhabited by one of the oldest Christian communities in the world, which has shrunk in recent years due to turmoil and threats.

The birthplace of both King David and Jesus Christ, the 'Son of David', Bethlehem was also where Joseph, Jesus' step-father, was born. Joseph had to return to Bethlehem from Nazareth, about eighty miles, for the census. In those days, it took a few days for he and his Holy-Spirit-impregnated wife, Mary, to make the journey.

So far, the six travelers hadn't drawn the attention of any of the Palestinian Authority security forces, but that was likely to change momentarily as the shocked onlookers began to murmur and point. Without travel permits, they could be arrested as spies or infiltrators.

Abraham turned slowly around to soak in the sights around Manger Square, the focal point of the long but narrow city of Bethlehem. On one side was the Church of the Nativity countered by the Mosque of Omar on the other side.

At first glance in the late afternoon sun, the weathered, rather ugly two-story church looked more like a stone-walled fortress, but then Abraham saw the two bell towers with crosses on top, not realizing that these were actually part of the adjacent Armenian monastery. The mosque, on the other hand, was a newer, narrower, taller building with an eight-story tower capped by a minaret.

The Church of the Nativity is one of the oldest churches in the world still in everyday use. It has seen a variety of custodians over the centuries, including the Persians and the Crusaders, all of whom attempted to preserve the church and even expanded it to its current large footprint of almost 130,000 square feet.

Today the church is governed by three Christian denominations: the Armenian Church, the Roman Catholic Church and the Greek Orthodox Church. Each has control over different sections of the building. Despite its historic and spiritual significance, the Church of the Nativity is on the Endangered Sites list of the World Monuments Fund, largely because of a leaky roof which threatens to damage the relics within the Basilica.

Just then Aly spotted two uniformed Palestinian police officers pointing their way from across the plaza. "Quick, into the church."

Vy and Aly quickly backed their way along the mammoth stone wall, providing cover for their charges, hands poised over their weapons. The facade of the Church of the Nativity is encircled by the high walls of three convents: the Franciscan on the northeast side, the Greek Orthodox and the Armenian Orthodox, on the southeast side. The facade has three doors, two of which were walled up.

They ran toward the remarkably unimpressive main entrance, unsure whether this could actually be the primary way inside. The low entrance, called the Door of Humility, was constructed at the beginning of the 16th century, in order to prevent the entrance of horses into the building. The one sleepy guard blinked nervously as the group of six crouched through the entryway.

They found the narthex, or lobby, divided into three compartments, with a single wooden door providing access to the interior. Once inside, they quickly surveyed the rectangular basilica which was about 175 feet long by 85 feet wide. Two rows of Corinthian pillars lined either side of the basilica, forty-four in total, each about 20 feet high and constructed of the white-veined pink limestone common to the area. Thirty of the nave's forty-four columns carry Crusader paintings of saints and the Virgin and Child.

There wasn't much time to think through their options, so Gabriel led a charge up the center aisle toward the first of several altars. Most visible at the far end was the High Altar. To the right in the rounded portion of the transept, was the Armenian altar, called the Altar of the Three Kings, which is presumed to be the place where the Magi dismounted. Next to it was the Altar of the Circumcision. In the left arm of the transept was the Altar of the Virgin, devoted to Mary.

These areas were too open, too exposed, so Gabriel led a charge down the stairs into the Grotto of the Nativity. As many believers and non-believers have observed, there's a special, inspirational atmosphere as one enters the grotto, causing many to be overcome with emotion. Even now there were several tourists standing in stunned silence while a couple of worshipers lay prostrate facing a 14-point silver star in the white marble floor which indicated the precise spot where tradition says Jesus was born.

Of the 15 lamps burning around the recess, six belong to the Greeks, 5 to the Armenians and four to the Roman Catholics. The Chapel of the Manger is situated on the right side of the Grotto. The mouth of a cavern gapes open at the end of the Grotto. A doorway led to two other chapels, the first one dedicated to St. Joseph, in memory of the vision he had when an Angel came to him and told him to take the Virgin Mary and Baby Jesus to Egypt to flee Herod's executions.[100] The second chapel is dedicated to the Holy Innocents, the children and infants whose lives were taken by Herod in his attempt to eliminate the Christ child.

The cavern has been honored as the site of Christ's birth since at least the 2nd century. Vy signaled that they should seek shelter in the cavern, although he felt it might be sacrilegious to do so. But Gabriel had come to a complete halt, overwhelmed by the spiritually intense environment. As urgent footsteps resounded behind them, Gabriel fell to his knees.

"Do not be afraid," Gabriel cried out toward the manger, "for behold, I bring you good tidings of great joy which will be to all people. For there is born to you this day in the city of David a Savior, who is Christ the Lord. And this *will be* the sign to you: You will find a Babe wrapped in swaddling cloths, lying in a manger."[101]

Suddenly, there was the sound of a multitude of heavenly host praising God and saying: "Glory to God in the highest, and on earth peace, goodwill toward men!"[102]

Behind them, the two Palestinian policemen and a retinue of guards and priests stumbled and also fell onto their knees, weeping uncontrollably. The heavenly choir continued to fill the Grotto with choruses of praise. Abraham rubbed at his moist eyes, singing along with the invisible angels. No one even noticed when Gabriel rose to his feet and looked around. As the choir wound down, he signaled to the others to go back up the stairs.

They had to step aside to avoid the crowd of people streaming toward the Grotto. When they reached the door to the narthex, they glanced back and saw that a bright golden light was shining forth out of the stairways leading to the Grotto. Scores of people were being drawn to the light, believers and non-believers, tourists and residents alike.

Back outside, they could see that the holy light shone like a beacon through the few windows. Even Muslims were pouring out of the mosque and running across the square toward the church. No one seemed to notice or care about the six pilgrims standing off to the side.

****

Almost simultaneously across the globe, Juanita and Brandon were making their way down Mt. Lee Drive to the hilltop where the famous sign overlooked Hollywood in the early morning light. The vista that spread before them was starkly barren and yet teeming with pockets of life at the few rebuilt tourist areas.

As they walked to the edge of the overlook, the Holy Spirit came upon them with such force that they staggered to their knees, no longer able to keep their balance. Filled to overflowing, both held their hands out in unison over the devastation and false life below.

Unseen by their mortal eyes were rays of heavenly power streaming through strategically positioned angels, flowing into and out of God's anointed. While it was Jesus Himself who directed and empowered the angels, it was the prayers of human beings that were the activating agent. Because God had given Adam and Eve dominion over the earth,[103] He would not violate humanity's free will. And so Jesus, who had regained the title deed to the earth from Satan through His sacrificial death,[104] awaited the freely offered prayers of the saints that opened the window for His judgments to fall upon the earth.

Brandon and Juanita were so immersed in the Holy Spirit that they were unable to speak coherently. Instead, they cried out in jumbled words and syllables that they themselves didn't understand. But the Holy Spirit translated the passion of their hearts and the groaning of their spirits into clearly understood heavenly language.[105] That was all Jesus needed.

A low rumble began to resound across the flat plane below the hillside, unheard by the instigators but causing a number of tourists' ears to perk up. As the rumble grew louder, a slight vibration rippled across the streets of Hollywood. More ears and many feet started to tremble in fear. Some raced to their vehicles while others sought shelter.

Jesus sat in His crying room, shedding tears and trembling in His own right. Oh how He wished that even now, even at this late stage, hearts would turn to Him. He wished that none should perish but come to everlasting life.[106] But the time was drawing nigh when He would begin to break the remaining three seals on the scroll of damnation. The timeframe His Father had called "the beginning of sorrows" was drawing to an end. Soon sin would have run its course to fulfillment and forevermore be stamped out.

Even as He stretched His hand out toward the abhorrent place called Hollywood, His Spirit cried out to those who were at the brink of death, to snatch them from the fires of eternal damnation. His Father, who knew things from the beginning to the end, told Jesus that there would be a few, precious few. His Spirit joined with Brandon and Juanita to pray for more.

The rumbling grew inexorably in volume until it sound like a freight train. The ground shook violently. Buildings swayed, people cried and scrambled for safety in all directions. Some fell on their faces and cried out to God for salvation and were visited by angels of light and visions of Jesus. Most simply ran or hid blindly, while a few even cursed God.

Suddenly, gaping holes began to open up in the ground here and there, swallowing up cars, people, streets and buildings. Fortunately for the two prayer warriors above, they were so entranced in the Spirit that they did not hear the screams nor see the disaster unfolding before them.

The sink holes spread until some began to join together. Soon there was virtually no ground that was not moving, shaking or sliding. Dust and debris rose and filled the air until nothing was visible from the hilltop above.

When Juanita and Brandon eventually opened their eyes, all sound had died away. All they could see was the dark, angry cloud covering the area that used to be Hollywood. But in the Spirit, the Lord also gave them spiritual eyes to see the souls of the few who had been snatched from the gates of hell rising up out of the devastation below within a golden beam of light that drew them upward into heaven.

Chapter Fifty-Four

Jim and Abby sat together on a bench that he had constructed for them on a ridge that overlooked a small valley just beginning to blossom with early spring foliage. The air had taken on the sweet smell of new life, a welcome change from the mechanically refreshed atmosphere in the underground complex hidden beneath the verdant valley floor.

With CIA-East now fully functional, the time had come for them to extend their perspective outward, reversing the inward focus that had consumed them for so many months. "Are we ready?" Abby wondered aloud.

Jim's face scrunched up in thought, one hand rubbing his chin while the other slicked back his thinning, graying hair. Abby relished the pleasure she took in watching Jim in all his various mannerisms, most of which he was unaware.

Finally he turned and looked down into her sweet face. He was continually taken aback by his good fortune to have found the perfect wife, or more likely that God had found for him. He couldn't help but smile as he mentally reviewed how much each of them had grown in such a short while. Nor could he not revel in the irony of having moved from the secular CIA to God's CIA.

Jim knew that they also made a perfect pair to lead this Counter Insurgency Agency. His penchant to be overly optimistic and even reckless was balanced by Abby's predilection to be too cautious. He had been chomping at the bit to charge into action for some time, but had waited as patiently as he could for Abby to reach the point where she felt even marginally satisfied with the foundation they'd built together.

He'd also prayed over and over for the Lord to reveal his perfect plan and timing. Now it appeared He had. Even without Jim's prompting, Abby too had seen the hand of the Lord moving them to the brink of battle.

Jim brushed back the hair that the light breeze had spread across her face. "I think the issue is more whether the Lord thinks we're ready."

Abby smiled, still astounded at Jim's transformation from Satan's henchman to God's helper. "Yes, and I think we've both prayed enough to realize that this is the open door we've been waiting for. But I'm scared, nonetheless" she admitted.

Jim reached around and pulled her close. "It is a bit scary," he acknowledged, "but if the Lord is for us, who can be against us?"[107]

Abby laughed, always pleased to hear God's Word coming out of Jim's mouth. "So, I guess we should talk to Randy."

Jim nodded, silently thanking the Lord for bringing Randy Klingsmart to them to head up their newly formed militia. "Yes, and Randy will be quite relieved to finally get a chance to have his troops move on from all that monotonous training."

Abby snuggled even closer into Jim's arms. Even though she knew the time had truly come, it made her more aware of the spiritual war raging on outside this peaceful sanctuary. As their troops moved out, would the war be drawn to their very doorstep.

Jim felt Abby shiver and thought it due to the chill in the breeze. "Well, let's get back inside and meet with Randy."

As they had both expected, Randy was quite excited by the prospect of springing into action. Jim and Abby explained how Sir William was closing in on finding the location of CIA-West, and how simultaneously his Satanic hordes back in Washington, D.C. had tracked down the general position of the Havenwood1 hideaway in Woodbridge, Virginia.

"So you're sure that Fran's intelligence is reliable?" Randy asked.

Jim and Abby both chuckled. "There's no one more capable or reliable than Fran," Abby answered. "If it wasn't for her, none of us would be able to function."

"But don't you think that it's too much of a coincidence that they would set up a Detention Center within a stone's throw of the hideaway?" Randy asked, his military training leading him to question everything.

The former General Randolph Klingsmart had a distinguished resume fighting and overseeing guerilla-style warfare from Vietnam to Iraq to Afghanistan. However, a roadside IED (improvised explosive device) outside Kabul took a leg, ended his career, but more significantly led him through severe depression into the saving arms of Jesus Christ.

"I'm beginning to understand that there really are no coincidences," Jim observed thoughtfully. "When seen from a spiritual perspective, ideas we think are our own often come from the Holy Spirit or the demonic realm."

Randy pondered that for a few moments. As a relatively new Christian, he appreciated that his two "bosses" had themselves been down the same road not all that long ago. "Okay, I'll accept that for now as a working hypothesis. So, what I hear you saying is that you want our militia to set out with three primary objectives, all at the same time? That's quite a lot for any military action, but especially for our very first mission."

"Yes, you're right, of course," Jim admitted. "But that's only from a secular viewpoint. With God, all things are possible."[108]

Randy sighed. It was hard mixing his worldly training with spiritual perspectives. "Okay, I'll accept that for the moment, but I'll have to pray about it before I fully commit myself to it."

Jim and Abby both nodded their approval.

"But let me be sure I've got it straight." Randy continued. "First of all, you want to create a distraction that will bring Sir William back east and take his attention away from CIA-West. Second, you want us to protect the Havenwood1 hideaway, and third, attack the nearby detention center."

"Yes, that's right, except for one thing," Jim responded. "It's not us who want this, but the Commander in Chief." Randy sighed again and nodded. "Yeah, yeah, yeah. I'll pray about it."

As the three prepared to leave the conference room, Randy suddenly stopped and turned around sharply. "Say, I just had an idea for the distraction. We suspect that Sir William has some top-level Christian leaders incarcerated in the basement jail in his mansion, like he once held Pastor Gabriel and you, Jim. Let's attack there first and take over his headquarters. Not only will that bring him running back, but he will probably call upon some of the detention center troops to try and retake his mansion, which we'll let him do while we attack the depleted detention center. With that accomplished and so many Christians released, I think that will create enough to occupy Sir William's attention and he'll forego further attempts to find the hideaway for awhile."

Jim and Abby positively beamed back their approval. "See, you've already gotten confirmation from the Lord, and it's not a coincidence," Abby laughed.

Chapter Fifty-Five

"For Pete's sake, whoever he might be, please get a grip on yourself, Mr. Global Czar, sir," Pope Radinsky said in disgust. "Stop obsessing over those two witnesses. We knew something of this sort would happen, and we also know it doesn't matter in the long run, so what's your problem?"

René stared in contempt at their noble leader whose eyes were glazed over in hatred after receiving the reports from Bethlehem. Whatever respect she'd had for him was in steady decline. Now it just died.

"Look, soon we're going to use our holographic system to keep your image on permanent display and demand that everyone who passes by bow in obeisance to your throne," Radinsky continued in a more soothing tone. "So you need to look your best when we shoot those images and you give your short speech this afternoon."[109]

Suddenly, Alexis' body shuddered and was thrown violently to the floor behind his massive desk, where he writhed and contorted in great agony. René just watched, enjoying Master Lucifer's retribution. Radinsky scowled and went over to the windows overlooking the Dome of the Rock so that he wouldn't have to watch the spectacle.

Within the Global Czar's mind, Lucifer's angry voice rebuked him severely. "Listen you snot-nosed pantywaist, I'm the one in charge and I'm the one who's still got things under control. Oh ye of little faith! Pull yourself together or else I'll raise up a replacement. Keep your eyes fixed on me, not on what others are doing. This is not your battle, it's mine. You are simply my pawn, my shell for this end-game."

D'Antoni's body gave one last shake and then slumped into a pitiful heap. Soon his rapid breathing slowed and he opened his eyes. The glaze was gone, the focus back. He blinked a few times and then struggled to his feet and plunked down in the massive desk chair.

"Okay, you can wipe that smirk off your face," Alexis growled at René. "I'm back to myself. You have no idea what it's like to be totally possessed by him. It's schizophrenic. One moment I feel I could conquer the world, then when he leaves I feel so empty that my worst fears take me over."

"Yeah, sure, whatever," René responded, totally uninterested in however Alexis chose to rationalize his weakness.

Eager to move past the embarrassing incident, Alexis spoke to Radinsky's back. "So, what was it you needed to meet about?"

The illicit Pope, aka the False Prophet, sighed and turned toward the Czar. "I'm afraid Mustafa is getting to be a real problem. I think he's starting to believe that our fake Mahdi and Dajjal are real and that the ridiculous prophecies are true."

"Well, he must have been pretty gullible to be taken in by the likes of you in the first place," Alexis snapped irritably.

Radinsky sighed again, rubbed his tired eyes and sat down on the couch. Ignoring the insult, he continued, "I think that we'll need to eliminate him right after the Madhi's 'miraculous' appearance, but I didn't want to initiate my plan without checking with you first."

"Yeah, sure, whatever," Alexis snarled, mimicking René.

Chapter Fifty-Six

Gus hesitated before opening the door to Sir William's hotel suite in Denver. Frankie had relayed to the security team that the boss was in one hellatious mood.

Taking a deep breath and gritting his teeth, Gus knocked softly and slipped inside, bracing himself for the inevitable onslaught.

"Good God, man, don't slink around like a wuss. You're supposed to be one of my tough guys, so at least try to look like it," Sir William said from the reinforced desk chair they'd had to requisition after the standard hotel issue had collapsed under its heavy load.

"Yes, sir, I'm sorry." Gus squared his shoulders and stood at attention.

"So, don't just stand there like a mute. Did you get the information I requested?"

"Yes, sir," Gus stammered and cleared his throat. Delivering bad news was known to be hazardous duty.

"Our operatives in D.C. have confirmed that your headquarters, your home, was captured last night by a well-armed and well-trained special ops team that caught us by surprise." Gus swallowed hard.

"By surprise? Surprise??" Sir William bellowed. "No one in a security team should ever be surprised by anything. Did any of them escape?"

"Yes, sir, Gordy was able to avoid capture. That's how we got the details."

"Have him executed," Sir William growled, his eyes glowering in fury. Gus cowered, hoping he wouldn't be next.

"Has the assault team arrived yet from the Woodbridge detention center?"

"Yes, sir, plus some marines from Quantico and soldiers from Fort Belvoir . They should be ready to retake headquarters by the end of the day with overwhelming force."

"Okay, but make sure our people are in charge. I don't trust those military types. Hard to know where their loyalties are these days," Sir William snapped. "And don't worry about destroying the mansion. We can always rebuild it, but make sure you capture the leaders alive. They have information we'll want to extract."

Thoughts of torture and locating the east coast centers of resistance brought some soothing comfort to an otherwise annoying morning.

"And what about the rumor we heard about Hollywood?" Sir William asked, reaching over to the coffee table to down another Twinkie.

Gus cleared his throat. "It appears the rumor is true. One of our operatives in Century City just called in. The entire area collapsed into a giant sink hole, probably a delayed reaction to the effects of the tsunami."

"Ah well, no big deal, just a bunch of clowns out there anyway." Sir William actually appeared to be somewhat pleased about its demise. After gorging a second Twinkie, Sir William waved at Gus to leave.

"Uh, sir, one more item has come to our attention," Gus said tentatively and stiffened to deflect the verbal assault certain to come.

"Well, out with it man, or will I have to beat it out of you?"

"Uhm, well, we've heard that Las Vegas was almost totally destroyed by a tornado, and what was left standing is now burning out of control."

Sir William sat back. "Interesting. Another hell-hole vanquished. It appears that the enemy has stepped up the pace."

"The enemy, sir?" Gus queried in spite of himself.

Sir William looked up and glared at the imbecile. "God and the Christians, you idiot. Why do think we're trying to lock them all up? This is war and you don't even know who the enemy is? You're useless, absolutely useless. Get out of here before I fire you or worse."

Gus gratefully scrambled back outside the suite. Before Sir William could finish off the last Twinkie, the phone rang.

He listened for a brief moment and then screamed in rage. "What do you mean the detention center was taken? How? When?"

Sir William listened for a few more moments and then slammed the phone down, angry at himself for being suckered by the enemy. He should have known that attacking his mansion was not the primary objective. After all, Dobson, Wildmon and Limbaugh were not such valuable resources to risk an attack.

Diluting the team at the detention center had been a terrible mistake, one his superiors would hold over his head for a long time. He'd overreacted because his attention had been divided by his obsession with finding the enemy's west coast center of operations. So close, so very close.

He took a deep breath to slow down his palpitating heart and clear his head. He'd have to go back east, but he'd leave this team of bird-brains to continue to close in on their Colorado quarry.

Maybe this was an opportunity, not a disaster after all, he finally decided. With the east coast operatives out in the open, surely they would catch some of them and get them to talk. Then they could search out and destroy both the east and west coast centers at the same time. That would more than make up for the immediate failings.

Reassured, he popped open another can of cola and reached for the leftover breakfast croissant.

*****

As the elevator doors opened underground in the Tennessee Valley, the band piped up and the crowd cheered, stomped, whistled, clapped and otherwise expressed their approval of the militia, just returning from their first triumphant mission.

Randy positively beamed as he led Dr. James Dobson and Rush Limbaugh out of the elevator along with their other rescued captive, Don Wildmon. As head of the Alliance Defense Fund, Wildmon had been a major legal nuisance for the New World Order until he and most of the other leaders had been arrested on trumped-up charges. All three men seemed weary and weak, but not in obvious distress.

Each group of militia that arrived on the elevators was greeted and treated as conquering heroes. When all had arrived, they were escorted to the dining room for an all-day shindig. Soon, Jim, Abby and Randy slipped away for a full debriefing.

About one hundred detainees were freed from the detention center and transported to the remote camp in the Blue Ridge Mountains. They could either remain there or get assistance in returning to their home states if they wished, although most had lost home and family by this point.

When Randy concluded, Jim asked for more detail about the casualties. "The two men you lost in your attack on the detention center, you have their bodies down below?"

"Yes, we were able to retrieve their bodies for a proper burial. Both men were single, so we'll contact their parents or closest relatives to see how they want to handle the funeral. Of course, we can't invite them down here, so we'll hold a special ceremony before taking their bodies back home."

"And the man you lost in D.C.?" Jim prompted.

Randy's lips pursed in regret. "He was wounded, but mobile. Someone got the drop on him and managed to get away with him. I'm afraid that they will torture him and find out our location."

Abby reached over and took the general's hand. "Don't worry, we serve a big God. We'll pray for him and expect that, one way or another, the Lord will have a way of escape or perhaps premature death."

Randy's moist eyes glanced up at her. "I keep forgetting that death can be a reward It's such a disparity from how we in the military treat it only as a complete loss."

"Yes, for us to die is gain,"[110] Abby said, reinforcing the upside down ways of the Kingdom. "I'm sure the Lord will have an even greater party than we are for those two brave men who laid down their lives for their fellow man."[111]

Chapter Fifty-Seven

Events were suddenly accelerating all around the globe. Freakish weather was pummeling every continent. Almost daily earthquakes were destroying many cities and regions. Even as the polar icecaps continued to melt, equatorial tropical regions were experiencing rare freezes and snowstorms. Rising sea levels had swamped New York City, Tokyo and all of the Netherlands. It was as if the earth itself was protesting the New World Order.

Although for the first time in recorded history there continued to be no wars anywhere, except for the ongoing persecution of

Christians and Jews, this was soon to change. Mustafa's plans were working to perfection, and even the elements seemed to be confirming their truth. One of the so-called 'minor' signs of the Mahdi's coming was that there would be great suffering across the earth, and now millions upon millions of people had been dislodged or killed by nature herself under the orchestration of Allah, or so Mustafa thought.. These added to the Ebola-like plague that Mustafa's cohorts released in several Muslim nations.

The Islamic world had already noted with anticipation the emergence of the Sufyani from Damascus, a descendent of Abu Sufyan named Urwa bin Muhammad, just as foretold. He and his army of dissidents had spread tendrils of corruption and disruption across many Muslim nations, culminating in an epic battle in Mina, Saudi Arabia, the traditional gathering place for the Hajj pilgrimage three miles east of Mecca. Meanwhile, the mysterious Yamani had emerged out of Yemen and was reviving terrorist attacks and suicide bombings in the major capitals of the world.

When the Euphrates was unexpectedly diverted by an underground pipeline explosion, the predicted 'mountain' of gold that Mustafa had sown was discovered and a great inter-tribal struggle for the treasure resulted between Sunnis and Shias, just as the hadiths foretold. Mustafa waited until the last possible moment for Allah to send the luminescent star but grew impatient and ordered the rocket fired. As the skies lit up across Arabian skies, expectations for the Mahdi's appearance reached a crescendo, fueled by a barrage of Tweets and Internet conjectures posted by Mustafa's staff.

Then, just as the hadiths prophesied, the Mahdi announced himself between the corner of the Ka'ba and the station of Abraham near the al-Haram Mosque in Mecca just after Ramadan had started. The small army of followers waving the Islamic Black Flags of battle were there to greet him and stir up end-time hysteria across all of Islam. Even as the Mahdi led his army and many new recruits to Kufa in Iraq, the Dajjal abruptly appeared in Jerusalem in front of the Dome of the Rock and the many news reporters Mustafa had planted in advance.

With the unseen cooperation of the Global Czar and local Imams, Masih ad-Dajjal and his followers took over the Temple Mount and the Al Aqsa Mosque in the name of the God of Abraham, Isaac and Jacob. From there, he announced to the world that he was Jesus Christ come to free Jerusalem for the Jews, the Hebrew Messiah coming for the *first* time to reclaim Israel as its earthly and heavenly King.

All of which threw the world into a great furor. Debate raged across the airwaves into every community about whether the Islamic Mahdi and Jewish Redeemer had indeed appeared or whether it was all a fabrication or a product of mass hysteria.

The Global Czar discounted and denounced both as imposters. "There is no god, and there are no saviors from heaven. These are nothing but mere mortals stirring up trouble and attempting to undermine worldwide peace. We will employ the Global Military Command to put down these insurrections immediately." Pope Radinsky added fuel to the fire by declaring the two new redeemers to be nothing but charlatans.

****

Nowhere was the debate more focused than in Egypt where Abraham, Gabriel and their entourage had settled after replicating the flight of Joseph, Mary and Jesus after King Herod had ordered that all the infants in Bethlehem be killed. They had been able to sneak in and out of Jerusalem again to follow Jesus' path when Mary and Joseph took the holy infant there to present Him to the Lord according to the law of Moses: "Every male who opens the womb shall be called holy to the Lord."[112]

Blaine had been confused enough about the journey to Egypt, let alone the Biblical events of Jesus' early days. "You mean that the three wise men did not pay homage to baby Jesus in the stable, or cave, whichever it was, but months later in a house?"

Gabriel laughed and shook his head. "It's a pity how traditional myths have supplanted Biblical truth. Matthew 2:11 clearly says the three wise men visited the infant in a house."

"Nor did the Magi follow a star *in* the east, but *from* the east," Abraham interjected. "Since they were coming from Asia, they travelled from east to west, so to them the star appeared in the western sky. *They* were 'in the east' not the star."[113]

"Then, after the wise men departed, not reporting back to Herod as he'd hoped, an angel appeared to Joseph in a dream warning him that they needed to flee to Egypt to escape Herod's wrath," Carmelita added.[114] "That fulfilled Hosea's prophecy that, 'out of Egypt I called my Son.'"[115]

"I'd never heard about them being in Egypt," Blaine noted. "I guess that's not part of the traditional story. How long did they stay there?"

"Until King Herod died," Gabriel answered. "There are different estimates based on historical records about when he died and, therefore, the length of their stay, but it was at least several years."

"Amazing," Blaine said, shaking her head in disbelief, not of the Scriptures but of humanity's propensity to substitute myth for truth.

"And so now, here we are in the midst of the Muslim world while the Mahdi and a false Jesus appear," Abraham said, also shaking his head in wonder.

"What do you make of it all?" Carmelita asked, snuggling up against the husband she had missed for so long.

"Well, clearly the enemy is at work sowing confusion. The 'father of lies' wants the world to see that these are all myths so that they will also conclude the Biblical Second Coming of Jesus must also be a fable," Abraham answered in repugnance.

"And yet Pope Radinsky represents the Christian faith?" Blaine continued to probe her confusion.

"He has to maintain his cover," Gabriel explained. "*We* know he's a fake, the actual False Prophet, but to the world he must maintain some semblance of Catholicism in order to remain credible."

"But surely the Jews are not going to accept the Islamic Dajjal as their Messiah?" Blaine declared, staring at Abraham for agreement.

"Oh, I wouldn't be so sure about that," Abraham mused, deep in thought. "Taking back the Temple Mount was a major victory. The Jews still want their King more than a Savior. Most have become so secularized over the years and so anti-Christian that many will grab hold of any notable candidate who delivers them from servitude to predominance. That the Dajjal claims to be half-Jewish and half-Muslim is being seized upon by the world as an opportunity for reconciliation of the two faiths."

"What a world, what a mess," Blaine finally concluded, frowning in antipathy.

"Yes, indeed, and getting messier all the time," Abraham concurred. "That's the nature of the end-times, with Jesus coming back just before the world is completely destroyed."

"So, what do we do now?" Carmelita wondered. "Surely we don't have to stay years here in Egypt?"

Gabriel chuckled. "No, we're not going to replicate the timeline, just the journey," he said reassuringly. "Otherwise, we wouldn't get it done before we're raptured out of here prior to the Day of Wrath."

"However," Abraham added, "with Jerusalem and the Islamic world careening out of control, I think it's wise to stay hidden away here until things settle down a bit."

Chapter Fifty-Eight

Reverend Wainwright and Rabbi David conferred in a small makeshift room in the underground basement. Wainwright had fully moved in and brought a number of his constituents too. They were all aghast at the chaos in Jerusalem and their congregation was demanding answers.

Fortunately they were prepared for a long siege. With the general water supplies tainted by blood thanks to their own two witnesses, they were tapping into storage tanks they'd buried below the basement floor some time ago. However, outside their secure hideout, turmoil was rampant.

Large crowds of seekers had gathered on and below the Temple Mount to hear the one-eyed man who claimed to be Jesus Christ. The Old Testament prophets had said the Messiah would be homely, so his deformity was perhaps a sign. That he denied the first imposter who had duped the early Christians and fomented the world's largest, but fraudulent religion spoke into the deepest yearnings of both Orthodox and secular Jews.

For centuries they had endured the claims of Christians that they were blind to their own prophetic Scriptures. Surely they could see that the first Christ fulfilled all the prophecies. How dumb could they be? Well, smart enough to see through the charade, many now countered. The reclusive Essenes had created a Messiah from their midst, many proclaimed, carefully contriving events to recreate the events foretold in the Old Testament. Risen from the dead? Hogwash! The imposter had simply been rescued from the tomb and whisked away for carefully staged appearances later.

Here was the real deal. According to birth records posted on the Internet, the Dajjal had indeed been born in Bethlehem and grew up in Nazareth. The one-eyed boy had been hidden away by his parents, not only because of his deformities, but also because an angel had told them he was the Messiah. And now he had claimed his throne, ridding the Temple Mount of the hated Muslims.

"How can your people be so easily fooled?" Reverend Wainwright asked as gently as he could, not wanting to rile his host.

Rabbi David leaned back in the worn chair, prompting even more stuffing to poke out of its seams. "Ahh, so sad, so sad. To be blind, to have a veil over one's eyes, is to be open to deception.

Now my people are really thrust into the 'valley of decision.' Before I had my vision restored through an angelic encounter, I too could find numerous ways to reject and repudiate all the claims concerning Christianity. It was actually quite easy and it felt very right."

Rabbi David's eyes turned inward. Boris sat very still, not wanting to interrupt the flow. "My people have been so persecuted, so downtrodden for so long, that any glimmer of hope stirs an inner yearning that is like a drug, a spiritual aphrodisiac. Furthermore, Scripture also tells us that God Himself will send spirits of deception that will cloud the minds of those who He knows will never accept the truth."[116]

When Rabbi David appeared to be finished, Reverend Wainwright voiced a pet peeve that spoke to that last comment. "Many Christians have also been led astray by the concept of 'predestination,' not fully understanding that God has already seen the end and knows the decisions we will make of our own free will. That word has been mistranslated and misconstrued, but our world of time doesn't have the words to convey eternal principles. What it really means is that God knew from the beginning who would or would not be saved, but not because He made those choices Himself."

David's head tilted sideways as he took in this explanation. "Quite so. I hadn't ever thought about it quite like that, but knew in my heart that the so-called 'elect' always had the free will to make their own choices. God merely chooses, or elects, those whom He knows will respond to the call. But enough ruminating. We need to determine how we will respond to this new crisis."

"Well," Boris said reluctantly, "I suppose we'll need to stand up for the truth, in the absence of our two witnesses."

"Yes, we will," the rabbi concurred. "The question is not if, but when, where and how."

"Must we step into the middle of the tempest on the Temple Mount?" Boris said, grimacing at the prospect.

"I don't suppose there's any other choice," David lamented. "But let's pray about it. Perhaps we'll get a reprieve."

Chapter Fifty-Nine

Alexis stared in fascination at the wild scene spread before him from his unique vantage point high above the Dome of the Rock and the Temple Mount that had, at least for now, been restored to the Jews. All in a name, he mused to himself. Well, soon it would only be *his* name, not just as Global Czar but then as god himself.

In the meantime, he'd try to enjoy the antics below and not allow himself to get irritated about it all. What a bunch of fools, all of them, including Mustafa, Radinsky and René. But in the end, he'd eliminate all of them. For the moment, however, Mustafa would get to play a leading role. He'd better enjoy it, because it would be his last.

Inside the Al Aqsa Mosque, now being torn apart by the raging Jews, Mustafa stood off to the side evaluating his handiwork. With the Dajjal getting established here, he'd soon have to return to Kufa and meet up with the Mahdi to orchestrate the next event. But was it really him doing the orchestrating anymore? Things had taken on a life of their own.

And whenever he was with the Mahdi, pretending to be his servant, it felt real. When the Mahdi called him Isa al-Maseeh, something stirred in him beyond the pretense. More and more he couldn't get it out of his mind that perhaps that's who Allah had created him to be, only now emerging into the truth. If so, then he would soon have to return and destroy the Dajjal in order to fulfill the prophecies.

Shaking off the imaginations that enflamed his soul, he refocused on the present. Signaling to his band of assistants, he indicated that it was time for the Dajjal to make his triumphant ride through the streets of Jerusalem. Opening a side door, one assistant led a gigantic mule out onto the Mount where shocked worshipers backed away.

Mustafa laughed at the double joke. While fulfilling the hadith about the Dajjal travelling on a giant mule, it also mocked the myth about Jesus riding into Jerusalem on a donkey.[117] As prophecies went, a giant mule clearly trumped a puny donkey.

When the Dajjal, a brutish hulk of a man, mounted the large mule, they seemed fit to one another, two freaks of nature making one natural. Riding off the Mount, the well-placed flunkies spread palm branches and even coats across the Dajjal's path. A large cheering crowd followed, surprisingly including many Muslims.

No, not all that surprising, Mustafa remembered, because some of the hadiths said that the Dajjal, also known as the Great Deceiver, would perform deceptive signs that would lead Muslims to believe that the Dajjal is 'Lord.' It was so hard keeping all the prophecies in mind because some were supported only by the Sunnis, while others solely by the Shia, with many of them in conflict with one another. So Mustafa had to pick and choose, hoping to appease both groups.

So now on to the next 'miraculous' sign. Mustafa gave a wave to his assistants and soon a convoy left and headed off in a different route to get ahead of the Dajjal's procession through Jerusalem. When they had arrived at their predetermined destination, they opened a large door leading into the depths of an underground garage. When the Dajjal arrived there on the giant mule, they were led inside while his vastly growing number of followers were kept outside, being informed that 'Jesus' needed to pray.

Once the large garage door closed, the Dajjal and the mule got inside a large military vehicle that quickly left out a rear exit and rapidly traversed the city into the shelter of another garage from where they emerged toward a stage that was in the process of being set up. Soon the Dajjal was exhorting a new crowd seeded with Mustafa plants and broadcast by an Arab TV network that was cooperating with Mustafa. Then the Dajjal and his mule were surreptitiously airlifted to Tel Aviv where another surprise appearance satisfied yet another hadith, that the Dajjal would miraculous move in great speed from place to place. Mustafa skipped the Tel Aviv trip in order to meet up with Muhammad, the Mahdi, in Kufa, about 100 miles south of Baghdad.

Meanwhile, Rabbi David and Reverend Wainwright had been on a futile mission to address the crowds gathering around the Dajjal because they seemed to arrive at each location shortly after he'd moved on, only to pop up again some distance away. They concluded that they had been somewhat presumptuous in assuming they were to jump immediately into the fray, apologizing to the Lord, willing now to wait for Him to open the door or signal the right time.

Chapter Sixty

Sir William sat in his old office contemplating the mess. It disturbed his hardened heart and seared soul to have had his power and pleasure center violated to such an extent. However, on the other hand, it could be a lot worse, a whole lot worse. That the occupiers had willingly abandoned the premises once the detention center to the south had been taken was a personal blessing, although a severe blow to his career and Lucifer's plans.

The loss of the three retired Christian leaders didn't trouble him all that much, though his superiors felt otherwise. After all, the three no longer had a platform to spout their ridiculous drivel. Christian radio was a thing of the past and all major faith organizations had been forcibly shut down. The symbolic value of parading them before the media had already been attained.

No, the real problem right now was restoring his *own* sense of order. Without that, his mind and heart would be in turmoil and all the rest would suffer as a result. The *feng shui* of the carefully established atmosphere had been severely compromised. With that decided, Sir William called in his Japanese interior decorator. Soon a swarm of carpenters, painters, electricians and plumbers set about to repair all the damage and restore things to exactly the way they were before.

Well, not exactly, since some rare, expensive artwork and artifacts could not be duplicated. But they could be replaced with items of equal import. Money had never been a concern for Sir William. Born to leftover industrial-era wealth, he had made prudent investments over the years, most driven by insider knowledge resulting from being an integral part of the Illuminati, as had his father and grandfather before him.

Midst the beehive of activity that was music to his soul, Harriet knocked at the door. As usual, she was a sight to behold, dressed in a skimpy, tight outfit. Why he'd never thought to have a beautiful woman as his Chief of Staff before was hard to fathom. Now he was glad that Henri had been killed in the first attack. Not only was Harriet better looking, but she was smarter too. And he loved the way she teased him during the day and then delivered at night.

"Well, well, your royal highness, you finally have some color back in that handsome face of yours," Harriet cooed as she provocatively slid onto Sir William's lap.

"What kind of decorum is this for the top person in my organization?" Sir William snapped, trying to appear serious.

"Just the kind you like, big boy," she said as she pinched his ample cheeks. "But before we play, you have some serious business to take care of."

When Harriet jumped off his lap, he knew she wasn't jesting. "Okay, what is it?" he sighed.

"We've got that Christian prisoner singing like a canary," Harriet crowed.

Sir William laughed. He really enjoyed the way she spoke in cliché's, but even more so the way she took credit for everything. Now that was his kind of woman.

"Good, good. It's about time we caught a break. Do I need to go down there?" Sir William began to lean forward, hoping the answer was no.

Now Harriet laughed. It had only taken her a couple of days to figure out most of Sir William's ways. He was so self-focused, so pleasure-oriented, so transparently hedonistic, that everything else rested on that foundation. She was ambitious and ruthless and would do anything to be promoted into the upper echelon of the Illuminati. Sir William was her ticket there. For now she'd appease him in every way possible, but there would come a time when he'd be expendable.

"No, don't strain yourself," she smirked, "I've got it all under control."

Sir William eased back down again, relieved, but also wary. Harriet's ambition would become a detriment at some point, but until then he'd take everything she was willing to give.

"So what is our songbird singing about?" he queried with a come hither look that Harriet ignored.

"Oh, just the exact location of their little hideout in the Tennessee Valley," she answered, striking a sultry pose.

"Really? You're sure that he's not just making it all up?" he queried needlessly, even as his eyes checked out every part of her exquisite body.

"Oh, he tried that," she responded with a sultry pout. "But after we removed a few fingers, toes and other anatomical parts, I'm certain it's real. GPS coordinates, the location of their secret entrance and the bar code to get inside."

Harriet knew that torture details were a real turn-on for the sadomasochist. She'd withhold them until he begged, and then she'd extract yet another favor. "So, big boy, want to celebrate?" she said in a husky voice.

"Close the door," Sir William gasped, almost unable to speak.

Chapter Sixty-One

Abraham was pacing back and forth across the basement below the old Coptic Church. Gabriel found it amusing, but it was starting to drive Blaine crazy. Not only had she never liked being enclosed below ground, but she also was extremely averse to sitting around doing nothing for days on end. Worse was the fact that this damp, depressing repository used to be an Egyptian Pharaonic mortuary temple.

She shivered just thinking about it. She'd known something was odd about the massive structure the moment they'd arrived in the dark of night. She could feel it in her bones, in her spirit. Located on the west bank of the Nile, opposite the city of Luxor, Deir el Bahri was one of many ancient Pharaonic temples that were taken over by the early Egyptian Christians.

The world "deir" actually means church, Blaine was able to find out when their hosts allowed her to interview some of the Coptic elders. It felt good to fire up the journalistic skills that had been pushed to the backburner for awhile. What she'd found out had been absolutely mind-boggling and had kept her preoccupied for a few days.

Before Egypt became an Islamic state, it was mostly a Christian country. It was a land where Jesus and His family were known to have traveled, and where early Apostles came to spread His word, at first in Alexandria. Although tourists are attracted to a number of churches in old, Coptic Cairo, most of the ancient churches are located in monasteries and smaller cities throughout Egypt. Many of these are built on sacred ground where it is believed that the baby Jesus and His family made stops in their journey through Egypt.

The Copts, which now constitute the largest religious minority in Egypt, claim descent from the ancient Egyptians. The word *copt* is derived from the Arabic word *qubt,* meaning Egyptian. The Coptic language is the final stage of the development of the ancient Egyptian language. Tradition has it that Egypt was Christianized during the first century A.D. by the Apostle Mark, when the country was part of the Roman Empire.

As Christianity exploded across the region, a paucity of buildings led the early Coptic Christians to modify many of the ancient structures from the days of the Pharaohs. The Coptic Church that was currently the sanctuary for the two witnesses and their retinue was renamed Deir el Bahri. Beforehand, it was known as Hatshepsut's Mortuary Temple. They converted the massive temple into a Coptic monastery, Pa Phoibammon. The upper terrace was settled by Christian monks who used the large hall for worship services.

The monastery remained inhabited until around 780 AD, but was abandoned shortly after that. Most of the structure then deteriorated, to be rebuilt by modern craftsmen. However, the current Islamic state eliminated virtually all traces of its Christian time of occupation. With the crackdown against Christians, many literally went underground along the West Bank of the Nile. These people were known as "Anchorites," a term which was given to those who were unable to pay exorbitant taxes and as a result lost their homes and possessions. They often occupied the empty tombs, including the Hatshepsut's mortuary.

The Mortuary Temple of Queen Hatshepsut is situated beneath the cliffs at el Bahari on the west bank of the Nile near the Valley of the Kings in Egypt. The mortuary temple was dedicated to the sun god Amon-Ra. Hatshepsut's temple employed lengthy, colonnaded terraces, with the three layered terraces reaching 97 feet tall. Each 'story' is articulated by a double colonnade of square piers. These terraces are connected by long ramps which were once surrounded by gardens.

In ancient Egypt, the mortuary temple usually adjoined a pyramid built in honor of a deceased Pharaoh and had an open, pillared court, storerooms, five elongated shrines, and a chapel containing a false door and an offering table. In the chapel, priests performed the daily funerary rites and presented the offerings to the dead king's *ka* (protective spirit). Perhaps it was these spirits that were unnerving her so much, Blaine thought.

In order to get Abraham to stop pacing, she decided to ask him about such spirits. "Rabbi Abraham, surely the stories about the dead king's *ka* are just fairy tales, right?"

It was as if the rabbi hadn't heard a word. He kept right on pacing, never losing a beat. So Pastor Gabriel cleared his throat to gain Blaine's attention.

"No, not fairy tales," he began to explain, "but not the king's spirit either. Demons who resided in or near the king during his life, may remain behind for a variety of reasons. These are the ghosts people often report seeing or sensing, or the *chindi* the Navajos speak of."

Blaine remembered her own jousting with poltergeists that Reverend Wainwright drove away. "Can't we just chase them away?"

Gabriel smiled patiently. It took awhile to understand how Satan's network of demons functioned. It was not a subject that most Christians broached.

"Yes, we can, in Jesus' name and authority," Gabriel said. "But, it's only temporary. Because of their relationship to the deceased and those funerary rights, which are sheer witchcraft, they have earned a right to be here and so will return. Only when a person with legitimate rights to undo the past does so, will the banishment become permanent. I once had to clear out a demon who'd become a nuisance in a widow's home. She, thinking it the spirit of her dead husband, at first welcomed its presence. But when the lights and TV turning on and off got to be too much of a hassle, I explained it wasn't her husband. She then agreed to rescind her prior welcoming remarks and I cast it out permanently."

"But if we were to keep chasing them away, we could remain free of them while we're here, right?" Blaine asked hopefully.

Gabriel laughed. "Sure, but that's more effort than it's worth. They can't harm us, so I don't care whether they're here or not. But if it bothers you so much, you can continue to chase them away for as long as you like."

Blaine blinked nervously. "Me?"

"Yes, you. Mark 16:17-18 says *all* believers can cast out demons in Jesus' name, so you've got as much right and power to do so as I do. The only hindering factor is unbelief."

Blaine took that all in, but felt somewhat self-conscious about doing so in front of God's two witnesses. Maybe she didn't have enough belief. She'd give it a try that night when they were all asleep. Perhaps then she too would be able to finally sleep peacefully too.

In the meantime, she'd also pray that the Lord would give them release from this dreadful place as soon as possible.

Chapter Sixty-Two

Muhammad bin Abdullah, the Mahdi, the 'guided one' rode out of Mecca on a white horse trailed by an enormous crowd of wildly fanatical followers, many waving Black Flags, symbolic of an Islamic army heading off into battle. Although there were some well-equipped soldiers and terrorists among them, for the most part the mob consisted of everyday Muslims of all stripes, many of whom were also well-armed. They travelled in cars and trucks, on camels, mules and donkeys or on foot, headed where they had not a clue.

Just as the first Muhammad had done, this fake Muhammad's first steps were to raise an army and go to war. Although many of the Muslims along for the ride had, on the surface, espoused to the world that Islam was a 'peaceful' religion, in their heart of hearts they knew that slaying infidels and unbelievers was the highest calling of Allah. They especially looked forward to killing off all the despised Jews.

Left behind in the Mahdi's wake in Mecca were many who sensed there was something wrong, but couldn't quite prove their contention that this was all a staged show. Certainly many of the prophecies were being fulfilled before their very eyes, but still it all felt too contrived. However, their voices were drowned out in the euphoria that trailed behind the Mahdi like a bride's wedding train.

As the procession headed north, through Saudi Arabia, it picked up more and more followers virtually every mile of the journey. The Mahdi seemed to be superhuman, never stopping, eating or sleeping. Those on foot either dropped by the wayside or scrounged a ride in a vehicle or on an animal. People took turns driving so as not to stop except for gas and to pick up some food. Eventually, the train of people being dragged along by the Mahdi stretched back over one hundred miles.

After three days, the Mahdi and those followers on the lead lap arrived in Kufa, Iraq, about 100 miles south of Baghdad. Located along the Euphrates, it is just south of where the original city of Babylon first flourished, which now was just a pile of rubble covered with sand. It was just outside of Kufa that the 'mountain of gold' had been discovered, with Shiites and Sunnis contesting still ownership.

Although Kufa was largely populated by the Shia sect, the Sunnis to the north laid claim to the gold based on deeds that were written (most likely forged) back when Saddam Hussein ruled the land. When the Mahdi set up camp in a field adjacent to the river, local leaders begged for an audience to present their case for taking possession of all the gold. Like Solomon, Muhammad decreed that the gold be split, but not just in half. He would also take a third to finance his growing militia. No one seemed eager to dispute the decision, since it had been prophesied in the hadiths that the Mahdi would settle the matter.

The following morning, a disguised Mustafa arrived stealthily for a meeting with Muhammad. "Greetings, sire, may peace be upon you," Mustafa said as he bowed before his creation. Too many eyes and ears to do otherwise, but somehow it still felt right.

"Isa, I have been looking forward to being with you again. Congratulations on your handling of the Dajjal in Jerusalem."

Mustafa blushed with pride. Yes things were all going quite well. To have the Mahdi recognize it was something else entirely.

"How are things progressing in Damascus?" Muhammad inquired, placing his hand on Mustafa's shoulder.

"All the reports bode well, but I feel a need to check it out for myself," Mustafa answered with downcast eyes.

"Very well, do so. It is important for you to feel comfortable because this is the place and the time for you, Isa al-Maseeh, to make his debut."

When Mustafa dared to look up into the Mahdi's eyes, he saw a twinkle that gladdened his heart. *Oh Allah, I beg of you to allow me to fulfill this role with your blessing,* he prayed silently.

"But before you go, let us review the details of our plans to capture Jerusalem and then all of Israel," the Mahdi suggested. Although it felt like an order, he was pleased to be able to spend time with Muhammad.

"Although it is foretold that we will triumph," Muhammad added as he led Mustafa into the dining tent where a lavish meal was just being laid out, "such prophecies depend upon our fulfilling our roles with due diligence, using the superior minds Allah has given us for this very purpose."

Chapter Sixty-Three

Jim and Abby were awakened in the middle of the night by frantic knocking on their bedroom door in the underground fortress. Sandra, one of the night shift communication center technicians, looked almost apoplectic when the bleary-eyed Jim opened the door.

"Come quick!" she cried out urgently. "Fran is on the line. She says it is absolutely imperative to speak with you immediately. I think we're in some kind of danger."

Jim and Abby quickly put on their bathrobes and hustled down the hall to the central station. Like the Havenwood hideaways, CIA-East was laid out in hallways off a central communications hub, perhaps out of nostalgia, or more likely because it was very efficient. Unlike the hideaways, these halls were gleaming metal and glass with a tiled floor.

Although it was nearly two a.m., the hub was alive with activity. Since the enemy never slept, neither would the Counter-Insurgency Agency. Jim ran to the red phone that connected the eastern and western CIA centers.

"Fran, this is Jim. What's up?" His heart rate, that was up for sure.

"One of our technicians picked up a warning signal in one of the email accounts we hack into on a regular basis," Fran began breathlessly. "Apparently, your militia guy that was captured broke under torture. He's revealed your location and Sir William is mobilizing a strike force."

Jim's brain was still groggy so he took a few moments to digest the stunning news. "When?" was all his tongue could muster to inquire.

"Soon, but there's not an exact time set yet, most likely within the next forty-eight hours." Fran hesitated, and then said, "I hope you guys have a good defensive strategy."

"Yeah, so do I," Jim mumbled while Abby was poking his shoulder trying to find out what was going on.

"Thanks, Fran, you're a real treasure," Jim said, wanting to add more but was incapable of forcing his neurons to wake up faster.

He just stood there a moment in shock, until Abby shook him out of his trance. "Jim, what is it, tell me!"

After giving Abby the brief message from Fran, she was filled with questions. "How big a strike force? What kind of weapons will they bring against us? Are they going to employ aircraft or just come on the ground? A sneak attack or a major assault?"

Jim felt a bit sheepish. He should have asked Fran more questions. He handed the phone to Abby who redialed CIA-West over the special satellite link Fran's team had illicitly set up across government-controlled airwaves.

After she'd extracted what information she could, she gave her sleepy, shell-shocked husband and co-leader a reassuring hug.

Then she sent Sandra off to fetch Randy. While they waited for him, she brewed a fresh pot of coffee and took the thermal carafe with her to the conference room.

Jim gulped down a first cup and then poured a refill before sitting down. Finally his head was beginning to clear. When Randy arrived, he let Abby fill him in on the situation since she now knew more than he did.

"Fran says it's too soon to know how and when they're going to attack," Abby concluded. "But from all indications, it's going to be a full-scale air and ground assault, possibly with tactical nuclear weapons since we're in such an isolated area, not that the Global Government would worry about innocent bystanders."

"I assume she's going to keep an eye on things and will let us know if and when she learns anything more," Randy noted, not yet fully aware of Fran's capabilities.

Abby and Jim both nodded emphatically. "Oh, yes, she's the best resource we have," Abby stated categorically.

"So then, I guess we should go to Code Red?" Randy stated more than asked.

Jim nodded again. "Yes, even though we've got a little time, it's best to start early since we've never done this before except in drills."

"I guess we'll find out for sure whether this facility has indeed been designed to withstand bunker bombs and tactical nuclear weapons, although it may never come to that," Randy noted.

"Huh? You don't think the government will do everything in its power to wipe us out?" Jim responded in a voice of amazement. Did Randy still not get it? Did he not realize they had become enemy number one in America, along with their sister facility in Colorado?

"Yes, of course I do," Randy quickly answered, not wanting them to get the wrong idea. "It just depends on what Gregory told them."

"I think we should assume he told them everything," Abby stated. "Better safe than sorry."

Randy smiled enigmatically. "Absolutely, I fully agree. But what you don't know is that I gave our militia soldiers false information about our GPS coordinates and entry codes. It's possible that they might have discovered my ruse, but my officers were under oath not to reveal that information unless absolutely necessary. To date, that hasn't happened, at least that I'm aware of."

Jim and Abby both sat back stared at Randy for awhile and then broke out in wide grins. "You sly devil, you," Jim finally snickered.

"No, not of the devil," Randy quickly corrected the common idiom. "I felt that God had placed that idea in my mind while I was showering one morning."

"Probably so, probably so," Jim mumbled, a bit embarrassed to have unwittingly given the devil the credit.

"So, then, what GPS coordinates might they have?" Abby asked.

"To another valley about fifty miles southwest of here," Randy said with a satisfied smirk.

"Well, well, aren't we the clever one," Abby grinned.

"Still, we can't assume that ploy will work," Jim cautioned, although feeling quite relieved that there was a possible escape from the situation.

"That's right," Randy agreed. "So I'll get to work immediately to get locked down defensively and set up our counter measures should they actually attack us here. By the way, the escape tunnels are almost complete. We'll redouble our efforts and cut some corners to ensure a secure evacuation route in the next day or so."

Chapter Sixty-Four

The entombed entourage of the two witnesses was startled awake by two of the Copt priests. "Come quickly, trouble is on the way."

As they rubbed sleep from their eyes, Abraham asked, "Trouble? What kind of trouble?"

"The Mahdi has stirred up the entire Islamic world," the elder priest answered. "Muslims are rioting all over, destroying foreign property and hunting down infidels to kill."

"Infidels," Gabriel snorted, "meaning anyone who isn't a Muslim."

Abraham and Gabriel exchanged glances. Were they to use their powers or slink away like frightened fugitives? A quick check with the Holy Spirit quickened their spirits.

"We kind of like it here," Gabriel declared, a quixotic smile playing across his face.

"Are you crazy or stupid?" the younger priest blurted out in both surprise and disapproval.

The older priest smacked him on the arm. "Mind your manners. Do you not know who these men are?"

"It is not we who decide these things," Abraham gently offered to the younger priest. "It is the Holy Spirit, and He is telling us we need to make a stand for Jesus against this false redeemer and all he stands for."

"Don't say we didn't warn you," snapped the young priest as he turned and fled outside.

"Please excuse him," the elder priest apologized. "He's young in the Lord and hasn't yet experienced the power of His might. Fear has engulfed our entire Christian community. Dozens have already been beheaded, and a mob is headed this way. They tortured one of our priests who gave you away."

Blaine's tired eyes widened in concern. "Are you two sure about staying?"

Carmelita went over and sat next to Blaine and put her arm around her. "Remember, our two witnesses will not be overcome until after the mid-point of the Tribulation."

Blaine frowned. "Yeah, but the Bible doesn't say anything about those who stand with them."

"Well then, remember what happened in Bali," Carmelita suggested. "Every believer with them was protected."

Blaine chuckled at her own journalistic-bred skepticism. "Yes, but there are no Banyan trees or volcanoes here."

Now it was Carmelita's turn to laugh. "No, but it is not the trees, nor the volcanoes, nor even these two witnesses who provide the protection. It is the Lord God Almighty."

Blaine sighed. "Yes, I know, and I've already seen many miracles on this journey. But fear comes anyway and almost completely takes me over."

Carmelita glanced over at Abraham and her beloved husband who were kneeling together, holding hands and praying. Vy and Aly were standing guard with their automatic weapons at the ready.

Turning back to Blaine, she said, "Fear strikes at everyone. It's a natural reaction. But fear is only of this world. There is no fear in heaven. So we must put on our God cloak and seek His Kingdom within, and ignore what our natural senses tell us about the outside world."

Blaine found it difficult to shut off her logical mind and enter into the Spirit. "So what do I look for when I seek the Kingdom that's supposedly within me?"[118]

Carmelita held Blaine tight. So many new Christians struggled with the ongoing war between Spirit and flesh. Even the Apostle Paul wrote about it, how the spirit was willing, but the flesh was weak.[119] Only practice and experience provide the necessary lessons, and so many people avoid the very circumstances that would strengthen their faith.

"Seek God's love first and foremost,[120] because *"perfect love casts out fear."*[121] Only God has perfect, unconditional love," Carmelita whispered gently, not wanting to disturb the prayers of the two witnesses.

"Then," she continued. "after you connect your spirit to God's love, allow His power to flow through you. The Scriptures say that, *'God has not given us a spirit of fear, but of power and of love and of a sound mind.'*[122] We have to learn to live in this upside-down world from the inside out, allowing the spirit to rule the mind and heart, not the other way around."

Blaine closed her eyes to seek the Holy Spirit within her. As she opened herself up to His perfect love, she could almost feel a switch turned on. A wave of love so strong swept through her that she had to grab Carmelita's arm to keep from falling over. And indeed, as she allowed the love to flow, the fear dissolved away.

The sounds of the approaching mob began to echo inside the stone mausoleum. Abraham and Gabriel arose and waved for Carmelita and Blaine to follow them outside.

"Put away your guns," Abraham said to Vy and Aly. "We won't be needing them."

The raging torrent of angry, bloodthirsty voices had grown to a feverish pitch. When the two witnesses emerged onto the lower terrace, the crowd had just reached the bottom of the stairs.

"There they are!" several screamed and led a charge toward the reviled Christians.

In unison, Gabriel and Abraham waved their right arms outward toward the charging throng who immediately were thrown backward, much like Jesus did when the rabble first came to arrest him.[123]

The mob was stunned, but in their demonic fury they picked themselves up, pulled out their swords and guns, and renewed their charge up the stairs.

Again, the two witnesses simply waved their arms and the hundreds of frothing Muslims were thrown back even further. Some sprang to their feet to fire their weapons, but the witnesses merely held out their right palms and the guns froze, the triggers refusing to budge.

As the voices stilled in shocked silence, Gabriel spoke up. "We do not wish to harm you. You can try all you want, but the Creator of the universe, the One True God will not allow you to carry out your Satanic desires."

Blaine turned to Carmelita. "I didn't know Gabriel spoke Arabic."

Carmelita's face was aglow. "He doesn't. The Holy Spirit is enabling him to speak in another language just like disciples at Pentecost."[124]

Several tried to fire their weapons again only to throw them down in disgust. "Allah Akbar!" many others shouted in defiance.

"Allah is *not* great," answered Abraham, also speaking fluent Arabic. "Allah *is* Satan and you have been deceived. Allah is a god of hatred and violence. Jesus is a God of mercy and grace.[125] Feel His love and forgiveness flowing out through us. He alone offers the promise of redemption and salvation. It is a free gift. Come and receive it."

There was a restless stirring in the crowd, confusion mingling with revulsion, anger and hope vying for supremacy. A few began to openly weep, only to be struck and rebuked by the remaining zealots. Suddenly, the focus of the mob turned inward and a great fight broke out.

About a quarter of the mob broke free and began to run away from their tormentors, up the stairs toward the two witnesses who calmly waited for a moment of separation between those who sought truth and those who were married to the lie.

The remaining fanatics hesitated to follow the deserters onto the stairs, remembering all too well the power that had driven them back twice already. That created space between the two groups. Abraham and Gabriel simultaneously clapped their hands, as the Holy Spirit had shown them in their prayer time.

Loud thunder roared as bolts of lightning shot down from the cloudless morning sky and consumed those who continued to swear allegiance to Allah. When the smoke cleared, there were only mounds of ashes where once several hundred zealots had stood.[126]

Those who had responded to the Holy Spirit's call threw themselves at the feet of the two witnesses. "See that you do not worship us. Worship only Jesus. Repent of your sins and receive Him now as Lord of your life."

Gabriel and Abraham proceeded to minister individually to each of the weeping converts and then led them in a glorious procession down the hill to the banks of the Nile where they baptized them all.

Crowds lined the banks to watch, having been drawn by the awesome lightning display. Many of them also responded to the Holy Spirit's call and splashed out into the water to be saved and baptized. By nightfall, an enormous crowd of new converts gathered to hear Abraham and Gabriel preach God's Word on the steps of the mortuary temple.

Chapter Sixty-Five

Mustafa was nervous. The time of reckoning was almost upon him. Fortunately, the flight from Bassel Al Assad International Airport, north of Damascus near Latakia, was smooth and quiet giving him a chance to think about the momentous occasion to commence in just another fifteen minutes or so.

He and Muhammad, the Mahdi, had selected the northern, quieter airport over the Damascus International Airport to maintain secrecy. But this also gave Mustafa the opportunity to survey the area from the air. As a young man, he had spent some time in Damascus. It was where he'd come to know his spiritual calling as well as his sexual orientation.

Since homosexuality was contrary to the precepts of Islam and against the law specifically in Syria, his underworld contacts had led him to a Church of Satan where he felt accepted and loved. The chief priest there was also a member of the so-called 'black priesthood' within the Catholic Church. This in turn led him to Cardinal Radinsky before he became Pope.

Yet now he was returning to his roots, soon to rebel against the Pope and embrace his role within the Islamic end-time revolution. His sexual proclivities had not been an issue, and were even an asset within the dark underpinnings of Catholicism. Nor did they pose a political or spiritual dilemma when he was orchestrating the emergence of a fake Mahdi and a phony Islamic apocalypse. So how could he now reconcile himself with the Qur'an?

Somehow, the Mahdi had almost convinced Mustafa that his role as Isa al-Maseeh was not an act, but real. He'd gone along with the delusion to encourage the Mahdi to fully embrace his role as the Islamic messiah, never expecting to question whether his own role was more than an illusion. Yet here he was entertaining the notion that all of this was real, that it wasn't him organizing events but rather Allah directing him.

Well, real or not, the die was about to be cast. Perhaps then he'd resolve his conundrum. He sighed, took a deep breath and glanced down at the northern suburbs of Damascus spread out below him. The "City of Jasmin," the capital of Syria, was widely considered to be the oldest continuously inhabited city in the world. And what a bizarre, topsy-turvy history it had.

First it had become a battleground between the Hittites to the north and the Egyptians to the south. Then the Phoenicians, the "Sea Peoples" had taken over. Later, Aramaic kingdoms were formed as Aramaeans abandoned their nomadic lifestyle and formed federated tribal states, one of them Aram-Damascus. The Hebrew Bible recounted the many battles between the Jews and

Aramaeans, with Israel gaining control after Ben-Hadad II was captured after besieging Samaria. A treaty with King Ahab of Israel led to a jointly won battle against the Assyrians.[127]

However, by the 8th century BC, Damascus was engulfed by the Assyrians and entered its own 'dark age.' Nonetheless, it remained the economic and cultural center of the Near East. After subsequently being taken over by the Babylonians, it fell to Alexander the Great only to be retaken by the Seleucidites. In 64 BC, the Roman general Pompey annexed it into its league of ten cities known as the Decapolis and became an important center of Greco-Roman culture.

It was during the Roman occupation that Saint Paul received his vision on the road to Damascus from Jerusalem, being struck blind and subsequently converting to Christianity.[128] Little remained of Roman architecture, but the Old City borough of Bab Tuma where the Apostles Paul and Thomas both lived for awhile was well-preserved. Bab Tuma was also the birthplace of several Popes and still houses ancient churches devoted to the two Apostles.

Damascus was later conquered by the Arab general Khalid ibn al-Walid in 635 AD, although the population remained mostly Christian for some time. However, more and more Arab Muslims from Mecca, Medina and the Syrian desert began to change the face and makeup of the city as time went on. In 715, construction of the Umayyad Mosque, the Grand Mosque of Damascus, was completed over the site that had originally been the Christian Cathedral of St. John, dedicated to John the Baptist.

Damascus soon entered a confusing time of constant turmoil as various Arab groups and Muslim sects vied for control. However, stability returned in the late 11th century when the Seljuk Turks took over and were successful in resisting the Crusaders who had conquered Jerusalem, Lebanon and Palestine. The Mongols invaded in 1260, only to fall to the Egyptians a few decades later. The Black Death plague in 1348-1349 wiped out almost half the city's population.

In early 1516, the Ottoman Turks reclaimed Damascus and ruled for the next 400 years, except for a brief occupation by Ibrahim Pasha of Egypt in the 1830s. The massacre of Christians in 1860 was one of the most notorious incidents of these times when fighting between Druze and Maronites in Lebanon spilled over into Damascus. The Druze began as an offshoot of Islam, but later incorporated other philosophies to become an "Islamic reformatory sect." The Maronites were from the Lebanese Catholic church, founded in the 5th century by a Syriac monk, Saint Maron.

In the early 20th century, the legendary T. E. "Lawrence of Arabia" drove the Turks out of Damascus and named Faisal ibn Hussein King of Syria. After World War I, the French made Damascus the capital of their League of Nations Mandate of Syria. When the Druze revolted in 1925, the French suppressed them brutally, bombing and shelling the city. In 1941, Damascus was captured from the French by the Allies during the Syrian-Lebanon campaign of World War II. In 1945, the French once more bombed Damascus, but the British forces intervened and the French agreed to withdraw, leading to the full independence of Syria in 1946 with Damascus as its capital.

As Mustafa reflected on this tumultuous past, it was no wonder that it was a peripatetic place of befuddled identity. Though three-quarters of the population were now Sunni Muslims with over 2,000 mosques, the alcoholic drink Arak was a popular beverage served at most occasions, and coffee houses proliferated. While the city itself contained 1.7 million people, the surrounding metropolis had grown to over 4 million inhabitants.

He glanced back down at the ground below. The semi-arid plateau was located in the eastern foothills of the Anti-Lebanon mountain range, which separates Syria from Lebanon, the name being derived from the Greek word 'anti' meaning 'opposite.' He saw the almost dry Barada river snaking its way southeast into the heart of Damascus. Under the almost dark skies of the early morning hour, the flat metropolis spread far from the core of Old City Damascus where he was headed.

Soon he could see the massive Umayyad Mosque on the horizon. He stared closely at one of the largest and oldest mosques in the world, located on one of the holiest sites in Damascus. Mustafa recalled his shock when he first saw the shrine within the mosque which contains the supposed head of John the Baptist, honored as a prophet by Christians and Muslims alike. He was there with Cardinal Radinsky in 2001 when Pope John Paul II visited the mosque, primarily to visit the relics of John the Baptist. It was the first time a pope paid a visit to a mosque.

The spot where the mosque now stands had been a temple of Hadad in the Aramaean era. The three minarets were now visible as dawn's early light began to glow. The footprint of the huge, almost square structure encompassed approximately two city blocks on each side. The mosque was arranged around a vast courtyard that connected to different areas of the mosque.. The courtyard is famed for its pavement of black and white geometric patterns and the façade is decorated with intricately cut and variously colored stones. The courtyard contains two ablutions fountains.

Inside, the prayer hall consisted of three aisles, supported by tall columns. The interior was mostly plain white, although it contains what is thought to be the largest mosaic in the world at over 4,000 square meters. The minaret in the southeast corner is called the Minaret of Jesus because many Muslims believe that it is here Jesus will appear at the end of the world. And it was to this minaret Mustafa was headed.

The camouflaged glider in which he rode floated along effortlessly behind the dark tow plane high above the mosque, invisible to the naked eye below in the partial light. Mustafa checked the harness of his hang-glider and then stood up and launched himself out of the glide plane. The chute was all black, but Mustafa was dressed in a phosphorescent white robe which fluttered around his body as he maneuvered his way in circles down toward the mosque.

As Mustafa approached the top of the southeastern minaret, the tow plane fired off a special flare rocket into the partly cloudy skies. The bright flash of light rippled through the clouds and across the entire sky, drawing the immediate attention of Muslims kneeling in morning prayers at all the mosques in Damascus, but especially at the Umayyad Mosque directly below. All eyes turned upward where they saw a white apparition descending from heaven and alighting atop the Minaret of Jesus.

Mustafa had trained over and over and over again for this mission. Now all the training paid off as he grabbed hold of the tall spire rising out of the conical crown of the minaret. Quickly releasing the black cables and chute which fell back onto the roof, he caught his balance and spread his hands outward over the astonished Muslims below.

First they gasped and then they roared with understanding. Just as the hadiths foretold, first the Mahdi had come to Mecca and now Isa al-Maseeh, the Muslim Jesus had arrived in Damascus.

Chapter Sixty-Six

"Why do you always have to call in the middle of the night?" Jim's sleepy voice scolded.

"Because that's when the enemy conducts all their secret doings," Fran snapped back. She too had been awakened from a sound sleep by her round-the-clock staff.

"Oh, yes, I guess that makes sense," Jim admitted.

"Okay, now that we've got the amenities out of the way, perhaps you'd like to know what Sir William's plans are?" Fran prodded, still a bit annoyed.

Jim scrunched his face and shook his head, trying to drive the sleepiness away. Abby impatiently grabbed the phone from him, knowing that it took awhile before Jim began to fully function after being awakened.

"Fran, this is Abby. What's going on?"

Relieved, Fran got right into it. "Sir William's strike force is on the move under the leadership of General McGiver. From what we've been able to gather from a few documents and emails here and there, it will be an air and ground assault commencing just after dark tomorrow, or I guess, actually, later today."

Despite having prepared for this eventuality, Abby was stunned. Would Randy's GPS ploy work? Or were they to be overrun just after their first successful mission?

Abby shook herself out of aimless speculation and quickly called Randy on their walkie-talkie system. Randy answered right away, not able to sleep in anticipation of the battle to come. He quickly sat up inside his camouflaged tent as Abby filled him in on the latest intelligence info.

"Well, we're in position and ready as we'll ever be," Randy noted. "We'll do all we can and pray that the Lord is with us."

"Yes, we'll get the prayer teams going here and all across the country," Abby added and quickly called all the hideaways and remote camps, as well as CIA-West and the Holy Trinity Monastery, their prayer engine in Kansas.

Randy waited till daybreak to wake his militia commanders and prepare for the impending confrontation. Then they inspected their fortifications on the hills surrounding the valley under which CIA-East lay hidden. With Alan Morrison's deep pockets and contacts in the technology sector, in addition to the standard weapons of the day they were equipped with experimental laser and sonic weapons. They had been able to perform some limited testing, but Randy wasn't certain how they'd work at extended ranges.

He called ahead to the advance teams in the east and west that were monitoring the only two dirt roads leading into their isolated valley, updated them on the expected timing of Sir William's approach, and ran through a readiness checklist with them. After that there was nothing to do but wait and pray.

The day passed slowly both inside and outside the underground compound. Nerves were brittle and tempers short. Fran tweeted coded updates documenting the movement of the troops and the launch of aircraft. Just before dawn, after an early breakfast, Abby led all nonessential staff into the lowest level of the underground complex near the entrance to the escape tunnel. They each packed a "boogie bag" containing enough individual supplies to survive for three days out in the wilderness.

Jim remained behind with a skeletal communication crew to monitor updates from Fran who was now watching events through a clandestine hookup to overlooking satellites. Jim would then relay relevant information to Randy.

As dusk began to settle over the valley, Randy heard the drone of aircraft in the distance. His advance teams didn't see or hear any evidence of ground troops yet. The anti-aircraft artillery was readied while the sonic and laser weapons were revved up.

Everyone tensed involuntarily as the droning of the aircraft grew louder. "Do *not* fire your weapons unless I give the signal," Randy repeated.

Soon the ground shook as low-flying helicopters appeared over the horizon. Higher up, the bombers and fighters could also be seen.

"Hold your fire," Randy said through clenched teeth into the walkie-talkie.

Muscles and fingers tensed almost to the breaking point.

But then they began to relax as the helicopters passed overhead without slowing down or changing direction. On they flew as did the other aircraft.

"No troops in sight," relayed the two advance teams.

Randy breathed a sigh of relief. The GPS ploy had worked.

Chapter Sixty-Seven

"What do you mean nothing was there?" Sir William bellowed into the phone.

He listened for a few moments more and then flung the handset across the room where it shattered against the far wall, joining dozens of other phones of different stripes in phone-yard hell.

Harriet went to smooth Sir William's furrowed brow with her hand, but he swiped it away and pushed her off the desk.

"This is your fault!" he raged. "Your prisoner's information was false!!"

Harriet stumbled, recovered her balance and glanced up into a face that brought shivers of fear from her head down to her toes.

"You're fired. Pack your bags and go. Count your blessings I don't have you killed."

Harriet was immobilized, unable to function. How could it all be over so soon? She struck a vampish pose in desperation.

"Get out before I change my mind!" Sir William roared and threw his Masonic paperweight at her. The point of the compass struck her just above the eye. She stumbled backward, reeling from the blow, blood dripping in her eye.

As Sir William reached for the desk clock, Harriet scrambled out the door. He slammed it back down on the desk, shattering the glass face.

He picked up his cell phone and clumsily dialed his security chief downstairs. "Call a cab for Harriet and bring the prisoner up here to me," he demanded sharply.

While he waited, Sir William allowed his rage to metamorphose into a white hot steeliness that turned his eyes black and his countenance dark. It was at these times that he felt at one with Abbadon, the destroyer, Satan's chief henchman.

When Gustav, his security chief entered the office, he immediately recognized the look on Sir William's face and knew that the prisoner was a goner and that other heads would likely roll as well, with Harriet's first on the chopping block.

Behind Gustav, two burly security officers carried in the prisoner, Gregory Heinz, who was in no shape to walk. The disheveled man was already missing several toes under the blood-soaked bandages. Sir William stonily waved for them to place the prisoner on the couch. Sir William rolled across the floor in his massive desk chair and sat directly opposite the partially conscious man.

Gregory's eyes eventually rolled past Sir William, paused and then returned with a little more focus, and then quickly roamed around the room. A look of hope gradually splayed across his face. This wasn't a cell but an office, and the huge man in front of him wasn't one of his torturers. Perhaps he would live after all.

That was exactly what Sir William was waiting for. "Mr. Heinz, it is good to see that you're still alive," he said kindly, although his eyes betrayed him. But Gregory's eyes couldn't focus well enough to see beyond the veil of hope that clouded his mind.

"I have brought you here to offer you the opportunity to live, to be free," Sir William continued in a soft, cajoling tone. "No more torture. In fact, I'll even arrange for hospitalization and surgery until you're fully recovered. And, since you won't be able to work for awhile, I'll see that you receive a stipend of $100,000 a year for the rest of your life."

That was music to Gregory's soul. Was it really possible he could escape from this hell? Had his prayers been answered?

"Now I know you feel badly about giving up the coordinates of your secret location, but I want you to understand that no one would have been able to withstand the severe torture you experienced."

Sir William paused to watch Gregory's expression shift to shame and then guilt, knowing that all devout Christians believe they should be able to endure anything for Christ like their Biblical hero, Stephen.[129] But Sir William had learned through experience that precious few had faith that strong.

"You don't need to beat yourself up about it, because we were able to negotiate a truce with them before any shots were fired," Sir William said with as warm a smile as he could muster.

Gregory's eyes lit up. "You mean they're all alive?" he gasped.

"Yes, no one was hurt," Sir William assured the confused prisoner who was now grasping at any possibility of hope. "And, they'd really like to see you, so we'll take you back down there. Of course, we'll transport you to the Mayo Clinic in Rochester afterward for the surgeries you'll need."

Despair fully gave way to thankfulness for this most unexpected rescue from the pit of hell. It was time to weave the last strand of the web Sir William had so skillfully woven.

"Gustav will drive you to see them after you've had your wounds dressed, filled your stomach with some nourishing food and gotten some of your strength back."

"Thank you, thank you so much," Gregory gushed in relief and gratitude.

Sir William signaled for the two henchmen to carry Gregory back out and then spoke quietly to Gustav. "When he's strong enough, drive him down into the area, get lost and have him direct you to where they really are. Then kill him and call me with the real coordinates."

Chapter Sixty-Eight

"Well, we blew it last time," Rev. Wainwright declared with a grimace as he and Rabbi David gathered together to pray for divine guidance.

David chuckled. "Boris, you're quite refreshing. All too often I buy into the notion that as a leader I must be perfect all the time."

"I don't know about you, but I'm less than perfect most of the time," Boris observed with a twinkle in his eye.

David nodded in agreement. At first he'd resented having to share leadership with this gentle man who often played the buffoon, but he'd come to realize it was all an act. Boris was actually quite intelligent and knew how to deflate tension with a bit of humor and a dash of honesty.

"You've got to admit that these are very confusing times," Boris added. "It's hard to tell the players without a scorecard."

David had to process the American's idiom for a moment and then got it. "Yes, you're right. We've now got two characters running around claiming to be Jesus."

"Well, you're the Muslim expert," Boris said, bowing his head in mock acknowledgement. "So explain, please."

David gathered his thoughts and then began, "The Islamic prophecies about the end-times are themselves quite confusing and, in some cases, contradictory. The Qur'an itself has little to say about it. The hadiths, that is, the sayings and deeds of Muhammad, are the only place these end-time characters are referenced. The Mahdi, who is the second coming of Muhammad, is mentioned in only one of the six books of hadiths, and that one is only recognized by the Shiites."

"So the Mahdi is the Islamic version of Jesus?" Boris asked.

"Yes and no," David laughed. "We see it that way, but they don't, because they also see Jesus returning too. That's who supposedly descended from heaven in Damascus."

Boris rubbed his chin. "But I thought this lunatic with one eye riding the giant mule was supposed to be Jesus."

"Not to the Muslims. They call the Dajjal the Great Deceiver, because he claims he is Jesus, but is not."

"Well that's clear as mud," Boris groused.

"Yes, that's an accurate depiction of the bewildering, paradoxical state of Islamic end-time prophecy," David chortled in agreement.

"So why do you think Jews here in Israel are buying into the Dajjal as their Messiah?"

"Ah, that's a tough one," David sighed. "You'd have to be a Jew to fully comprehend the long-term, generational impact of constant persecution. It's like your saying of being on the short end of the stick – all the time. That's led to a repressed hunger for the Messiah to come and raise up Israel above all the nations of the earth."

"That's Biblical, isn't it?"

"Yes, at the time of the end. But it's like the early Jewish followers of Jesus wanted him to become King right then and there, regardless of all the prophecies that said He must suffer and die first.[130] Ultimately, it comes down to a lack of knowledge of what the Old Testament actually teaches."

"*'My people are destroyed for lack of knowledge',* saith the Lord God Almighty." Boris quoted.[131]

"Precisely," David heartily agreed. "That was true in the past and it's just as true today."

"So, back to the Islamic beliefs. This Dajjal, this Great Deceiver claiming to be Jesus, even the Muslims know he's an imposter, but they believe that this new guy in Damascus is the real deal?"

"Yes, they've always believed in Jesus as a great prophet, but not as the Son of God. It's all more understandable if we look at Islam as Satan's counterfeit of Christianity. In counterpoint, they have a fake savior who is Muhammad, *not* Jesus. Then, to refute Jesus' claims to being part of the Godhead, they have a fake Jesus who proclaims that he is *not* the Son of God, but rather a supporter of Muhammad. And then, to deceive and ultimately attempt to destroy the Jews, they even have a fake Jesus who says this is his *first* coming, to satisfy those who do not believe Jesus has come yet."

"Wow, what a mess. No wonder the Muslims are so confused."

"Indeed, and with the Sunni and Shia sects having different end-time beliefs, that's why they are back to fighting among themselves even as their savior has presumably arrived," David added.

"That's also Biblical," Boris noted, "because Genesis says that Ishmael's descendents, the Arabs, *shall be a wild man; his hand shall be against every man, and every man's hand against him.*"[132]

"And so it is, they fight against us *and* against each other."

"Back to us." Boris said, redirecting the conversation. "I have the feeling that you and I are supposed to do something about all of this, but I don't have a clue what it is."

"Yes, I agree. Perhaps it's just us not wanting to stay cooped up down here on the sidelines, or maybe it's the Holy Spirit trying to tell us something or prepare us for something."

"Then let's pray about it. But before we run off on another futile mission, I suggest that whatever we think we hear from the Lord should be verified by your prayer group," Boris suggested and David nodded in assent.

Chapter Sixty-Nine

"You have done well, Isa," Mahdi Muhammad said to Mustafa after arriving in Damascus with hundreds of thousands of followers trailing behind.

Mustafa felt more like Isa than his former self, but not quite like Jesus, although he was far along in the process of rationalizing it all. He had no memory about having walked the earth in a previous incarnation, but perhaps the spirit of Jesus was within him.

"It is time for us to appear together for the first time, are you ready to play your part?" Muhammad asked.

"More than ready, sire. Eager and excited," Mustafa declared, bowing low before his savior and then following the Mahdi out of the Umayyad Mosque into the massive courtyard that held thousands of Muslims all cramped together.

An ornate platform had been assembled in the middle of the courtyard with a red carpet leading through the screaming throng. As the Mahdi led the way with Mustafa following behind, hands strained to reach over the restraining ropes to simply touch the Prophet. Many fainted upon doing so.

The Arabian television broadcaster, Al Jazeera, had set up several camera stands from various distances and angles to provide the awakened Muslim world with live coverage of this historic event. All disputes among the various Islamic sects and factions were temporarily set aside to see whether the prophecies would be fulfilled.

From the podium on the platform, Muhammad spread his arms over the crowd and beckoned for a silence that took several minutes to take hold. Then they fell to their knees, facing Mecca with their foreheads on the ground.

"Alhamdu lil lahil lazi Ahyaana baasa ma amatan wa ilaihinnushooro (All praise to Allah, he who revived us to life after giving us death, and to him we shall have to return)," the Mahdi prayed. The congregation rose on their knees, repeated the prayer and bowed down again.

Muhammad turned to Mustafa. "Isa al-Maseeh, Jesus, has returned to us from the heavens above." The crowd cheered "Allahu Akbar" for several long minutes.

When they had quieted, Muhammad said to Mustafa, "Isa, will you please lead us in prayer?"

Mustafa bowed low. "It is not I who should lead, but you Muhammad bin Abdullah, may peace be upon you."

The Mahdi, his black hair and beard glowing in the bright sun, bowed back. The twelfth and final Imam, his broad forehead and prominent nose giving him an other-worldly appearance, then turned back to the congregation and led them in prayer.

In concluding the morning prayer session, Muhammad prayed, "Allah! Umma antas salaamu wa minkas salaamu hayina rabbana bissa laame wa ad khilna daarassalaam tabarakta ya zaljalali was ikraam, samena ataana ghufranaka rabbana wa ilaikal maser (Allah! Thou art the author of peace and from thee comes peace and peace returns towards thee. Keep us alive with peace, and let us enter the house of peace. Blessed and exalted art thou o lord of glory and honour! O our lord! Hear us and grant us pardon.)"

After the congregation had repeated the well-known closing prayer, Muhammad beckoned to Mustafa. "Isa, please come and address our loyal brethren."

Mustafa, fully into his new personality, stepped up to the microphone. "Greetings in the name of Allah, who has sent me down from heaven again in order to refute the many lies and blasphemies perpetuated by the blasphemers, the Jews and Christians who will roast in hell."

The lusty cheers shook the very foundations of the courtyard and shook the walls of the mosque. Isa waited till they had calmed down and continued. "To say that I, Jesus, am the Son of God, is a complete falsehood that has been taken out of context. We are all sons of Allah in that he has given birth to everything in the world. But I am not a god, simply a prophet – and not even the greatest prophet at that," he said and bowed once again toward The Prophet.

After the roar subsided, he added, "Nor is Allah split into two or three parts. He is one. His spirit resides within him. There is no trinity, no Holy Spirit. I have come again to set the record straight, to erase the lies of the infidels to whom we give this one last chance to renounce their false beliefs and accept Allah as the one true god and Muhammad as his prophet and savior."

This time there was no containing the screams and shouts of praise. Midst the tumult, Mustafa humbly followed the Mahdi back inside the mosque.

Chapter Seventy

René snapped off the plasma screen with an extreme look of hatred and contempt. "Why don't we just bomb them all into oblivion?" she asked rhetorically.

Alexis sat back in his desk chair. "You know the answer to that. It's not time yet. They have a role to play and are being directed by our master Lucifer himself. Remember that a house divided will fall."

"Yada, yada, yada," René pronounced having heard it all before. "That doesn't mean I have to like it."

"Don't worry," Pope Radinsky cajoled, "soon they'll all be dead and the crowd of fanatics will be cheering for us."

René glared at the False Prophet. "It's not their cheers and adulation I want, it's the power to do to them what I wish and what they deserve. Just sitting by and watching is very frustrating."

"See, that's just how I feel about those two witnesses who are off converting Muslims in Egypt. I'd like to strangle them with my bare hands, but have to sit on my hands instead until the right time," Alexis explained, looking for a little sympathy.

René turned and gave Alexis the evil eye before stomping out of his office. "I sure pity whoever she plans to take out her frustrations on today," the Global Czar said and forced a laugh.

Radinsky studied his partner for a few moments wondering if he had the stomach for his next major scene. Would he have enough faith to carry out the crucial part destiny would force him to play?

****

"How are things progressing in Turkey?" Muhammad asked Mustafa.

"Very well, my lord. The Yameni and Sufyani have joined forces and raised up an army of nearly half-a-million and will begin their march on Israel tomorrow," Mustafa bowed and answered.

"Then we had better assemble our forces as well and prepare to move on Jerusalem the following day," the Mahdi stated.

Mustafa and the two Islamic Republican Army generals set off to do so.

****

"Is the prisoner well enough to make the trip?" Sir William asked his security chief.

"He won't croak, if that's what you mean," Gustav laughed. "We've got him juiced up on morphine and the poor fool truly believes that he's going to be reunited with his compatriots."

"See that he keeps on believing," Sir William warned. "Oh, and have one of your boys see to it that Harriet has a little accident. We don't want her blabbing about how we do things down here."

****

Rabbi David and Rev. Wainwright stared at each other awhile, their eyes wide with alarm.

"Well, that's a first," Boris finally uttered. "Seeing the same vision at the same time. Will wonders never cease?"

"It would be nice to know how it all turns out," David sighed.

"Nonetheless, I think we know for sure what we have to do," Boris emphasized. "Still, let's have your team pray about it too. They might get a little more insight."

****

Carmelita and Blaine rubbed their tired eyes awake. "Now?" was all Blaine could say.

"Yes, the Lord has just shown us that we need to be in Jerusalem the day after tomorrow, so we'll need to get going right away," Pastor Gabriel said, the urgency clear in his voice and his countenance.

****

The celebration at CIA-East was well underway when the proceedings were interrupted by an urgent call from Fran. *Not again,* Jim griped to himself.

Abby saw the expression on his face and headed him off on the way to the communication center. "Let me get this one," she said gently. Jim recognized his annoyance and realized she was right.

"I thought we were safe now," Abby said as she picked up the secure line connecting the two counter-insurgency centers.

"It's not you I'm worried about this time," Fran answered in a rush, "it's the world. Turn on your TV. The Muslims are marching against Israel."

****

Millions around the world were glued to their televisions. A massive army of Muslims and mercenaries was on the move south out of Turkey, while the Mahdi was leading an equally huge contingent westward out of Damascus, Syria. Simultaneously, the Dajjal had assembled a large following of Jews and Palestinians moving north out of the Gaza Strip.

Other Muslim forces were on the move from out of the many small republics like Kazakhstan, Uzbekistan and Chechnya that had once been part of the Soviet Union, eager to join up with their brethren for the final demise of Israel. Not wanting to be left out, the Iranians were on the move through Iraq picking up troops and volunteers along the way.

"It's not clear at this point whether all these Islamic armies are aligned together," the CNN anchor related, "or whether the various sects they represent will be competing against one another for supremacy."

"Meanwhile, there has been precious little word from the Global Governance Committee. However, sources inside the Global Palace, speaking anonymously for fear of retribution, revealed that there are insufficient troops on the ground to withstand the assault on Israel because the Global Army is spread all around the world."

****

"Good job, Christine," Alexis said and put his arm around his spokesperson and favorite new toy. "We need to make it look like we're weak and confused. That will encourage more Muslims to come running from all corners of the globe to participate in what they think will be the annihilation of Israel and their assuming control over world government."

"And then we can bomb them into oblivion?" René asked, almost salivating at the prospect.

"Yes, indeed," the Global Czar assured her. "But not until they wipe out most of the Jews. Then we'll strike with aircraft and missiles to rid the earth of these Muslim vermin. Two birds with one stone, as it were."

****

Rabbi David and Reverend Boris stood on the Temple Mount observing the chaos all around them. No longer were Jews and Muslims contending with one another over ownership of the most prized spiritual possession in the entire world. Instead, the plaza was empty.

Inside the Aqsa Mosque, Muslims were crowded in prayer seeking Allah's favor in aiding their forces to retake Israel and crown Jerusalem as the Islamic capital of the world. Likewise, the new, Third Temple, was packed with Jews praying to Jehovah for divine intervention and protection.

Outside, there wasn't a Jew in sight. Either they had run off to follow the Dajjal, their phony messiah or they'd hunkered down to endure the coming siege. The Israeli military had been dismantled after the Global Peace Pact was signed, with the Global Czar and the Global Army taking over responsibility for Israel's defense. Because of the global peace that ensued, this had seemed, on the surface, to be reasonable and just.

However, now that it appeared the Global Army was not going to repel the Islamic uprising. The Jews were in a panic, cursing one another for their lack of foresight in surrendering their fate to the Gentiles, although in retrospect, they had been given little choice in the matter.

****

Gustav stopped the Humvee in what seemed like the middle of nowhere. He shook the prisoner, Gregory, awake. "I've gotten lost and the GPS unit has stopped working. I need you to guide me the rest of the way."

Gregory's feverish eyes surveyed the area. As one of the advance scouts in the militia, he had spent months training in the mountains surrounding CIA-East.

"I can't tell anything from here. You'll have to find a hilltop so I can look around."

While Gustav drove in circles for awhile and finally located a dirt trail leading up to the top of the highest point in the area, Gregory tried to force his afflicted mind to remain conscious. Something didn't seem right about all of this, but his headache was severe and his brain was close to short-circuiting.

The only thing he could think of to do was pray. *Lord God, please forgive me for not being strong enough to withhold the GPS coordinates from the enemy, but help me now to do the right thing, whatever that might be.*

****

"This just in from the Middle East," the TV anchor intoned in a hushed, ominous tone. "The Islamic forces have converged on Israel with only token resistance from remnants of the once mighty Israeli military. The only global forces in the area have retreated to surround and protect the Global Palace, where the Global Czar has been holed up, remaining strangely silent."

The anchor grabbed another sheet of paper that had just been handed to him. "The Turkish forces have swept through Lebanon, picking up additional numbers along the way and are moving now against Tel Aviv. The Mahdi's army has crossed the Golan Heights where fierce fighting has broken out. Meanwhile, the Dajjal is closing in on Jerusalem, apparently headed for the Temple Mount."

****

"We're not going to get there in time," Gabriel said to Abraham off to the side of their enlarged travelling party. "And I think we need to drop the hangers-on"

Abraham nodded in agreement. "We'll have to ask the Lord to transport us once again. Let's gather our core group together for prayer on that hilltop over there."

Gabriel went to fetch Carmelita, Blaine, Aly and Vy. When they joined Abraham on the hill overlooking the Gaza Strip they were appalled at what they saw.

After most Palestinians had left to follow the Dajjal to Jerusalem, others had remained behind to loot and destroy. Acrid smoke rose from many sections of the poverty-stricken enclave.

The group of six joined hands in a circle and sought the Lord's guidance and assistance.

****

"This is where we part ways, Isa," the Mahdi said to the former Mustafa. "May Allah be with you as you follow destiny's path."

"And with you, sire, may peace be upon you," Isa al-Maseeh answered as he humbly bowed before his lord and savior.

Chapter Seventy-One

Boris and David had remained standing alone on the Temple Mount for quite some time, praying and claiming it for the One True God.[133] But now, in the distance, they could hear the growing rumble of the vast mob following the Great Deceiver through East Jerusalem, wrecking and ransacking along the way.

Muslims and Jews began to spill out of the Al Aqsa Mosque and the Third Temple, immediately confronting one another. Boris and David stepped in between the rival factions.

"In the name of Jesus Christ, the True Savior of the world, lay down your hatred and your arms and receive his gift of eternal salvation before you all are killed and go to hell," Reverend Wainwright cried out.

The two groups stopped in their tracks, both alienated by the same blasphemy.

One of the Jews shouted, "The Messiah is coming right now to take Jerusalem as his righteous possession. It is you who need to repent and receive *him* as your savior."

A Muslim spoke up in turn, "No, he is the Dajjal, the Great Deceiver who only claims to be Jesus. The true Jesus, the true savior is coming right now from the north leading Muhammad's mighty army."

"No," Rabbi David shouted, "these are both imposters, just as Jesus warned us in Matthew 24!"

Just then, a voice cried out from atop the Dome of the Rock. "Yes, that is what I said, and that is exactly what has happened."

All eyes turned upward and saw Isa al-Maseeh glowing in his white robe, his long hair flowing in the gentle breeze. The Muslims fell to their knees and pressed their foreheads to the ground. The Jews were stunned, but then quickly began to denounce the Islamic blasphemer.

Just as they were about to attack the prostrate Muslims, the Dajjal and his followers reached the foot of the Temple Mount. Astride his giant mule, the Dajjal rode up between the Jews and Muslims and glared up at Isa.

"You are an affront to god and humanity," the Dajjal growled and waved his followers to storm the Dome of the Rock. "Drag him down from there and tear him apart limb by limb," he ordered.

As the mob surged forward, overrunning Jew and Muslim alike, David and Boris huddled together praying for peace in the midst of the pandemonium.

Isa stretched forth his hand toward the Dajjal. "I am giving you one last warning. Stand down or prepare to meet your maker."

The Dajjal roared in laughter, his one eye scrunched closed. Before it could blink open, a bright streak whistled down out of the sky, striking the Dajjal and blowing him to pieces.

Yet another prophecy fulfilled, the *real* Muslim Jesus thought to himself, a satisfied smirk playing across his face as he surveyed the chaos below.

****

Just a little to the north, the Global Palace was completely surrounded by the Mahdi and his rag-tag army which consisted of Islamic soldiers, terrorists and ordinary Muslim people. Muhammad thought it somewhat odd that they had encountered only token resistance on their march through Israel, but rationalized that the will of Allah was at work.

Many shoulder-fired missile and grenade launchers were aimed at the palace. Muhammad mounted the steps onto the front portico and signaled his vast army to quiet down. Then he raised an electronic bullhorn to his lips. "Alexis D'Antoni, Global Czar, your reign is over. We call on you in the name of Allah to come out and surrender peacefully."

After a short pause without any response from inside the palace, the Mahdi repeated his demand, adding, "If you do not surrender within the next two minutes, we will destroy the palace and all who are inside."

Just before the deadline expired, Alexis walked out onto the front portico followed by Pope Radinsky and René. With a stone face, the Global Czar walked calmly up to Muhammad, stood silent for a few seconds and then declared, "I will not surrender peacefully or otherwise. Your little fun and games are over. It is you who must capitulate.

The Mahdi's eyes blazed with anger and hatred. He quickly pulled out the ceremonial sword he wore at his side and plunged it into D'Antoni's midsection, once, twice, three times. Then he pulled the blood-soaked sword back and watched Alexis sink first to his knees and then face forward on the marble floor.

A hush fell over the scene and across the world, as the Al Jazeera cameras zoomed in on the expanding blood pool beneath the fallen, extinguished Global Czar.

****

Gregory had been scanning the horizon for some time now, propped up against the Land Rover. Gustav's patience was exhausted. "Enough, already. You said you knew the Tennessee Valley like the back of your hand. So let's get on with it. Your friends are waiting to see you and to hail you as a hero."

The severely wounded, confused, erstwhile prisoner turned his face back toward his one-time torturer who now pretended to be his friend. Gregory's weakened brain couldn't quite figure out what had happened, but he knew that he could not and should not lead Sir William's security chief to the CIA-East location.

As he continued to pray for guidance, he felt a quickening of his spirit. As his strength was renewed, he realized that this was the end of the line for him. No longer afraid to die and feeling forgiven for having given up the GPS coordinates, he smiled at his tormenter. "Go to hell."

Gustav was furious. He never thought this ploy would work, but perhaps more physical persuasion would do the trick. He grabbed Gregory by the shoulders and began slamming him against the side of the vehicle. Instead of screaming in agony, as Gustav expected, Gregory stared off into the distance as a broad smile broke out.

Gregory saw a semi-transparent figure who looked much like Jesus, or at the least an angel of the Lord, floating above the ground, holding his arms out and beckoning Gregory to come to Him.

A perplexed Gustav turned to follow Gregory's gaze, expecting to see some of his friends coming to the rescue. But he saw nothing.

Turning back to his prisoner, he prepared to strike the smile off Gregory's face but stopped when the face before him went blank and the body sagged slowly to the ground. Gustav felt for a pulse but there was none.

He turned back around with an eerie sense that somebody was out there, but his spiritually blinded eyes couldn't see Gregory's glorified body being embraced by the Son of Man.

****

The shocked crowd of Jews and Muslims stood frozen on the Temple Mount, staring at the remains of the Dajjal and his giant mule, unaware of the drama unfolding at the Global Palace.

Into the midst of the silence, Rabbi David and Reverend Wainwright stepped forward. "This Dajjal was indeed the Great Deceiver, being neither the Jewish messiah nor the Muslim redeemer. But so too is that imposter up on the Dome. He also is a deceiver," David explained.

"But the real Jesus Christ, who will return after this Tribulation period, is alive and His Spirit is here right now offering each of you a final chance of forgiveness and eternal salvation," Boris added.

With that, many of the Jews and Muslims were whipped into a frenzy by the deceptive demons goading them into action. They charged toward Boris and David, intent on ripping them apart with their bare hands.

Suddenly, there was a flash of brilliant white light that temporarily blinded their eyes. As their vision slowly returned, they saw that the two ministers were now surrounded by six more people.

Before the stunned mob could figure out what to do, Abraham and Gabriel stretched out their hands toward Mustafa, high above them, still upon the Dome. A surge of fear and revelation suddenly came over the phony Isa al-Maseeh. It had all been a dream, an illusion. He was and would always be just Mustafa, a black priest, a servant of Satan. And now he would die and join him in hell.

Just as that last thought crossed his mind, a bolt of lightning flashed down from the sky and completely incinerated him, his ashes drifting down gently on the soft breeze. Down below, several fell to their knees and wept, crying out to Jesus as His Holy Spirit moved upon them. Most, however, were oblivious to the final offer of redemption, their consciences seared with hatred and lies.

Unseen except by the two witnesses was an angel of the Lord receiving the saved souls and leading them upwards to heaven. All that the rest of them saw was a covering of light that descended over the two witnesses and their entourage just before the whine of missiles drew their attention for a split second before they were all destroyed.

****

Back at CIA-West, Jim and Abby were transfixed by the images on the plasma screen. Several of the residents behind them screamed when they saw the missiles strike the crowd on the Temple Mount, followed by blackness as the al-Jazeera cameras were also snuffed out.

But then the screen popped back to life, as the cameras at the Global Palace zoomed back out from the Global Czar's dead body to show the Mahdi and his followers chanting, "Allahu Akbar, Allahu Akbar!"

Midst the frenzied celebration of conquest, few noticed Pope Radinsky crouch beside the blood-stained body of the Global Czar. He rolled the body over and placed one hand on the forehead of Alexis D'Antoni and the other on his mid-section, wet with blood, the gaping wounds clearly visible.

In a clearly supernatural way, Radinsky's voice cut through the bedlam, sending shudders into the bystanders as well as the worldwide TV audience. "O mighty Lucifer, god of this age,[134] prince of the air,⁽¹³⁵⁾ I call upon you now to heal your devoted servant and display your awesome power!"

Then, before millions of eyes, the wounds slowly closed, the blood dried up and the Global Czar sat up. The Mahdi stepped back, aghast, afraid. The shocked mob of Muslims retreated backward away from their worst nightmare.

Radinsky held out his hand and helped D'Antoni to his feet. The Global Czar then stared hard at the Mahdi, and then into the television camera. "Allah, your time is up," he proclaimed in a cold voice.

He then turned toward the Global Palace, looked up and yelled, "Now!"

Windows on many floors and on all sides of the palace flew open. Automatic gunfire, grenades and mobile missiles flew down into the thousands of Muslims gathered there, continuing to rain down until not one of them was left standing. Simultaneously, bombers and fighter planes swooped over the Sufyani and the Yameni and their huge army, likewise destroying them all.

Many CIA residents gasped, screamed and cried. "What in the world just happened?" Randy asked, his ashen face swollen with fear.

Jim whispered to Abby who ran to get her Bible. "Listen up, everyone. There is no need to be afraid. The Bible has once again triumphed over the Qur'an, Truth has won out over lies."

He waited as Abby flipped open the Bible and found the right passage and read aloud from Revelation 13:11-14: *Then I saw another beast coming up out of the earth, and he had two horns like a lamb and spoke like a dragon. And he exercises all the authority of the first beast in his presence, and causes the earth and those who dwell in it to worship the first beast, whose **deadly wound was healed**. He performs great signs, so that he even makes fire come down from heaven on the earth in the sight of men. ¹⁴And he deceives those who dwell on the earth by those signs which he was granted to do in the sight of the beast, telling those who dwell* *on the earth to make an image to the beast who was **wounded by the sword and lived.***

Appendix A – Scriptural References (NKJ)

1. 1Samuel 15:22, Deuteronomy 28:2, Exodus 19:5
2. Psalm 18:28, Psalm 27:1, John 8:12
3. 2Corinthians 4:3-4
4. Revelation 13
5. Luke 21:19, James 1:2-4
6. Psalm 51:6, Proverbs 2:6-7, 3:13, 4:5, Ephesians 1:17, James 1:5, 3:17
7. John 15:26, (KJV), 1Cornintians 1:3-4
8. Isaiah 28:29, John 16:13
9. 1Corinthians 1:18-25, 2:14
10. James 3:14-16
11. Proverbs 8:17, Matthew 7:7
12. Psalm 139:23-24
13. 1John 1:9, Romans 14:11
14. 1Samuel 15:26
15. Matthew 17:15-18
16. Matthew 16:19, 18:18
17. Psalm 91
18. 1John 4:18
19. Ephesians 5:26
20. John 4:10-14
21. Hebrews 9:13-14, Matthew 26:28, Ephesians 1:7, Isaiah 53:5
22. Ephesians 5:15

23. Ephesians 5:25-32
24. Genesis 2:24, Matthew 19:5-6, 1Corinthians 6:16
25. James 1:6-7
26. Matthew 18:3
27. Psalm 27:14, 37:9, 37:34, Isaiah 8:17, 40:31
28. Luke 21:36, 1Corinthians 10:13
29. Isaiah 9:6, 11:2
30. Ephesians 1:17, 1Corinthians 12:8
31. John 14:26
32. 2Corinthians 10:4-6
33. Matthew 16:19, 18:18
34. Matthew 12:29
35. Psalm 18:2, 40:17, 70:5, 144:2, Romans 11:26
36. 2Corinthians 1:20
37. Zephaniah 1:15
38. Acts 12:5-10, 16:25-26
39. Luke 4:29
40. 1John 4:18
41. Mark 5:1-13
42. 2Corinthians 12:7-10
43. Matthew 9:32-33, Mark 9:25
44. 2Corinthians 10:5
45. 2Corinthians 2:11
46. John 6:53
47. John 6:35, 48
48. Revelation 3:20

49. 1Corinthians 10:17, Hebrews 3:14, 6:4, 12:10, 1Peter 4:13, 5:1, 2Peter 1:4
50. 2Corinthians 12:9
51. Ephesians 5:18, Luke 1:5, 41, 67, 4:1, Acts 2:4, 4:8, 31, 9:17, 13:9, 52
52. 2Corinthians 11:14
53. Ephesians 4:26
54. Hebrews 12:14-15
55. Ephesians 4:27 (NIV)
56. Exodus 34:29-35
57. Acts 2:1-4, 4:24-31
58. Revelation 13:8, 15
59. 2Corinthians 5:17, Ephesians 4:22-24
60. Jeremiah 1:5, Psalm 139:14-16
61. Ephesians 4:18 (NIV)
62. 2Corinthians 5:18
63. James 4:7
64. Isaiah 40:31
65. Ephesians 2:8-9
66. Luke 12:11-12
67. Joshua 3:11-17
68. Revelation 1:16, Psalm 149:6-9, Hebrews 4:12
69. 1Corinthians 1:27 (KJV)
70. 2Corinthians 4:4
71. Luke 17:21
72. Romans 12:2
73. John 15:14-15

74. Matthew 3:4
75. Matthew 11:14, Mark 9:11-3, Luke 1:17
76. Revelation 11:2
77. Revelation 13
78. Joel 3:14
79. John 3:16, 2Peter 3:9
80. Matthew 23:37
81. Revelation 11:6
82. John 10:10
83. Matthew 3:10
84. Luke 21:16, Mark 13:12-13, Matthew 19:29
85. Matthew 12:49-50
86. Isaiah 52:12
87. John 12:4-6
88. Luke 9:58
89. John 1:46
90. Matthew 21:11, Luke 24:19
91. Mark 6:3
92. Matthew 13:57, Mark 6:4, John 4:44
93. Luke 1:31-32
94. Luke 1:50-55
95. Matthew 1:20-23, Isaiah 7:14
96. John 8:44
97. Galatians 6:7-8
98. 2Kings 2:11
99. Acts 8:39

100. Matthew 2:13
101. Luke 2:10-12
102. Luke 2:13-14
103. Genesis 1:26-28
104. Revelation 5:1-5
105. Romans 8:26
106. 2Peter 3:9, John 3:16
107. Romans 8:31
108. Matthew 19:26, Mark 9:23, 14:36
109. Revelation 13:15
110. Philippians 1:21
111. John 15:13
112. Luke 2:23
113. Matthew 2:1-2
114. Matthew 2:13
115. Hosea 11:1
116. 1Kings 22:20-23
117. Matthew 21:1-7
118. Luke 17:21, Romans 8:9
119. Galatians 5:16-17, Matthew 26:41
120. 1John 4:8-16, Matthew 6:33
121. 1John 4:18
122. 2Timothy 1:7
123. John 18:6
124. Acts 2:6-11
125. Hebrews 4:16, Psalm 107:1

126. Revelation 11:5
127. 1Kings 20:1-34
128. Acts 9:1-20
129. Acts 7:59-60
130. John 6:15, Isaiah 53:3-5
131. Hosea 4:6
132. Genesis 16:11-12
133. Jeremiah 10:10, John 17:13, 1John 5:20
134. 2Corinthians 4:4
135. Ephesians 2:2

Appendix B – Pre-Wrath Rapture Timeline & Justification

Quick Reference Guide (Scriptural justification in the following section).

1. The days leading up to Jesus' second coming are called the last days, the end-days or the end-times, what Jesus called the "beginning of sorrows." This is where we are now.

2. The so-called Four Horsemen in Revelation chapter six are already running rampant, bringing disease, death and financial disaster upon us.

3. Before the 7-year Tribulation starts, there has to be a major war in the Middle East, then a peace treaty, and a one-world government. Then the 7-year Tribulation starts.

4. There won't be a pre-Tribulation rapture because many verses show that the saints will suffer during the Tribulation (see next section).

5. This peace treaty will bring a 'false' peace that will last for the first three-and-a-half years and give rise to the anti-Christ..The Jews will be allowed to rebuild their temple, but not the outer courts. It is a false peace because there will be no rest for Christians, only persecution.

6. There can't be a mid-Trib rapture because we would know in advance when that would occur since we can mark the beginning of the 7-year Tribulation to the signing of the peace treaty. Jesus said we wouldn't know the day or the hour when He is coming back to resurrect the saints.

7. After the first three-and-a-half years of 'peace,' the anti-Christ will commit the "abomination of desolation" in the Temple by declaring himself to be god.

8. This initiates a time of great warfare and suffering as Jesus begins to open the remaining seals.

9. When the sixth seal is opened, the sun turns black and the moon red, ushering in the Day of the Lord, the Day of Wrath, a "great and terrible day" – a 'great' day because that's when the rapture occurs, right before the wrath of God is unleashed on the earth.

10. This 'day' is not necessarily a 24-hour day but more likely a short time period during which the trumpet and bowl plagues decimate the earth, the period Jesus called the Great Tribulation.

11. At the end of the 7-year Tribulation, a new earth and a new Jerusalem descend from heaven and Jesus establishes his reign on earth for the thousand-year Millennium.

12. Following the Millennium, Satan is released from the 'bottomless pit' and then finally terminated for good in the 'lake of fire.'

Biblical Analysis – Part 1 – The Great Tribulation

The Bible teaches that Jesus is coming back a second time to take permanent possession of the earth. At that time, all people will come before the **Great White Throne** for judgment:

> *Then I saw a great white throne and Him who sat on it, from whose face the earth and the heaven fled away. And there was found no place for them. And I saw the dead, small and great, standing before God, and books were opened. And another book was opened, which is the Book of Life. And the dead were judged according to their works, by the things which were written in the books. The sea gave up the dead who were in it, and Death and Hades delivered up the dead who were in them. And they were judged, each one according to his works. Then Death and Hades were cast into the lake of fire. This is the second death. And anyone not found written in the Book of Life was cast into the lake of fire.* (Rev. 20:11-15)

Unbelievers, all of whom had the opportunity to make a choice, will be cast into a hell of **eternal torment**:

> *And the smoke of their torment ascends forever and ever; and they have no rest day or night, who worship the beast and his image, and whoever receives the mark of his name.* (Rev. 14:11)

Believers will then have their works **judged by fire**. What comes through the fire represents their heavenly treasure:

> *For no other foundation can anyone lay than that which is laid, which is Jesus Christ. Now if anyone builds on this foundation with gold, silver, precious stones, wood, hay, straw, each one's work will become clear; for the Day will declare it, because it will be revealed by fire; and the fire will test each one's work, of what sort it is. If anyone's work which he has built on it endures, he will receive a reward. If anyone's work is burned, he will suffer loss; but he himself will be saved, yet so as through fire.* (1 Cor. 3:11-15)

The days leading up to Jesus' second coming are called the last days, the end-days or the end-times. Jesus spoke about these times in his Olivet Discourse in Matthew 24. He separates these days into two phases. The beginning stage He calls the "**beginning of sorrows**."

> *And you will hear of wars and rumors of wars. See that you are not troubled; for all these things must come to pass, but the end is not yet. For nation will rise against nation, and kingdom against kingdom. And there will be famines, pestilences, and earthquakes in various places. All these are the beginning of sorrows.* (Matt. 24:6-8)

These days are characterized by **wars, earthquakes, pestilence** and the like. A time of **great deception**, when many will falsely say "here He is, or there He is." We see a lot of that today, when all sorts of erroneous ideas concerning Christianity will spread great **confusion**, a primary tactic of Satan.

> *Take heed that no one deceives you. For many will come in My name, saying, 'I am the Christ,' and will deceive many… Then if anyone says to you, 'Look, here is the Christ!' or 'There!' do not believe it. For false christs and false prophets will rise and*

show great signs and wonders to deceive, if possible, even the elect. (Matt. 24:4-5, 23-24)

- o Note: The Greek form of the word "if" suggests that it *is* possible for the elect to be deceived

The deception will be so great that there will be what the Apostle Paul calls a great "**falling away**."

➢ *Let no one deceive you by any means; for that Day will not come unless the falling away comes first.* (2Thess. 2:3)

This means that believers will have their faith **undermined by false teaching** and drift away into **unbelief**. That's why Scripture tells us we need to "**hold fast**" to our faith (1Cor. 15:2, Heb. 3:6, 4:14, 10:23, Rev. 2:25, 3:3, 3:11). Jesus tells us we must **"endure"** to the end:

➢ *But he who endures to the end shall be saved.* (Matt. 10:22, 24:13)

Paul also wrote to Timothy about what these last days would be like:

➢ *But know this, that in the last days perilous times will come: For men will be lovers of themselves, lovers of money, boasters, proud, blasphemers, disobedient to parents, unthankful, unholy, unloving, unforgiving, slanderers, without self-control, brutal, despisers of good, traitors, headstrong, haughty, lovers of pleasure rather than lovers of God, having a form of godliness but denying its power. And from such people turn away!* (2Tim. 3:1-5)

That describes kind of where we are today. But things will get progressively worse. The so-called **Four Horsemen** in Revelation chapter six are already **running rampant**, bringing disease, death and financial disaster upon us. It's happening now and will get progressively worse.

Jesus also said that He would not come again until the gospel had been **preached to all nations**, all people groups. Through the advent of the **Internet** and **satellite** communication, this has largely been accomplished.

> *And this gospel of the kingdom will be preached in all the world as a witness to all the nations, and then the end will come. (Matt. 24:14)*

Then Jesus says the '**Great Tribulation**' will come upon us, punctuated by a terrible earthquake <u>after</u> the "**abomination of desolation**" occurs:

> *When you see the 'abomination of desolation,' spoken of by Daniel the prophet, standing in the holy place… there will be great tribulation, such as has not been since the beginning of the world until this time, no, nor ever shall be. (Matt. 24:15,21)*

It is from the prophet Daniel that we get a detailed **timeline** of that terrible period. Daniel 9:24-25 starts by telling us that we're talking about a period of **seventy weeks**. Actually, the precise translation of this is "seventy-sevens" with **each week** being seven **years**, for a **total of 490 years**.

> *Seventy weeks are determined for your people and for your holy city, to finish the transgression, to make an end of sins, to make reconciliation for iniquity, to bring in everlasting righteousness, to seal up vision and prophecy, and to anoint the Most Holy. Know therefore and understand, that from the going forth of the command to restore and build Jerusalem until Messiah the Prince, there shall be seven weeks and sixty-two weeks; the street shall be built again, and the wall, even in troublesome times. (Dan. 9:24-25*

Daniel's starting reference point is when King Artaxerxes gave the decree to **Nehemiah to rebuild the temple** in 445 BC. Verse 25 tells us there will 7 weeks and then 62 weeks. The seven weeks, or 49 years, brings us to 396 BC when the temple was completed.

Verse 26 refers to a subsequent 62-week period after which the Messiah, **Jesus will be 'cut off.'**

> *And after the sixty-two weeks Messiah shall be cut off, but not for Himself; and the people of the prince who is to come shall*

destroy the city and the sanctuary. The end of it shall be with a flood, and till the end of the war desolations are determined.

These 434 years bring us to 37 or 38 AD, depending on whether there is a year zero or not. Jesus was actually born in either 3 or 4 AD and lived 33 ½ years. Jesus was indeed "cut off" or killed **right when this prophecy says**.

After the 'people of the prince' (i.e. Satan) destroy the city (Jerusalem) and the sanctuary, (the temple) which occurred in 70 AD, there is **an indeterminate length of time before the seventieth week.** This is to allow enough time to **'finish the transgression'** as Daniel wrote or when 'the transgressors have reached their **fullness'** as he wrote in chapter 8, verse 23-25.

> *And in the latter time of their kingdom, when the transgressors have reached their fullness, a king shall arise, having fierce features, who understands sinister schemes. His power shall be mighty, but not by his own power; he shall destroy fearfully, and shall prosper and thrive; he shall destroy the mighty, and also the holy people. Through his cunning he shall cause deceit to prosper under his rule; and he shall exalt himself in his heart. He shall destroy many in their prosperity. He shall even rise against the Prince of princes; but he shall be broken without human means.*

The Bible refers to **Satan** as the 'prince of the air' (Eph 2:2) or the 'god of this age' (2Cor. 4:4) in the New Testament, so we know Daniel is talking here about the devil being the **'power'** behind this **'king'** whom John calls the **'antichrist'** (1John 2:18,22; 4:3, 2John 1:7)

Several prophets, primarily Ezekiel, tell us that a **major war in the Middle East** will break out involving Israel and the Arabs, Persians (i.e. Iran) and Russia (Ezek. 38-39). Out of this a **"Beast"** will arise as described in Revelation, chapter 13.

> *And I saw a beast rising up out of the sea, having seven heads and ten horns, and on his horns ten crowns, and on his heads a blasphemous name... So they worshiped the dragon who gave authority to the beast; and they worshiped the beast, saying,*

"Who is like the beast? Who is able to make war with him?
(Rev. 13:1,4)

Daniel 9:27 says that this man will '**sign a covenant with many**' meaning a **peace treaty** which will last for one week, or **seven years**. The 7-year Tribulation begins when the peace pact is signed. This peace treaty will bring a '**false**' **peace** that will last for the first three-and-a-half years. We call it a false peace because there will be no peace for Christians, only persecution.

> *Then he shall confirm a covenant with many for one week.* (Dan. 9:27)

Jesus says that the first 'forty-two months' or three and a half years, the '**beast' would be in control** and form a **one-world government**, as described in Revelation 13:5-7. This will actually be a time of peace – for everybody except the Christians.

> *And he was given a mouth speaking great things and blasphemies, and he was given authority to continue for forty-two months. Then he opened his mouth in blasphemy against God, to blaspheme His name, His tabernacle, and those who dwell in heaven. It was granted to him to make war with the saints and to overcome them. And authority was given him over every tribe, tongue, and nation.*

Then, Daniel states in verse 27 that, in the **middle** of the 7-year Tribulation (i.e. after forty-two months), the anti-Christ will '**bring an end to sacrifice and offering**.'

> *Then he shall confirm a covenant with many for one week; but in the **middle** of the week he shall bring an end to sacrifice and offering.*

This implies and is confirmed elsewhere that, as a result of the peace treaty, Israel will be allowed to **rebuild the temple**, the so-called 'third temple,' the first two having been destroyed. However, this will only be the temple building itself, not the inner and outer courts because they will be **overrun by the Gentiles** (i.e. non-Jews) as described in Revelation 11:2. Even now, orthodox Jews in Israel have reconvened the Sanhedrin, their leadership council, and are training priests to prepare to start up their complex system of sacrifices last performed in 70 AD.

In addition to ending sacrificial ceremonies in the third temple, this is also when the so-called **'abomination of desolation'** occurs, as referenced in verse 27 of Daniel 9b as well as by Jesus in Matthew 24:15.

> *And on the wing of abominations shall be one who makes desolate, even until the consummation, which is determined, is poured out on the desolate.* (Dan. 9:27b)

This occurs when the anti-Christ sits in the Jewish temple and **declares himself to be God**, as described by the Apostle Paul in 2Thessalonians 2:3-4.

> *Let no one deceive you by any means; for that Day will not come unless the falling away comes first, and the man of sin is revealed, the son of perdition, who opposes and exalts himself above all that is called God or that is worshiped, so that he sits as God in the temple of God, showing himself that he is God.*

Part 2: The Day of Wrath

The "abomination of desolation" precedes the **'great and dreadful day of the Lord'** described by Malachi and other Biblical prophets, which is also referred to as "that day" and "the day." Both the Hebrew and Greek words used in this context can mean a **twenty-four hour day** or some **indeterminate amount of time**, usually of **short duration**. So it's not entirely clear whether it's a literal 24-hour day or not, but that goes along with the overall premise that we won't know exact dates and times in advance.

Effectively, **God's hand of restraint is removed** (2Thess. 2:7), **sin** erupts in **fullness**, and cataclysmic events begin to happen when Jesus opens the 'seven seals' of judgment. Here are some additional verses that describe that day. These are just a few of many verses that refer to this day:

> Psalm 110:5 *The Lord is at your right hand; He shall execute kings in the <u>day</u> of His <u>wrath</u>. He shall <u>judge</u> among the nations.*

- Revelation 11:18 *The nations were angry, and Your <u>wrath</u> has come, and <u>the time</u> of the dead, that they should be <u>judged</u> and that You should <u>reward</u> Your servants the prophets and the <u>saints</u>, and those who fear your name, small and great, and should destroy those who destroy the earth.*

- 1Thessalonians 5:4 *But you, brethren, are not in darkness, so that this <u>Day</u> should overtake you as a thief.*

- Ezekiel 30:3 *For the day is near, even the <u>day of the Lord</u> is near; it will be a day of <u>clouds</u>, the time of the Gentiles*

- Joel 3:14 *Multitudes, multitudes in the valley of decision! For the <u>day of the Lord</u> is near.*

Let's look at a few verses that show us how truly **dreadful** this day will be for **unbelievers**:

- Isaiah 13:6,9 *Wail, for the day of the Lord is at hand! It will come as <u>destruction</u> from the Almighty... <u>Cruel</u>, with both <u>wrath</u> and <u>fierce anger</u>, to lay the land <u>desolate</u>; and He will <u>destroy</u> its sinners from it.*

- Jeremiah 46:10 *A day of <u>vengeance</u>... the sword shall <u>devour</u>.*

- Joel 2:11 *The day of the Lord is great and very <u>terrible</u>; who can endure it?*

- Joel 2:31, Acts 2:20 *The <u>sun</u> shall be turned into <u>darkness</u>, and the <u>moon</u> into <u>blood</u>, before the coming of the great and awesome day of the Lord.*

- Matthew 24:21-22 *For then there will be <u>great tribulation</u>, such as has not been since the beginning of the world until this time, no, nor ever shall be. And unless those days were shortened, no flesh would be saved; but <u>for the elect's sake those days will be shortened</u>.*

> 2Peter 3:10 *The <u>heavens will pass away</u> with a great noise, and the <u>elements will melt</u> with fervent heat; both the earth and the works that are in it will be <u>burned up</u>*

There are even more verses that speak about how awful it will be. But let's look at a couple of important points contained in these Scriptures, beyond how awful it will be. First of all, notice what it says in Acts 2:20 which quotes Joel 2:31.

> *The **sun shall be turned into darkness**, and the **moon into blood**, before the coming of the great and awesome **day of the LORD**.*

A major, cataclysmic event will blot out the sun and cause the moon to appear red. There's been lots of speculation about how this will occur, from volcanic eruptions to nuclear war. But that's just speculation. We're more concerned about *when* this will occur. Revelation, chapter five, beginning at verse twelve says:

> *I looked when He opened the <u>sixth seal</u>, and behold, there was a great earthquake; and the <u>sun</u> became <u>black</u> as sackcloth of hair and the <u>moon</u> became like <u>blood</u>. And the stars of heaven fell to the earth... Then the sky receded as a scroll... and every mountain and island was moved out of its place.' Then in verse seventeen, 'For the great <u>day</u> of His <u>wrath</u> has come, and who is able to stand?*

We can see that this event, which is **triggered** when Jesus opens the **sixth seal**, fulfills Joel's prophecy, with verse seventeen tying it to the 'day of wrath.' Jesus also refers to these signs in Matthew 24:29-31:

> *Immediately after the tribulation of those days, the <u>sun will be darkened, and the moon will not give its light</u>; the stars will fall from heaven, and the powers of the heavens will be shaken. Then the sign of the Son of Man will appear in heaven, and then all the tribes of the earth will mourn, and they will see the Son of Man coming on the clouds of heaven with power and great glory. And He will send His angels with a great sound of trumpets, and they will gather together His elect from the four winds, from one end of the heaven to the other.*

Part 3: The Rapture

We can see from the above verses that the '**day of the Lord**' involves Jesus coming to **execute judgment** on the earth with **great wrath**, but the **saints will be rewarded**. In several other Scriptures, we're told that we don't receive our rewards until we are in heaven (Matt. 5:12, 19:21). That's why it's a '**great**' day for Christians, because that's when we are "**raptured**" into heaven.

When Jesus returns, he will appear in the clouds all over the earth, all at the same time. Then, we will be '**caught up**' into the clouds with him. This is what we call the **rapture**, a word that is derived from the Latin translation which uses the word '*rapieumur*' to convey the sense of being '**caught up**' into the clouds."

> ➢ *For the Lord Himself will descend from heaven with a shout, with the voice of an archangel, and with the trumpet of God. And the dead in Christ will rise first. Then we who are alive and remain shall be caught up together with them.* (1Thessalonians 4:16).

The so-called **pre-Trib rapture** is a terrible mistake foisted upon us by the devil so that the Church won't rise up to do its job, content to remain **apathetic and complacent**, simply awaiting our trip home to heaven. 2Thessalonians 2:3 says:

> ➢ *Let no one deceive **you** by any means, for that Day will not come unless the falling away comes first, and the man of sin is revealed, the son of perdition, who opposes and exalts himself above all that is worshipped, so that he sits as god in the temple of God, showing himself that he is God.*

This says that the **Christians will see these referenced events**, which take us up to at least the midpoint of the seven-year Tribulation. In addition, Revelation 13:7 tells us that the anti-Christ will *'make war with the saints and overcome them.'* For that to happen, the saints need to still be around and not raptured away before the Tribulation.

Back in Matthew 24:15, Jesus says, *'so when **you** see standing in the holy place the **abomination** that causes **desolation**'* He is referring to what Daniel says is to occur at the **mid-point** of the 7-year Tribulation. This is written to **believers**, so we're obviously going to be around for the first three-and-a-half years. Furthermore, Rev. 7, verses 9 and 14 speak of the *"**multitude… who come out of the great tribulation**" – out of*, not before.

But the rapture **can't happen at the exact midpoint** of the Tribulation, or otherwise we would know the exact time. We will know the day the Tribulation started, that is when the **"peace pact with many"** was signed as prophesied in Daniel 9:27. So I believe the rapture will occur sometime after the mid-point and **right before the so-called Day of the Lord**, or the **Day of Wrath**, which I believe is when Jesus opens the sixth seal.

We also know from Daniel 9:24-27 that the Tribulation is to last seven years. Therefore, **we will be able to say with certainty when the midpoint of the Tribulation will occur**. This violates Jesus' admonition that we won't be able to predict the day of the rapture, and since He is not a liar, there can't be a mid-Trib rapture.

So the rapture will occur sometime **after** the middle of the Tribulation, after the "abomination of desolation." Of course, we **don't know the exact time** when this will occur. It'll come 'as a **thief in the night**' and catch us by surprise (1Thess 5:2, 2Peter 3:10).

But for the *'elect's sake,'* that is for believers, those days will be *'shortened'* by the rapture, the catching away of the saints prior to the terrible devastation wrought when Jesus opens the seventh seal, the so-called trumpet and bowl plagues (Rev. 8,9,16)

> *If those days had not been cut short, no one would survive, but for the sake of the elect, those days will be shortened.* (Matt 24:22)

Fortunately, a **new earth**, and a **new Jerusalem** descend from heaven (Rev. 21:1-2) to usher in the thousand-year **Millennial** when the saints will **reign with Jesus** (Rev. 20:4-5). After the thousand years, Satan is released from the 'bottomless pit' before being finally terminated for good in the '**lake of fire**' (Rev. 20:7-10).

Made in the USA
Columbia, SC
06 January 2025